# HOSTAGE TAKER

# HOSTAGE TAKER

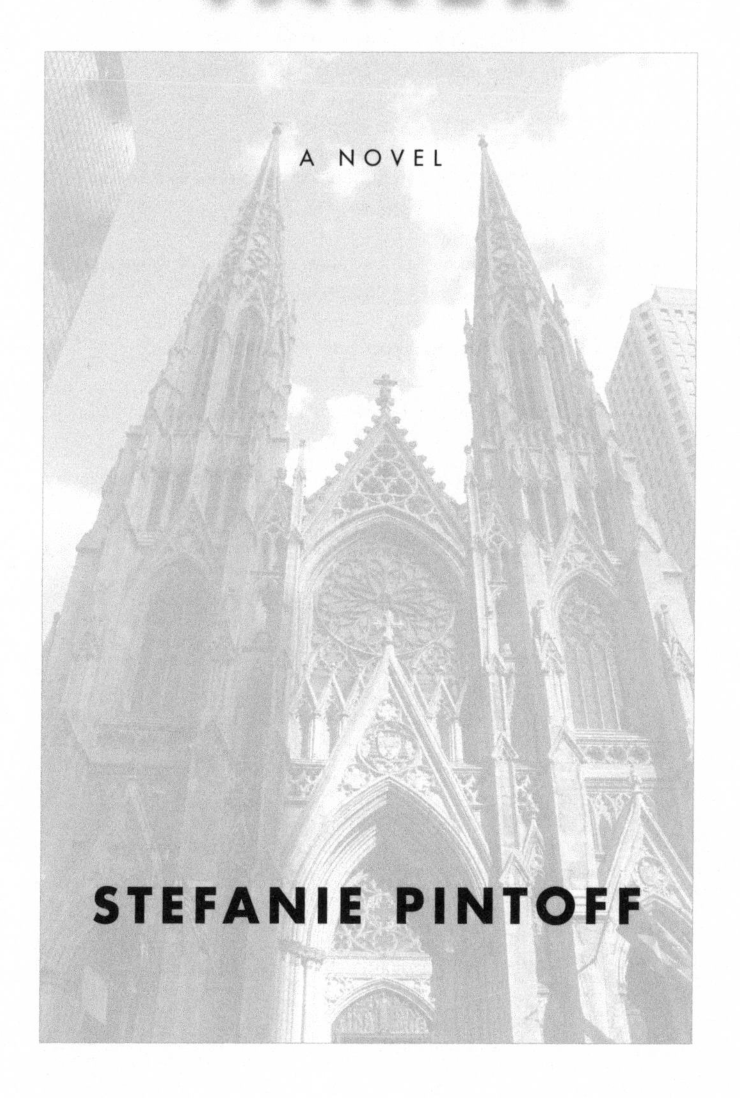

A NOVEL

STEFANIE PINTOFF

BANTAM BOOKS NEW YORK

Published in the United States by Bantam Books, an imprint of Random House, a division of Penguin Random House LLC, New York.

BANTAM BOOKS and the HOUSE colophon are registered trademarks of Penguin Random House LLC.

Library of Congress Cataloging-in-Publication Data
Pintoff, Stefanie.
Hostage taker : a novel / Stefanie Pintoff.
pages ; cm
ISBN 978-0-345-53140-7 — ISBN 978-0-8041-7993-5 (ebook)
I. Title.
PS3616.I58H67 2015
813'.6—dc23
2015001375

Printed in the United States of America on acid-free paper

randomhousebooks.com

2 4 6 8 9 7 5 3 1

First Edition

Title-page image: copyright © iStock.com/© zinchik
Book design by Victoria Wong

*In memory of Jake—who loved a good story.*

*And to Craig—for believing I could write one.*

# HOSTAGE TAKER

# Prologue

*What are you guilty of?*

*I already know.*

*View the files on the enclosed flash drive. They will apprise you of the situation and what you personally have at stake.*

*Your first instinct will be to call the police.*

DON'T.

*Your next impulse will be to call a friend.*

*That would be unwise.*

*Be assured of three things:*

1. *I don't hurt those who do as I ask.*
2. *I won't kill the undeserving.*
3. *Obey my demands, and I will protect what you hold precious.*

NEWS NEWS NEWS NEWS NEWS

PART ONE

# ZERO HOUR

6:47 a.m.

Good day, New York!

It's 41 degrees right now in Midtown, with heavy rain and fog for your morning commute. Luckily, we expect these soggy conditions to be out of here by lunchtime. But bring a fleece lining for those raincoats, because temperatures will continue to plummet throughout the day.

Today is a Gridlock Alert Day, due to tonight's Tree Lighting ceremony at Rockefeller Center, which we'll have live coverage of beginning at seven p.m. We expect tens of thousands of people in the area, so do yourself a favor and take mass transit today . . .

# Chapter 1

Cristina Silva had never been a believer.

When she was a girl, she didn't believe in fairy tales or unicorns or Santa Claus. Then she grew up and didn't believe in miracles. Or magic. Or the myth of the American Dream.

Cristina had always known better than to believe in God.

But she had faith. The kind she'd learned to live by in AA: *If you can't believe, just make believe.*

At this moment, staring down the steps of Saint Patrick's Cathedral toward Fifth Avenue, she was make-believing with all her might. Because nothing short of magical thinking was going to help her now.

She took timid steps forward and blinked the water out of her eyes. Daylight had not yet broken. It was still raining, and drops fell through the gaps in the scaffolding directly above her. The winter sky was murky gray and the streets were blurred by mist. She could barely make out Fifth Avenue, stretching for blocks in front of her.

*Deserted.*

Cristina concentrated on looking around her. Hoping for some sign of life out there in the gloom. She saw none. If there was one time this city ever took a nap, it was near dawn.

Massive bronze doors closed behind her with a forceful thud. Several thousand pounds of metal—and the images of half a dozen saints—now separated her from the rest of them. Those unlucky fools who, like her, had gone to Lady Chapel this morning. As soon as the Cathedral opened.

Then she had been singled out—for what, she wasn't quite sure.

*Where was he?*

Her blood, humming in panic, created a fierce rushing noise inside her head. It was like the ocean, only louder—and more distracting than the gusts of wind and rain that buffeted her cheeks.

A drenched passerby scurried down Fifth Avenue, buried under a green golf umbrella.

Cristina opened her mouth, but no sound came out.

"Help!" she silently pled.

The passerby did not turn. In the teeming rain, he couldn't be bothered with glancing toward gothic spires or intricate marble façades. Never mind a woman wearing a yellow rain slicker and carrying a wooden sign with HELP ME painted in a brilliant shade of red.

Cristina took a cautious step forward.

Another umbrella passed, this one black. Then two cars.

No one slowed.

*Just make a call,* she prayed. *311. 911.* Report the crazy lady standing in the rain. The one at Saint Patrick's—a landmark, tourist destination, and religious refuge, all rolled into one.

She took another step. Craned her neck through the gloom toward the scaffolding high above.

*Was he watching?*

Another step.

Tears welled in her eyes, mingling with the rain. She knew that Saint Patrick's was a symbol. The sign she carried was a symbol, too. Even the confession she'd been forced to make was only a symbol. And for all her nonbelieving, she was terrified that she was about to die as a symbol.

Of God-only-knew-what.

A block away, Angus MacDonald got off the M4 bus, straight into the chilly puddle that snaked around the corner of Fifty-second Street and Fifth Avenue. Aware of the rain leaking into his supposedly waterproof trench coat, he made a run for it.

At least, he tried to. Thanks to the arthritis in his joints, sometimes his legs just refused to get with the program. Whoever had coined *mind over matter* obviously hadn't hit seventy-four.

Ahead of him, Angus saw virtually nothing. Only a traffic light that creaked and groaned as it swayed. This wasn't just Midtown at its quietest. The weather had made it a ghost town.

Then a man wearing an NYPD rubber raincoat emerged from the fog. Angus watched him cross Fifth Avenue in the middle of the block. Racing for the Cathedral. Not wanting to be late for seven-o'clock Mass.

It was a reminder that Angus had better move faster—or he was going to be late, too. He cut a forty-five-degree angle. Crossed the avenue.

The cop made it halfway up the stairs of Saint Patrick's Cathedral. Stopped.

There was a woman there. Just standing. Her canary-yellow raincoat stood out, even with the elaborate scaffolding that covered the entrance. Angus squinted. She was at least in her mid-twenties, he decided. She looked scared. So tense she didn't even respond to the cop staring at her. Like he wasn't even there.

She just stayed frozen in place, looking around.

The cop looked around, too.

There was nothing—and no one—to see. Only rain and fog and mist and the occasional headlights of a passing cab. And, of course, Angus.

The cop broke away with a shake of his head—as if there was nothing he could do. Then he turned and walked into the Cathedral.

The cop had been a big guy with a ruddy face, maybe six-one, maybe two-fifty. More suited to taking out street thugs than talking down distraught women.

Angus resigned himself to being late to Mass. In his experience, young women loved creating drama. He could see his niece pulling a stunt like this: standing in the rain with some silly sign, just to prove a point or get attention after a breakup gone bad.

"Hey, lady—why don't you come in out of the rain?" he called when he was within earshot.

She was so startled she whirled and faced him.

She'd obviously been lost in her own world, because Angus wasn't the type to scare people. With his wrinkled black skin, crinkled gray hair, and generous beer belly, he'd even pass for Santa Claus, given an appropriate red suit.

He reached out a hand to help her—but let it drop when she didn't move. Since the scaffolding provided scant shelter, he moved toward the massive bronze doors, shaking the worst of the water off his coat like a wet dog.

She stayed rooted in place, but she angled her head to watch him.

"My name's Angus. What's yours?" He bunched his hands in the pockets of his coat, huddling against the downpour.

She didn't reply, although she continued to look at him with an intense stare. Like she wanted to say something, but couldn't.

"Just tell me your name. That's not so hard, right?"

A whoosh of wind pushed away her bright yellow hood. Her hair blew wildly, and was instantly soaked, but she made no move to cover herself.

"You'll catch your death out here," Angus scolded. "Come inside with me."

Again, she didn't answer. She cocked her head, like she was trying to listen to something. But the only sound came from the driving rain as it pounded the marble steps.

"It's time for Mass," he said. "Whatever's wrong, whatever's upset you, let's talk about it inside, where it's warm and dry."

She looked up, eyes searching the levels of scaffolding.

"Your sign says HELP," he pointed out. "I'll help you. Let's go inside together."

She tried to raise her arms. It was a futile gesture. For the first time, Angus noticed: The sign she held was bound to her hands with tightly wrapped wire.

A troublesome sensation settled in his gut. *No way did she do that to herself.*

High above the Fifth Avenue skyscrapers, there was a flash of light, followed by a booming sound. Something in the atmosphere changed.

He needed to get help. He needed that cop. The giant bronze doors had just been open. He reached for the door on his right—the one with Mother Elizabeth Seton—and tugged.

It didn't budge. Not even when he pulled harder.

He tried again with the door on his left—the one with the Blessed Kateri Tekakwitha—and failed. He'd have to try one of the side entrances.

But these doors shouldn't be locked. Not right before seven-o'clock Mass. Not when he had just seen the cop go inside. Something was wrong.

Angus forced himself to think straight. Whoever had done *this* to the woman must be inside the Cathedral. But it would be all right. The cop was a big guy. Surely a big cop could handle whatever threat lurked inside. Angus should focus on the situation out here.

He turned back to the woman, who was now facing him.

Her eyes fixed on Angus's.

He was trying to decipher the mute plea in them when he noticed a funny red dot dancing on her forehead. It looked just like the laser pointer he used when he taught algebra class.

Then she was gone.

The shot was silent as it sliced through her forehead. She crumpled, and suddenly there was slick blood everywhere, mingling with the rain that puddled on the Cathedral steps.

Angus felt a terrible stinging in his head, though he knew he hadn't been hit.

His legs stopped working and he fell to his knees, collapsing beside her.

*The sacrifice of His body and blood,* Angus thought, fumbling for his cellphone. Words from the Mass service that he was missing.

The rain-swept morning was hushed and still. The streets remained deserted.

Hands shaking, Angus managed to call 911.

It was another seven minutes before help arrived for the dead woman with the wire-bound hands, still gripping her small wooden sign.

It would be another nine before the responding officer would notice something else. That the sign she had carried held a message.

Not the public plea for HELP that she had shown the world. There was a note—a private communication taped on the back of the sign.

The officer didn't understand it.

But he was smart enough to radio it in.

NEWS NEWS NEWS NEWS NEWS

# HOUR 1

8:17 a.m.

Good news for your morning commute, New Yorkers: Rain and fog should be lifting within the hour. We'll have gray skies most of the day, with a slight chance of snow showers by this evening.

But if you're headed downtown to work, you might want to avoid Fifth Avenue below Fifty-seventh. We're receiving reports of police activity in that area . . .

# Chapter 2

A hundred blocks uptown, in the downpour that drenched New York City, Eve Rossi placed a stone on top of her stepfather's grave. It was a custom—albeit one that she didn't understand. She'd been told that the stone symbolized her memories, durable and everlasting. She'd also heard that it kept demons away. One superstition even held that the stone's weight would keep the dead man's spirit grounded in this world. As if Zev Berger would ever have wanted to stick around as a ghost.

Eve believed none of it.

Still, Zev had followed certain traditions, so Eve honored this one now. Instead of an ordinary stone, she'd chosen a clamshell from Zev's favorite beach—a secluded spot on the South Shore of Long Island where piping plovers nested and rough waves crashed into a black rock barrier.

Clamshells were beautiful, but not in a traditional way: Their irregular purple-and-cream stripes appeared textured. She always expected to *feel* those brilliantly colored ridges—and yet the shell was perfectly smooth to her touch. Not unlike Zev himself, a tough CIA veteran who never stood for being crossed—but who had always yielded to Eve or her mother.

Eve stood motionless in the rain. She didn't pray or talk. But she *remembered.* And if she imagined that she and Zev had a wordless conversation, that was only because she had once known him so well. Under the bleak December sky, her past and present bled together.

She'd made it through four of the five stages of grief. She had denied it, ranted at Zev, bargained with a God she wasn't sure she believed in, and learned to live with her dark thoughts. Now all that was left was acceptance.

*Acceptance is a gift not always granted,* a man in New Delhi had told her.

Eve didn't know about that. But her every instinct was to avoid accepting that Zev was forever gone. She couldn't face setting foot in Zev's home. Or returning the probate lawyer's calls. After Zev's funeral three months ago, she'd boarded a flight leaving JFK for Rome and kept on moving.

It seemed Zev had died holding a Scheherazade's store of secrets—and she was resolved to uncover the important ones. She *wanted* to understand his life; she *needed* to understand his death. So she started in Rome and Madrid. Then Paris and Bruges. Followed by Munich, Prague, Amsterdam, Copenhagen, and eventually Athens and Shanghai. It was only after she'd reached Hong Kong—and felt the twist in her throat, watching men in the park play mah-jongg, as Zev had once done—that she realized the answers she needed were at home.

So she returned to New York. She visited this cemetery. That had to count for something.

She closed her umbrella and turned away from the grave. The morning's teeming rain had finally stopped, but a thick fog filled the air and the temperature was dropping. Shivering, she pulled her gray jacket tighter around her and started walking north alongside the Riverside Drive retaining wall.

The huge cemetery had been deserted, except for her. Now she noticed two men approaching through the mist.

No reason to think they were a problem. There were plenty of graves in this cemetery. Plenty of potential mourners. So what if a couple had decided to show up for an early-morning visit?

Nevertheless, she quickened her steps. Pushed her tangled blond hair away from her face. Took a closer look.

The men were walking south from West 155th Street.

She headed east toward Broadway.

From the corner of her eye she saw: They switched direction and went east as well.

Definitely not here to pay respects.

Her eyes scanned the landscape. No one was around. Just her—and these two.

She picked up her pace. They followed. Closing in fast.

She cut an angle toward the southeast. Used her peripheral vision to observe them.

They walked with a straight bearing. Authority in every step. A slight bulge near each of their waists betrayed the weapons they carried. Law enforcement, she decided.

*What did they want with her?*

She walked faster. Still watching. Still wary.

The one on the left, she determined, was plainclothes NYPD. He had gone days without shaving. And while once he might have had the body of a linebacker, he was now starting to go to seed. But he walked with swagger and confidence—still the man on the field, despite his lack of uniform.

The man on the right was smooth-shaven and clean-cut. He walked a half-step behind his partner. Because he had been trained to blend in, not stand out. FBI, definitely.

Two men working together—a model of interagency cooperation. The new norm in a post-9/11 world.

She wished they would just go away. But she knew they had to be dealt with—so she slowed and allowed them to catch up with her.

The NYPD officer arrived first. "Special Agent Rossi? I'm Rick Connor, and this is Special Agent Chris Anders." Connor thrust his NYPD ID in front of her. Anders flashed his FBI shield. "We need you to come with us."

Eve stopped abruptly. "I'm on leave."

"This is important."

"I'm on leave," she repeated. "Bereavement. You need to ask someone else."

"Director's orders," Anders persisted. "He wants to see you."

"Henry?" Eve raised an eyebrow. Her attitude toward a command from FBI assistant director in charge Henry Ma was no different from her view about stones on graves. She would follow the custom—or the command—only as she saw fit. Not because she lacked respect for the job Henry did or felt that his work was unimportant. But the man was a political schemer who couldn't be trusted. "Tell Director Ma that I'm sorry, but I'm not available." She started walking away from them.

"It's an emergency."

Eve's heartbeat quickened. They didn't mean a personal emergency. She was the only child of now-deceased parents, responsible for no one. Anders hadn't bothered with pleasantries or wasted words, so Eve didn't, either. "What kind of emergency?"

"A woman is dead."

"There are other profilers—"

"It has to be you. I'll explain on the way to the car." He indicated an unmarked sedan parked just up the hill. It was scarcely visible through the fog.

"How did you find me?" Eve didn't move.

"It's our job. Now we need you to do yours."

"I'm not on payroll." The government offered thirteen days of paid leave. Eve had already taken six times that amount, unpaid. And she fully intended to take more. "I've also got an appointment downtown." She made a point of glancing at her watch.

Connor found a cigarette in his pocket, lit it, and sucked in deeply. Like he was more desperate for nicotine than air. "There's more at stake than the dead woman. Director Ma said your presence was critical."

"Why?" Eve demanded.

"Hostages. We think the victim was a hostage. We're worried there are more like her." Except Connor didn't sound concerned. He was the kind of cop who had lost all ambition. She knew the type well. He performed his duty and counted down time: the minutes until quitting time, weeks until vacation time, and years until pension time.

"If you're worried, then you're not sure."

"It's complicated." Connor stood, smoking, staring at Eve like *she* was the problem.

Eve shook her head. She didn't want anything complicated. She had even less interest in a crisis involving hostages. Maybe at one time she would have been considered the top hostage negotiator in New York's FBI field office.

Not now.

She'd left that work for a more unconventional assignment, put it behind her. No, this was a situation she wanted no part of.

"I haven't worked a hostage case in over a year." She turned away from them. "Pick someone currently on HRT." The FBI's Hostage Rescue Team was top-notch. So was the NYPD's.

This time it was Connor who spoke. "This is going down at Saint Patrick's Cathedral."

In spite of herself, Eve felt a prick of curiosity—but she trained a blank expression on the NYPD officer. "I heard nothing on the news." In her home, growing up, at least three televisions had always been on so Zev could monitor the different news channels. Another family tradition she now followed.

"The media haven't broken the story. But you should have received an encrypted message with the particulars."

Eve's fingers reached into her pocket for her phone—and she saw to her surprise that Connor was right. Even though this phone received only personal email. She opened the first page and swiftly scanned its contents. The spare words of the official report grabbed her interest and held it. This was complicated.

She looked up. "How long since the Hostage Taker barricaded the Cathedral?"

"Initial report came at seven-oh-nine a.m. After the first victim was killed."

"How?"

"Gunshot. We took a preliminary suspect into custody—but looks like he's clean. The shot was fired from high in the Cathedral scaffolding—which is a patchwork of steel and wood, in the process of coming down." Connor dropped his cigarette butt to the ground. It sparked until he squashed it under his heel.

"The area's contained?"

"Completely. NYPD and a half-dozen officers from HRT have established a perimeter. No one inside is getting out."

"Victim ID?

"Still working on it."

Her interest flickered again—but Eve dropped her phone back into her pocket. "I've been out of the game for too long. Besides, I'm too busy."

"Because that seven-mile run you've taken the past three mornings can't wait? Sounds a little selfish to me." Connor's smile mocked her.

She turned to Anders with a cold stare. "Since when does the FBI spy on me?"

"Since early November," the agent answered with a shrug. "That's when the top brass started wondering if there was a problem. Why you were visiting so many foreign countries. If you were ever coming back."

"Give the lead negotiator my number. I'll share my thoughts if anyone needs some support," she lied. She had no intention of getting involved.

Anders wouldn't let it go. "You're not understanding us. It's possible that Ma will need *you* to be lead negotiator."

"Out of the question," Eve said firmly. The last time she'd worked a hostage case, she'd made the wrong call—and people had died. Eleven in all, including children. It was not an experience she cared to repeat.

Connor fixed her with a withering stare. "There may be a number of people inside Saint Patrick's this morning who need you to reconsider your answer."

"Sorry." Eve started back up the path.

"The Hostage Taker left a message."

"Give it to someone else."

"Can't," Connor called out after her.

"Why not?" She threw the words over her shoulder, still walking.

"He asked for you by name, Agent Rossi."

**VIDOCQ FILE #A3065277**

**Current status: ACTIVE—Official Bereavement Leave**

**Evangeline Rossi**

Nickname: Eve
Age: 34
Race/Ethnicity: Caucasian, Italian
Height: 5'5"
Weight: 117 lbs.
Eyes: Hazel
Hair: Blond

**Current Address:** 348 West 57th Street (Hell's Kitchen).
**Criminal Record:** None.
**Expertise:** Behavioral Science and Criminal Investigative Analysis, subspecialties in kinesics and paralinguistics. Seasoned interrogator and hostage negotiator.
**Education:** Yale University, B.S., and M.S., Clinical Psychology.

**Personal**

**Family:** Mother, Annabella, deceased. Stepfather, Zev Berger, recently deceased, former CIA operative. Father, unknown.
**Spouse/Significant Other:** None.
**Religion:** Agnostic.
**Interests:** Addicted to crossword puzzles. Concert-level pianist. Avid runner who has finished four NYC marathons.

**Profile**

**Strengths:** The stepdaughter of a CIA spook, Eve was born into the business and is passionately dedicated to her work, believing that it makes the world a better place. Her instincts and training give her insight into the criminal mind that most agents of her age and experience do not possess.

**Weaknesses:** A perfectionist. She likes control and does not delegate well.

**Notes:** Subject to debilitating migraines triggered by stress, lack of sleep, or caffeine mismanagement. Claims medication keeps condition under control. Suffered a crisis of confidence following failed hostage negotiation resulting in multiple fatalities (case history #175137662). Currently on Personal Leave of Absence after Vidocq Unit was disbanded.

**Assessment prepared—and updated—by ADIC Henry Ma. For internal use only.*

NEWS NEWS NEWS NEWS NEWS

# HOUR 2

9:31 a.m.

This just in. We have a developing situation in Midtown.

Police and first-responder activity is causing multiple street closures in the vicinity of Fifth and Madison throughout the Forties and Fifties.

Our Sky Chopper is in the air to bring us this live shot of the area. There's a crush of emergency vehicles—including multiple fire department vehicles—jamming both Fiftieth and Fifty-first Streets on either side of Fifth Avenue.

Over to you, Jim. From your vantage point, can you tell whether the incident response seems directed to Rockefeller Center—or to Saint Patrick's Cathedral?

*JIM:* All I can say right now is that we're seeing a massive emergency response on the ground, centered on Fifth Avenue between these two major tourist destinations, especially busy at holiday time.

# Chapter 3

The man who'd summoned Eve was pacing back and forth under Atlas—the enormous bronze statue who held up the heavens—at Rockefeller Center, directly across the street from Saint Patrick's Cathedral. Watching him, Eve realized: The timing of this crisis was bad, but it could have been far worse. They were fortunate that the area had been secured before tens of thousands of visitors swarmed the site for that evening's world-famous Tree Lighting ceremony.

This was Midtown Manhattan's prime tourist arena, transformed into a brilliant holiday spectacle. Normally the smell of roasting chestnuts would fill the air. The jingle of bells from Salvation Army Santas would compete with the Christmas carols played by every store.

Dazzling window displays demanded attention, each more ornate and magnificent than the last. And every building would be decorated with an extravagant array of Christmas lights, red ribbons, and ubiquitous green wreaths. Even the most jaded New Yorkers found it extraordinary—and they joined tourists who came to spend the day shopping at Saks, ice-skating at Rockefeller Plaza, or wandering through Saint Patrick's.

Eve returned her attention to it: an enormous neo-Gothic cathedral with stunning stained-glass windows and graceful twin spires soaring more than three hundred feet into the air, disappearing into low-hanging clouds that lingered after the rain. Though dwarfed in size by the skyscrapers encircling it, the Cathedral's grandeur ensured that it easily dominated the block. Even obscured by scaffolding—part of a massive restoration project designed to rehabilitate the Cathedral inside and out—the building retained an almost mystical aura. It didn't matter to Eve that she wasn't Catholic, or even particularly religious. The building itself was so uniquely beautiful that she had always found peace there.

Not today.

Fifth Avenue between Forty-ninth and Fifty-second Streets was transformed into a circus of police cars, emergency vehicles, equipment vans, and dozens of unmarked government sedans. The seventy-one thousand twinkling white lights of Saks competed with the flashing of crimson-and-blue emergency vehicle lights as first responders from different organizations—NYPD, FBI, Homeland Security, EMS—swarmed the block. They created a secure perimeter around the front of Saint Patrick's.

As expected, all approaches to Saint Patrick's were blocked off. Beyond the perimeter, concrete barricades manned by police in full body armor held back the crowds and the members of the press with their video cameras and microphones. Detoured drivers were honking, and somewhere a car alarm was blaring. Meanwhile, an elderly woman, upset she was not allowed through, wielded an umbrella like a weapon in her futile argument with a cop.

"I need that barricade moved two blocks uptown, hear me?" Henry Ma shouted into his radio. "Get rid of those cameras!" The director shrugged off his raincoat and thrust it at the assistant who followed him, clipboard in hand. Then he wiped the sweat from his brow—overheated, despite the increasing chill in the air. He wore his usual bold red tie and spit-shined shoes, but he had put on at least fifteen pounds since Eve had last seen him three months ago. His suit barely fit, his shirt was unironed. And his wedding ring was missing.

Eve waited for his eyes to find her. Then he froze—and motioned toward a tactical response van. It was a signal. The assistant with the clipboard retreated, and a Hispanic woman in plain khaki pants and a black fitted coat stepped out of the van, nodding to the cluster of officers. She was in her early thirties; her long, dark hair was in a simple ponytail; and she carried no weapon. But her chest was thick, out of proportion to the rest of her slender body—a telltale sign of bulletproof armor underneath.

This woman was an NYPD negotiator.

Henry straightened his tie and stalked toward Eve. "I wasn't sure you'd come." Maybe he regretted the way he had abandoned her when the political winds shifted during their last case. Or maybe he didn't. Either way, this was as close to an apology as Eve would get.

"I didn't want to. I wasn't given a choice," Eve replied.

"Because there isn't one. They told you about the message the dead woman carried? There was a note on the back of her sign. Asking for you."

Eve nodded. "Yes. Why would the Hostage Taker ask for me?"

"We were hoping you could tell us. Maybe you've crossed paths with him before."

"What do you think we're dealing with?"

Henry made a noise of frustration. "Who the hell knows. The guy inside could be a criminal or a terrorist or a religious nutjob with some beef against the Catholic Church. Take your pick. I've got one team combing surveillance video and another trying to get eyes and ears inside. Tactical is standing by. We can't get our infrared to penetrate the walls of the Cathedral."

"What about the military?"

Henry bristled. "Our equipment is military-grade—the latest technology. It's just no match for those walls. They're made of about ten feet of granite and marble, concrete and brick."

"Any word yet on how many are inside?"

"There's no telling. This situation unfolded shortly before seven-o'clock Mass, so we suspect there are multiple hostages. At least the bad weather may have limited the damage. I would be surprised if too many people braved this morning's monsoon."

"Any IDs?"

"The media hasn't broken the full story. When they do, we'll drown under tips about people known or suspected to be at Saint Patrick's."

"What about the Hostage Taker? Anyone claim responsibility?" The Hostage Taker—or Takers, if there were more than one—would need to show his hand before long.

"We've got nothing. Just the message asking for you."

"The Cathedral would be a difficult space for just one person to manage," she said, thinking aloud.

"Try *impossible.* Security cameras and guards. Multiple entrances and exits. Hordes of tourists. And over two hundred skilled restoration workers on a typical day."

"How many doors provide entry to this building?"

"Seven, not counting access from the Parish House and the Cardinal's Residence."

"You've evacuated those buildings?"

Henry nodded.

"And the Cardinal himself?"

"Fortunately he's not in residence; he's visiting the Vatican, together with the rector and all his pastoral staff. But because of the timing, shortly before first morning Mass, we believe the substituting Monsignor—Father DeAngelo—may be among the hostages."

"The Hostage Taker gave no warning—made no demand of any sort—before he killed the woman?"

"Not in a traditional sense." Henry hesitated. "You might learn something from the old man we took into custody. We cleared him of involvement in the hostage taking—but he claims he talked with the victim before she was shot."

"You've communicated with the Hostage Taker?"

"Soon. Believe me, Tactical is considering all options."

*Tactical* was considering options? Henry's reluctance to begin negotiations struck Eve as off base. The first order of business—always—was to establish a line of communication with the Hostage Taker. It wasn't just the best way to learn about who he was and what he wanted. It was also the best way to minimize casualties among hostages. Because when the Hostage Taker was talking, he wasn't shooting or worrying about defending his barricade from tear gas or a full-out assault.

"I'm confused, Henry. Why didn't you immediately reach out to the Hostage Taker?"

Henry cleared his throat, realized he was standing in a puddle, and scowled at his custom-made shoes. "I'd like you to meet Sergeant Martinez. She will attempt first contact."

"Henry, *you* asked *me* to come here. Because the Hostage Taker demanded it." Eve felt herself slipping off the rails of her control.

"We can't give in to his first demand. You know that, Eve. But I still need you close by—in case that message with your name on it means something."

*Of course it means something,* Eve thought. Otherwise she wouldn't have come.

She wanted to point out two things: If the Hostage Taker, unprovoked, had already murdered one victim, then substituting another negotiator for one he requested would be a mistake. And Henry's excuse for not putting her in was complete bullshit.

But she knew the deal: Henry was looking out for himself. He was poised to take over the crisis—and put Eve in play—the instant doing so benefited him. But so long as there was potential for this crisis to turn into an explosive mess, he was happy for the NYPD to shoulder the blame.

"With all due respect, Henry—"

"My decision is made," he snapped, cutting her off. "Annie Martinez is a capable negotiator with the Hostage Negotiation Team. You know their reputation is impeccable."

"How long has she been on the job?"

"Almost two years."

"She ever negotiate a release?"

"She's a bit wet behind the ears. But she's had two completely by-the-book releases that impressed the top brass—kind of like the way you started, Eve. Plus, she managed it when it really counted. I read her file. Seems her father battled mental illness most of his life. Her senior year of college, she came home for spring break and found Mom shot to death. Dad was holed up in the garage with a shotgun and her little brother. She spent the next thirteen hours sitting and talking with him until he gave himself up."

"She's got the right temperament, then." Eve was impressed. "The problem is: This Hostage Taker asked for me."

"Which is why you're here if we need you." Henry said it reasonably. He missed—or more likely ignored—her lingering concern. Instead, he gestured for the slim ponytailed woman to come forward and made the introductions. Then he glanced at a group of officers who were working with an electronic device. They motioned him over. "Excuse me for a moment."

"Looks like they almost have the throw phone ready," Annie Martinez remarked. The device wasn't an actual phone—not anymore—although the colloquial name for it had stuck. It was a combination microphone/speaker, rugged enough to withstand a significant drop, but highly sound-sensitive, capable of transmitting through doors and walls and windows. It didn't matter if the Hostage Taker didn't want to talk. As long as you positioned the throw phone in the general vicinity, the Hostage Taker would hear you. If you were lucky, nearby hostages would, too.

"How are you getting it inside?" Eve asked Annie Martinez. Between those ten-foot-thick marble-and-granite walls and bronze doors that weighed more than nine thousand pounds each, the Cathedral seemed like a fortress.

"One of the stained-glass windows has a small crack in a corner. The tactical team plans to enlarge the break, then drop the device." Annie shot Eve a rueful look. "There's already a guy here from Landmarks Preservation. He won't be happy."

"No," Eve agreed. "And just wait until the Church gets involved. But that's not your problem."

"By the way, it's great meeting you." Annie blushed. "What you did with the Marsh case is in all the casebooks. Your words and phrasing—and the way you established a bond with him. It's the model for how to start a negotiation."

Eve shrugged. "I'll be here if you need me. If my name comes up again—and I'm hoping it won't."

Annie started to say something—but their attention was drawn by a flurry of activity in front of the statue of Atlas. An officer securing the scene barked an order. Two approaching cops stopped in their tracks. A half-dozen Feds rushed out of the tactical van—and instantly halted. The attention of every single first responder was now directed at one point.

The center bronze door of Saint Patrick's—where a boy, maybe eleven or twelve years old, had been thrust outside.

He wore jeans and a puffy blue jacket, and he'd gelled his hair so it spiked straight up. His eyes blinked in response to the flashing lights. He seemed terrified by the vast number of police and emergency personnel who had converged around him.

The boy took four cautious steps forward until he stood at the top of the stairs. He held a cellphone clutched in his right hand. His left clenched a sign reading HELP. Eve wondered if it was identical to the one the previous victim held.

Two groups of officers began to come toward him. Many had raised their weapons.

Startled, the child tensed. "No!"

It sounded like *nor*—but without the emphasis on the *r.*

"Don't m-m-move! I've got to do what he says or he'll shoot."

The officers slowed. One issued an order; a few took a step back.

Snipers would be in position. Alert for the Hostage Taker, should he reveal himself behind the scaffolding.

The boy waved the phone. His voice cracked. "He wants to talk with Agent Rossi. Eve Rossi."

*To* was only a *t*—with a breathy *uh* at its end. And the *th* was dropped entirely. Definitely a British accent. *Yorkshire?* A tourist—which meant he probably had a mother or father still inside.

The boy put the phone back to his ear and listened. "He says you have exactly ten minutes to get her on the line. Starting now."

*He* again, not *they.*

Eve glanced at Henry Ma. He was having an agitated conversation with an NYPD sergeant. They came to a decision fast. "Martinez! You're on."

Annie Martinez lifted her shoulders and walked toward the steps.

*It was a mistake.* Eve could sense it, more than she could rationalize it.

"Hi, there," Sergeant Martinez called, addressing the boy. "My name is Annie, and I'm a negotiator with the New York Police Department. I'm here to help you. I know you must be scared."

The child's eyes followed her, but he said nothing.

"What's your name?"

No response.

"We've asked Agent Rossi to come. But she can't get here in ten minutes. Not in the kind of crazy traffic we have this morning. Agent Rossi's on her way, but it's going to take her some time. Maybe you could tell him that. Assuming it's a *him,* of course."

The boy just stared ahead.

"Ask him what he'd like me to call him," Annie urged. "You can let him know my name is Annie."

*Good. Not Sergeant Martinez. Not even Annie Martinez. Just his friend, Annie—friendly and approachable.*

Despite the political game he was playing with the NYPD, Henry had been technically right about one point: It was a common negotiation strategy not to cooperate with the Hostage Taker's first demand. Stalling for time was the name of the game—and that was what Annie was doing now. She would do everything in her power to string the minutes into hours, and hours into days. Her goal was simple: to tire the Hostage Taker out. If he got sleepy, he might make mistakes. If he got hungry, he might make concessions for food. Then the balance of power would switch and the negotiator would gain control and get results. That was how these crises typically played out.

But on such a public stage, could they afford to let this drag out for more than a few hours? The whole world would be watching. And the shock waves from this situation would grind all of New York City to a halt.

Annie took another step forward. "Why don't you give me the phone? That way I can talk to him, grown-up to grown-up. You don't need to be part of this."

The wind whistled as it gusted up Fifth Avenue. Multiple sirens wailed. At first, Eve barely registered the sound, she was so focused on the boy in front of her. It took her a few moments to realize that more emergency vehicles were approaching from Rockefeller Plaza.

The boy shouted, "Don't come closer!"

Annie stopped. She nodded. "I'd like to explain to him how we can resolve this. Or if he prefers, he can use my phone. I have a special one that connects directly to me, personally. Will you let him know?"

The boy didn't reply. He held the phone to his ear.

Emergency vehicles flashed red and blue lights around the secure perimeter. Both Annie and the boy were caught in their reflection.

"I'd like to tell him that we're working on getting Agent Rossi here. Meanwhile, I can help him."

The boy closed his eyes, listening.

"He just needs to talk to me." Annie waited, unmoving. This was all part of the stalling game.

The minutes were slipping by. That was supposed to be a good thing, because time was usually the negotiator's friend.

Except nothing about this particular situation was usual.

Annie Martinez was handling the crisis exactly according to textbook. She had focused on calming the hostage and establishing contact with the Hostage Taker. Her body language was relaxed, her voice patient and respectful. With every word, she was conveying her willingness to help.

Paramedics and NYPD officers were jockeying for position next to Eve at Rockefeller Plaza. Everyone wanted to be close enough to help the boy.

Radios squawked and cellphones trilled. In the distance, horns continued to honk and sirens shrilled. The crowd behind the cordons swelled.

But the storm of sound seemed far removed from the boy, who remained mute. He shivered and swayed, buffeted by the wind. Then his HELP sign dropped to the ground, clattering down the marble stairs.

Eve usually prided herself on being logical. And rationally, she knew: Everything was going exactly as it should. It took time to learn about the Hostage Taker, to convince him that you understood his problems, to establish yourself as his friend. Annie was doing a great job. Nothing Eve could put a finger on was wrong.

Still, glancing at the sign the boy had dropped, she couldn't shake the sense that she was watching a tragedy unfold. *This was no fairy tale. There would be no happy ending today.*

# Chapter 4

Penelope Miller had crossed the Atlantic because of Fulton Sheen. Specifically, she'd come to New York City—and Saint Patrick's Cathedral—in order to pray with him.

Never mind that the good father had been dead the last several decades. Penny figured they needed each other.

Father Sheen was buried in the Crypt, right under the Cathedral altar, in the company of several other archbishops. The difference was: He was on the fast track to Sainthood, with one miracle already credited to his name. Still, he needed a second miracle if he was going to be canonized.

That was where Penelope came in. Her husband Stu had stage IV lung cancer; he had exhausted all medical treatment. He was a perfect candidate for divine intercession—and if Father Sheen's first miracle had been to revive a stillborn baby, why couldn't his second involve curing her husband's cancer?

So she had made the arrangements: taken her son Luke out of Ludgrove, booked the airfare and hotel, and convinced the Monsignor to meet her last night to take her into the Crypt of Saint Patrick's.

She supposed she ought to have noticed right away that something was wrong. But she had got caught up in the moment. Felt special because she and Luke had been granted this private visit underground.

The priest had opened the massive bronze doors just for them—as expected, since their visit was after proper closing hours. Luke had dallied, asking questions about the saints on the double doors.

He'd wanted to know about Mother Elizabeth Seton. Specifically, what had she done to earn her place on the lower portion of the door on the right? *Daughter of New York,* her inscription read. There was a rosebush to her right and an inscription to her left.

The priest had sidestepped Luke's question.

Then Luke wanted to know what the motto next to Mother Seton meant.

*Sequere Deum.* Follow God.

Priests knew Latin, so a real priest would have known that. Just like a real priest would have appreciated Luke's interest. Except *this* priest couldn't be bothered.

Penelope should've grabbed Luke's hand and left right then and there—but all she could think about was what she planned to say to Fulton Sheen when she reached his vault in the Crypt. She needed the perfect words to make him see that Stu was worthy of help. Otherwise, Father Sheen would ignore her. Just like all the penitents who'd come before her.

They were halfway down the staircase when Luke stumbled.

When he went tumbling, rolling all the way down, landing in an awkward sprawl at the bottom, she thought he must have tripped. She had rushed toward her son and then she felt the bite of cold steel against her neck.

"Freeze," the priest had said softly. "Or I'll blow you to Kingdom Come."

When she awoke later, she remembered the blinding light when something had slammed into the back of her skull. Now her head was throbbing.

And she was alone.

Somewhere in the bowels of Saint Patrick's. Hog-tied to a chair—with a set of colored wires running from her to a black box fastened to the paneled door behind her.

She twisted her neck around.

*No sign of Luke.*

She saw only a small marble room illuminated by a soft yellow light.

She listened.

No voices. No footsteps.

*Where had the priest-who-wasn't-a-priest taken her Luke?*

Then she heard a ringing noise that sounded odd. It seemed to echo from within the walls.

*Was that even possible—or was she hallucinating? Had her attacker drugged her?*

Penelope remembered something Father Bryant at home said once: that every Church had a few hidden passages, hollow walls, and secret doors. A long-standing tradition. The invention of masons alone. Never part of the blueprints.

Because even a Cathedral had its ghosts, and ghosts needed a place to call home.

# Chapter 5

Eve watched as Annie continued talking to the boy on the steps in a compassionate, calm voice. "Why don't you just come down the stairs? Bring me the phone."

The boy didn't move. He stood, trembling, holding the phone to his ear. Waiting for his next instructions.

Annie was asking the boy if everyone inside was okay. If anyone needed medical attention. She wanted to know how many people were with him.

The boy didn't respond. Eve knew that he wouldn't. Eleven-year-old boys from Yorkshire, England, didn't go to Mass by themselves. Someone important to this child was still inside—and that meant that he was going to do exactly what he was told.

Eve stepped closer to get a better look. As close as she could get without someone from Tactical objecting.

She noticed that the boy's wrists were red and chafed. He had been restrained, just like the first victim.

Now Annie was asking if anyone inside needed food or water. Saying it was really important if anyone was diabetic or needed medications.

She was still following the textbook: trying to build goodwill while gleaning important information. If this were a simulation, Eve's old instructor down at Quantico would have graded her an A+.

The problem was: This was real life, not a test. And this Hostage Taker was not reacting to Annie's script.

"You have f-four minutes to go." The boy's voice was halting.

"Honey, please tell me your name," Annie responded.

Eve shook her head. The time deadline was a warning. Annie needed to adjust her approach.

*Where did Henry go?*

"Where is your family?" Annie asked.

Eve needed Henry to clear her to go in, right now. Not because the Hostage Taker had demanded it. Because doing the unexpected was this boy's only chance.

"How many people are with you?" Annie was still on script.

The boy's voice trembled. "You have three minutes."

Eve considered running to join Annie. Then some instinct of self-preservation reminded her: She wasn't in official dress or carrying a badge. Not one of these sharpshooters knew her. Going rogue would be the fastest way of putting herself out of commission for the duration of this crisis. Or of getting herself killed.

The kid dropped to his knees. Started to pray. *Our Father, who art in Heaven, hallowed be thy name.*

Eve cursed under her breath, spun on her heel, and went to find Henry.

He was not with the NYPD lieutenant and his crew.

He was not with the HNT support unit.

He was not with the Homeland Security team.

She found him inside the tactical van, monitoring the action via live video feed. "You need to put me in," she told him. "*Now.*"

He pursed his lips. "Stand down, Eve. From my vantage point, Sergeant Martinez is doing an impressive job."

Eve didn't reply. They watched on-screen as Annie asked, "What does the man on the phone with you want? I can't help him if I don't know."

"She's doing what she's been trained to do." Eve jabbed a finger toward the screen. "But that's exactly the *wrong* approach for this situation."

"This is why we have training," Henry replied reasonably. "So negotiators have a script to follow when they are out in the field. If you were out there, you'd do it no differently."

Eve shook her head. "No. I'd give this guy exactly what he wants."

"That's the fastest way to give him the upper hand when the crisis has barely started. You learned that in Negotiation 101."

"He's going to shoot," Eve insisted. "He killed the first hostage. Now he's going to kill the boy."

"You're losing it, Eve. Maybe you've been out of commission for too long. Do you know how many snipers we have in position? Not to mention officers on the ground? No way is anyone going to get a shot off to harm the boy. The kid's safe as can be on those steps."

For an instant, Eve doubted herself. Then she heard Annie speaking, and she pivoted back to the screen. "Just let me talk to him until Agent Rossi arrives," Annie was saying.

Eve sucked in a breath. Annie should *never* have reminded the Hostage Taker about his unmet demand. Next to her, Henry squirmed.

The boy had finished the Lord's Prayer. He listened to his phone, then looked up. "You have one minute to go." He passed the phone from his right hand to his left. Then he made the sign of the cross.

*This can't be good.*

Without another glance at Henry, Eve spun away from the screen and raced out of the van. She turned the corner and then walked briskly to the area right behind where Annie was standing.

"I have information that she needs," she told an officer holding the perimeter. He had big ears sticking out from his hat; they had turned a painful red from the cold. "I'm FBI. I was briefed with Sergeant Martinez just before she initiated engagement."

She could hear Henry's order—*Stop her now!*—bark over the radio.

"It'll have to wait," the officer snapped.

"It can't," Eve insisted.

"Orders are orders."

"That boy's life depends on it." Everyone was trying to stick to the script—when they most needed to improvise.

The officer pressed his weapon against her chest. "Lady, back off!"

She looked up at the boy. He was trembling. He dropped the phone, then announced, "Time's up."

The officers surrounding the steps divided swiftly into two groups. Half raised their weapons to the sky, bracing to take out any shooter who lurked behind the scaffolding. The other half rushed toward the steps and the boy.

It wasn't that they were too late. They were simply unprepared.

Not one of them saw the shot. It came from an invisible position on high.

With utter precision, the bullet found its target, right between the eyes. One minute, life was there; the next, life was gone. The body slumped forward and a halo of blood began to grow around it.

People screamed. Others ran.

Officers swarmed and covered the weeping boy with their flak jackets.

Amid the commotion, Eve simply walked forward. No one stopped her this time. She took the marble stairs, one step at a time, toward the bronze doors.

When she reached the lifeless body of Sergeant Annie Martinez, she circled wide.

Right where the boy had been when his life was spared—where officers clustered, their eyes searching the scaffolding—she announced in a loud, clear voice, "My name is Eve Rossi. Pass me that phone on the ground. I want to talk immediately with the guy inside."

# Chapter 6

Once Eve had the cellphone the boy had carried, she turned away from the chaos on the steps. Her gaze drifted up, along the scaffolding, above the magnificent stained-glass windows, to areas where stone and mortar repairs had recently been completed.

*Where had the shot come from?*

She pushed the button that would redial the last call received. Annie Martinez had been wired—outfitted with a super-sensitive device that could record both sides of any conversation. Had she succeeded in establishing direct contact with the Hostage Taker, voice-recognition software would have almost immediately begun to analyze his speech patterns and word choices.

Now Eve was jumping in blind—relying solely on her ears and powers of deduction. It was far from ideal, but she was convinced time was of the essence. The Hostage Taker had made his point: He was commanding the action, and law enforcement couldn't even protect their own. Eve hoped to shake his sense of control by making an unpredictable move. In this case, by responding faster than he would anticipate.

The phone rang once. Twice.

Three, four, five, six, seven times.

Then a click. And a voice, rich and deep. "Good morning. Who is this?"

A male voice. Educated, with the *g* articulated at the end of *good morning*. And the phrase: *Who is this?* Not *Who the fuck is this?* or *Who's this I'm talking to?*

Eve took a breath. "This is Eve Rossi. I understand you want to talk with me." Her voice sounded all right to her ears. Calm and firm. Respectful.

"Glad you decided to join the action, Agent Rossi, not just stand by."

She listened to the voice, paying close attention to what she heard. *Self-confident. Cool. Slight New York accent—maybe from the Bronx or Brooklyn. He punches his initial consonants, like he wants to start a fight.*

"Speaking of action, you've brought together quite a crowd this morning," Eve remarked.

"That's because everyone loves a good train wreck, don't they? They don't want to watch, but they can't turn away."

"Yes, but train wrecks are accidents. It doesn't strike me that anything you've done is accidental, Mr. . . . What should I call you?"

She held her breath, waiting. Expecting him to sidestep the question.

"Mister?" He laughed. "Nice manners, Eve. Your parents taught you well. Sorry for your loss, by the way."

He'd done his homework on her, too. *Smart. Calculating. Prepared.*

"Plenty of people here are qualified to talk with you," she replied evenly. "Why do you want me?"

"I don't think we know each other well enough for personal questions, Agent Rossi. We haven't even begun to get acquainted. I don't know your favorite food; you don't know whether I root for the Giants or the Jets."

*He knows the playbook.*

According to the manual, the negotiator's first goal was to build a connection and establish a rapport with the Hostage Taker. To find out what was important to him: Family? Job? Hobbies? A special place, like the mountains or the lake? Eve's task was pretty simple: win him over, convince him that she understood him, get inside his mind, and eventually wear him down. She would need to know him so well that she could predict his every word and anticipate his every move.

That was the hardest part—though not because she wasn't good at it. She just never liked it. And she'd never done it when the Hostage Taker was in on the game.

"Why do you want to hurt people?"

"Who says I do?" He sounded surprised.

"Your two victims," Eve answered tersely.

He clucked his tongue. "You're not much for following protocol, are you, Agent Rossi?"

He was right. Standard operating procedure was to avoid all mention of the crisis. Keep the conversation light and off-topic. But she knew already: The usual methods would never work with this guy. "You didn't strike me as one for small talk," Eve said. "But sure, we can discuss the rotten weather. Or how the Knicks lost again last night."

He laughed. It was a small sign of rapport. "Fine. You were honest with me. So I'll be honest with you. The two people I've killed are dead because they didn't do as I asked. The boy lived because he did."

"But how did Sergeant Martinez—"

"I won't discuss the house mouse," he interrupted. "That's all you get. This was a productive first conversation."

"Not for me. I still don't know what you want."

"First, I want you."

"That's easy; I'm here. Now can we let those hostages go?"

"Ever watch YouTube, Eve? You should take a look at the recent entries for Saint Patrick's. You won't learn everything I want, but you'll see what I'm capable of."

"I've already seen something of what you're capable of. If you keep killing your hostages," Eve persisted, "then I've got to assume they're already as good as dead. I'll authorize an assault team to take you out and end this crisis."

He laughed again. "I can kill as many hostages as I want—and I'll still hold the biggest ace of all. Saint Patrick's itself. Why, I'll bet you've already got Landmarks and Church people shitting themselves because bullets are flying outside their precious building." His voice turned deadly serious. "I'll call you back in thirty minutes to discuss my demands. I've done my homework. Time for you to do yours."

There was a click—and he was gone.

. . .

Eve brushed past Henry Ma as she stepped into the tactical van.

"Of all the foolhardy things I've ever seen you do," he sputtered. "No vest. No protective gear. No wire. Completely exposed."

She pulled a notebook filled with blank paper out of her bag. Slapped it on the desk, grabbed a black marker, and started a list. In the first column, she wrote *Educated. Confident. A planner who did his homework.* In the second, she put *Important: Watching a train wreck.*

Henry jabbed the notebook with his index finger. "You aren't explaining this to me."

Eve shook her head. "I don't have a handle on this guy. At least, not yet." She turned to the Tactical Management Team, which consisted of four men and a woman, all wearing black jeans and matching weatherproof jackets. They were different ages, different ethnicities, different physical builds. What they had in common was their chosen profession and their ability to maintain a poker face around Henry Ma. "I need a chronology of everything that's happened in that Cathedral, beginning with when security ran their final check last night. I need full ID and background on the two victims. Forensic analysis of the bullet trajectory in both incidents. And blueprints: I want to know every inch and corner of Saint Patrick's, including all plumbing, electric, and sewer lines."

No one moved; then Henry nodded his approval. The woman tapped a button and opened a new window on her computer; the man next to her picked up the phone and began dialing.

"I need to talk to the man you took into custody this morning," Eve said.

"Angus MacDonald," Henry interjected. "He's with Medical right now; he was having heart palpitations."

"Then I'll begin with the boy. I need a private room—and space to work."

"Fine by me. What else?"

She stood straighter. "We agree that I'm in charge of negotiations."

"It's your show, Eve. No one will question the Feds taking the lead. Not after the NYPD just failed so spectacularly." A tight smile spread over Henry's perfect white teeth.

It reminded her again of how much of a political animal Henry was. And how the agents surrounding her were men and women whose allegiance he had carefully cultivated—or perhaps outright bought. They had followed her orders—but only after Henry gave them permission.

She needed her own agents. Agents loyal to her, not the FBI. Or to the rigid protocol found in the playbook. "This is an unusual situation—and I'm going to need unconventional help."

Henry's smile faded. "Your guys have moved on."

"Then I'll track them down."

"You can't be sure they'll come back."

"That's *my* problem, not yours. I just need you to do one thing: officially green-light the Vidocq Unit."

NEWS NEWS NEWS NEWS NEWS

# HOUR 3

10:36 a.m.

We continue to follow a developing situation in Midtown Manhattan, where we are talking with our correspondent on the ground, Dave Bledsoe.

He's at Fifty-seventh and Fifth Avenue, where hundreds—perhaps thousands—of people are being held behind police blockades. Dave, what can you tell us?

*DAVE:* I'm standing here with Ali Murtag from Commack on Long Island, and her ten-year-old daughter, Chloe. Their story of a disrupted day—and disappointed plans—is typical of many I'm hearing this morning. Ali, what can you tell us?

*ALI:* It's Chloe's birthday, so we came into the city to do some Christmas shopping, see the holiday window displays, and have a special breakfast at the American Girl Café. We've been here since 8:30, but the police aren't letting anyone through—and no one at American Girl picks up the phone!

*DAVE:* For those of you tuning in from outside the New York area, the American Girl Place is just one block south of Saint Patrick's Cathedral, across the street from Rockefeller Center, where a major incident appears to be unfolding. Stay tuned for details as we have them . . .

# Chapter 7

Eve divided her attention between the two computers now set up in her temporary offices in the Bureau's Mobile Response Unit. The MRU had just arrived and it was a technological marvel on wheels—complete with encrypted satellite Internet access and an independent power grid—and large enough to house at least eight agents. They parked in front of Banana Republic, the clothing store on the northwest corner of Fiftieth and Fifth, opposite the Cathedral. She had a direct view of Saint Patrick's from her small bulletproof window, but she didn't watch as the forensic and medical technicians gathered their evidence behind protective shields.

She'd just seen a woman she barely knew die in front of her. She'd just had a conversation with a man who took a life as reflexively as he might swat a mosquito. She already felt a hollow pit in her stomach and a familiar pounding in her head.

She reached into her bag for the small white pill that would relieve her headache, swallowing it dry. She knew there were likely many more hostages in the Cathedral. She didn't want to worry about them. She didn't want to watch any of them die. In fact, the less she thought of them, the better—or she'd be distracted from what was now her sole priority.

*The Hostage Taker.*

First, she needed to do her homework: find his message, scour the Cathedral's blueprints, and analyze the forensic report. Second, track down—and win back—the members of her former team. Third, learn what she could from the only two eyewitnesses to date: the boy and the old man.

*Am I really up for this?*

It didn't matter. The Hostage Taker had given her no choice.

There was plenty she couldn't change. She would never bring the dead back to life. There was no guarantee that she could save the still-living. But that didn't mean she couldn't try.

She toggled screen after screen, searching among videos. Filtering her search by *time* didn't help. In just the past forty-seven minutes, no less than eight people had gotten around to posting video of themselves at the Cathedral during the Saint Patrick's Day Parade. Never mind that it was almost Christmas and their videos had been shot last March.

*Maybe I should put a junior agent on this?*

She rejected the thought almost as soon as she formed it. She was looking for something specific—and she trusted only her own instincts to lead her to it. Plus, she preferred keeping control of her own information.

Eve knew that within the FBI she was considered a lone wolf. A far cry from other, more stable agents who had developed the right relationships—with superiors who protected them, trading favors when necessary. She'd trained as a profiler after discovering that she had a gift for understanding people—and manipulating them, when necessary. But Eve had never been a political player; she lacked patience for empty talk and games. She had experienced a meteoric rise in the Bureau early in her career, propelled by the number of hostage situations she had successfully defused. It all came to a screeching halt when a high-profile case went bad.

With the right connections, her career might have gone in a different direction. Instead, after a brief leave, she had accepted an invitation to head a secret, unconventional, and highly controversial unit.

*Vidocq.*

Modeled after the example of Eugène Vidocq, one of France's most notorious criminals of the late-eighteenth-century, who later in life was convinced to use his considerable talents on behalf of the police. Vidocq became a legendary crime fighter and head of the French Sûreté.

Established after the First World War, the FBI's Vidocq Unit brought together a unique group of thieves, forgers, blackmailers, and murderers—with extraordinary talents—who could solve crimes using methods that ordinary agents never could. The deal offered them was simple: put their skills to work for the government—or do hard time in prison. They were spectacularly successful, credited with everything from arresting German saboteurs in the 1930s, within days of their submarines landing off the Atlantic Coast, to taking down several members of New York's Five Families. Vidocq continued to adapt to the times, recruiting team members from diverse backgrounds with unique specialties, from weapons and munitions to all methods of high-tech security.

At first, Eve had felt completely unsuited to lead them.

She played by the book. They laughed at the rules.

Bureau training had drilled into her a sense of her own unimportance. They had oversized egos.

She had learned how to compromise for the good of the unit. The word *team* was not in their vocabulary.

In other words, she had absolutely nothing in common with them. Except they shared her impatience for bullshit, they were uniquely good at what they did, and, more than anything else, they relished winning.

Vidocq was a unit designed to serve the FBI during moments of crisis. Whenever they needed someone to save the day. Or, failing that, when they needed someone to blame.

Eve steeled herself, picked up the phone, and dialed.

# Chapter 8

Three and a half miles uptown at the public courts on East 106th Street, Mace—born Julius Mason but nicknamed after his favorite player—dominated the high-stakes two-on-two basketball game. From the top of the key, he dribbled hard toward the man on defense. He stopped, spun 180 degrees, and lobbed the ball to a tall, bald, stocky player. Massive hands caught the ball, then launched it into a long arc that dialed it in long distance with a swish through the net.

"Get the popcorn ready. It's showtime," crooned the player known as Area Code.

"Arrogant son of a bitch." The player who'd been dominated grudgingly forked over a couple of Benjamins.

Area Code grinned, revealing a gold front tooth. "I ain't *arrogant*. I'm just *good*." He pocketed one bill.

Mace snatched the other, frowning. Their take so far had been good, not great. And he was in the hole, big-time.

He'd been born with two talents: One for dealing. The other for Hoops.

He could return to the black-market trade—and if he was lucky, he'd be rolling in dough like the old days. That was what everybody expected. They'd been laughing for years at the notion he'd gone straight. Figured he'd come back to it when things got tough and he had to choose between paying his rent and feeding his rescue dogs at No Bull Pit.

But he also knew: If he got unlucky, this time they'd send him to Rikers to do hard time. And while his teeth rotted and his brain went soft, his dogs would end up back in the fighting ring, bloodied and probably dead.

That left streetball. Which in East Harlem took basketball to a whole 'nother level.

He pulled Area Code aside. "Listen, I've got to go big or go home. Ain't never gonna get what I need with hundred-dollar games. You in for five grand?"

"Mace, these ain't the guys you school downtown at the Cage. They play ball, but they got backup on the street. Where we gonna find that kinda dough if we lose?"

"Let me worry about that. You in?"

"Why not? All I gotta do is run faster than you if we lose." Area Code smirked.

Mace grabbed the ball and walked to center court, spinning it on his finger. Looked around. Let his eyes take everything in.

The rusted goalposts.

The fraying nets.

The four men besides himself and Area Code, all standing around the perimeter, silent. Wearing plain sweatshirts and layup shorts and fuck-you expressions. Mace didn't know their real names. Only their street names and reputations.

The Professor was rail-thin and five-foot-nine and not much of a talker. A lot of people thought he was stupid—that his nickname was a joke. But Mace figured out long ago that quiet was different from dumb, and sometimes silent guys were the most dangerous. That's why he suspected that the Professor was actually the brains behind the Queen Street Bloods. Opposite him stood Flash, who had a broad, easy grin—but his skin was covered in knife scars and he was fueled by an anger that could blaze up faster than any match. But the Professor and Flash were foot soldiers and they played average ball, so Mace decided not to worry about them. It was the other two guys—Grasshopper and the Shield—who were dangerous. Off the court, both were known for their hair-trigger tempers, bad impulse control, and heroin dealing. On the court, Grasshopper was average height, but he could jump; the Shield was a meat slab, a three-hundred-pound heavy who blocked everything coming his way.

Right now all four were staring at Mace with menace.

"You lookin' at somethin'?" the Shield glowered.

*Ghosts,* Mace thought. *Past, present, and future.*

Somehow, he always ended up here. Sure, he'd dabbled in black-market deals. Got caught and did a gig with the Feds. Maybe even found a spark of good in his soul by saving animals with No Bull Pit. But none of it mattered like *this.*

Was it pure love of the game? He guessed no other reason made sense.

It wasn't like he enjoyed hanging out with the guys: He wasn't a people person. He hated their damn lies and snap judgments.

And it wasn't like he wanted to be part of a group. Mace didn't join things. Never had.

But he was addicted to the adrenaline high he got when the ball flew through the net. Proud of how he could size up a player's strengths and weaknesses, figuring out how one brother's speed and quickness could trump another's tough physical play. Most of all, he liked talking trash and fucking with their minds.

When easy money was involved? Well, that made the game irresistible.

"Just lookin' around to see who's gonna finish second," he answered, oozing confidence. "Five grand says me and my buddy here can take any of you. Standard rules."

Everyone knew the deal. Each basket worth one point, game to eleven. Loser had three hours to pay their debt. After that, it would be paid in blood.

Mace spun the ball again. "Who's got the balls to man up?"

The other four huddled, clearly interested in making some quick dough themselves. Grasshopper and the Shield emerged from the pack.

Mace grinned—and launched the ball toward Area Code.

"Grasshopper's got your number," Flash said.

"Nah, I'm unlisted." Area Code dribbled away with the ball.

Mace focused on defense against the Shield. It was hard work. Mace might be imposing—six-foot-seven and roped with muscle—but he gave up a full head to the Shield. Still, streetball was a mind game, not just a physical game. Talking trash helped—even though some players just ran their mouths.

"You gonna build a house with all those bricks?" Mace grabbed the rebound after the Shield missed his third shot, passed it to Area Code.

Area Code took the ball at the top of the key. What he lacked in size and strength he made up for with speed and a sweet jump shot. He lobbed the ball back to Mace, who caught it one-handed—then dribbled toward the Shield, spun 180 degrees, and arched the ball fifteen feet toward the hoop. It swished through the basket, nothing but net. "In your face!" Mace shouted.

Grasshopper took the ball and sent a bounce-pass to the Shield, who was backing up Mace in the post.

Mace didn't give an inch.

The Shield sent the ball back out to his partner, but Area Code flashed into the lane, intercepted the pass, and sent a beautiful rainbow for a swish. "Somebody better call the cops; I just stole the ball!"

They won the first game no contest. Then agreed to play for higher stakes.

Twenty grand to Mace and Area Code if they won. Enough to clear all Mace's debts.

Only five grand owed if they were to lose. Even so, five grand they didn't have.

The Professor came in for Grasshopper. "Class is back in session," he announced, before grabbing the ball and rifling it into Mace's chest.

Then he backed it up with a series of jump shots, acrobatic layups, and dunks. He didn't talk anymore smack. In fact, he didn't talk at all. He just dominated the rest of the game.

And when he sent the winning shot through the hoop with a reverse layup, he smiled for the first time.

"We're fucked," grumbled Mace.

"How're you gonna pay up?" asked the Shield.

"That's my problem, not yours. I'll be back here with the dough in three hours." Mace gave them all an embarrassed grimace.

The Shield glared. "You shittin' me?"

Mace shrugged. "Standard rules."

"Standard rules for Queen's Blood. You ain't been part of Queen's Blood for years."

"What're you saying? My word's no good?"

Grasshopper rested his knife-scarred hand on Area Code's arm. "I'm sayin' we're takin' a security deposit."

Area Code ducked low, moved to launch a blow.

The Shield and Flash were right there. They flanked Area Code, close.

*Shit.*

Area Code shot a panicked glance at Mace.

*Great.* Now he didn't just owe eight grand to Diggs, a loan shark with two-foot-long dreadlocks and arms wrapped in skull and snake tattoos. He also owed five thousand to this crew. And he'd gotten Area Code into a pile of dog crap.

"You know I ain't friends with him," he answered calmly, trying to read their body language, but coming up short.

"Don't gimme that bullshit." The Shield's face was innocent, but his eyes were cruel as he flashed a knife. "You bring me the money. Three hours. Or I'll open him the fuck up."

Mace looked up into the dead winter sky, like maybe there was some kinda answer up there. Behind him, cars on the FDR were honking. Six teenage punks were coming onto the court, swaggering and arguing. An old woman in a cherry-red coat struggled to push a cart of groceries down the block. Problems came in all shapes and sizes.

Just then Mace's phone sounded. His ringtone was the opening to "Black Dog" by Led Zeppelin.

He glanced down.

Didn't recognize the number.

But the call was a welcome distraction, so he answered it anyway.

He listened to the voice on the other end. Then—despite the predicament he was in—his face lit up with a sunny grin.

A solution to his problem had just presented itself.

**VIDOCQ FILE #A30652**

**Current status: ACTIVE**

**Julius Mason**

Nickname: Mace
Age: 43
Race/Ethnicity: African American
Height: 6'7"
Weight: 230 lbs.
Eyes: Brown
Hair: Black
Prominent features: Three-inch scar by left ear

**Current Address:** 1883 Lexington Avenue (East Harlem).
**Criminal Record:** Multiple felony convictions—conspiracy to import and traffic illegal contraband. Sentence: fifteen to twenty-five years.
**Expertise:** Clandestine movement of goods across borders. Specialized knowledge of smuggling networks for weapons, narcotics, and exotic wildlife.
**Education:** Attended Bronx Regional High School (Hunt's Point, South Bronx).

**Personal**

**Family:** Mother, Dolores. Father, unknown. Brother, Marcus, deceased (gang violence); brother, Duane, deceased (drive-by shooting). Pit bulls—Romeo, Ace, and Danger.
**Spouse/Significant Other:** None. Numerous female partners.
**Religion:** Baptist.

**Interests:** Regular player, pickup hoops. Founded No Bull Pit, dedicated to helping rescue pit bulls from dog-fight rings.
**Other:** Abandoned longtime gang, the Bloods, when they became involved in dog-fighting.

**Profile**

**Strengths:** Loves nothing more than the thrill of a close game—and winning it.
**Weaknesses:** Doesn't play well with others. A loose cannon with no respect for authority. Operates by his own rules, preferring instinct vs. planning. Soft spot is love for animals.
**Notes:** His good-natured personality predominates over his intimidating physique. Wants to train his rescue dogs for the FBI K-9 program.

**Assessment prepared by SA Eve Rossi. Updated by ADIC Henry Ma. For internal use only.*

# Chapter 9

When Eve next dialed her telephone, it was to headquarters downtown. Tersely, she explained what she wanted and how quickly it was needed.

There was an uncomfortable pause on the other end. Then a voice said stiffly, "I know Director Ma authorized whatever you wanted. But this is highly unorthodox."

"You disburse larger amounts for Special Ops all the time," Eve pointed out.

"Sure, but for *operations*. Not new hires."

"Just repeat back my instructions."

"We are to allocate fifteen thousand dollars as a signing bonus, with five grand of that available in cash today from our discretionary fund." Another hesitation. "Agent Rossi, are you—"

"Please have the cash ready for pickup within the half-hour," Eve interrupted. Then she clicked off.

Before making her next call, Eve returned to the video search.

In the past thirty-six hours, five Midnight Masses from Christmases past had been uploaded to YouTube's Saint Patrick's archive.

She scrolled through each, wondering: *Where is your message, asshole?*

# Chapter 10

*Hangovers are a bitch.* Eli Cohen staggered through the door of his fifth-floor apartment at 123 Orchard Street, downed three Tylenol with a bottle of Power-C Vitamin Water, yanked the shades down, and collapsed onto his unmade bed. The mattress creaked in protest under his weight—at least sixty pounds more than his doctor preferred.

He wanted to fall asleep. Or at least to lie in peace. Instead, he felt like a knife was slicing into his brain.

Eli closed his eyes—and groaned.

While he waited for the Tylenol and Vitamin Water to work their magic, he found himself replaying the events of last night. The party was like a bad movie he couldn't bring himself to shut off.

There he was again: watching nervously as a woman wearing a black-and-gold sequined dress and bright red lipstick swayed straight toward him, armed with a pink fizzy drink and a wide smile.

There went his stupid idea that this holiday party might go okay.

He could have said it wasn't his kind of party. Or that these people weren't his usual kind of friends. But to tell the truth, he just wasn't a party kind of guy. He never had been. He had simply grown from an overweight, socially awkward kid into an overweight, socially awkward forty-something. It had been a natural progression.

"Are you Eli?" the woman had asked.

"That's me," he answered bravely.

"My name is Barbara. John has told us so much about you, I feel I know you already." She reached out and enveloped him in a perfumed one-armed hug. Miraculously, her drink did not spill. "You looked so lonely over here. Hasn't John introduced you around?"

Eli's eyes had drifted over to where John was drinking eggnog and singing "I'll Be Home for Christmas" with his two brothers. *Like three Long Island tenors,* Eli thought. The crazy thing was: They actually seemed to get along. No sign of petty jealousies or long-held resentments. Maybe that was because the liquor was flowing nonstop, lubricating relations among a large Irish Catholic family that was twenty times the size of his Jewish clan. He'd met more of John's cousins and aunts and uncles and family friends than he could possibly remember. Their names were one long, mindless blur.

He plastered a smile on his face and tried to look happy. That was what everybody expected, and this party—well, all parties, really—were about trying to live up to what people expected. Surely he could fake it for a couple hours. "Yeah, John introduced me."

The woman didn't seem to be listening. "I want you to meet my daughter." She gripped his right arm. "She's divorced," she added in a conspiratorial whisper.

Eli wasn't sure why that was relevant. Then again, most things people gossiped about weren't relevant.

Spotting no good exit strategy, he had no choice but to follow. Her fingers were tight on his arm. He noticed bloodred fingernails and a multi-carat diamond ring. He also saw the large mustard stain on his tie—probably from those mini–hot dogs. How had he already managed to ruin the sky blue Hermès tie John had picked out for him? They hadn't even sat down to dinner yet. *No way am I going to get through this without embarrassing myself,* he decided.

Of course, if John was going to be scared away by Eli's abysmal lack of social skills, better to know sooner than later. It had been three whirlwind weeks since Eli had gone to The Taste of New York and sat next to the good-looking tax attorney with thin-wire spectacles who appreciated fine food and wine. Eli couldn't tell a chardonnay from a sauvignon blanc, never mind whether the flavor was oaky or had hints of vanilla. He just liked to eat.

Amazingly, John hadn't cared. They'd hit it off—and by the end of Bobby Flay's gourmet meal, Eli had fallen hard.

Now here he was, meeting John's family already, trying to fit in—or at least trying not to stand out like a mustard-stained sore thumb.

Barbara steered him ruthlessly toward the drink station, where a rail-thin woman was nursing her champagne. She wore a green dress and a distracted expression. Eli immediately pictured a fragile glass teetering at the edge of a table, on the verge of losing its balance and falling off.

"This is my Meaghan," Barbara explained. "She'll be wonderful company for you." Then she waved to someone who had just entered the room and left.

Eli extended his hand. "Nice meeting you. John is your . . . ?"

Meaghan stared at him curiously. Either he'd met her before and had already forgotten—or she was someone John probably told him about. Who was he kidding? He was doomed.

"Cousin. Same age. Grew up next door." Meaghan tilted her half-empty champagne flute toward him. "Want a drink?"

He looked around. Everyone else had a drink. *Just try to fit in,* he reminded himself. Plus, maybe a drink or two would loosen him up. Help with the small talk.

He was desperate for a beer, but he settled for vodka with soda. That way, when he spilled it on himself—or, God forbid, somebody else—it wouldn't show or stink too bad.

"How long have you been seeing John?"

"A few weeks."

Meaghan smiled indulgently. "You're in the honeymoon period. I remember the night I met my ex. I was an undergrad at Saint John's, and I'd gone out with a friend to celebrate her birthday. He was there, drinking with his police buddies, and he asked me to dance. He was a lot older than me, but the band played a slow song and he put his hand on the small of my back and I knew: We belonged together." Another gulp of champagne. "You know how at every wedding, people say the couple is so great together? Half the time, it's just empty words. But when it's real, it means that you're actually better and stronger with this other person than you are alone."

Eli wasn't sure about that. But he'd once experienced its opposite:

a bad relationship in which he only became an uglier and more despicable version of himself.

Eli wracked his brain for what to say next. He'd never been any good at making small talk. "You still live around here?" he managed.

"Long Island born, bred, and stuck in my parents' house." She took a noisy gulp of champagne.

He'd pegged her all wrong. Forget *distracted.* Make that *intoxicated.*

"I've got you beat. I'm Lower East Side born, bred, and I've lived my whole life in my grandma's apartment," Eli offered.

Meaghan raised an eyebrow. "Seriously?"

"It's rent-controlled. Crazy cheap. And I'm unemployed." The instant he said the words, he wished he could take them back. Why did he always talk too much when he was nervous? He loosened his tie.

"How long have you been out of work?" Another gulp of champagne.

There were a couple different ways Eli could answer that question. *Since I was arrested for insider trading eight years ago. Since the only job that would have me disappeared three months ago.* He had nothing good to say. He wished John would stop singing those silly Christmas carols and come rescue him. "Sorry, I'm bad at parties."

A faint smile. "But you're good with ordinary social interactions?"

"No," he admitted right away.

That generated a laugh. "Didn't think so. That's okay. What do you do?"

"Told you: nothing right now."

"So what *did* you do? Let me guess—law, like John?"

Eli shook his head.

"Accountant?"

Suddenly, Eli was seized by the desire to feel important. Just for a moment, even if only in the eyes of John's lush of a cousin. "I actually worked for the FBI. A secret division."

That got her attention. She stood up a little straighter. Opened her eyes a little wider.

She waited for Eli to say more, but he was done. In two sentences, he'd broken every confidentiality agreement he'd ever signed. Though, come to think of it, did those rules even apply, now he had been fired?

"Let me get you another drink," he said.

He expected her to pass him the now-empty champagne glass she held. Instead, Meaghan leaned in so close he worried she was going to kiss him. Her lips mercifully stopped within inches of his ear. "Tell me the juiciest case you ever investigated."

Eli allowed himself another desperate glance in John's direction. Opposite the piano, where John was still singing with his brothers—the tune had changed to *Deck the Halls*—there was a small seating area. It had chocolate leather sofas and was near a massive flat-screen TV that made Eli wish he could just settle in with a beer to watch the Knicks game. And ignore all these people. "I don't think you'd find anything I did very interesting."

"Try me." She waved to a woman teetering across the room in silver sandals with stiletto heels. They looked hard to handle sober, much less after a couple drinks. "Hey, Lori—come over here.

"Meet John's new boyfriend." Meaghan slurred the words, but managed the introductions. "He was a secret agent with the FBI, and he's about to tell me all about his favorite case."

"I really can't do that." Eli slid off his tie and stuffed it into his pocket. Lori had steely blue eyes that seemed to pierce right through him, and he didn't want to advertise that mustard stain.

"We're all friends here," Lori purred. "I'd love to know what a secret agent does."

Two other women heard the word *secret,* and suddenly four women were watching Eli expectantly.

Eli thought that they were all missing the concept of the word *secret.* He answered, "By *secret,* I really mean under-the-radar. We were guys who got the job done without attracting attention."

"You don't *look* like an FBI agent," a woman with curly brown hair and a nasal voice pointed out. "What did you do?"

"Boring stuff. My expertise was money. Unraveling complex financial schemes."

"I thought agents had to pass fitness tests every year." Lori gave Eli's beer belly a pointed look. "Like firefighters."

"Not for my job," Eli said.

"Sounds like it wasn't regular FBI, then." Lori's eyes narrowed suspiciously.

That was true. Eli wouldn't have lasted a month in a regular Bureau job—even if anybody was willing to give him one. The bureaucratic machine at 26 Federal Plaza would almost certainly have chewed him up and spit him out. He needed the freedom—what fancier people called carte blanche—that the Vidocq Unit had given him.

"Good thing the NYPD doesn't require annual requalifications," Meaghan remarked, "or my ex would be screwed. Is that why you got fired?"

"I never said I was fired," he protested stiffly.

His eyes scanned the room. *Where is John?*

"But you're unemployed. Is it some kind of suspension?"

Meaghan meant it as a challenge to Eli, but she hadn't counted on Lori's interest. "Like your ex?" Lori placed a sympathetic arm around Meaghan's shoulder. The blast of jasmine perfume nearly made Eli sneeze.

"Internal Affairs is still investigating." For Eli's benefit, Meaghan added, "They think he stole from the evidence locker."

"What do *you* think?" Lori demanded.

Eli watched Meaghan take a moment to answer. When she did, she stumbled. "Yes. No. I don't know."

"Maybe the secret agent here could help," Lori said sarcastically.

All eyes turned to Eli.

He was used to being made fun of, so he struck a reasonable tone. "Not like that. I told you my job: I tracked down money. Unraveled finances."

Meaghan shook her head. "Internal Affairs can take their time. I can't. For God's sake, he has my daughter every week."

"Does *she* think her father did it?" the curly-haired woman asked.

"I won't poison her relationship with him by asking that. But I need to know, all the same. I don't know who he is—not anymore." She drained her glass, then explained. "Last year, he was coming off a double shift. Tired and distracted. His car struck a pedestrian crossing the street. He wasn't charged with a crime. He was sober and she was crossing against the light. But the man who left me to go to work and the man who came home that night weren't the same."

No one said anything. There was nothing to say.

Meaghan wanted someone to tell her whether her ex-husband was still a responsible father. The problem was: Nobody was in a position to do that.

Eli could sense the sadness as Meaghan stared off into some place he couldn't see.

"Don't you at least have a contact who might help?" Lori asked Eli.

Eli shook his head. He was disappointing all of them.

Lori jumped in. "I know you!" Her mouth hung open and her eyes were wide.

Eli put down his drink. It was time to leave.

"I recognize you," she insisted. "From the papers. White-collar crime. Money laundering. Tax evasion."

They were all staring at him with a mix of holier-than-thou attitudes and pity.

"I remember now," the brunette piped up. "They covered your trial on the front page of *Newsday* for weeks!"

The crowd around him was growing. "Deck the Halls" had finished. John was rushing toward him from the other side of the room.

"The headlines said they'd locked you up and thrown away the key," someone contributed. "How the hell did you get out?"

Eli just stood there, clutching his chest. A worthless schmuck. "You're right. I was in jail. But I *did* work for the FBI."

Then John reached him and hustled him away.

That morning, lying in bed, Eli was still running through all the things he wished he'd said. Different choices that might have led to a less disastrous night.

He had nothing: No job. No self-respect. And after last night, probably no boyfriend.

That's when his phone rang and everything changed all over again.

CLASSIFIED

## VIDOCQ FILE #A30888

### Current status: INACTIVE

**Eli Cohen**

Age: 46
Race/Ethnicity: Caucasian
Height: 5'8"
Weight: 237 lbs.
Eyes: Hazel
Hair: Red

**Current Address:** 123 Orchard Street (Lower East Side).
**Criminal Record:** Multiple felony counts for embezzlement, tax evasion, and money laundering. Sentence: thirty-five years.
**Expertise:** Corporate financial systems and the clandestine movement of money.
**Education:** City University of New York, B.S. and Fordham University, MBA.

**Personal**

**Family:** Parents deceased. Estranged from extended family after coming out of the closet in March 1990. Remains in touch with sister, Elaine.
**Spouse/Significant Other:** New relationship with John Murphy, a tax attorney.
**Religion:** Nontraditional Jewish, devotee of the mysticisms of Kabbalah.
**Interests:** Comics and fantasy baseball.

**Profile**

**Strengths:** Enjoys the challenge of deciphering complex financial models.

**Weaknesses:** A loner who doesn't bond well with others. Excessive preoccupation with his health (nondiagnosed hypochondria) compromises his abilities and work habits. History of depression. (In 2010, he was hospitalized for seven weeks following a failed suicide attempt.)

**Notes:** Isolated and misunderstood. Will attach himself to someone who understands him. His fundamental insecurity makes him vulnerable to the influence of more dominant personalities—including hostiles resorting to bribery or other coercion methods.

**Assessment originally prepared by SA Eve Rossi. Updated by ADIC Henry Ma. For internal use only.*

# Chapter 11

Searching the Midnight Mass uploads on YouTube yielded no results. But within the last seventy-two hours, five people had uploaded videos of the construction work at Saint Patrick's Cathedral. Eve fast-forwarded through each, scanning footage of stained-glass cleaning and concrete repairs.

Nothing stood out as remarkable.

*Am I just missing it? Is the Hostage Taker's upload among footage I've already reviewed?*

She desperately needed information if she was going to have any chance of defusing this situation.

She scanned videos uploaded for tourists coming to NYC. Still nothing.

Then Eve toggled through three YouTube videos of the Saint Patrick's Cathedral choir in performance and finally found the video posted by the Hostage Taker.

The clip wasn't long. Only three minutes, eighteen seconds in duration. She forced herself to watch it four times.

First, she focused on the wires.

Second, she focused on the detonators.

Then, she focused on the grainy figures who were doubtless the hostages.

The fourth time, she focused on the stone images. These were the most disturbing of all: stone sculptures that appeared to be part of a wall of the Cathedral. Except rather than depicting the usual saints or the Virgin Mary or even Saint Patrick, the sculptures showed the destruction of New York City itself.

The Brooklyn Bridge breaking in half.

People running in panic beneath the Stock Exchange.

The Statue of Liberty being swallowed up whole into the water.

*Is this terrorism?* Impossible not to think so. After 9/11, almost anybody would.

Unless she didn't understand the images carved into the stone. Was it possible these statues were a part of Saint Patrick's that she had never noticed? That no one talked about?

The Hostage Taker's message made Eve want to call another member of her former team—Frank García. A former Army Ranger, he was the one man who could possibly handle a Special Ops mission, given these particular challenges.

But a few clicks on the computer made it clear: García was not available. At least, not right now.

Divorce proceedings with Teresa had been contentious, and apparently he had threatened her. She obtained a restraining order against him—then agreed not to press charges if Frank would enter a program to treat his PTSD and alcohol dependency. He'd chosen one at New York–Presbyterian.

Eve felt a twinge of guilt, reading it all. She had known about García's issues. The problem was: The same paranoia and hypervigilance that had cost García his family also made him extremely good at his job.

She couldn't bring herself to dial after she closed García's digital file. Now that she knew where to find him, she could afford to wait.

She picked up the phone all the same. She had saved the hardest call for last. Her history with Haddox was complicated. So she planned to keep the conversation simple.

# Chapter 12

The rain that had drenched New York City early that morning had reached Boston when Corey Haddox woke up late—drowsy, satiated, and craving a smoke. He stretched his legs over the side of the bed and pulled on his white undershirt and jeans, listening to water gurgle down the drainpipe outside the window.

*Where is my shirt?*

Not on the floor.

Not on the chair.

Then he looked to his right on the bed and found it on the stunner who was snoring softly beside him.

She was wearing nothing but a shirt. *His* shirt. It looked grand on her.

He pulled a Marlboro Red out of his pocket, lit it, and sat—just savoring the moment. Taking one last look at the redhead beside him. A great kisser, phenomenal between the sheets. He was tempted to put his hand under her shirt one last time, knowing *this* woman's skin was lean, firm, warm.

Yes, he would have loved to spend more time with Bridget Malone. But he needed to get moving.

He appreciated how lucky he'd gotten. And Haddox knew one thing about luck: It always ran out.

He took a long, final draw on his smoke, then ground it into the makeshift ashtray—a soap dish with a pink seashell on it—that she'd given him for the nightstand. Found his shoes where they'd been flung across the room. Threw his leather jacket on. Tiptoed down the hall—and offered a silent prayer that she wouldn't wake up. Because now he had a job to do. And maybe it was the romantic in him, but he wanted Bridget Malone to believe *she* had chosen *him* at the Emerald Inn last night. She ought to remember him for what he'd seemed to be—a charming Irishman briefly in Boston to visit old friends.

It was gloomy outside, so Haddox was forced to turn on a brass lamp in the living room. He surveyed the room. Bridget's decorating style was pure Pottery Barn. Sofas with loose, easy slipcovers and cabinets with fake apothecary drawers. Brand-new, but designed to look old.

She was also a neat freak. The remote control sat in a special holder on the end table. Magazines were on the coffee table: *Pointe, Dance Spirit,* and *Time Out Boston.* They were displayed in a half-fan position, organized by date, with newer issues on top. This was good. Even better than he could have hoped for. A girl who organized her magazines probably had a special place for her bag.

*Where is that purse?*

He scanned the room, came up empty.

*Is there a hall closet?*

No. Which wasn't really a surprise, not in an old building like this.

He walked toward the front door. There was an umbrella stand and bench just beside it. A quilt was folded and draped across its length.

He lifted it up. Found nothing underneath.

He should've stuck to his original plan, which involved only chatting her up at the bar and pinching her phone. Problem was, he liked women—and he'd liked this one, in particular.

On the floor, he saw the simple ballet flats she'd worn, and his memory flashed to last night. They'd come in the door, she'd kicked off her shoes—and . . .

*Then what?*

The answer came: *Kitchen. Look in the kitchen.*

Her bag was there, dropped on the counter. A small zippered pouch by Michael Kors. Not much in it. Pink lipstick. A pack of Trident, spearmint flavored. He fished out her wallet, opened it, and found five twenties and six ones. Usual array of credit cards: AmEx, Visa, and Discover. Driver's license.

His heart took a hopeful leap in his chest—but the address was for this apartment. The one he was standing in, not the one he was searching for. *Damn.*

There were no photos or receipts or scraps of paper. This was the electronic age. What he needed was going to be on her cellphone.

From the street outside, he heard voices. Loud and angry.

He scanned the countertops. It was a tiny kitchen. Barely enough room for a coffeemaker and a roll of paper towels. Definitely no cellphone.

He returned to the living room, scanning all the electrical outlets.

*Nothing.*

He stole a glance out the window. The rain was still teeming. Three Ford Explorers were lined up at the curb. The doors opened and six men wearing raincoats got out. Two from each car.

*Not good.*

He wondered if he should return to the bedroom. If it was possible he had missed seeing the phone there.

*No, I searched there when she was in the bathroom. I was quick, but thorough.*

He heard the slam of car doors closing. The six men gathered briefly in a circle. One of them looked up toward the window where Haddox stood.

He shrank into the shadows.

*Definitely not good.*

They would be coming up now.

Two seconds later, the intercom buzzed from the street. Haddox waited—then hit the button and ran his fingernails over the microphone. He said nothing—and the voice that answered was unintelligible.

Bridget lived on the third floor of a walk-up. That meant four flights of stairs and two landings.

He could count on sixty to ninety seconds. No more.

*What do I know about you, Bridget, darlin'?*

Everything with a place. And everything in its place.

The purse had been in the kitchen.

He turned back into the kitchen.

*Think,* he told himself.

More noises. Voices. Coming this way.

He slid open drawers. One for silverware. One for dish towels. And one for exactly the thing he needed.

It was a charger drawer—equipped with its own electric outlet.

*Clever,* he thought.

There was loud creaking from the stairs outside the apartment.

He hadn't wanted to steal her phone. It was the information on it he was after, nothing more. Problem was: He had to get out of here. Fast.

He pocketed the phone and headed for the window. Flicked the lock clasp to the left. Tugged.

*Nothing.*

Looked down. Saw the window was painted shut.

He still heard stairs creaking. Voices coming closer.

He slid his pocketknife out of his jeans. Ran the blade around the perimeter of the window.

The six men were heavy. The stairs and landings groaned under their weight. Their wet shoes made loud squeaking noises.

He heard them make the turn. Reach the final landing.

He pushed at the window—hard. It resisted—then gave.

He slipped out onto the fire escape, into the downpour, at the exact moment they rang the bell.

Shut the window behind him. They'd figure it out—but maybe beautiful Bridget would take a while to answer the door. And buy him a little more time.

Most people would have gone down, made for the street. So Haddox went up. He practically tiptoed up the slick metal stairs—but they still clanged under his weight.

*A giveaway.*

He decided if he couldn't be quiet, then he'd better be fast.

He clambered up the escape, past the fourth and fifth floors, and onto the roof. He cleared it before he heard the sound of Bridget's kitchen window being opened.

He froze. Listened.

*Nothing.*

His shoes were full of water. His leather jacket was ruined.

Better his clothes than his life.

His eyes scanned the horizon. Five-to-six-foot brick walls separated this building from the three next to it. Nothing he couldn't manage. But then he'd need to find a way down. The fourth building, with its slippery slanted roof, was beyond his skill level.

Haddox was a Level One computer hacker—someone with expert coding skills, an intuitive understanding of how machines operated, and a unique ability to infiltrate impenetrable targets. He'd gotten where he was for one reason only: He always did the unexpected. It was the rule he'd lived by—so he applied it here, too.

When they figured out that he'd gone to the roof, they'd expect him to run as far as he could—to Building 3—before finding a route back down to the street. Or to be so impatient as to risk Building 1. So he made a different choice: He picked Building 2.

He swiftly scaled the first brick wall and crossed rapidly through someone's private roof-deck garden. It was washed by the rain and nicely landscaped with teak furniture and a propane grill that probably was illegal. The renter must pay a pretty penny for so much green in an urban jungle, Haddox decided.

He scrambled up the second brick wall and found himself on a roof that was exactly the same size with exactly the same view but a completely different approach. Nothing there but asphalt and a single lawn chair and a small telescope. Someone's simple urban retreat, just sky and stars.

He stole a glance down the street. The six guys had split up. Three were in front of Bridget's building. They'd be checking the side alleys soon. Which meant three would be headed to the roof.

The fire escape down was right there. Haddox thought he had time to make it—assuming he hurried.

Haddox wasn't entirely wrong. He set foot on the ground in plenty of time, splashing into a puddle. But he couldn't escape the back alley where the fire escape had taken him. One of the six was pacing by its entrance. Smoking. Moving like he was waiting for instructions.

Or company.

Haddox wasn't a fighter—not in a traditional sense. He'd weathered the occasional barroom brawl without too much damage, but he didn't fancy his odds against the six large men who worked for Jimmy Malone. But against one guy, and with the element of surprise, he'd take his chances.

He made his way down the alley toward the street. He knew he'd have to be quick. He'd have one hit only—because a long battle would invite company.

Hit the guy once and take off running. That was the plan. He rehearsed it in his head.

He moved to the mouth of the alley. Saw his opponent was about two hundred fifty pounds of muscle.

Kept moving forward. Out of the alley, into the open.

When he was right where he wanted to be, he said, "Got a light?"

The man turned as expected—but he had no time to formulate a plan.

Haddox jerked forward and kicked the guy full-on in the groin.

The move folded him in half.

Just for good measure, Haddox followed with an elbow full of torque to his head. That brought him down into a heap.

Haddox took off running. Past the three Explorers, around the corner. Saw Bridget's yellow Mini with the racing stripe. Right where she'd parked it last night.

He pulled out a small device the size of a cellphone. Wet, but still working.

He ducked into a second alley—and sent the wireless signal.

Most new cars today were just computers on wheels. And Haddox was in possession of a device—made of parts costing less than twenty bucks—that allowed him to seize control of a car's internal network. Last night, he'd used the Mini's Bluetooth connection to install the malware while Bridget was driving them home.

The small device connected to the car's controller area network. Haddox sent the signal to unlock the doors. Then started the car. And made a run for it.

He leaped over a puddle.

Heard footsteps running behind him—but not gaining.

He had just enough time to slide into the driver's seat and start moving.

In fact, he'd have had plenty of time—except for one problem.

Bridget Malone's car wasn't empty.

Jimmy Malone was already sitting in the passenger seat with a gun with a silencer pointing right at Haddox through the window, looking plenty pissed off. Haddox backed away from the car. Five thugs filed behind him, forming a tight arc. They looked equally unhappy.

"Shite," he said.

"Shite indeed," bellowed Jimmy Malone. He muscled his three-hundred-pound frame out of the tiny car. "Feckin' piece of shite. You skip-tracing bastard low-life scum, taking advantage of my daughter. Using her to find me." He came around the front of the car, spread his meaty hands wide. "Well, you found me, you bastard. Happy now?"

Five thugs were closing the arc behind Haddox. He was out of options.

Someone snapped his head back. Haddox felt his spine turn to jelly. This was not going to go well.

He was dimly aware of his cellphone—ringing—as it clattered to the street.

Someone clipped his jaw with a powerful right.

Haddox lost his balance, fell into a second guy. Started scrabbling at the thug's shoulder. No way was he going down without a decent fight.

Suddenly a large, fleshy hand was on his shoulder. Spinning him around. "What's this?" Jimmy Malone thrust Haddox's own phone into his face. Raindrops streaked its screen.

There was a missed call. His caller ID said it all: *Eve Rossi—FBI.*

"You a Bureau informer? Is that why you've been after me?" Jimmy doubled him over with a savage punch to his gut.

Haddox coughed and spat into cement. Jimmy had it wrong, but Haddox didn't think it would help the situation much to admit he was working for Billy McCourt. Jimmy's nemesis.

"You want us to get rid of him?" Haddox heard one of the thugs ask. He felt arms keeping him still while the others landed enthusiastic blows. He lurched toward a storm sewer; it was clogged with dead leaves, overflowing with water.

"Not yet. Let's see what he's got on us first." Jimmy delivered another bone-and-flesh-crunching blow. "And I thought you were just a dumbass liar for hire." He swiped the rain from his brow. "Take him to the warehouse," he ordered.

Haddox couldn't move. He could barely think. But he could recognize an opportunity when he saw it.

"Call the lady back," he managed to choke. "Tell her you made me. She just might make a deal you'd be interested in."

**VIDOCQ FILE #Z77271**

**Current status: NEWEST RECRUIT**

**Corey Haddox**

Age: 39
Race/Ethnicity: Caucasian/Irish
Height: 6'1"
Weight: 178 lbs.
Eyes: Blue
Hair: Brown
Prominent features: cleft chin

**Current Address:** Unknown.
**Criminal Record:** Convicted under the Gramm-Leach-Bliley Act of multiple counts of computer hacking, bank record pretexting, and identity theft. Sentence: twenty-five years.
**Related:** Though never charged, Haddox was suspected of killing his brother-in-law—a habitual drunk, wife-abuser, and leader of the splinter paramilitary Real IRA (RIRA). In retaliation, the RIRA has issued a death warrant for Haddox in Ireland.
**Expertise:** A rare talent in the world of computer hackers. Combines personal charisma with cyber-genius to become the ultimate skip tracer and con artist.
**Education:** Trinity College, Dublin, B.Sc. (honors), Information Systems.

**Personal**

**Family:** Father, Duncan (in Dublin nursing home with multiple ailments), and sister, Mary. Mother, Emily, deceased.

**Spouse/Significant Other:** None. Commitment issues.
**Religion:** Catholic, lapsed.
**Interests:** When not immersed in the cyber-world, plays guitar with whatever Celtic blues band he can find.

**Profile**

**Strengths:** Motivated by the need to expose hidden secrets and codes—the more complex, the better. Follows the thrill of the chase, which takes him job to job and place to place.
**Weaknesses:** Unpredictable. He resists being pinned down to anyone or anything. Deep-seated fear of flying.
**Notes:** Haddox is extremely comfortable in his own skin and extraordinarily perceptive. He cannot be motivated through traditional means. He'll be more likely to stay in the game if he's kept off-balance. He exhibits compassion for women in need, but will easily find any effort to play the "damsel in distress" transparent.

**Assessment prepared by SA Eve Rossi. Updated by ADIC Henry Ma. For internal use only.*

# Chapter 13

"Let's see if I understand." Henry scowled at Eve. "Getting your team back together has just cost me fifteen grand?"

"Not including the private helicopter from Boston. Or—"

He cut her off. "I don't want to know. When do they get here?"

"I expect Eli and Mace within the hour. Once Haddox reaches the heliport, it's a seventy-five-minute trip."

"Just get the job done. Assuming you can."

"Always appreciate the vote of confidence."

Henry's rigid smile contained an understanding that chilled her. "The fact that this Hostage Taker took control of the Cathedral at all has demonstrated superb planning. Yet he's murdered a hostage and a negotiator. Most troubling of all, he's made no demands."

"Except to talk with me."

"You know what this means."

"He's taking the kind of risks that suggest he's willing to die in there—never mind who else goes with him." She closed her eyes and thought yet again how the Vidocq Unit was designed exactly for these kinds of desperate situations. Sometimes it took a criminal to stop a monster.

And failing that, her team of ex-convicts was expendable—as Henry and the top brass had already proven.

*No, she did not trust Henry and the FBI. Not anymore.*

Henry turned to leave. "I have to go talk to a representative from the Church. Someone sent to be sure we mind our *P*'s and *Q*'s and don't destroy any part of the Cathedral. Meanwhile, EMS says the boy is ready for you. His name is Luke Miller and he's eleven years old. They got that from his passport. Because the kid himself? He isn't talking."

Six minutes later, Eve was sitting across the table from a child.

The boy with the spiked hair had been brought to her by a protective senior agent with a sour face and a box of tissues. Luke Miller sat down, fidgeted uncomfortably, and stared at Eve with reproachful eyes.

He looked small—his thin frame swallowed whole by an oversized NY Yankees sweatshirt. And scared—his smoky gray eyes churned with fear and hurt. Complex emotions Eve would never fully understand. Her degree in psychology and advanced training in criminal profiling had taught her a good deal—and her own sense of empathy filled in the rest—but the truth of someone else's pain would always be a mystery. Every person, she knew, experienced it uniquely.

But Eve could guess: Luke wanted this all to be over. He wanted to go home. Most of all, he wanted his mother. And right now, Eve probably symbolized everything that was getting in the way of all that.

EMS had given Luke a cursory medical check. It was their opinion that the boy had not been harmed while held hostage inside Saint Patrick's Cathedral.

Not physically, anyway.

Running his passport number had turned up his mother's name: Penelope Anne Miller. She had checked herself and Luke into the Holiday Inn Midtown two days earlier. A search of their room had turned up ticket stubs showing their recent activity. They'd toured Ellis Island. They'd seen *The Lion King*. They'd visited the dinosaurs at the American Museum of Natural History. Eventually, of course, they'd ended up at Saint Patrick's.

Despite having no ID as of yet on the first victim, Eve at least knew it wasn't the boy's mother. Penelope Miller's passport photo bore no resemblance to the woman shot and killed this morning.

Luke clutched an uneaten bag of peanut M&M'S—what some agent had scrounged up to help him feel more at ease. Eve had the harder task: finding the right words. Especially when there *were* no right words. Not for this situation.

Eve moved her chair so it was at a diagonal. She crossed her legs. Struck a conversational pose. "My name is Special Agent Eve Rossi. And I'm told you're Luke Miller—come all the way from Sheffield, England. That's South Yorkshire, right?"

Luke's gaze flickered down.

"How old are you, Luke?"

Silence.

"Eleven?"

Nothing. Luke wasn't talking.

Eve was the stepdaughter of a CIA spook, but she was also the child of a classical musician, and she had learned: Listening could be even more powerful than talking. To be a good listener, Eve knew you had to understand more than words. You had to observe. To pay attention to what excited people—or frightened them. To notice where they hesitated—as well as where they rushed ahead. To watch as a person revealed himself in hundreds of different ways. Hands. Eyes. Gestures. Expressions. Movements. Body language made it possible to figure out almost exactly what someone else wanted. Even if that person never uttered a word.

Now she watched as Luke ripped open the M&M'S bag and dumped its contents onto the table. He made one large pile of browns and yellows, reds and blues, oranges and greens. He shored up its sides until he had created an M&M'S mountain.

Luke began dividing the M&M'S by color into six separate piles. The brown pile was largest, followed by the yellow and red.

"The brown ones were always my least favorite," Eve remarked casually. "But I'd eat them fast because there were so many of them. Did you know, scientific studies have shown: There *are* more brown M&M'S in every bag?"

Luke didn't answer, but she noticed that his thin shoulders relaxed.

He separated the three smallest groups from the others. Orange, green, and blue circles were moved to his far left. Red and yellow partnered in the middle. Brown—the largest circle—stayed to the right.

Little. Medium. Big.

The tale of *Goldilocks and the Three Bears* flashed into Eve's mind: Papa Bear, Mama Bear, and Baby Bear.

She was still only watching. But now she had a plan.

She'd never spent much time around children, so she didn't pretend to understand them well. But she recognized something in Luke's M&M'S game. Not just an affinity for patterns. A certain precision of thought. She had no idea if all kids organized their thinking this way—but she thought this kid might. Because when she was a child, she once had.

She had been seven years old when she irritated her mother by insisting that no, she did not have *Gym* on Tuesdays. What she had was *PE*—which her mind classified as an entirely different activity. Some children focused on the literal. Maybe that was just what was required.

"I understand you're here with your mother." Eve made it sound conversational. "I know she's still inside the Cathedral. I'm going to get her out, but I could really use your help to do it faster. I believe you want to talk to me—but the man inside the Church threatened to hurt your mom if you did."

Luke looked up, cautiously.

"If I have it right," Eve suggested, "would you move one of your M&M'S toward me?"

She recognized his deer-caught-in-the-headlights expression for what it was: pure panic.

"He said you couldn't talk. But I'll bet he said nothing about M&M'S."

Luke gnawed his lower lip. Then a look of determination crossed his pale face. He nudged a brown M&M across the table toward Eve.

"That's great, Luke. I'm going to ask you some general questions. The answers will help me get your mom free. But I promise: You won't have to say a single word. The man inside the Church will never trace your answers back to you."

Luke nodded.

"How many other hostages were with you inside? Did you notice? I bet you did. You could show me with individual M&M's."

No M&M'S moved.

Eve waited patiently.

Then Luke tapped his forefinger on the table, twice, and started moving the M&M'S one by one. Spreading them apparently haphazardly around the table.

"So everyone is held separately? Green for *yes,* red for *no,* yellow for *I don't know.*"

A green M&M moved toward Eve. *Yes.*

"Can you describe any of the other hostages?"

A yellow M&M slid toward Eve. *I don't know.*

"Is there a priest among the hostages?"

Yellow crossed the table.

"Did you see anyone helping the man who took you hostage?"

A red M&M came to Eve. *No.*

"Tell me more about that man. Was he tall?"

Green. *Yes.*

"Did you see his face?"

Red. *No.*

When Eve felt they had built enough rapport, she asked the one question that would help her most. She wanted to know why the Hostage Taker had chosen *this* boy. The Hostage Taker was more than willing to kill. Yet with Luke, he had been willing to release.

Had it been random—because the boy was positioned nearest the main door?

Had it been tactical—because with his mother inside, the boy would be easily controlled?

Or was it a rare display of sympathy for a child?

Other answers would come soon enough. Given time, she would learn who was inside the Cathedral—and identify the Hostage Taker. But meanwhile, she would be negotiating with him. And if she knew the answer—*Why Luke?*—then she would have a much clearer idea of whom she was dealing with.

"Luke, I have one more question for you, but it's not a yes-or-no answer. It's your *opinion.* I want to know why you think the man inside the Cathedral decided to release you?"

Luke shuffled his sneakered feet.

"Whatever you believe, it's just between you and me. I promise not to tell anyone else what you say. But I need your help, Luke, to get your mother out of there—and back to you—as fast as possible."

Luke glanced toward the two computers Eve had been using earlier. The image of *Goldilocks and the Three Bears* flashed again into Eve's mind.

"Maybe you'd like to write a story?" she suggested. "A tale about a monster who invaded a church?"

He seemed to silently debate how to respond.

Eve added, "It would be pure fiction. Just a story. Nothing that would break any promise you made. Because writing a story is different from talking about a hostage-taking, isn't it?"

Luke slid off his chair. He walked over to the computer on the left.

"Yes, that one's fine," Eve assured him. "Let me close out my work and get into basic word processing."

Fourteen minutes later—after Luke had finished typing and the social worker had taken him to a nearby hotel with the promise of chocolate-chip ice cream—Eve read what the boy had written. His story was about a Wolfman who answered the door of a big church one evening wearing a priest's robe. The Wolfman smiled, but he didn't look friendly. The Queen didn't notice, so the Prince followed her into the gray, ghostly place. It was empty. Closed for the night. The priest took them to the basement, because they'd made a special appointment to pray with the Saints. They didn't notice when the Wolfman attacked. He hurt them and tied them up. Later, the Wolfman let the Prince go because the Prince was a good boy. A boy who wouldn't dare disobey.

The story had all happened more or less as she expected—but for one detail.

*The timing.*

They had been assuming the crisis started in the early-morning hours. Sometime before the first victim was killed on the steps of Saint Patrick's just before 7:09 a.m.

*What if that was wrong? What if the whole thing started last night?*

She put in a call to Information Technology and directed them to forward to her all street surveillance video starting the night before.

"Sure thing, Eve. Beginning what time?"

The agent talking with her was Tom Barrow. He had worked in IT since well before Eve joined the New York office—and she had always liked him. He was calm and steady, and he read technology data the way she did people: watching and listening from a thousand different angles.

So what time should she tell him to start searching? The Cathedral officially closed for the night at a quarter-to-nine. "Focus your efforts after eight p.m.," she decided. "But scan the footage from the entire day. And if you notice any large materials being transported in, particularly any trucks or vans nearby, please send me that as well. And Tom?"

"Yeah." His voice was distracted. He had already started work.

"I need this as quickly as you can get it."

"Understood." And he clicked off.

*Time.*

So often the negotiator's advantage. Except here, the Hostage Taker acted as though he had all the time in the world. In fact, if Luke was right, the Hostage Taker had taken control of the Cathedral last night—but not bothered to reveal his presence until morning, near sunrise. Why?

Most troubling of all: He'd still made no demands other than to speak to Eve.

*What did he want? How many people did he hold? How could they find out?*

Those were the questions Eve was puzzling over when the phone trilled.

Not hers. Not the FBI's.

The one Luke had been given by the Hostage Taker.

NEWS NEWS NEWS NEWS NEWS

# HOUR 4

11:37 a.m.

We have an eyewitness on the telephone right now. Vinnie is on the building staff at the Olympic Tower, the fifty-one-story building on Fifth Avenue next door to Saint Patrick's Cathedral.

Vinnie, can you tell us what you saw?

*VINNIE:* Well, before we got evacuated about an hour ago, I was working on the thirty-fourth floor, and I had a pretty good view of the roof of the Cathedral and Fifth Avenue. I can confirm for you that there's an ongoing incident inside the Cathedral. I didn't just see emergency personnel and NYPD officers. I saw what looked like SWAT teams surrounding the building. And some kind of temporary command post is set up on Fifth Avenue, right across from the Cathedral.

Vinnie, tell us about your building's evacuation.

*VINNIE:* NYPD handled it, assisted by some firemen and FBI. It was real orderly. Nobody panicked. They took us out the back entrance and told us to keep walking north. Away from the Cathedral.

# Chapter 14

Eve checked to be sure the recording device was active. Then she answered the ringing phone. "I thought you'd forgotten about me. You said thirty minutes. It's been forty-eight."

"I've been busy. You found my message?"

"I did. What's going on in there?"

"I needed to be sure you understood the situation. So you wouldn't be tempted to try anything stupid."

"I need you to understand something. I've taken your message offline. Before the media noticed it." She waited, practicing patience. Now that she'd challenged him, she would find out: Did he have a hair-trigger temper? Or was he truly an ice-cold planner?

"Careful, Eve." There was a hard element in his voice that betrayed the tension. But he maintained a tight rein of control. "Remember, the world is watching. Whether you want it to or not."

Eve replied coolly, "I'm not sure you actually understand what so much attention means. Helicopters circling overhead with telephoto lenses will be relentless."

"You've done a nice job keeping the media at bay. But I'm an open book."

"Then tell me your name."

"This is about my message. Names aren't important."

"The only message you've sent—and it isn't particularly original—is that you have Saint Patrick's Cathedral under your thumb. You've booby-trapped all access points with explosives rigged to hostages."

"Because you need to know the stakes: If you breach the Cathedral, people will die. And when your tech analysts finish analyzing the video, they'll verify that the explosives I've used are sufficient to bring down the Cathedral, too."

"I understand you mean business. But what do you *want*?"

"You have pencil and paper, Eve?"

"That sounds old-fashioned."

"I'm going to give you a list; it contains the names of five people you need to bring to me."

"My job is to get you and your hostages *out.* Not bring more people *in.*"

"Haven't you figured it out yet, Eve? This might be the greatest show on earth, but it's my show and it needs an audience."

"You said it yourself: The world is already watching."

"The world is not enough. I need these five. Let's call them *witnesses.*"

"Why do you need specific witnesses?"

"Not your concern. Your job is to bring them here to me. You have until seven p.m.—or more hostages will die."

"I need more time," Eve said quickly. "There's no predicting how long it might take to track someone down."

"I'll reassure you: No one on my list is vacationing in L.A. or honeymooning in Paris."

"We can put them in touch with you remotely. We live in the age of Skype and FaceTime."

"Do you know what a witness is, Eve? A witness must be present to see an event. Personally. To confirm the truth of it."

"I cannot bring people—*witnesses*—here. That's preposterous."

"Did you not understand the implications of that video, Eve? You saw all those images of New York's destruction? If you don't do as I say, they'll have to add Saint Patrick's to the deadly montage. You *will* bring these people here. Set them up in a bulletproof bubble, put them in the damn Popemobile. I don't care. But they have to show up to *see.*"

"See what, exactly?"

"The first name is Blair Vanderwert."

They were being recorded. Eve scribbled it down anyway.

"Luis Ramos."

"What about you? Once these witnesses arrive, will you need a helicopter or armored car? I can help you get out of there."

"The third name is Alina Matrowski."

"How do you know these people?"

"The fourth name is Sinya Willis."

"Do you have a particular message for them?"

"The final name is Cassidy Jones."

"How do I reach you, if I have questions? Like if two Blair Vanderwerts live on East Eighty-sixth Street and I don't know which one you mean?"

"You'll figure it out."

"Why me?"

"Because you came very highly recommended. Better get started, Eve. The clock is ticking."

"Wait! Is there anything you need for the hostages? Food? Medicine?"

The line clicked, then went dead.

Blair Vanderwert
Luis Ramos
Alina Matrowski
Sinya Willis
Cassidy Jones

Five people. He'd called them witnesses.

*Put them in the damn Popemobile,* he'd said. Was this about the Church?

Why did the Hostage Taker want these particular five people brought here?

Four and a half minutes later, Eve heard Mace's deep, husky rumble. "Well, now I've seen everything. Eli Cohen come to work in a *suit*?"

She swung open the door to find a pudgy man in his mid-forties standing awkwardly as another man approached. The first was wearing a burnt-orange jacket that made a fiery contrast with his red hair and beard—and did not match his olive-green pants. The other was a six-foot-seven-inch-tall African American, lean, with solid-cut muscle, who moved with rough, jagged motions like he was still playing offense on the courts.

"Looks like you raided your dad's 1975 collection, mothballs and all," Mace continued. "Dude, where'd you find that outfit?"

Eli tugged at his collar. "This isn't a suit. It's a sport jacket. The latest style, I might add."

"It's *orange*. Looks like you spilled your breakfast on it." Mace's eyes zeroed in on a dark coffee stain.

"My jacket's *tan*. So what if I dress better these days? You should try it." Eli's gaze rested with disapproval on Mace's gray hoodie and layup shorts.

"Eve sounded like she was in a hurry." Mace flashed her a wink before taking two giant steps and wrapping her in a hug that could easily have snapped her spine. "Me and *Welcome Back, Kotter* here, reporting for duty."

Eli gave her a shy nod. "Can't believe I actually agreed to work with this group of morons again. Who's the nutjob inside? Terrorist? Or religious fanatic?"

Eve allowed her eyes to wander along the wet, windswept landscape—first up Saint Patrick's twin spires, then back down along Fifth Avenue. Receding fog framed a scene that felt oddly surreal: the heart of Midtown Manhattan, frozen to a standstill at the height of the Christmas season.

A block uptown, the Cartier building was wrapped in a fourteen-foot-wide giant red bow. A block downtown, Saks was adorned with wreaths. And thousands of white lights created glittering snowflakes all over the building—a breathtaking spectacle to complement its iconic window displays, which this year brought back Yeti, the magical snowmaker. And just behind, a seventy-six-foot Norway spruce from Connecticut awaited its ritual lighting. Fifth Avenue should have been packed with thousands of people—tourists and locals alike—who'd come to enjoy the city at its most festive. Instead, all activity had slammed to a halt.

Traffic was stretched to a standstill for forty blocks in either direction.

Police in flak jackets and ballistic shields kept back gawking onlookers.

A siren wailed and a policeman shouted instructions into a bullhorn.

Keeping a wide perimeter, a helicopter circled the Midtown area.

Everyone was watching. Waiting. While Eve worked to resolve this crisis on the most public stage of her career.

"The hell if I know who we're dealing with." She opened the door to the Mobile Response Unit. "Come on inside, you two. Help me figure this out."

# Chapter 15

*I look down onto Fifth Avenue and imagine Eve inside a little box, racked with indecision, wondering what to do.*

*I sympathize with her.*

*How can I not? She has no good options.*

*Some situations don't offer any.*

*Seventy-three days ago, I was riding the M104 bus uptown around half past three. Dismissal time for the area schools, which had just started back after Labor Day. I had a window seat to myself near the rear exit. Students piled in, girls from a local middle school, pushing one another forward and shoving.*

*Rude little bitches.*

*I noticed the smallest one, wearing black leggings and an oversized pink T-shirt with sparkles on the front. She wasn't pushing or shoving; she was lagging at the rear. Kid had a thin face and sad eyes, and she was struggling under the weight of a purple backpack, brand-new, with no marks or tears in the fabric. It must have weighed as much as she did.*

*She wanted to sit down. She looked right and left for an empty seat, found one, and headed for it—an aisle seat two rows in front of me.*

*"You can't sit there." A fat girl with braces and frizzy hair dropped her leg over the seat.*

*"There's room if you move over," the smaller girl said nicely. She shifted the weight of the backpack from one shoulder to the other.*

*"Better get your vision checked, 'cause this seat's taken."*

*"You're screwed up. Who'd want to sit by you anyway?"*

*The bus moved forward and the small girl lurched in the aisle, struggling for balance. She almost fell.*

*I reached out my arm. She grabbed it instinctively—like she was reaching for a lifeboat in a storm.*

*With that single action, I helped her plenty. More than most people would.*

*She steadied herself and started to walk to the rear exit, where she'd stand until she reached her stop.*

*She jerked her chin up, trying to ignore the taunts coming from the back.*

*"What's wrong, can't walk?"*

*"One foot in front of the other, loser."*

*"You must have cooties—no one wants to sit with you."*

*I've never liked bullies. I despise the way they have a sixth sense for weakness. Some uncanny ability to identify those with shaken confidence and bruised egos—and target them.*

*I've also never liked standing by and ignoring a problem when something could be done to fix it. Most people don't care about trying to make a difference.*

*But what's the point of that?*

*Inaction is still a kind of action. Just like indecision is still a decision.*

*I counted nine different problems on that bus, but I figured taking care of the main one would solve the rest.*

*I started by getting up and offering my seat to the girl. Her cheeks went pink, but she took it with a shy smile and a soft "thank you." Then I walked toward the ringleader—the girl with the frizzy hair who'd denied her an empty seat. Who still had her chunky leg stretched out across the whole bench. Before I sat, I reached down and grabbed that leg. Then I twisted it and shoved it hard into her other leg, at an angle, so she couldn't kick me. The space wasn't big, but I had just enough room to jam her tight against the window.*

*"Hey!" she yelped.*

*I looked straight ahead. Kept my face calm. The other passengers didn't even care. They were too busy trying to ignore the raucous girls. Three girls talking might be loud. Six girls laughing and shriek-*

*ing could be deafening. But nine teenage girls? The noise they produced was inhuman.*

*Next I leaned in, grabbed Chunky's left wrist, and twisted. It wasn't a natural movement, given the tight quarters. But when it came to hand-to-hand combat, years of training made my movements fluid and instinctual. With my free hand, a quick blow to her solar plexus was payback for her actions.*

*She couldn't scream, though I knew the pain and shock must be stunning.*

*"Could've done much worse, but I think you get the point," I whispered.*

*She was sobbing now, great heaving gulps, snot running from her nose.*

*I stood. My stop was nearby.*

*The small girl in the pink shirt had been watching me with cautious eyes, not sure what to think.*

*I stared at her. "Backing down is never an option. 'Cause somebody like that? If they're hurting you, then they're hurting somebody else, too."*

*She nodded, uncertainly. She had no real idea what I'd done.*

*She had less idea why.*

*The bus screeched as it slowed by the curb. The middle exit doors rattled, then hissed when I shoved them open.*

*That's how I live my life. I take matters into my own hands.*

*The fat girl was a little brat, but I took no pleasure in hurting her. It wasn't about that.*

*There are no good options in a bad situation.*

*But inaction is still a form of action. Indecision is still a decision.*

*And justice is in short supply these days.*

NEWS NEWS NEWS NEWS NEWS

PART TWO

# HOUR 5

12:18 p.m.

This just in, from the AP newswire . . .

The incident in Midtown Manhattan that we've been following closely is now confirmed to be a hostage situation. We repeat: We have confirmation of a hostage situation inside Saint Patrick's Cathedral.

We have no numbers—no idea of how many individuals may be held inside the Cathedral. And no details on the identity of the person or group responsible.

In this day and age, the first questions that come to mind are: How is this possible? Who are the hostages inside? And could this be a terrorist act?

We are told the mayor will be holding a news briefing shortly . . .

FILE #B7685

## ANALYSIS

### SAINT PATRICK'S CATHEDRAL

**Location:** Full city block between Fifth & Madison Avenues, Fiftieth and Fifty-first Streets. Neighboring buildings are Saks Fifth Avenue to the south and the Olympic Tower to the north. Situated directly across the street from Rockefeller Center (facing the statue of Atlas).

**Capacity:** This massive structure can accommodate 2,200 people.

**Hours:** Daily from 6:30 a.m. until 8:45 p.m.

*(*Special hours may be announced on holidays as well as on the day of the annual Rockefeller Center Tree Lighting.)*

**Cathedral Layout:**

- Built of brick and clad in Tuckahoe marble.
- Structure is the shape of a cross.
  - * The long stem is the nave (332 feet long).
  - * Shorter cross-arms are the Transept (174 feet wide).
- Two spires rise 330 feet from street level.
- The Lady Chapel sits at the top of the cross. (Note: The Lady Chapel was not part of James Renwick's original plan.)
- The grand choir loft and organ are located at the bottom of the cross (second floor).
- Two additional structures abut the Cathedral:
  - * Cathedral Parish House, also known as the Rectory, adjacent to the upper left corner.

* Cardinal's Residence, adjacent to the upper right corner.

**Cathedral's History:**

- The land was purchased in 1810.
- The cornerstone was laid in 1858, signaling the beginning of construction.
- Work was halted by the Civil War and resumed in 1865.
- The Cathedral was completed in 1878.
- The spires were added in 1888.
- The addition to the Cathedral, including the Lady Chapel, began in 1900 and finished in 1906.
- The last major renovation was in 1931 (the organ was added and the sanctuary was enlarged).
- The Cathedral was declared a National Landmark in 1976.
- The Cathedral contains numerous stained-glass windows, sculptures, and other works of art that are considered priceless and irreplaceable.

**Blueprints:**

- No complete set of plans is available.
- The disjointed construction of the Cathedral (interrupted by the Civil War) and later renovations resulted in an incomplete compilation of building blueprints.
- Multiple architects. Hundreds of stonemasons.
- The cornerstone has been completely lost. Other details of the original construction are unknown.

**Alternative Access Points:** In addition to normal access points around the Cathedral's perimeter, there is underground access from the Rectory and Cardinal's Residence.

**Note:** Rectory and Cardinal's Residence Tunnels are easily secured.

- There are no other known access points, although rumors persist of a subterranean tunnel system with access to the Cathedral.

**Renovation Work:** Began in 2012 at an estimated cost of $177 million. Interior work ongoing. Exterior work nearing completion. Scaffolding fills the gallery to provide access to the numerous masons and wood craftsmen who are tasked with this meticulous, ongoing renovation. Exterior scaffolding in the front of the Cathedral—above the bronze doors—is in the process of being removed.

**Miscellaneous:**

- The massive bronze doors each weigh 9,200 pounds and measure 16½ by 5½ feet. They feature carvings of six saints: Saint Joseph, Saint Isaac Jogues, Saint Kateri Tekakwitha, Saint Patrick, Saint Frances Cabrini, and Saint Elizabeth Ann Seton. They were dedicated and blessed by Cardinal Spellman.
- Nineteen Cathedral bells, with a range of nearly two octaves, ring twice a day: at noon and at 6:00 p.m. Once rung by hand, they are now played from a small keyboard.
- There are more than seventy windows, many of which have frontage to Fifth Avenue.
- The Cathedral was named after the patron saint of Ireland.

**Analysis prepared by SA Kendall Longworth for SA Eve Rossi. For internal use only.*

## Saint Patrick's Cathedral Floor Plan

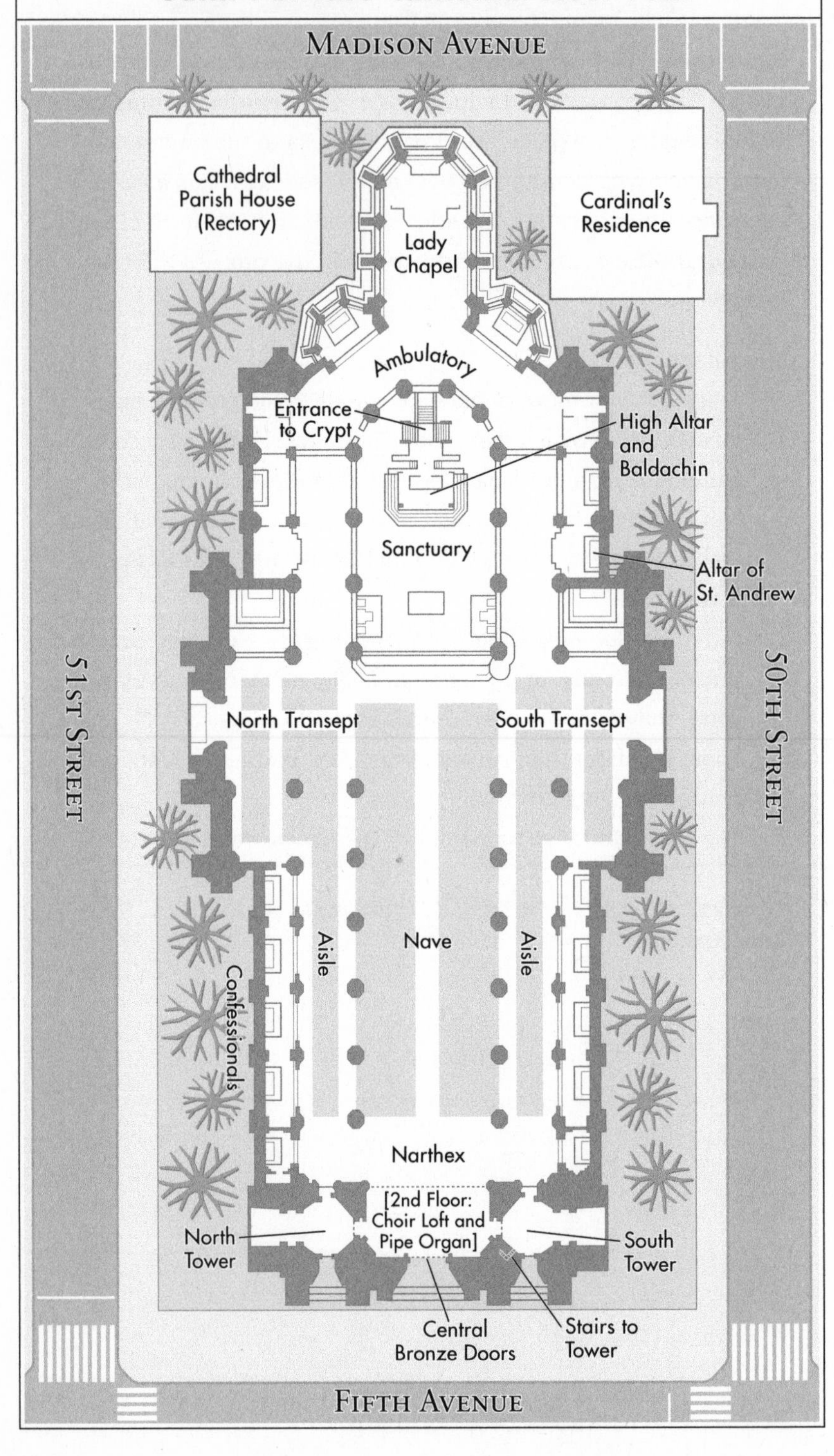

# Chapter 16

"We have two videos showing a limited view inside Saint Patrick's," explained Neil Brodsky, the FBI tactical liaison assigned to brief Eve. He stood ramrod straight between two computer screens, his wound-up-tight nerves on overdrive. "On the left, you see the YouTube footage uploaded by the Hostage Taker. On the right, you see the video that Special Ops managed to obtain. Individually, neither tells us much—and we certainly don't trust what the Hostage Taker may have staged for pure theater effect. But taken together, we gain a better understanding of conditions inside."

"*This* is how we're gonna figure out how many hostages are holed up in there? Can't tell a damn thing from that grainy feed," Mace groused. His enormous frame was stretched back in his chair, sneakered feet on the table. Completely relaxed.

Unlike Neil, who flinched every time Mace spoke.

"W-we confirmed that the Hostage Taker's video is largely accurate." Neil stumbled nervously over his words.

"Hope you've got equipment that shows something better than snow." Mace shook his head in exasperation.

"Since when did you become a tech expert?" Eli challenged Mace.

"Calm down, Kotter. Gotta see the ball to make the call. We need a high-def recording."

"Can you stop calling me that already?"

"Then don't wear that seventies jacket."

"Do you always have to be such a pain in my ass?"

"Who—me? I'm two hundred thirty pounds of muscle, sweetness, and light," Mace retorted with a grin.

Eve was convinced they never actually listened to themselves. She planted her elbows on the table and refocused on Neil. "Can you walk us through the details?"

The question seemed to please him. "W-we snaked a flexible fiber-optic pinhole camera through a sm-small opening inside the construction zone on West Fifty-first Street. A spot where repairs to crumbling stonework are incomplete. We obtained video showing an unobstructed view of what the Church has named the North Transept Entrance. That's the one on West Fifty-first Street nearest Fifth Avenue. We're calling it Door Number Four." Using his cursor, Neil moved a neon-orange dot on-screen to point out the area. "As far as we can tell, the Hostage Taker has taken the necessary steps to deter our entry. All g-gaps around the door have been filled with what's probably a construction adhesive; you see that here."

"Yes." Eve's eyes followed the orange dot.

"That d-deters our cameras as well as our ability to inject anything small—including gas—through the doors. Then do you see what looks like barbed wire, attached with concrete fasteners?" Neil pointed out wire loops that created a perimeter surrounding the door frame. "That's actually concertina wire. Which is expensive—and far more lethal than barbed wire. It's the choice of prison and military bases. Places where the highest level of security is required."

Eve thought: *Possible military or security background.* She said only, "Tactical must have the capability to get past it."

"Absolutely. It's just window dressing. Since it's *inside* the church, we believe its purpose is to discourage any hostages from foolishly trying to escape. Except here's the problem: He's placed additional obstacles. Do you see the motion-based mercury switch? That's the detonator. It's connected to a thin copper filament that's strung the length of the door. Notice how it then attaches to the scaffolding that covers the north side of Saint Patrick's—and crisscrosses, rung by rung, until it reaches the pews."

"Yeah, we see it." Mace stretched his arms.

"Watch. Two paired wires are connected to that copper filament. We follow the wires along this path . . ."

Eve's gaze followed Neil's orange pointer as it led to what looked like a package. Next to a pew. And sitting in the pew was a figure—with hands and feet bound. Almost as if posed for the NYPD and FBI to see. A visible deterrent. *Proof of life.*

Medium height. Medium build. Short hair.

Hard to tell from the angle, but possibly a woman. Eve thought she detected a flash of jewelry on one of the fingers.

"What's he got rigged there?" Eli squinted, nudging his eyeglasses up his nose.

"Basically, if we breach that door, the motion-based detonator will trigger and the hostage in the pew will die." Mace said it flatly.

"You're only partly right," Neil continued to explain. "Keep following the wire."

"So we can see more hostages? What I wanna know is: How many are there? When are we gonna talk about getting them out?" Mace slammed his palms onto the table, ready for action. He considered himself effective only when he was in the game, playing offense—not planning the next play on the sidelines.

"We only had a small window of v-visibility, so we couldn't learn how many hostages are inside. But we have to assume there are others, likely restrained the same way," Neil cautioned soberly. "All that is a challenge enough, but watch this." The video feed advanced. "Other wires and more packages are attached to the columns that make up vulnerable points, according to the architects. The whole system is basically a set of IEDs that form a daisy chain. If one point on the chain is tripped, a series of explosions will result."

"Kind of like a roadside bomb in Iraq or Afghanistan?" Eve hazarded.

"Worse. Basically, the whole system is what we call an HBIED. That's House Borne Improvised Explosive Device. And you're right that it comes from the Middle East—specifically, the military practice of clearing houses. Insurgents fought back by rigging entire houses to detonate and collapse moments after our guys entered." Neil turned to face Eve, frowning. "The problem here is that the house in question is Saint Patrick's Cathedral."

"Does this Hostage Taker really have the explosive capability to blow that building up?" Eli shook his head. "Seems way too big—way too much stone—to be brought down."

"People have said that about buildings bigger and sturdier than this," Mace countered. "Like the Twin Towers on 9/11. Didn't stop them from collapsing."

"Anything's vulnerable when you have the right explosives, placed strategically at the weak points," Neil confirmed. "And I'm telling you: This guy knows what he's doing."

"How did he manage it, anyway?" Eli asked. "It seems . . . preposterous that anyone could. How much help do we think he had?"

Eve said, "We don't know. As I figure it, and the details are still coming in, he succeeded by having extremely good timing. He must have entered the Cathedral before it closed for the day at 8:45 p.m. That's also when the night security guards arrive to change shifts with the day guards. Except the real night guys had each been phoned and told their schedule had changed this week, due to construction. No one showed. The day guys were ready to go home after a long day, so when a new guard clocked in and said others were coming, just delayed because the subways were having signal problems, no one asked questions. That left the Hostage Taker—and anyone helping him—alone in the Cathedral. He had already entered their secure network and disabled the security cameras. He would have secured the doors. Poured concrete to block the plumbing and waste lines. Rigged all access points with explosives. All he needed to take total control."

No one spoke.

Mace cursed. "How'd he get explosives and concrete inside?"

"We checked with the supply company that delivers materials for the renovation project. Turns out one of their trucks was stolen yesterday morning," Neil explained. "Except here's the odd thing: When we reviewed the surveillance tapes, it would appear that the same afternoon, a shipment of materials from a truck with the same license-plate number was delivered to the Cathedral. Forensics is checking the vehicle now, but I expect they'll find trace evidence of explosives. With hundreds of different workers involved in this project, no one would question the arrival of a shipment from the usual supplier at the usual time—disguised among the usual delivery of plaster materials."

Mace whistled.

"This nutcase has skills you can't imagine. I just wanted you to be aware of what we're up against," Neil warned. "Bear it in mind when you're negotiating."

Eve was thinking fast. "So while I'm trying to talk with the Hostage Taker, Tactical is going to explore different options for a breach."

"How are you going to do that," Mace demanded, "without jeopardizing lives? Just the vibrations from an approach could trigger an explosion."

"If we can identify vulnerable points, we'll stand a decent chance," Neil explained. "Basically, the Cathedral is buttoned up tight at ground level and below. But because of the construction, the upper areas may have some gaps."

"Like a big slice of Swiss cheese," Eli said.

Mace wasn't buying it. "Any hole in particular you're thinking about?"

"There was a stained-glass window behind the organ loft—invisible from anywhere inside the sanctuary, not indicated on any set of blueprints—that was 'rediscovered' during the restoration project. Maybe we can find something similar."

Eve frowned. "So a point of access the Hostage Taker may be unaware of—but at the cost of a historic treasure."

"Exactly."

"What about those symbols of New York in the Hostage Taker's video? The ones that look like they're from a stone pillar?"

"You mean here." Neil switched videos, then toggled forward until the screen showed a marble column. At the very top, there was an image of the Twin Towers collapsing—tumbling into the Chrysler building. Further below, cars tumbled off the Brooklyn Bridge, which was split in half. The Stock Exchange was in a panic, and the Statue of Liberty was drowning. The art was deeply disturbing. "The destruction of New York—or, at least, its fabled landmarks."

"Where *are* these images?" Eve demanded. "Are they part of the restoration work?"

"We asked both the architecture firm and the GC doing the work. Neither was familiar with them. They swear those stone carvings are not from Saint Patrick's."

"So they're either just a way for the Hostage Taker to make a threat—or they're from a secret part of the Cathedral that even those who know it intimately can't identify." Eve drummed her fingers on the table. "It makes me worry what else we're not aware of."

"Plenty, I'm sure," Eli grumbled.

Eve ignored him. "I've heard rumors all my life about various tunnels and catacombs that run throughout this city. Under the public library. Beneath Grand Central. Even within the first Saint Patrick's—Saint Patrick's Old Cathedral—in Little Italy on Mulberry and Prince. It's still an active parish—it has been ever since *this* Cathedral replaced it—and people say it's got hidden tunnels in its walls and catacombs, chock-full of ghosts."

"How'd you learn this shit? Part of your special-agent training, for the day you'd need to tunnel under a city monument?" Mace asked.

Eve shook her head. "Part of being my stepfather's daughter." Zev Berger had owned property in upper Manhattan where the original owner, a Turkish tobacco importer, had built a tunnel from the house to the Hudson River to handle the arrival of illegal shipments from abroad. Some later owner sealed up the tunnel, but Zev promptly reopened it. Its covert access to Riverside Park and the Hudson River had proven useful in his own work for the CIA. "His home was one of many buildings in this city with secret passageways."

Eve clicked a succession of keys and loaded a map of the Cathedral. She was trying to do what she did best: Think outside the box to accomplish the impossible. "We know of two underground entrances to the Cathedral, running from the Rectory and the Cardinal's Residence into the Crypt." She traced it with her cursor. "Rumor has it there's more. I need to talk with someone who thoroughly knows the ins and outs of that Cathedral. Maybe the project manager in charge of renovations?"

"I've spoken with him extensively," Neil said.

Eve leaned forward. "And?"

"The Cathedral is a unique challenge. Full of surprises that aren't documented on any map."

"But the workers who've had access to the Cathedral in recent months would surely know."

"We're talking about over two hundred workers each day. Rotating, depending on their expertise. Given enough time, it's entirely possible we might learn something from one of them. But—"

"Then I just need someone who loves the building and cares about its history—every single nook and cranny. What I really need is a priest."

Behind her, a door had opened.

Eve looked up to see a man with serious eyes, dark hair, and a cleft chin walk into the room. He was thirty-nine years old, six-foot-one inches tall, and wore a T-shirt that had once been white and was now spattered with blood. Despite a nasty bruise on his left cheek and a jagged cut under his lip that had only recently stopped bleeding, he was grinning.

In a musical Irish brogue, Corey Haddox said, "A priest, luv? No one's ever confused me with a man of the cloth."

# Chapter 17

"You look like shite."

Haddox smiled in spite of himself. He'd said those same exact words to Eve three months ago when they first met in a park outside FBI headquarters. She had been a stunner, despite looking all business and briefcase—there had been sharp intelligence in her hazel eyes and a complete absence of vanity in her tangled blond curls. He'd missed her. Probably because he hadn't yet figured out what made this woman tick. "It's grand seeing you again, too, luv. I figured it was only a matter of time before you'd come calling."

Nothing changed on her face. "*I* didn't come calling. This is about a case."

Haddox quirked an eyebrow. "Huh. First time a *case* kept my mobile number on speed dial."

"Lucky for you I don't purge my contacts on a regular basis. Or it's unlikely you'd be standing here at all—given you'd have two broken kneecaps. Now, take a seat."

He preferred to stand. "What'd you have to give Jimmy Malone to save my mug?"

"Remember that saying: The enemy of my enemy is my friend? Turns out we had a common enemy—and I promised Malone the Feds would take care of that enemy. If he'd just give us one rogue Irishman with an ego too big for his shoulders."

He'd forgotten how much he liked the sound of her voice. Warm and nuanced. "Sounds like I owe you one."

"Only one?"

Mace and Eli had been watching them go back and forth like it was a volleyball match. Finally Mace broke in. "Damn, Eve—you've been even busier than I thought this morning." He leaned past her and gave Haddox a fist bump, saying, "Relax, bro—she's been radio silent with us, too. Right up 'til this morning."

"Yeah," Eli added glumly, "and I could've used something to do these past three months."

"What are you sayin'—that you actually missed us?" Mace teased.

"Did a basketball hit you in the head and scramble your brains? All I'm saying is that I was bored. We still don't think alike, work alike—or even like each other. Only butting heads with you guys beats sitting home, having no life."

"So none of you stayed in the game?" Haddox was genuinely surprised. Not because Eli wasn't right about Vidocq. They were all self-absorbed, half-cocked pains in the arse. But somehow, despite all that, the sum was greater than its parts. He couldn't imagine them anywhere else than right here.

"Not worth it." Eli shook his head. "Besides, Eve wasn't in town." He turned to her. "I heard you went everywhere—from Hong Kong to Copenhagen."

"Don't forget Rome," Haddox chimed in. Wanting an explanation he knew he wouldn't get.

She shot him an exasperated look. He supposed he deserved it.

"I wasn't gonna work for some Fed asshole without Eve," Mace reasoned.

"We worked for several Fed assholes before Eve," Eli reminded him.

"Yeah, 'cause they all had a judge's order saying they could put my ass back in jail. Then Henry disbanded Vidocq and we all got a free pass."

"Look, Eve, we're all here now, except for García—" Eli began.

Mace interrupted, "Yeah, what happened to Frankie? On an extended bender?"

Eve ignored him. "Before we can resolve this, what I really need is information. First, who is the Hostage Taker?" She pointed to the whiteboard, where she'd listed only four descriptors. *Unknown subject. Male voice. Educated. Possible Brooklyn or Bronx native.* "I need identity. Background. And most important—motive."

"What about surveillance cameras in the area? They must show something," Haddox said.

"In the immediate vicinity of the Cathedral, they were disabled around six o'clock last night. We're going through other footage within a fifteen-block radius. But without exactly knowing what we're looking for, it's like searching for a needle in a wheat field," Eve replied.

"What did the security guards say?"

"The day guards from yesterday claim it was business as usual." She filled him in on the rest. "Our guy emptied out Saint Patrick's of all guards, bypassed the security system, and buttoned everything down tight—and in just one evening. We still haven't determined the number of hostages inside. Definitely too much for one man." Eve began pacing in front of the large whiteboard. "All that we really have at this point is his demand. He wants these five 'witnesses.' We don't know why—it's a crazy request—but they're the key to this crisis."

"Look, *witnesses* doesn't sound too bad—but who the hell knows what this guy wants to do to them," Mace insisted. "You can't give him what he wants."

"I don't like it, either." Eve stopped pacing. "Usually the Hostage Taker just wants to trade his hostages for something more valuable. A helicopter to go somewhere. A prisoner he needs released. TV time to spotlight his cause or his politics."

"So what is he?" Eli asked. "Terrorist? Religious nut?"

"I vote religious nut," Mace decided. "Eve said it: This was all super-*planned.* He picked Saint Patrick's Cathedral for a reason. Wired it to explode to Kingdom Come. Plus, he's talking to her about Popemobiles and posting Armageddon images involving this city."

"Even his idea of 'witnesses' sounds religious," Eli offered.

"We need to track them down and bring them here all the same. Interview them and figure out their connection—which may reveal what this Hostage Taker is really after. Plus, if they're here, I can use their presence as a show of good faith. To buy more time." Eve looked at each man on her team. "Bottom line, we need information. That's the only thing that will give us the upper hand."

"Mace, can you run the weapons angle? The Cathedral is rigged with military-grade explosives. Ask the right questions of the right people in the right places—and maybe we'll get a lead on who might've recently accessed that kind of equipment."

"*No problemo.*" Mace was halfway out the door. He wasn't built for sitting at a desk.

"Eli, you can start tracking the money trail the moment Mace gets a hit. Meanwhile, can you look into the stone carvings of New York's destruction that are featured in the Hostage Taker's video?"

Eli frowned. "They scare me. The fact they're in stone? Makes them seem more important. Like they're unchangeable."

"Find out what their religious significance may be—and whether they're part of Saint Patrick's at all."

"Got it." Eli stood, stretching.

"Guess that leaves just you and me," Haddox sat at the table, kicked the chair next to him out for Eve. "Partnering up. You know, like Fred and Ginger?"

"Astaire and Rogers?" She raised an eyebrow.

"People said she gave him sex appeal, he gave her class."

"And she did everything he could, except backward and in heels. You still follow that eight-eighteen rule of yours?"

Haddox never made commitments more than eight hours, eighteen minutes in advance. That used to be how long he could stay inside a secure government database without being noticed. The habit had stuck: In his line of work, he preferred to stay on the move. "I'll let you know in eight hours, nineteen minutes." He flashed a smile again.

Eve ignored it. "Good. Because the Hostage Taker has only given us seven hours. And we have five hours, fifty-seven minutes left. I need you to do what you do best." She handed him the Hostage Taker's list. "Skip trace these five 'witnesses' he's given us."

"Witnesses?"

"The whole thing is nuts," Eli muttered.

"No problem, luv. Not that I can't handle it on my own, but I thought you intended to help?"

Eve slid a file in his direction. "I just got a message. Angus MacDonald regained consciousness at the hospital. And he has something to say."

# Chapter 18

Haddox eased himself gingerly into the nearest chair. He was no longer wet, but his body was a mottled mess of bruises and abrasions from his near-death experience in Boston. He popped four Advil into his mouth, settled himself in front of the computer, and took a sip from his double espresso. It wasn't bad—from Dean & Deluca in Rockefeller Center, courtesy of one of the dozens of NYPD officers securing Midtown. He tried to block out the racket from outside. Sirens blaring, helicopters chopping, officers shouting—so many noises created an almost deafening cacophony. He needed silence in his own mind in order to focus. The scribbled list of names Eve had given him was taped to the monitor. Everything he needed for now.

He let the screen refresh, ran through a series of password protocols, and called up an online directory managed by the FBI. One that drew from a multitude of different data sources.

Haddox hacked in to this directory all the time. But today would be the first time in months that he'd accessed it legitimately.

Then he considered the list.

Blair Vanderwert
Luis Ramos
Alina Matrowski
Sinya Willis
Cassidy Jones

He decided to begin with Alina Matrowski. First, because she was female—and, well, he liked women. Second, because her name was unique. Even in a city of more than eight million people, he doubted there was more than one Alina Matrowski.

She was a twenty-nine-year-old pianist pursuing a master's degree at the Manhattan School of Music. Born in Moscow; immigrated to the United States with her parents when she was six. Her family remained in Falls Church, Virginia; she now lived only a block from her school, on Claremont Avenue and 121st Street. Her website boasted the usual array of recitals and performances—and she had begun forming a small studio of young students.

*Why would the Hostage Taker want you as a witness, Alina?* No idea Haddox came up with made any sense. And when things didn't make sense, he knew he didn't have the whole story.

Haddox scanned all available documents in the database. She had no apparent tie to Saint Patrick's Cathedral. She wasn't Catholic. She wasn't even Christian. According to the many papers her family had filed with the government over the years, her family background was Jewish. Although—based on a redaction of her father's citizenship interview—it seemed the Matrowskis were "culturally Jewish." They observed traditions of food and family, not Temple and prayers.

*Maybe you had a connection to the Hostage Taker?* He'd never know 'til he asked her.

Alina's home address and professional details offered a good start—but given their deadline, he needed to know where she was *now*, not at ten o'clock tonight when she might finally return home.

He found her cellphone number easily. Dialed. Listened to multiple rings, then a voicemail message. And clicked off.

That was okay. He had enough for now: Alina's number and her wireless service provider. Like most people, she had a cellphone plan with a regular carrier—entitling her to a discounted upgrade every two years and a certain allotment of data and minutes every month.

Unlike Haddox.

His motto was "one and done." Every day or two, depending on usage, he ran through a burner phone—a throwaway phone with a temporary, anonymous number. The choice of coke dealers, Russian gangsters, and people who just didn't like having their movements tracked. Whether by the government or by someone like him.

Only once had Haddox ever made an exception to his rule. He'd yet to rid himself of the burner he'd been using in Rome. He'd tried—even going so far as to toss the damn thing in Saint Mark's Square in Venice. But he'd immediately regretted it—and then spent a nasty fifteen minutes sorting through garbage, while fending off aerial assaults from the scores of pigeons that had laid a similar claim to the tourist scraps. The one person who had the number to that burner was Eve, and he'd found himself unable to sever the connection. Thinking of his last-minute rescue from Jimmy Malone, he decided maybe it was a good thing that he was a stupid sap.

It was amazing what you could learn about people just by accessing their cellphone records. Because what most people thought of as a cellphone was actually a tracker.

It didn't matter that Alina hadn't joined the generation that embraced check-ins with Facebook or Foursquare. Between built-in GPS technology and a proliferation of smartphone apps, her phone had captured a hoard of data beyond who she texted and called: what she ate and where she ate it, what she bought and where she bought it, the miles she walked, the books she read, the friends she emailed. When Haddox was tracing a mark, he used this data—and it was easy to figure out whether his target was a churchgoer or a gym rat, an alcoholic or a philanderer. Companies angling for marketing strategies called it "predictive modeling" when they used this data to forecast a person's habits. Haddox just called it "doing his job."

His fingers danced over the keys.

The computer hummed in front of him as he manipulated the data. Crafted a down-and-dirty algorithm to decipher his subject's movements.

When it yielded information about Alina's exact whereabouts, he would improvise.

Meaning he wouldn't lie—he would just put a creative spin on the truth.

It came naturally. He was Irish, after all—he'd been taught from birth never to take too strict a view of the facts.

# Chapter 19

At the opposite end of the MRU, Eve sat forward in her chair and adjusted the brightness of the video feed on her monitor. She couldn't afford the precious minutes it would take to visit the hospital in person. Even via the videoconference, Eve could tell that Angus MacDonald looked tired and weak in his hospital bed, surrounded by tubes and monitors. But he was alert.

"Mr. MacDonald, I'm glad you're feeling better. I'm Eve Rossi, the special agent in charge of the situation at Saint Patrick's. I know you've already told your story to another officer. But I'd like to hear it again, directly from you."

So Angus told her everything, starting from the moment he stepped off the M4 bus in the pouring rain. He told her about the woman in the yellow raincoat who looked so distressed but refused to talk. About how he'd tried to reason with her, get her to go inside. About how the center bronze door had been locked. About the funny red light dancing on the woman's head in the moment before she was shot.

Eyewitness testimony was often radically different from the forensic facts. Eve was pleasantly surprised when they actually corroborated each other. The ballistics report was on the table in front of her. The victim had been shot with a bullet considered standard for the M14 semiautomatic rifle—specifically, the M14s taken out of U.S. military storage after 9/11 and the advent of the War on Terror. The rifles had been rebuilt as precision semiautomatics for sniping use. Further analysis of the angle of entry would pinpoint the shooter's exact location.

"There's one thing I don't understand about what you describe," Eve said.

"What's that?"

"Why would the woman you saw stand on the steps—and not make a run for it?"

Angus grunted skeptically. "You got me. Maybe the same reason she wouldn't move out of the rain. People are strange. Sometimes there's just no figuring them out."

"Mr. MacDonald, I can tell you're a thoughtful man. And based on our conversation now, it's clear that you don't miss much. Even if it's just a guess, can you help me understand what you think happened?" Eve wanted to validate his emotions. To open his mind—and his memory—to possibilities he would otherwise hesitate to share.

He closed his eyes slowly and exhaled, clearly exhausted. "I knew something was wrong in there. I guess I was naïve thinking the cop could handle it."

Eve's fingers had been tracing the makeshift blueprints of Saint Patrick's. They suddenly stopped. "What cop?"

Angus's official report had not mentioned a police officer.

Angus opened his eyes again. "I saw him trying to talk sense into the woman. I was still a couple blocks away."

"Did she respond to him?"

"Ignored him, best I can tell. Like she did me."

"How did he respond to that?"

"I got the impression he was exasperated. No patience. So he went inside."

"Did he call it in?" Eve made a few clicks at the keyboard to pull up all of the initial police reports once again. Maybe she had missed it.

*Unlikely.*

"I dunno. Don't think he had time. Maybe he meant to, once he was in. It was raining cats and dogs."

"What did he look like?"

"White, I think. About my height, so maybe six-foot-one."

"Why did you think he was a cop?"

Angus shifted slightly. "He was wearing one of those NYPD rain slickers."

*Something anyone could buy on eBay,* Eve thought.

Then Angus added, "Plus, he moved like a cop. With authority. Like he'd dealt with wackos too many times. Like he was beat after a long shift. I think that's why he wasn't very patient with the woman."

"And he definitely went inside the center bronze door?"

"Yeah. Guess he was the last one in before somebody locked it."

The reality of it dawned slowly on Eve. They had so many unresolved questions about who was inside the Cathedral. It was a relief finally having one answer—even if it was incomplete. Despite the enormous odds stacked against them, maybe there was a cop inside.

A trained ally. One of the good guys.

But lacking patience. Not the right sort of temperament to be helpful at all.

And possibly disabled. Because a cop would surely have been a target. Who knew what had happened to him, once he went inside?

NEWS NEWS NEWS NEWS NEWS

# HOUR 6

1:19 p.m.

For our viewers just tuning in now, we're bringing you the mayor of New York with an urgent update on the emergency response effort under way to contain a hostage crisis at Saint Patrick's Cathedral . . .

*THE MAYOR:* Today is, obviously, a difficult moment for our city. On what should be a joyous day, when thousands of tourists and locals come together to mark the beginning of our Christmas season with the annual Rockefeller Center Christmas Tree Lighting, we're instead confronting an emergency at one of this city's most beloved landmarks.

As this is an ongoing crisis, we will be taking no questions at this time.

However, before I turn this over to the police commissioner, who will update you on the city's response and closures in the area, I want to broadcast a special number. If you have concerns about friends, family, or coworkers who may be impacted by the events of this morning at Saint Patrick's Cathedral, please call 212-555-6699.

*UNIDENTIFIED REPORTER #1:* How did this happen?

*UNIDENTIFIED REPORTER #2:* Has FBI or NYPD taken control of the scene?

*UNIDENTIFIED REPORTER #3:* Is this terrorism?
*UNIDENTIFIED REPORTER #4:* How many people are inside?
*UNIDENTIFIED REPORTER #5:* What are the terrorist's demands?
*UNIDENTIFIED REPORTER #6:* Can you tell us if there are casualties? We heard a woman was shot.

# Chapter 20

One witness down. Four to go.

Haddox punched Cassidy Jones's name into the database next. With a name like Cassidy, he bet she would be young and interesting.

He waited as the computer whirled through DMV records. Tax files. Arrest records. Visa applications. Social Security numbers.

Meanwhile, he ran a search on the Web, including Facebook, Instagram, ask.fm, and other sites. And immediately saw that he had a problem.

*Stumped.*

There were too many Cassidy Joneses. The New York area had them in spades. Maybe not quite as bad as results would be for Joe Smith or John Doe—a name for which, surprisingly, there were plenty of the genuine article around.

Without information to narrow his search, he didn't know how to proceed. Guess Eve was going to have to ask the Hostage Taker for clarification. And unless he happened to call her, she was probably going to have to do it herself the old-fashioned way: in front of the Cathedral with a sign or a bullhorn. Because so far, the Hostage Taker hadn't called from the same cell number twice. He was cycling through burners.

Haddox glanced at the cellphone the Hostage Taker had used to communicate—first with the boy, then with Eve. And his thoughts snagged on a half-remembered conversation. Despite the throbbing pain that the Advil had yet to quell, he grinned with anticipation.

Maybe there was a different way.

It was a long shot that he would be able to do anything. Of course they had identified the original number the Hostage Taker had called from, using the phone Luke Miller had used. Both burner phones had been manufactured by Nokia and were part of a batch sold in the Netherlands. Both operated on GSM—the Global System for Mobile Communications—and thus were able to work anywhere in the world. Both had been purchased with cash, so no personal data was exchanged. And if the Hostage Taker were anything like Haddox, he would have purchased a store of these—procured not just from the Netherlands but from around the world.

Based on something he'd once learned from an NSA hacker named Shadow Fox, Haddox knew that it was possible to gather information on a target who routinely cycled through random cellphones. You looked for phone numbers on the network that had been used for single, unique contacts—and you focused on the time each call started and ended. Basically, you looked for a sequence of calls that had distinctive characteristics. Shadow Fox called them *lonely calls*. Onetime calls from onetime numbers that were never used again. Each call would be short, lasting a limited amount of time—and after it went dead, another unique, lonely number would come online. If the analysis worked out right, you could identify a whole series of burner phones that—taken together—created a portrait as unique as a fingerprint.

This was going to be a challenge.

A completely irresistible one.

And the only place to start was with what he already knew.

Haddox's screen refreshed with the details of the burner phone they had recovered from the boy.

Its first call was received at 10:12. That was the Hostage Taker on the line with the boy, giving him instructions. Its last call was made at 10:23. That was Eve reverse-dialing the Hostage Taker after the NYPD negotiator was shot. Giving them two cell numbers in the sequence.

The key question now was: Could he identify the other burners in the Hostage Taker's control?

Every cellphone identified itself less by its mobile identification number—the number assigned by the service provider that was similar to a landline number—than by its electronic serial number. Called the ESN, that number was a thirty-two-bit binary number assigned by the manufacturer. Unlike mobile numbers, it could never be changed. And when manufacturers sent phones to suppliers, they tended to sell them in large blocks. So if the Hostage Taker had bought more than one phone from each supplier—which seemed likely—Haddox would be able to track him down by running all the ESNs in that shipment.

Assuming the Hostage Taker had left the batteries inside—charged up and ready to go, of course. Because even if a cellphone was turned off, so long as its battery was present, it emitted a signal looking for base stations within range. That signal—a "ping"—lasted less than a quarter of a second. But it contained both the mobile identification number and the ESN.

Haddox focused his attention on the monitor and called up a new search. It yielded a screen covered with numbers.

His fingers raced over the keyboard, typing in the parameters for two different searches. One was designed to search for any ESNs that were close enough to the cellphone they had in hand, so as to be part of the same supply shipment. The other was designed to search for any ESNs within close range of the cell tower nearest Saint Patrick's Cathedral that were active but had never been used. Primed for action but not yet in the field. The screen split in two. Each contained a string of numbers that flashed by fast, blurring into green psychedelic lines.

Eight minutes later, he gestured for Eve to join him. "You want to call the Hostage Taker—or should I?"

She frowned. "I don't follow."

"We need to ask him *which* Cassidy Jones. Because there are currently forty-seven Cassidy Joneses in Manhattan, never mind Brooklyn, Queens, Long Island, or Connecticut."

"And you found the Hostage Taker's number? So you can just dial him up whenever you want?"

"Better than that. I've got a whole series of numbers he's either already using or is just about to use. In other words, luv, I've given you the upper hand." With a wink, he passed her the phone. "You can thank me later."

# Chapter 21

Mace wiped off a park bench and sat, eating two double cheeseburgers and slurping a mega-size strawberry milkshake. The rain had finally stopped, but the sun hadn't pushed through the clouds and the temperature was dropping fast. Behind him, the dollars were flowing as the chess hustlers ran their games. He watched a homeless man with gray hair resembling an overgrown shrub push a grocery cart along the path, peering into one garbage can after another for discarded cans and bottles. An NYU student tour, led by a tall, perky blonde, made a wide semicircle to avoid him. The kids in the tour continued chatting and sloshing through puddles. A handful of parents—probably visiting for the first time from some flyover state—gawked.

His bench was near the center of Washington Square Park. The heart of Greenwich Village. Bordering NYU. A lot of real estate that you had to be LeBron James to afford. And right next to the East Village, which still had some of the city's best watering holes. Mace usually came around when he was heading to a pickup game at the Cage—a public court on West Fourth Street where some of basketball's best talent cut their teeth. Today he'd come to meet Sweet Pea. She was a former Knicks City Dancer. Twenty years ago, she'd had a dancer's body—lean, loose-limbed, and damn . . . he still remembered those legs. When her dancing gig ended, she'd opened her own East Village bar. Except hers wasn't filled with wannabe punks sporting tattoos and piercings. Hers attracted two kinds of guys: NYPD's finest and guys deep in the game. That meant she had her ear to the ground when almost anything happened. White Hat or Black Hat side, didn't matter.

"Hey, baby." She sidled up behind him. Planted a kiss on his head before coming around to join him on the bench. It groaned in protest.

Mace flashed her a wide smile. Sweet Pea might've traded a size six for a size sixteen, but that meant only that her style was less Tyra Banks, more Oprah Winfrey. A fine woman either way. "You're lookin' good," he said, and meant it.

"Don't you know it." She gave him a sly smile, then edged a few inches closer. "How's things at the Bull Pit?" She meant No Bull Pit, the organization Mace had started up a few years back when he'd found himself rescuing one dog—then another, and another—from the fighting rings. He healed them, rehabilitated them, and trained them to be working canines: detecting explosives and drugs. Someday, it might be a living. Meanwhile, he was having fun.

"Same old. How's things at the Blue Parrot?"

Sweet Pea took a bottle of water from her tote bag, swallowed a gulp. "Business is good. No complaints."

"You still shoot the shit with Freddy and the boys?" Some of Mace's former contacts in the black-market trade. They dealt in all kinds of contraband and stolen goods. But especially weapons.

"Most every night."

"They talk recently about somethin' interesting?"

"What interests you these days, darlin'?"

"Anything involving concertina wire and explosives. The kind you might use to make an IED."

"Sounds military to me."

"Yeah, but the military ain't in the resale business. Least, not to regular guys." He leaned in a little closer. Caught her scent: something lemony and lavender. It made him remember the night they'd met. She'd stopped by the Cage to watch her boyfriend—and witnessed one of Mace's best moments ever. He'd gone one-on-one against his namesake—the original Mace-in-your-Face—and won. Later that night, she'd said goodbye to the boyfriend and let Mace buy her a drink. She'd chosen him that night. And then kept coming back for more. 'Cause Mace's skills didn't end on the basketball court.

She tipped her head back and laughed. "Regular guys don't buy military-grade stuff."

"But supposing they did?"

"You wanna know where. This have anything to do with what's goin' on today at Saint Patrick's?"

Mace put a leg up on the bench. "Maybe . . . assuming you heard people talkin'."

"Freddy and the boys are quiet. If they got anything goin' on, they ain't runnin' their mouths."

"But?"

She let out a noisy breath, like the weight of the world was escaping her. "The fuzz is another matter. Drug Enforcement guys were in last night."

"I'm not lookin' for missing drugs."

"Will you shut up and listen? Stuff's been goin' missing from their evidence locker for a few months now. Meth. Coke. Ecstasy. Even outright cash. But last night, they were talkin' 'bout a different kind of theft. Few months ago, they chalked up a huge bust. High fives all 'round, special commendations, 'cause it was a big, influential dealer. Took a lot of manpower, too. Drug dealer had partnered with guys just come off a private security detail in Iraq to guard his stash. So in addition to the drug haul, they took in all kinds of shit. Military-grade stuff—including explosives, barbed wire deterrent, the works."

"Shit that got stolen."

She nodded sagely.

"Which precinct division?"

"Midtown West logged it in. And here's the kicker: It's the same locker where the drugs got stolen, too."

"They know who did it?"

"They got a line on somebody, but who the hell really knows?" Sweet Pea heaved herself to her feet. "I gotta get back. New staff learnin' the ropes today." Her smile flashed. "You know where to find me. And if you do, you won't be disappointed."

# Chapter 22

There were moments when Eli was ashamed of himself. Sure, he felt bad that not a hundred yards away from him, people were suffering, their lives in imminent danger. But there was one part of this hostage crisis that he could get used to: the food. Because Eve's team was expected to work around the clock until this thing was resolved, a junior agent—so young and inexperienced that the ink on his college diploma still hadn't dried—had brought him lunch. And not just an ordinary lunch: a pastrami-and-corned-beef combo, dripping with mustard and sauerkraut, coupled with a cream soda. Eli willed himself to eat it slowly, savoring each bite, as he rebooted the Hostage Taker's video on the open computer in the adjacent MRU.

Eli paid close attention, taking in everything on the video. But he was distracted by the quality of the recording. It made his heart sink with disappointment. Dimly lit, with grainy pixels. Not a professional effort. *Focus on the message, not the medium,* he scolded himself.

His finger pressed a button. The video slowed, each frame moving forward at a careful pace.

There was no time stamp. No frame division. First the camera flashed on a hostage or two—so quick, he couldn't really tell—and the explosives threatening them.

Then it didn't.

It centered on two stone columns with some pretty disturbing pictures.

He slid his chair closer, pushed up his glasses. They wiggled, so—eyes still on the screen—he pulled a piece of tape out of his pocket and wound it around the left temple. The added bulk filled in the gap behind his ear.

Then he reviewed the footage.

What did he *really* see? The Brooklyn Bridge was breaking in half as a bus plummeted into the water. Waves from the rising water crashed over the city skyline. People ran hell for leather below the New York Stock Exchange. And next to the people, a scorpion, snake, and other vile creatures swarmed around a skeleton. Meanwhile, the Statue of Liberty stood by, apparently unaware that she was drowning.

Eli burped. Guess he wasn't eating his sandwich slowly enough.

What else did he see? Images that were even more unsettling. The city skyline—including the Chrysler Building, Citigroup Center, and the former Twin Towers—was swaying wildly, with plumes of smoke over it. What looked to be a big church was underneath its looming shadow.

*Saint Patrick's Cathedral?*

And if so, what the hell did this Hostage Taker want everybody—and particularly his five "witnesses"—to see?

Eli closed his eyes and exhaled. He'd lost his appetite.

Maybe it was just because he was a New Yorker who didn't like seeing his home depicted this way. Maybe it was because he'd lost friends on 9/11. But this didn't feel like the work of a religious nut, like Eve thought. This felt like something else.

*Terrorism.*

# Chapter 23

The sounds from outside were deafening. Officers barked orders. Phones trilled. Motors hummed. Somewhere overhead, a chopper was circling. So much activity, so many vehicles actually generated a *smell.* An odor somewhere between grease and transmission fluid.

And the temperature was continuing to drop. Inside the drafty MRU, Eve could tell that the air was growing more frigid. The wind was whipping with more velocity.

Eve dialed the last number the Hostage Taker had used. There was no response. As expected, he'd removed the battery and trashed it. Time to use the advantage Haddox had given her.

Eve tried the first number on Haddox's list. One from the Amsterdam shipment. And the moment she dialed, all trace of the world around her faded away—and everything was an eerie calm.

Eight rings. Then a message that the wireless number had not been activated.

"Keep going," Haddox instructed. "One of them is the magic number. Linked to the phone he has charged up, ready to use next."

She kept trying. Another six from Amsterdam. Four from Dallas. Five purchased in Bangkok. Seven from San Francisco. A large shipment of twelve from Munich. Just when she was starting to think Haddox had it all wrong, she hit pay dirt with a number from the Barcelona batch.

Someone answered. She knew because the ringing stopped. But this time, there was no recording. Just the soft rasp of someone breathing. The person on the other end of the line was waiting.

Eve didn't.

"It's me," she said, forcing an intimacy into her voice that she didn't feel. Creating the illusion that they had a relationship—that they could trust each other—was part of the game.

"How did you get this number?" Her heart leapt. It *was* the Hostage Taker.

"You asked for me. Specifically by name. Did you doubt I was good at my job?"

"Your job is to find my five witnesses." He sounded hoarse, but something else, too. Skittish.

"Actually, that's why I'm calling. Cassidy Jones."

"Do your job already."

"Wait. I need to know *which* Cassidy Jones. There's dozens in the tri-state region alone. And that's assuming you don't mean the ones in California or Texas who live so far away there's no hope of them getting here before your deadline." *Unless your deadline is just a red herring. As ridiculous as your demand to bring "witnesses."*

Silence.

"I'm not playing games with you. You gave me a deadline. I've got five hours, seven minutes to go. Are these witnesses your real demand? Or is there something else going on we should discuss?"

Silence.

She acted on instinct. "Well, if you want me to help you, you know where to find me."

She pressed a button. Ended the call.

Then waited.

Five seconds. Ten seconds. Fifteen . . . Twenty . . . Twenty-five . . .

Fifty-two seconds later, when she had almost given up, the phone in her hand trilled. She answered. "You decided to help me?"

"I like to see you when we talk, Eve." His voice was cold. "Come outside."

"I'm not looking for a long conversation. Just info. An occupation. A street name. An address. Something to keep me moving forward with Cassidy Jones. Assuming that's still what you want." She held her breath.

"Outside, Eve. *Now.*"

She shrugged off his fury before she even felt its heat. She had been right: He needed to be in charge. Or to have the illusion of being in charge.

She kept the line open as she strode to the door of the MRU and stepped outside. A bearded agent she'd never met before offered her a bulletproof jacket. She shook her head to indicate *no*—and ignored the shouts and frantic waves of protest that several agents signaled.

*This was about creating the illusion of control,* she reminded herself. What the Hostage Taker wanted—no, *needed*—if she was going to manipulate him into reassessing his plans. One step at a time.

She felt the worried eyes of dozens of officers on her, moving with her. Reminding her that she was not alone.

Only when she made her way to the steps of the Cathedral did the Hostage Taker's voice crackle in her ear once more. "No bulletproof vest? I'm impressed, Eve, by your bravery. Or is it just foolishness?"

"I don't believe in wasting time on something that doesn't matter," Eve said coolly. She looked up into the scaffolding. Tried to imagine him in the recesses of the Cathedral looking down at her.

"So your life doesn't matter?"

"I didn't say that. But you took down your first two victims with shots that most people would find impossible. Right to the head—from a bad angle, in worse weather. That means you're a professional. You know what you're doing. And if you want to kill me, you will—bulletproof vest or not."

The Hostage Taker laughed.

Then a great gasp. It came from the crowd—the mix of federal agents and NYPD officers and EMS technicians and FDNY personnel who were standing by.

Eve knew, though she couldn't feel it: Right now, there was a red dot dancing on her forehead.

She heard the crackle of a command behind her: *Find that damn sniper and take the bastard out!*

"Stand down!" She made her voice loud, clear, confident. Even though inside, she was so frightened she felt her knees buckle. She stabbed the mute button on her cell. "I need everyone to *stand down.*

He's not going to hurt me. He's upset. He's reminding us that he's in charge here. But he asked for me, specifically. No one else. Ultimately, he still wants my help."

She unmuted her phone. And waited—praying she was right.

There was a lull. She kept staring upward, eyes raking each branch of the complicated scaffolding. The rain had made its rungs oily and black—which only served to remind her of the semiautomatic weapon that lurked there in the shadows.

She opened her hands, making a show of her submission.

Five seconds became ten. Fifteen. Twenty . . .

She was testing him more than she'd expected to at this early stage. *What does he want? Am I as important to him as he'd claimed?*

If the answer was *no*—if he was a terrorist or a fanatic who'd been making demands just for a distraction—then she'd just played a losing hand.

But if he was something else?

*The illusion of control—and trust—was paramount.*

She was establishing both. Once she had them, she could work to find out things she could use to manipulate the situation. Extremely carefully, of course. Because illusions worked both ways—and if she wasn't vigilant, she might end up being played for a fool.

After the longest seventy-three seconds of her life, she heard the crowd around her breathe in relief.

She forced herself to do so as well. The icy air filled her lungs and felt good. She spoke into her phone again. "It's a two-way street. So I can help you, help me. We can do this together. *Which* Cassidy Jones?"

"She's a wannabe actress. Lives in Astoria."

"I appreciate that information," she said.

"And just so you don't bother me again: The Luis Ramos I want uses a middle initial. *J.* Works as a window washer at Trump Tower."

"I'd like to do something for you, as a gesture of goodwill. You must be getting hungry. Can I send you some food?"

"Eve, Eve, Eve. Haven't you learned anything? Nothing's getting in or out of this building without blowing it to Kingdom Come."

"I get that. But I'm out here talking to you because I want to get you—and everybody inside—out of the Cathedral without getting hurt. You must be holding—what?—at least a dozen people. By now, they're probably tired. Hungry. Starting to complain." That last was a calculated gamble. She usually preferred to avoid all mention of hostages—and she *did* avoid mentioning the cop. But the invisible presence of those hostages—still unidentified in name, unknown in number—weighed heavily on her mind.

"You're not bringing me food," he said. "You're not delivering secret messages to my hostages. You're not going to launch your best assault team. Because if you try any of these things, I will detonate the explosives you know I have." His voice was rising.

Eve took one shaky breath. Then another. Forcing herself to think through her options. She hated this part of the job. Figuring out how far she could push. Deciding when to dangle a carrot—and when to threaten a stick. The smart move was to stop contact now. Let him consider his alternatives.

"Call me when you want to talk about your options." She turned and started walking back to the MRU.

But before she closed the line, she heard him say one last thing.

"Just find the Jones bitch and bring her here."

# Chapter 24

The symbols of Armageddon in the Hostage Taker's video were definitely above Eli's pay grade, so he wasted no time getting on the phone with Damian Galla, a professor of religious studies at Brown University. The fact that Professor Galla was also a longtime family friend didn't hurt. As a child, Eli liked to tiptoe to the top of the stairs to eavesdrop on Professor Galla's spirited debates about theology with his father. Eli's father was among the most respected Talmudic scholars at Temple Beth David on the Lower East Side. And Professor Galla's visits stretched into the wee hours of the morning, typically leaving young Eli fast asleep on the staircase.

Eli hadn't seen him since his father died, but he doubted the man had changed: Professor Galla had always been small and bald, full of tics and eccentricities. The man never set foot outside unless he wore a suit and a red bow tie. His meals were eaten at the same time, in the same seat, at the same diner. And he answered every phone call not with "hello," but with "What's your question for me?"

To Eli, that was actually a relief. He had little interest in hashing through inane pleasantries. Not so soon after John's family Christmas party. Plus, he was pretty sure that Professor Galla didn't like him. Probably thought Eli was greedy; definitely blamed him for the way his father's health had declined following Eli's insider-trading indictment. "My question's about some disturbing symbols carved into a column at Saint Patrick's Cathedral," he said, going on to explain about the Twin Towers and the other disturbing scenes of New York City's destruction carved in marble.

"I'm at my computer," Professor Galla said. "Can you send me the images?"

Eli complied with a few clicks of his keyboard. While it was sending, he also explained that the images were part of a larger message from the Hostage Taker at Saint Patrick's Cathedral.

There was a pause. When Professor Galla spoke again, he sounded irritated—though it might have just been the gravel and phlegm that lived in the old man's throat. "Well, those are famous—or perhaps I should say *infamous*—carvings."

"If they're so famous, how come I don't know anything about them?" Eli demanded.

"Inadequate education, perhaps?"

No, the professor definitely didn't like him, Eli decided.

"They're from a New York Cathedral, but not *your* Cathedral. They're carved into the west end of Saint John's Cathedral uptown."

Eli wasn't a total dolt. He knew about the Cathedral of Saint John the Divine. It was up on 112th and Amsterdam, near Columbia University. Started in the late nineteenth century, it was both one of the largest cathedrals in the world and still unfinished. He'd gone there once with a friend to see the annual Blessing of the Animals. There had been a baby kangaroo. "So why is this guy pretending they're at Saint Pat's Cathedral?"

"I'd say they have a meaning to him that Saint Patrick's was lacking," the professor responded dryly. "A lot of cathedrals have incorporated images of the End of Days. The practice came about in the Middle Ages. The images were meant to be read, just like scripture. And don't forget: Saint John's Cathedral is named after the presumed author of the Book of Revelation."

"So famous Cathedrals in Paris and Rome have images showing their cities being destroyed?"

"I have to admit, what we see here is unusual," the professor conceded. "And highly disturbing—which is why these carvings from Saint John's have become a magnet for conspiracy theorists. They look at the swaying Twin Towers and they see 9/11. Then they look at the waves overtaking the city and they see the damage caused by Superstorm Sandy."

"Can't say they don't have a point."

"Sure, but that misses the entire context."

"Which is?"

"Simon Verity was the artist who designed the images. His vision focused on Saint John the Divine himself standing on top of the Four Horsemen of the Apocalypse. Everything surrounding him was contemporary—and he even included representations of people from the neighborhood."

"When did he do all this?"

Professor Galla took a moment to look it up. Eli could hear him clicking at his keyboard. "Stonemasons started in the late 1980s; finished about 1997."

"Four years before 9/11."

The professor made a dismissive noise. "Stuff and nonsense."

"Then tell me what it means."

"Can't. There's not much documentation about it. And the rest of Saint John's contains plenty of art with strange symbols alluding to catastrophes. I think your question is: What does it mean to the man who made this video?"

"Don't have to be a rocket scientist to conclude that he's sending a message that he wants to destroy New York City."

"Then why did he pick Saint Patrick's Cathedral?" Professor Galla shot back.

"Major New York City landmark."

"If his only goal is to destroy something, he could've gone for Rockefeller Center across the street. Or the Empire State Building. Or half a dozen other secular landmarks. He also didn't need to send you a video about it."

"Meaning you think this is religious?"

"Hard to imagine there's not some religious component to it. He's sent a message with apocalyptic images. You tell me he's demanded you bring 'witnesses.' You can't ignore the possibility."

"He wants *specific* witnesses. He's named them."

"You know, throughout history, almost every society, religious or not, believed some inner spiritual force exists inside us. The soul. The Holy Spirit. The conscience. The psyche. The anima. The Force."

"In one sentence, you take us from church to *Star Wars*?"

The professor ignored him. "Theologians question whether this spiritual force is something God-given, pure and whole. Or whether it's shaped by our own experiences and desires."

"I don't even know what that means. Not in this context," Eli said flatly.

"I'll make it simple: Does something inside your Hostage Taker lead him to believe that God's telling him to do this? Or is he acting from his own desires?"

"What difference does it make?'

"If it's the latter, Eli, your negotiator's got a chance of getting him to see reason and may resolve your crisis peacefully. But if it's the former, you've got no chance in hell." The professor snorted. "My latest book focuses on the root causes of religious zealotry. The case examples included a man who attempted to hijack a plane because God told him that killing all the passengers would rid the world of the devil. A serial killer who had no remorse for his crimes—in fact, was scarcely aware of them—because he believed God commanded him to kill certain individuals to eliminate evil. And a kidnapper who took a young girl from her bed at night on orders from God."

Eli let forth a low whistle. "You know something, Professor? Your brain is filled with some weird shit."

# Chapter 25

The world was deathly gray. The glittering white lights of Saks had been snuffed out. Their holiday windows had gone dark. The Olympic Tower and Rockefeller Center were now unlit. It was as though someone had flicked a switch and blacked out Fifth Avenue's celebration of light.

All in the name of security, of course.

"What the hell were you doing out there?" Henry Ma spoke in a low rumble the moment Eve was in earshot. "You could've got yourself killed."

"You know exactly what I was doing," she replied coolly.

"That kind of hotheaded move can get you booted right out of the field. Worse: The news media might have caught it. Their long-range lenses pick up everything."

"I *was* out of the field. You're the one who brought me back in. Is this about your disagreeing with my judgment—or just a public-relations issue?"

"I'd call your actions ill-advised on both counts."

Except Eve knew: It was the prospect of public judgment that annoyed Henry. And he didn't like this case already. It wasn't straightforward. The city was in chaos. They still had no ID for the suspect. No clear motive. No resolution in sight.

"There's a casebook we study at the Academy in Quantico," she told him. "I believe you know it. Your name's on the spine as a coauthor. If you think about it, you'll recognize that what I did falls strictly under chapter three, section two."

Henry shook his head. "So what exactly did you learn from that stunt you just pulled?"

She continued walking back toward the MRU. The area around the secure perimeter was filled with officers moving around—some in ballistics gear, some wearing fluorescent vests, others in plainclothes. Their faces were uniformly pale, concerned. It was increasingly cold. From somewhere beyond Rockefeller Plaza, a Christmas carol played. The notes of "God Rest Ye Merry Gentlemen" danced like snowflakes in the air above.

She glanced at Henry, who followed her closely. "I learned who we're dealing with. You'd call him a control freak—and he is. But here's what's important: His need for control tells me about his background. Now I know we're looking for someone with gaps in his history. Possibly from a broken home. Possibly he's grown up with multiple parent figures. As an alternative, he may have moved around a lot as a child. Maybe a military brat, which would figure into the sniper training. Maybe he followed his father into military service—or similar law enforcement or security professions."

"So you've just narrowed our field of subjects down to—oh, what?—almost half of America?"

"It's not about narrowing the field," Eve replied, ignoring his tone. "It's about knowing your subject. Experiences like I just described will make the subject very protective of his physical and emotional space. Like we just saw."

"And you can manipulate that?"

"That's the plan."

"What if this is all smoke and mirrors—and he's not actually holding anyone inside the Cathedral?"

"And what if he's got three dozen people in there?" she countered. "There must be more we can do to find out."

"Believe me, I'm working on it." Henry glanced up Fifth Avenue to the roadblock where police in riot gear now controlled growing crowds of unhappy onlookers. Headlights blazed beyond the blockade. Horns were honking; people were shouting; traffic was snarled up for blocks. "There are two individuals we strongly suspect to be inside. The boy's mother. And the priest who would've presided over this morning's Mass. No one can reach him."

"Don't forget the cop—assuming our eyewitness is right about that. Anything else?" Eve put her hand on the door to the MRU.

"Just this. A preliminary coroner's report on the first victim is in—obtained in record time, due to the urgency of the situation. No toxicology yet, obviously. But plenty of information we can use—including ID."

Eve took the manila folder from him. "So who is she?"

"Name's Cristina Silva. And identifying her was a breeze. Turns out she had a criminal arrest; all her information and prints were on file."

Ignoring a tinny ringtone sounding "Jingle Bells" and the squawking radios of officers passing by, Eve stood and flipped through the file.

She flipped past Cristina Silva's vital stats and the medical examiner's certification to where the narrative began. Phrases jumped out at her.

*The body is clad in a torn green long-sleeve T-shirt, white bra partly bloodstained, gray pants, & black underwear.*

Presumably, this was a woman who'd wanted only to attend early-morning Mass—and found less solace than she'd bargained for.

*The body is that of a well-nourished Hispanic woman, sixty-five inches, 131 lbs., and thirty-three years old by report.*

Add to that: bound to a sign that asked for *HELP.*

*The corneas are clear, irises brown.*

With a handwritten note tucked on back of the sign, requesting SA Eve Rossi.

*The earlobes are cosmetically pierced.*

She had been chosen as the first victim.

*The fingernails are short, evenly cut intact.*

And one final succinct phrase—*Gunshot wound, penetrating, fatal.*

The preliminary autopsy findings were attached to selected Internet printouts. Cristina indeed had a record of criminal arrest. Five years and three months ago, on an eighty-five-degree summer day, she had forgotten to drop her fifteen-month-old baby girl off at daycare. Instead, she'd gone directly to work, leaving her daughter buckled into her seat in back of her Toyota. Seven hours later, she'd found her child—dead.

She'd been convicted of reckless endangerment. Sentenced to probation, counseling, and community service. Condemned by all in the press—but most of all by herself.

Cristina's background raised a question Eve hadn't wanted to address because it complicated matters so significantly. She'd assumed there were more hostages inside the Cathedral. She'd also assumed every hostage being held was random. Just a collection of strangers who had intended to attend early-morning Mass. She had worried only about who—and how many—the hostages were.

But was it possible these people represented something more to the Hostage Taker? That they had been chosen for a *reason*?

Her heart ached as she stepped back inside the MRU.

# Chapter 26

*Do people ever think about what's important?*

*There's one time when strangers willingly step in, no hesitation at all: when they have unsolicited advice.*

*I've seen it happen, particularly to young mothers—on the bus, in the grocery store, really any public place. "The baby needs more layers, dear; he's going to catch cold." "The child's too old to still be drinking from a bottle; you'll stunt his growth."*

*It's different for men, of course. At the bar, you'll hear variations on: "Think you've had too much, man. Better slow down." Others enjoy butting into personal relationships, asking the woman: "Is he bothering you?"*

*But when the stakes are real?*

*Those same worrywarts turn a blind eye.*

*Last summer, a homeless man ran up to a child in Riverside Park and shoved him. The child's father objected. The homeless man produced a knife and stabbed the father four times. The child cried as the father lay bleeding on the ground—and countless bikers, joggers, and dog walkers passed by.*

*It was nineteen minutes before 911 received a call, asking for help.*

*Don't you just love people?*

*Always there when you don't want them.*

*Never around when you do.*

*Hypocrites.*

NEWS NEWS NEWS NEWS NEWS

# HOUR 7

2:17 p.m.

On the line, we have Professor Menklin, a historian at Columbia University, who also sits on the city's Landmarks Preservation Commission.

Professor Menklin, as we wait to learn the identities of those individuals we believe are held captive inside the Cathedral—and what action law enforcement will take next—let's discuss the Cathedral itself. Is it safe to say this historic landmark is part of the Hostage Taker's plan?

*PROFESSOR MENKLIN:* Absolutely. You know, Saint Patrick's truly represents what this city is about. It was built because so many immigrants were arriving in New York who followed the Catholic religion—and also because this great city of ours required a great Cathedral to rival the best of Europe. So Saint Patrick's Cathedral represents the importance of Catholicism in New York—as well as the importance of New York City itself.

Professor, you raise an interesting question. Is the Hostage Taker targeting Saint Patrick's as a symbol of Catholicism—or as a symbol of our city?

*PROFESSOR MENKLIN:* Does it have to be an either-or proposition? Because it strikes me as possible: This madman might be doing both.

# Chapter 27

Outside, pearl-gray clouds covered the sky. It was definitely colder. Eli could see it through the tiny window at his workstation, not to mention feel the draft coming in through multiple gaps in the trailer's walls. Whoever designed these MRUs obviously had never experienced the way the wind whipped around skyscrapers during a Manhattan winter. He shivered.

It actually looked like it might snow. Light snow in this city was magical—especially when it came in December and lent atmosphere to all the wreaths and lights, window displays and holiday markets. But it had to be *light*. Heavy snow lasted too long—and made the sidewalks a dirty, slushy, treacherous mess.

He sighed, then returned to those crazy stone images of New York's skyline coming undone. He didn't understand how this hostage-taking could be motivated by religion—no matter what Professor Galla had said. Looked like the work of a garden-variety terrorist. Hell, though—he also couldn't begin to understand how a nutjob like this guy would think. That was why he liked following the money trail. That was his element. He understood how people felt about money: how they stole it, where they stashed it, and, ultimately, how to get it back.

He glanced at the clock: 2:19 p.m. He needed a real job to do. Get out of this freezing tin can on wheels. When was Mace going to call?

As if in answer to his question, his phone beeped. Except it wasn't a call. It was a text. There were three of them, all from John. Increasing urgency in every one.

Eli knew he was spinning wheels on the religious imagery, so he dialed John back. When John picked up, Eli didn't waste time on hello. "Hey. Everything okay?"

"Not exactly."

Eli tensed, waiting for the blow. Last night must've gone even worse than he thought. He recognized the reluctance in John's voice. The tone that made clear he didn't want to be having the conversation they were about to have.

And Eli knew that tone well: It usually came right before "We need to talk" or "This isn't working anymore."

Instead, John said, "I've got a problem. And I need your help with it."

"Of course." Eli almost gushed with relief. God, he sounded like a schoolgirl. "Let's meet after work tonight. Talk it through together."

"It can't wait."

"Really? Uh." Eli glanced around, self-conscious now. The room was bustling with activity. Other agents were doing six different things at once. It was definitely not the time to be on a personal call. "I can try to call you again, soon as things settle here."

"It'll only take a sec." Now there was a throaty, pleading tone in John's voice. Eli couldn't resist it.

"Okay. Let's hear the thirty-second version. And I promise I'll call back the moment I can talk more."

"I know you met my cousin Meaghan last night."

Thin as a rail. Green dress. Stiletto heels. Great memory for long-ago details in the crime blotter. Unfortunately, Eli remembered her all too well. "What about her?"

"Meaghan needs help. I thought of you."

"Help?"

"Her kid's missing. A thirteen-year-old girl."

"Sounds like she needs the police and an Amber Alert, not me." Eli was aware that a cop whose cheeks were liberally sprinkled with giant freckles was looking at him strangely. Probably wondering why he was on a personal call.

"She tried that. Didn't work. Officially, this is her ex-husband's custody week. He's not obligated to check in with her. So the police won't lift a finger until his custody period ends in another forty-seven hours."

"Is she on friendly terms with her ex?" Eli lowered his voice.

"They're amicable."

"Maybe it's his custody time and he doesn't want to be bothered."

"Fair enough. But her daughter? I know Georgie; she's a typical teenager—absolutely glued to her phone. She'd never ignore her mother's calls." There was a steely edge in John's voice that surprised Eli.

"Unless she's got a dead battery. Or is out of range. Or—"

"I get it," John interrupted. "There are plenty of logical explanations. Meaghan's considered all of them. She's still worried."

A half-formed memory thrust itself into Eli's consciousness. "Her ex . . . he was having some kind of problem, wasn't he?"

"He's been suspended from the NYPD. Both Internal Affairs and the D.A.'s office are investigating him. Theft. Drugs."

"So how come he still gets custody of the girl?"

John let out an exasperated sigh. "Because there's no proof. Not yet. Remember, this is America: We still consider people innocent 'til proven guilty."

"Uh-huh." Eli reached for a scrap of paper. "What's the daughter's name?"

"Georgie. Officially, Georgianna Murphy."

"Cell?"

John rattled off a 917 number.

"I'll look into it," Eli promised. "Soon as I can."

"Hurry," John urged. "You know how mothers worry."

Eli clicked off the line and shoved his notes deep into his pocket. This wasn't good. It was too soon for him to be navigating the treacherous ground of John's family issues. Frankly, never was probably too soon. Half the equation involved a missing kid. The other half involved a derelict ex-husband. Together, it all added up to a huge family drama.

# Chapter 28

Now that Haddox knew Cassidy Jones was an actress, finding her was a breeze. Cassidy shared an apartment with two other actresses in Astoria, Queens, above a Greek diner. She'd moved here from Georgia five years ago, searching for her big break. She was still waiting for it to come. But she had secured an up-and-coming agent at William Morris to represent her, putting her in a better place than most.

Cassidy wasn't home, but her roommate was. She gave her name as Chloe, and judging from the slow way she drawled her vowels, she was a Georgia transplant just like Cassidy.

"Cass is out," she told Haddox. No offer to take a message.

"Listen, I've just gotten off the phone with Bob at WME," Haddox improvised. Cassidy's agent, Bob, hadn't wanted to be bothered—and had actually hung up on Haddox. But strictly speaking, Haddox was telling the truth. "I really need to reach Cassidy, but she's not picking up her cell."

He heard the crackle of chewing gum. "That's cuz she's at work. She's not allowed to take calls during her shift."

"When does she finish her shift?"

"Six tonight."

"Listen, I'm with a crew at Rockefeller Center who wants to bring her on down, but six tonight is too late. Could you give me her work number?"

"You mean NBC?"

Haddox glanced at the building that soared to the sky behind him. "I'm in front of their studios right now." The most believable lies were actually half-truths. When you offered a small detail that could be interpreted several different ways, you could count on your listener to imagine what she wanted.

Chloe was silent. Haddox imagined her battling feelings of jealousy. Wondering why Cassidy was getting interest from NBC but the phone wasn't ringing for her. It was always tough on a friendship when one career took off and the other didn't.

Haddox scanned the files of both girls. Cassidy was a five-foot-eight platinum blonde, full-figured à la Marilyn Monroe with a Heidi Klum smile. Chloe was a five-foot-one former gymnast with short, dark hair—more of a ringer for Mary Lou Retton.

"There aren't many tall blondes like Cassidy available right now," he said. No reason, he figured, for Chloe to get bent out of shape over nothing. He also laid his brogue on thick. In his experience, women responded to musical Irish vowels.

This one was no exception.

"I can find the number if you give me a second to look." Another snap of the gum. Fourteen seconds passed; then Chloe was back, rattling off a 718 number.

"And where is this?" he asked.

"The Utopia," she replied. "It's a diner—and it's actually downstairs. If you have trouble reaching her, I can walk down and give her the message."

With memories of good times with Sweet Pea still dancing in his head, Mace strode up the steps of the squat brick station house on Thirty-fifth Street near Ninth Avenue. Midtown West Precinct. Still known informally as "the Busiest Precinct in the World," even though a few years ago some official made them take down the banner that advertised it. After all, these guys policed Times Square, the tourist traps and hotels, and all three transportation hubs: Port Authority Bus Terminal, Grand Central Terminal, and Penn Station.

They had another reputation besides being busy: These were the NYPD's bad boys, the black sheep who'd gotten caught doing everything from trading favors at the local strip clubs to going shopping at the trucking bays in the garment district. Where valuable stuff sometimes just happened to fall off the truck when the cops showed up. In

Mace's book, that made them slightly more interesting than the average cop.

He walked up to the receptionist. She was a no-nonsense woman who met his infectious grin—the same one most women couldn't help but respond to—with a frosty glare. She was going to be a challenge.

He kept his broad smile pasted on and said, "Think you could help me locate somebody?"

"You know how many people come through these doors every day?"

"More than I can imagine, I'll bet," Mace answered earnestly. "But I don't mean a *particular* officer. I just need you to point me toward someone who knows what's going on. Who has his fingers in all the cookie jars."

Her eyes narrowed suspiciously.

"You must know an officer who could help a brother out?" His smile broadened.

"I ain't nobody's babysitter."

He sighed. "Just looking for a little interagency cooperation." Mace pulled his old FBI ID out of his wallet.

No luck. The no-nonsense woman was immune to both his charm and his badge. She pawned him off to the nearest warm body. "Go see Sergeant Rodriguez over there." She stabbed a finger toward a weary-looking young man sitting at a desk buried in paperwork. "He handles general inquiries."

Mace almost agreed, figuring that was the best he'd manage to do. Besides, maybe Sergeant Rodriguez only *looked* like a dweeb who never broke the rules.

Then he hesitated—because something important had occurred to him.

How could he have missed the solution to his problem? It had been staring him in the face as he walked into the precinct house.

So he said "Maybe later" to the ice queen—and turned to leave.

Two down. Three to go. Blair Vanderwert—the next name on the Hostage Taker's list—was a cakewalk to locate. He was a New York City realtor who specialized in Upper East Side properties.

Haddox didn't think he would like him much. Vanderwert's website profile was the picture of a man who seemed far too pleased with himself. Bleached white teeth. Fake smile. Perfect hair. Tweed blazer and cotton plaid shirt. The man was probably incapable of killing a cockroach who invaded his kitchen, but he had dressed like he was going hunting with the hounds.

Still, Blair Vanderwert was nothing if not easy to find. He maintained an office with a receptionist. His email and cell number were posted all over the Internet. His latest tweet was eleven minutes ago.

Haddox didn't bother trying to call him now. Vanderwert would be there for the taking when he needed him.

At least, so long as Haddox played the perfect cover. And reading about Vanderwert's record-setting sales in twenty-two buildings and $150 million yearly sales volume, Haddox knew that wouldn't be a problem.

# Chapter 29

Four hours, thirteen minutes to go.

A security camera on the northeast corner of Seventh Avenue and Fifty-second Street had picked up the image of a cop matching the description given by Angus MacDonald. The cop was walking in the general direction of Saint Patrick's at 6:49. His head was turned—but the footage was being circulated throughout every NYPD precinct all the same.

Eve dialed the leader of Omega Team—an interagency SWAT team—on a secure line. Henry Ma had authorized a search-and-discovery mission. In the event that Eve failed to negotiate an acceptable outcome with the Hostage Taker, they urgently needed to devise a plan that would minimize casualties and damage. Both to any hostages and to Saint Patrick's itself.

Eve knew that this was the right move. While there had been small victories in her dealings with the Hostage Taker, she was very far from understanding who he was and what made him tick. Absent a breakthrough on her end, they desperately needed information. To know any vulnerabilities and possible entry points. The number and location of potential hostages. The position of the Hostage Taker or Takers.

But there was no question that this was high-stakes poker. A massive roll of the dice. If the Omega Team blew their cover, they would be back to square one—or worse. The fragile thread of trust between Eve and the Hostage Taker would be broken—and the lives of all hostages would be at terrible risk.

The Omega Team planned to approach from the roof of the Rectory at the rear of the Cathedral. They hoped to be out of sight of the sniper who had already killed two innocent victims.

"Heat seekers, cameras, microphones, anything you can use covertly," Eve explained to the Omega leader. "But if you blow our cover, we're screwed."

"You got it, Agent Rossi," the lead man promised. "Just hope what's up above is different from down below. We've never been stalemated like this before. The Hostage Taker's got every access point we can think of either locked down or loaded up with explosives."

"You had no luck with the sewers?"

"No, ma'am. We talked with Church officials and used the incomplete blueprints on file with the city. Checked every single drain and supply line listed. But he's poured concrete down every damn pipe. Didn't miss even one."

"So let's keep looking for something the Hostage Taker hasn't thought about," she told him. "The main thing is to figure out what's going on inside. In particular, we need to confirm how many people he's holding. And to your point, how many bad guys we're going to have to take out."

"Acknowledged. I'm sending the men up in groups of two—Team Alpha and Team Delta. Twenty minutes to green light order for Team Alpha."

Then Eve heard him talking to his Special Ops units. "Ready? This is terminal countdown: five, four, three, two, one . . . mark."

# Chapter 30

The whole point of Mace's visit to the Midtown West Precinct had been to find out who they suspected of stealing that mother lode of explosives that had gone missing from the evidence locker. The same mother lode that—just maybe—had been used to booby-trap Saint Patrick's Cathedral.

Then he realized: He didn't need one of New York's Finest to tell him about it. In fact, better to avoid the precinct house altogether—since his own odds were about fifty-fifty whether he would end up dealing with a standup guy or a total prick. And he didn't have time for bullshit. The deadline was going to expire. There were only four hours, two minutes to go.

It just so happened a better option was waiting for him outside.

Mace had noticed the girl sitting on the stoop of the plain squat five-floor building next door. She looked about ten years old.

All alone.

Just her and a deflated basketball that had lost its bounce.

Mace hadn't made the connection before. But then the lightbulb had gone off—and the timing couldn't have been better. The kid was the daughter of Vernon Brown. A guy the fellas in the Bronx called "the merchant of death" because he controlled virtually all arms deliveries to rival violent narcotics gangs in Morrisania. Mace made it a point to know the family members of all the kingpins of NYC. Never know when that connection could come in handy.

The girl watched Mace approach, tracking him carefully.

"Hey, kid. What's up?" Mace kept his tone casual.

"The sky."

Mace stopped. Made a show of looking up into pewter-colored clouds that threatened snow. Then looked down with a delighted grin. "What d'ya know? You're right. You play?" He pointed to the ball.

A scowl. "No."

"How come? 'Cause that ball don't work no more?"

The girl was quiet for a second. "No. 'Cause I'm too short. And I'm a girl."

Mace nodded. He'd gotten it wrong. The kid's face and voice were about fourteen. It was her body that had gotten stuck at ten. "Short don't mean you can't play ball."

"Means I can't play *well.*"

"You kiddin' me? Tell that to Muggsy Bogues. You know who he is, right?"

The girl looked down.

"He's only five-foot-three. Shortest player ever in the NBA. But he was the number-twelve draft pick his year out, and he played point guard in the big leagues for fourteen seasons."

"How'd he do that?"

"He was lightning fast, with great instincts. A ball hawk. Maybe you could learn to play like him. Your name's Ashley, right?"

"How do you know that?"

"I've heard your dad talk about you. There a court nearby where I could show you a few things?"

"Maybe." The girl flushed. "You any good?"

"I ain't LeBron James—but I can hold my own. Couldn't live without it, if you know what I mean." Mace pointed to the precinct house. "Your dad in there?"

"Yeah."

"When did they come for him?"

"Early this morning. Like they always do. Before sunup."

"He told you to come wait?"

"Nah. I just wanted to."

"School?"

The girl looked down. "I missed all morning anyway."

Mace lifted an eyebrow. "Guess you didn't wake up early enough, huh?"

"Dad needed me to do stuff."

"Who'd he tell you to call?"

"Snoopy."

That changed Mace's view of things considerably. If Vernon was guilty of what they'd brought him in for, he'd have wanted the message to go to Juice Gomez. Juice knew how to tidy things up. Essentially do damage control. But Snoopy? He was the guy whose job was to dig up dirt. Calling Snoopy meant Vernon had no intention of doing time for somebody else's crime. "How 'bout we play some ball—then you take me to Snoopy? I might have some info that would help him out with your dad."

For the first time, the kid's eyes lit up. "Cool. But Snoop's supposed to come here. In another"—she scrunched up her face, checked the time—"twenty-five minutes."

Mace nodded, then reached for the ball. He picked it up like a grapefruit, in the span of his right hand. "Just enough time to put some air in this baby and teach you a cool trick or two. Why don't you text him? Tell him to come to where we're playin' hoops."

Mace knew Eve would probably think he was playing around in the middle of a crisis. Not doing his job.

He liked to call it networking. It was important work.

Guys with suits did it at places like the Yale Club or Jean-Georges.

He did it with a basketball and a fifteen-foot jumper on the court.

Before Eli placed the call he'd been putting off, he popped a Tums into his mouth—hoping it would remedy the indigestion his pastrami and corned beef had given him.

"Principal Grady's office." The voice that answered was flat and uninterested. Definitely not wanting to be bothered.

Eli got straight to the point. Rattled off his name and FBI credentials. Then said, "I'm conducting a welfare check on one of your students."

"Name?"

"Name's Murphy. Georgianna Murphy."

"You got a warrant?"

"I just need to know that the kid showed up to school okay this morning."

"We don't share information about our students. Period. Not without a court order or a warrant."

"Perhaps I could speak with Principal Grady," Eli offered.

"She won't tell you anything different."

"Maybe not. But if this student is in trouble, she'd probably like to know. Sooner rather than later."

Eli watched the second hand sweep around the clock. He knew managing a school was one of the most important yet completely thankless jobs in the world. Administrators were overburdened, underpaid—and yet still keenly invested in the success and well-being of their students. Otherwise they couldn't do what they did every day.

Problem was: This receptionist was taking a helluva long time to remember that.

The second hand revolved seven times around the clock face. Then Eli heard a series of beeps as the transfer went through.

Three witnesses down. Two to go.

Haddox was grateful for small things. In this case, the fact that the Hostage Taker had been proactive in telling Eve that the Luis Ramos he wanted had a middle initial, *J*, and worked as a window washer at Trump Tower. Based on that, Haddox had his records in seconds. It seemed Luis had been caught committing a minor traffic violation. The problem was: Luis was an illegal immigrant, so he had been formally charged and threatened with deportation. Which had sent the window washer underground, where his trail went ice cold.

Three hours, fifty-two minutes left until deadline.

Haddox knew it wasn't going to be easy. But that was just the way he liked it.

The principal was named Julie Grady. Second-generation Italian, married to an Irish cop. Fourteen years on the job.

"Thanks for talking," Eli said, repeating his FBI credentials and emphasizing that he was calling on behalf of the Murphy family. Specifically, the mother.

"Mrs. Murphy needs to call me herself," Julie Grady said. "Student records—and that includes attendance records—are confidential. I'm sure you understand. I'm not authorized to talk with you."

"I know that," Eli said, "but she's already panicked. Listen, this isn't really about the child—or her record. It's about her mother. Just tell me she has no reason to worry." Eli explained about the ex-husband having custody, which blocked all official intervention until his custody period ended. How cops needed a better reason than "my daughter won't call me back" to issue Amber Alerts and warrants and take other preemptive action. "Do you have kids?" he asked the principal.

"Three. Where's this going?"

"Well, imagine we're talking about your daughter—and one day she just didn't check in. Even though she *always* made a habit of it."

"How about we trade some information?" Julie Grady said without hesitation, to Eli's surprise. "An answer for an answer. But *completely* off the record."

"Deal. We never spoke," Eli vowed. "You first."

"I've got reason to believe that Georgianna's home life is causing her difficulty. Am I correct?"

"Both parents appear to be facing some personal and professional challenges. To say that in English, Mom and Dad had a bitter divorce, Mom's unemployed, Dad's been suspended from work. Now my turn." Eli doodled with the pen on his desk. "Is Georgianna in school today?"

"No. However, Georgianna has a history of cutting class. In recent weeks, quite frequently. We left another message this morning with her father."

"So you're saying we shouldn't worry?"

"I didn't say that. Her teachers have been concerned. *Very* concerned."

"When did she go missing?"

"Day before yesterday. Sometime between lunch period and her two-o'clock history class."

# Chapter 31

Still three down, two to go.

Finding Luis Ramos was going to take ingenuity. So Haddox briefly turned his attention to Sinya Willis. It turned out to be a smart move—since unraveling her whereabouts was almost child's play.

Sinya Willis had worked as a nanny for every single one of the forty-three years since she'd arrived in New York City. From Jamaica. Haddox didn't talk with her—at least, not right away—but he did talk with Claire Abrams, who lived with her large family in a Classic Seven on West End Avenue at 104th Street.

Sinya's employer.

Sinya had cared for the three Abrams boys for about eight years, ever since the oldest was born. Claire was distressed to think the FBI might need anything from Sinya. She assured Haddox that Sinya was here legally. That she paid all her taxes and got nothing under the table; there were no nannygate issues. Sinya had had a little medical problem a few years ago, and that caused some debt to build up, but they were helping her and it would disappear very soon. Claire Abrams was clearly freaked that she was under investigation for either tax fraud or illegally employing a foreign national.

Haddox didn't have the heart to tell her that the truth was far worse.

Four witnesses down. One to go.

Eli crossed over to the MRU where Haddox and Eve were working. He'd lost what Mace called his *Welcome Back, Kotter* sport jacket. Now he just wore a crumpled dress shirt with the front left pocket—

normally filled with a pocket protector and pens—stuffed with candy. He pulled out a roll of Life Savers and offered a cherry one to Haddox, who shook his head.

"Do me a favor?" Eli asked Haddox.

"Depends on the favor," Haddox said automatically. He didn't lift his eyes from his computer screen.

"You know how to track a cellphone, even if it's not on, right?"

"Aye. Assuming its battery is still inside—and hasn't died."

"Can you try? Here's the number." Eli passed him a crumpled sheet of paper. Somehow during its time in Eli's pocket, it had acquired a red stain. Eli managed to control his instinctive panic that he was bleeding to death. Then he realized that it was just a nasty concoction of sweat and atomic fireballs.

"Who does this number belong to?"

Eli lowered his voice several decibels. "It's personal—sorry. Don't tell Eve."

Haddox shrugged. "No worries, mate. I'll run it in the background while I do the official heavy lifting."

The last witness.

The official file on Luis J. Ramos was paper thin. What little there was came courtesy of U.S. Citizenship and Immigration Services.

The Ramos file at least contained a list of LKAs—meaning Ramos's few last known associates. There weren't many. Luis had kept to himself: Worked hard and sent money home to Oaxaca, Mexico, which was one of the poorest regions in the country. It was also where his wife and five-year-old daughter still lived.

Haddox decided that was the key. Luis might have vanished underground to avoid his deportation hearing. But wherever he was, he was still working—and sending money home.

Assuming Luis had stayed in New York—and Haddox thought it was a fair assumption, given the number of no-questions-asked jobs to be had—there were several options for a Mexican worker to send money home. But one of the most popular was a remittance house. There was a section of Broadway in Harlem where there was a whole line of them—each advertising in Spanish how *they* had the cheapest rates to wire money straight from NYC to Mexico.

He'd have to visit, ask around, and see where a little luck and some charm took him.

That was as far as his planning extended. He'd have to improvise as needed from there.

Still four down.

Still one to go.

Three hours, thirty-two minutes until deadline.

# Chapter 32

Mace bounded into the MRU, where Eve, Haddox, and Eli were glued to a video screen. The Omega Team had just authorized the first team to take the roof.

"What's going on?" he asked.

"We're watching Special Ops Team Alpha go fishing," Eli explained.

"I caught a big one on my own fishing expedition."

No one said anything.

"I spoke with a guy who knew about a major stash of stolen weapons and explosives. The inventory seems to be a match with what we're dealing with here," Mace added triumphantly. "It's all straight from Iraq. A clear echo of the kind of explosives and techniques the guys use over there."

"Iraq," Eve said absently. Then stood up straighter. "Look—he's almost in!" She pointed to the screen. A man from Team Alpha was scaling the roof.

Everyone watched. No one seemed to be able to breathe.

"So looks like we're dealing with a vet. Specifically, a disturbed vet," Mace persisted.

No one turned.

"Or some wacko insurgent who's bringin' his fight to America," he added.

No one paid attention.

"Or a flying monkey with flames shooting out of his ass."

Nothing. They had eyes and ears for nothing but the men on the video screen.

"Problem is: Even the NYPD's got no proof how a big shitload of explosives got stolen. They just know it's gone." Mace cursed. "Not that any of you seems to give a damn."

He strode out of the MRU, slamming the door behind him.

Damn if he was going to waste time on shit nobody cared about. Life was too short.

He had just turned the corner, circling around Atlas, when he stopped short.

*Another hostage stood on the steps.*

He looked like a priest. At least, he was wearing a priest's collar and robes. He had to be freezing.

*Really a priest—or just dressed to look like one?* No way to know.

He was white, maybe early thirties. Brown hair, slightly curly, fell into his eyes. His face was a little too round, his body a little too soft. A guy with no discipline. A guy who hadn't visited the weight room in years, if ever.

The hostage looked around. Held up an index card. Started to read.

His hands were shaking. His voice was trembling.

"You have exactly ninety seconds for your assault team to reverse course!" he shouted. "If they do not, I will die! In Ninety. Eighty-nine. Eighty-eight. Eighty-seven . . ."

# Chapter 33

*Fifty-six. Fifty-five. Fifty-four . . .*

Eve stood in front of the hostage, on the street at the base of the broad marble steps, phone to her ear. "Stand down! Stand down! I repeat, Omega Team *stand down*!"

There was no acknowledgment on the secure line.

The priest didn't move, but only continued looking around. Uncertain. Counting. *Forty-nine. Forty-eight . . .*

Eve ignored the chaos around her. Radios were crackling. Officers in full body armor were crouched eight feet away. In the periphery of her vision, she was aware of sharpshooters in position.

"I need confirmation, Omega Team."

"Roger that." In the background, she heard the Omega Team leader repeat the order.

She heard Eli's shout from the MRU. "Team Alpha in full retreat. Team Alpha in full retreat."

She exhaled the breath she hadn't realized she was holding. She dialed the Hostage Taker's number. It rang—once, twice, three times, four times.

She redialed it again. Still nothing. She wondered if he'd switched to a different burner.

She took a step toward the hostage.

He seemed barely able to stand. His voice quavered, *Thirty-three. Thirty-two . . .*

"It's okay," she called up to the priest. "We just did what you asked. What *he* asked."

*Twenty-nine. Twenty-eight.*

"You can stop counting now. It's over." She stretched out her hands. "You need to come with me now, Father. You'll be safe."

The SWAT team was on standby. Men in full gear with shields. She had only to give the signal and they would whisk the hostage to safety.

*What was stopping her?*

She supposed the hostage himself. She could feel the priest's fear and apprehension; it was as palpable as if it were her own. As though she herself stood exposed on those steps, trembling in the crosshairs of a sniper's rifle.

*As she had been, not so long ago.*

*Twenty-six. Twenty-five.*

She empathized with the hostage—and reminded herself that empathy was a large part of what made her very good at her job. It wasn't just her ability to study people—to read their body language and intuit their thoughts. It was her ability to understand their fears. That formed the root of all her strategy—and it was what the instructors at Quantico had never been able to teach in the training room.

*Her training.*

In that instant, she recognized her problem. All her empathetic impulses were being misdirected to the *hostage,* not the Hostage Taker. For a negotiator, that was a mistake. A sometimes fatal mistake. Her training had taught her to assume all hostages were "homicides in progress." To be rescued, if humanly possible. To be sacrificed, if not.

Her empathy belonged solely to the Hostage Taker right now—and yet she felt lost, unable to reach him. The last time she'd been unable to connect with her opponent, too many people had died.

She needed to try harder.

"They're in full retreat, Eve. Teams Alpha and Delta." Eve didn't even recognize the voice that shouted the information.

*Nineteen. Eighteen. Seventeen.*

"You can stop counting now," she told the hostage. "Come to me. You'll be safe."

He didn't move.

*Fourteen. Thirteen.*

He had to be in shock.

The FBI's own snipers were in place. Forensic analysis was complete—so now their crosshairs were trained on the exact spot, a gap high in the fragmented scaffolding, from which the last two bullets had come. Upon seeing the slightest movement, they would fire.

*Ten. Nine.*

Eve gave the order. The SWAT members rushed the hostage.

Covered him with their flak jackets. Protected the air space above them with their shields.

Began moving him down the steps, away from the Cathedral and the bronze door.

Eve could still hear him counting. *Five. Four. Three . . .*

She was seized by a panic—an overwhelming sense of approaching calamity. She wanted to turn away. She did not want to watch.

*Two . . .*

*Had she heard the count? Or only imagined it?*

She felt the shock wave. Even though the men and women surrounding her were all seasoned professionals, she heard their collective gasp. Then somebody screamed—and the noise seemed louder than the explosion itself.

She didn't focus on the victims—although she knew there were three.

She was teetering at the edge of reality and memory—unable to shake the image of Zev and an explosion three months ago on the banks of the Hudson River. When the scream that had sounded had been her own.

She looked down at the priest and his would-be rescuers. She remembered Zev. All of them now in a place she could not reach.

Choking on the smoke, she collapsed to her knees in despair. Her pulse was pounding, her blood humming, her mind struggling to filter the chaos. In the split second before reality was permanently clouded by memory, she felt strong hands lifting her up—half dragging, half carrying her away.

*Haddox.*

NEWS NEWS NEWS NEWS NEWS

# HOUR 8

3:22 p.m.

This just in.

You are looking at a live shot of smoke rising from the front of Saint Pat's Cathedral. We are receiving multiple reports of an explosion there within the last few minutes.

We repeat, there has been an explosion in front of Saint Patrick's Cathedral.

We have no details yet on the extent of the damage or possible injuries.

We have no official word on whether this is believed to be an act of terrorism.

On the line, we have Rob Nichols, a retired FBI counter-terrorism agent. What can you tell us, Rob?

*NICHOLS:* I've been listening to your newscast for the past hour, and I know what everybody's worried about. We see smoke rising over the New York City skyline, and after 9/11, we all worry about terrorism. We hear there's a hostage situation at a beloved landmark, and we worry about the number of lives at risk inside.

But in my opinion, what we're seeing here is not the hallmark of terrorism. What tells me this is the timing. A terrorist would have aimed for maximum impact later in the day—when the Church was filled with hundreds of tourists, and Fifth Avenue was swarming with shoppers. In my opinion, this situation speaks of someone who very likely has a grudge against the Catholic Church.

# Chapter 34

Thirteen minutes passed in a blur of screeching sirens and dashing paramedics. Eve was aware of serious blue eyes watching as she sipped ice water, sagged against a makeshift wall of coats in the deserted MRU annex.

Those blue eyes confused her. And memory merged with reality all over again. She fought back tears.

"I've got questions," Haddox said soberly.

"A pint of Guinness. A fast car. A room at the Four Seasons."

Haddox shot her a quizzical look.

"You're the one who told me those were all the answers you'd ever need."

"Right. Usually they are." He half smiled at the memory. Then immediately grew serious again. "You were thinking of Zev out there."

She nodded. Her whole body seemed to sway with the motion. "Hard not to. Did anyone—"

"Notice?" he finished for her. "Only me and Mace. Everyone else was a little preoccupied. What day is it?"

"Excuse me?"

"Just making sure you're here. Not off in some other place."

"Don't be absurd," she snapped.

"Because for a few minutes there, I lost you."

"I'm fine."

"But you haven't been fine," he insisted. "Not for a while, luv. Am I right?"

"It's nothing."

"When was the first spell?"

*Rome,* she thought. *Two boys—one in a blue-striped shirt, one in yellow—playing in the Piazza Navona. Giggling. Teasing each other. Then suddenly standing up and running away—as the firecracker candle they'd lit flew thirty feet into the air. She'd heard the noise. Smelled the smoke. She had practically fallen into the Fountain of the Four Rivers—and emptied the contents of her stomach into its waters.*

Haddox was talking nonstop, not even waiting for her answer. "It's why you didn't come back to work, isn't it? Too many potential triggers."

"You're overreacting." This wasn't about her—or his appraisal of her during the past three months.

"Your leaving me in Rome? Your nonstop tour of the world?" His brow furrowed. He was making the connections.

Time to end this discussion. "Maybe your ego just can't accept that I left you."

Haddox raised his chin. "You'd never have left without a damn good reason, luv."

"Because what woman would leave you without one?" she mocked him.

"You said it, not me," he replied with a careless grin.

"Chalk it up to commitment issues," she said, finding a smile. "Mine."

"More like trust issues."

"You can't complain. You're the guy who doesn't stick around in one place, since the wrong people might find you. Who won't keep a regular cellphone, since the government might track you."

"Not might, *would,*" he corrected her. "Besides, life is short—and best spent on the move. How about we debate this over dinner tonight? When the crisis is ended?"

"That sounds overly optimistic."

"That you'll have dinner with me? Or that the crisis will end?"

"No chance this crisis will be over."

"But if it is?"

"My answer's still no. Maybe we'll talk when you stop calling me 'luv.'" She turned serious. "Did either of the agents surrounding the hostage make it?"

Haddox shook his head.

Her heart sank with a thud. She had known it; after all, they'd borne the brunt of the blast, saving others. But it still hurt, hearing it. "Omega Team?"

"All members safely back at home base."

"What puzzles me is this: He didn't shoot this time. Why change his methods?"

"Your sharpshooters had uncovered his position. So he changed his tactics."

She took a few seconds to think about it. "He cheated, you know."

"Who?"

"The Hostage Taker. We did what he asked. We recalled Omega Team."

"He didn't give a tinker's damn."

"He wouldn't answer my call."

"You broke his trust."

"He's a terrific shot. If Omega Team's breach was what bothered him, why not take one of them out? Why punish his hostage?"

"Because your Special Ops forces put their lives on the line all the time. It's their job. Whereas killing a hostage—an ordinary civilian? That makes headlines."

Stubbornly, Eve crossed her arms. "He cheated another way, too. The victim was counting down—but never made it to *one.*"

"Kinder that way, don't you think?"

Mace poked his head in the door. "All good?"

Eve managed a wobbly smile. "C'mon in. Tell me what you wanted to, before, about the weapons taken from the Midtown West storage lot."

"Gotta get one thing off my chest first. No disrespect, Eve—but after what just happened, do you really think you're gonna be able to talk this motherfucker down?"

*Am I?* she wondered. *When the connection I thought I'd made was just undone in a blast no one saw coming?*

"There's still a chance," she said.

"'Cause if we end up needing to get inside that Cathedral, I'm thinking you gotta call Frankie."

*Frank García—whose PTSD terrors from service overseas had landed him in treatment.* A smile played on her lips. "You—asking for García?"

"Don't get me wrong: I can't stand the guy. Don't want to work with him, don't want to be in the same room with him. But he's the only bastard I can think of who's got the chops to get into that Church without the Hostage Taker noticing."

Eve squeezed her eyes shut. What Zev's violent death had done to unsettle her, she wouldn't wish on anybody. Whatever haunted Frankie, she knew, was much worse.

Then she remembered how the hostage had trembled.

How the Hostage Taker hadn't taken her last call. She'd been foolish to think she could trust him; she'd been arrogant to believe she could predict his moves.

Omega Team had failed. If Eve and those helping her were going to succeed, then she needed someone whose abilities were as unpredictable and unconventional as her adversary's.

She turned to Mace. "You're right. We need García on this one. I'll handle it."

**VIDOCQ FILE #Z77519**

**Current status: INACTIVE**

**Frank García**

Nickname: Frankie

Age: 41

Race/Ethnicity: Hispanic

Height: 5'10"

Weight: 185 lbs.

Eyes: Brown

Hair: Black

Prominent features: Triangle of three tattooed dots on knob of right wrist (the symbol of *Mi Vida Loca,* My Crazy Life, the motto of the Latin Kings); tattoo on left arm (*I will never quit,* warrior ethos).

**Current Address:** 3884 Broadway (Washington Heights).
**Criminal Record (U.S. Army):** General court-martial for involuntary manslaughter, resulting in dishonorable discharge plus forfeiture of all pay and allowances. Sentence: ten years.

**Related:** *Military record makes clear that he loses respect for the chain of command when a superior fails to meet his exacting standards.*

**Expertise:** Member of elite team of Army Rangers (75th Ranger Regiment). Specialized hand-to-hand combatives expert (including knife-fighting training by experts in Apache knife techniques). Weapons expert and trained sniper.
**Education:** Graduated South Bronx High School.

**Personal**

**Family:** One of seven siblings (four brothers, two sisters). Two brothers, Jesus and Alex, are current members of Latin Kings. A sister, Emelina, died of lung cancer in 2006.

**Spouse/Significant Other:** Divorce finalized from spouse, Teresa. One son, Frankie Junior, age nine.

**Religion:** Devout Catholic.

**Interests:** Devoted to Frankie Junior and his extended family. Passionate about vintage muscle cars.

**Profile**

**Strengths:** A warrior who will fight to uphold his personal code of honor.

**Weaknesses:**

- Belief in irrational superstitions is a frequent distraction and cause for concern.
- Significant risk of PTSD meltdown or alcohol addiction relapse. Judicial order for inpatient treatment established October; future shared custody of Frankie Junior depending on successful completion of program.
- Isolated and distrustful of others.

**Notes:** A highly skilled individual with serious personal liabilities. García mistrusts alliances, having been burned first by the Latin Kings and then by the Army Rangers. Change his perspective and the result will be lethal—a Special Ops expert who will run through walls for his team.

**Assessment prepared by SA Eve Rossi. Updated by ADIC Henry Ma. For internal use only.*

# Chapter 35

*I have their undivided attention now. I feel like an orchestra conductor, making sure each different instrument in my symphony performs its individual role. Ensuring that the whole will be far greater than its parts.*

*From my perch on high, in the great choir loft over the front portals, this Cathedral spreads before me. An entire city's block of stone and stained glass, sheathed in scaffolding. I can't see them all, but I know the people I've positioned are waiting beneath.*

*They have no choice.*

*I reach into the back pocket of my pants and draw out a narrow vial of powder, sprinkling some on my hands, creating a perfect circle pattern. I rub my hands together, grab the nearest scaffolding pole, and begin climbing.*

*I go higher and higher, above the massive organ's thousands of brass pipes, until I reach a part of the wall where I know there's a gap. I peek through and see Fifth Avenue. It's closed to ordinary citizens, but NYPD and FBI and emergency responders are everywhere, like crazed ants.*

*Traffic uptown and downtown must be a nightmare. A mind-boggling standstill. Families will be disappointed—there will be no tree lighting at Rockefeller Center tonight.*

*A group of officers stares up—but I know they can't see me. They are watching the scaffolding. Maybe even admiring the twin spires of Saint Patrick's.*

*The world outside is chaos.*

*The world in here is peaceful.*

*My own eyes drift up the wall, focusing on each individual block of stone. Each layer of mortar binding them together.*

*I imagine my father's grandfather hard at work here with his brothers and cousins. All of them stonemasons from County Cork who came to a land of golden opportunity—and a city rising as fast as immigrant labor could raise it. My great-grandfather watched as the cornerstone of Saint Patrick's—now missing—was laid.*

*I wonder if I will be remembered for rediscovering that lost cornerstone. If they fail to follow my instructions, it may reveal itself.*

*Amid the rubble.*

NEWS NEWS NEWS NEWS NEWS

PART THREE

# HOUR 8 CONTINUED

3:47 p.m.

*MAYOR:* I've just gotten off the phone with the governor, who is en route by helicopter to the city this afternoon as the continuing crisis at Saint Patrick's Cathedral escalates. Both he and the president have personally assured me that this city will get whatever resources we need to bring this terrible situation to a safe resolution.

*UNIDENTIFIED REPORTER:* Can you comment on the explosion?

*MAYOR:* As I'm sure you can understand, since this is an ongoing crisis and investigation, we can't comment at this time.

*UNIDENTIFIED REPORTER:* What about casualties?

*MAYOR:* There have been casualties, but until all loved ones have been notified, we cannot provide further details. Our focus right now is to make sure all available resources are being deployed and that everything possible is being done to save lives.

*UNIDENTIFIED REPORTER:* How many people are inside? Have you confirmed their identities?

# Chapter 36

Three hours, eleven minutes to go.

Eve finished issuing instructions.

As her highest priority: She wanted the five witnesses on-site before the deadline. She wanted the Hostage Taker identified, with full background. She wanted to identify any and all secret access tunnels leading to Saint Patrick's. It might prove the only way to end the crisis without further cost to either innocent life or the Cathedral itself.

And they had confirmation of some of those innocent lives: A number of people had now been reported missing. People believed to have gone to Saint Patrick's for early-morning Mass. People who later missed meetings and appointments. People who never made it home.

The first name had always been on Eve's list of potential hostages: Monsignor DeAngelo, who was to have presided over the Mass.

So had the second: Penelope Miller, Luke's mother. A cousin in Philadelphia had arrived to take charge of Luke; she confirmed that no one in the family could reach Penelope.

Now there were other names.

Ethan Raynor. A sous chef at Café Bonne Nuit—reported missing by his coworkers.

Aiko Tanaka. A grad student in art history at New York University, doing a paper on Saint Patrick's—and reported missing by her roommate.

Jason Chitov. A priest from Vermont—reported missing by his mother, who lived on Staten Island.

One priest—DeAngelo or Chitov, pending official ID—was now dead. Plus the hostage cop—though no precinct had yet come forward with information to identify him. And when the workday ended—and others didn't return home—even more people might be reported missing.

Still, at least five hostages were now presumptively identified.

Eve was determined not to think about it. The weight of that responsibility would only distract her.

First, she delegated the lower-priority work to agents outside of Vidocq. She asked them to focus on identifying that cop—who, if not disabled, could be a potential ally. She directed Haddox, Mace, and Eli to tackle the higher-priority list. In their case, she expected quick results. Failure was not an option.

Springing Frank García from his hospital bed was squarely on her shoulders. She called the medical director in charge of García's treatment. Dr. Roger Albin had spent most of his career in private practice, treating those patients wealthy enough to afford his staggering hourly fees. His specialty had been women, particularly those with eating disorders.

Then his son Mike came home from a tour of duty in Iraq—completely unraveled. Where the doctor saw a familiar row of brownstones across the street, Mike saw a haven for sniper fire. Where the doctor saw ordinary garbage cans, Mike saw an IED receptacle. Where the doctor saw beautiful fireworks over the East River, Mike saw explosions.

Six months later, Mike's wife had left him, protesting that the separation was necessary to protect their four-year-old daughter from his explosive bursts of fury. Mike moved back into the doctor's basement. Fast-forward another nine months, and Mike was in the ground—having hanged himself in his grandmother's garage.

Roger Albin had determined to help others, as he wished he had been able to help his son. He'd given up his lucrative private practice and joined a special VA program servicing soldiers and veterans. He took his job seriously.

"It's important work we do here, Agent Rossi," he told her. "We help heroes who have served their country. And any disruption in treatment impedes our progress."

"Of course I understand," she assured him. "In any other situation, I would never interfere with a patient's treatment plan. But this situation is urgent. I need someone with Frank García's expertise."

"Find someone else, Agent Rossi. He's at a critical point right now. Even a temporary release could undo all the valuable progress he's made."

"I understand. But it's a risk we have to take."

"Mr. García suffers from severe post-traumatic stress disorder. He's frequently disoriented. His body may have left the battlefield, but his mind remains there. His custody issues—his ability to continue seeing his son—depend on successful completion of this treatment program."

"Which is why he will return immediately upon completion of this mission."

"Surely someone else—"

She cut him off. "There's no one else. If there were, I'd call them. The director's office has faxed over the paperwork. An agent will be by to pick Mr. García up within the half-hour."

His voice crackled with anger. "I don't actually have a choice, do I?"

"No, Dr. Albin. Today you don't."

# Chapter 37

Eve was desperate for air. Unable to stay inside the MRU another minute. And almost frantic to reestablish a dialogue with the Hostage Taker. Rebuild the trust the Omega Team had broken.

The secured perimeter was teeming with cops, firemen, Feds, and forensic techs. Eve brushed past them all, stumbling into a cop whose right hand was bandaged in gauze, thick and round as a boxing glove. She mumbled an apology, then found a space in between the statue of Atlas and Banana Republic. A singing, dancing Santa doll was on the ledge beneath Atlas's left foot, spitting out a tinny rendition of "Jingle Bell Rock." A poor replacement for the block's lavish holiday displays, now gone dark. Eve normally would have found it cheesy, bordering on ridiculous. Today she saw it as a small act of defiance—some first responders keeping alive the holiday spirit that the taking of the Cathedral had all but squashed.

She tried each of the numbers Haddox had rounded up after analyzing the Hostage Taker's lonely calls.

No luck. The Hostage Taker's cellphones—past, present, and presumed future—had been bricked. No way to reach him—unless she embraced the old-fashioned technique of the bullhorn, or shattered a priceless window and deployed a throwphone. She hated both options. One-sided conversations were never particularly effective, in her experience. To have a dialogue, you needed both parties.

Her cell chimed with an incoming text from Henry Ma. Attached was a file on Jason Chitov—now positively identified as the latest victim. Chitov had been a priest. Specifically, a defrocked priest.

Chitov had been convicted in 2008 of molesting an altar boy—

one he had befriended while assigned to Saint Mary's Catholic Church in southern Vermont. He had been released on parole in 2013 after serving eighty percent of his sentence.

The file stressed that Jason Chitov had been remorseful. Two days after the accusations against him were lodged, he leapt from the balcony of Saint Mary's in a suicide attempt. He was hospitalized and taken into custody following his recovery. He had accepted the plea deal that was offered him.

No additional details were available.

But it certainly raised the question: *Did the Hostage Taker know?*

# Chapter 38

Another MRU was brought in to house the witnesses as they arrived. They put this one in front of Façonnable, the high-end clothing boutique on the southwest corner of Fifty-first and Fifth Avenue. Like the first, this MRU's space was technologically equipped, linked to the FBI's secure network. But its original purpose had been the transport of cartel drug lords by the ATF—the Bureau of Alcohol, Tobacco, Firearms, and Explosives. That meant the van was also bombproof and bulletproof, and offered small enclosed cubicles where each witness could wait—or be interviewed—with some degree of privacy. There was even an ample-sized central area where they could meet as a group.

All that remained was bringing the witnesses to this secure location.

There was the sound of boots on concrete pavement. Then Eve watched as the three agents she'd summoned filed into the room, dressed for maximum protection, wearing full body armor.

"This is a search-and-secure mission," she explained to them. "You'll need to dress the part. Exchange your Kevlar vests for sport jackets and ties; you don't want to scare your targets. As far as we know, none of these five individuals did anything wrong. You need to use your wits, not your muscle."

The man to her left, Agent Morgan, was a short man with a large bald spot in the middle of his head. "What if they don't wanna come in? Are we authorized to use force?"

"As a last resort. Explain what's at stake first. At least five lives."

Haddox joined the conversation. "And one of the greatest landmarks in New York City," he reminded them.

"Agent Morgan, you will pick up Cassidy Jones of Astoria, Queens. You'll find her at work. A Greek diner named the Utopia. Ditmars Boulevard near Thirty-third Street." Eve turned to Hayes, the next agent in line. "You'll head to the Upper East Side. Blair Vanderwert will be waiting for you in the lobby of his real estate firm at Eighty-sixth and Lexington. Oh, and he thinks you're looking to drop ten million dollars on a new condo."

Turning to the third agent, Eve explained, "I need you to make two stops along the West Side. Alina Matrowski will be waiting for you at the Starbucks on Fort Washington Avenue and 181st Street. Next you'll find Sinya Willis in the lobby of her boss's building at West End Avenue and 104th Street. Take it easy on Ms. Willis. She's a bit jumpy."

"That's it?"

"Each of you has been sent an electronic file with your target's photograph. Remember, this matter is urgent. We need them here ASAP."

As the last of the three agents left the MRU, Eve turned to Haddox. "That's four of our witnesses. Where are we with Ramos?"

"Turns out he requires a delicate touch—and probably a bit of thinking on my feet."

"Thinking on your feet? Time is critical."

"Relax, I've got this."

"Sure, why worry? An illegal immigrant hiding in the shadows of Harlem—and only two hours, forty-seven minutes for a cocky Irishman to find him." Eve handed him a file. "Everything Immigration has on Ramos is in here. Unfortunately, there's no photo."

"Don't worry, luv. I'll be back before you'll get a chance to miss me," Haddox said as he walked out the door.

Haddox could have asked for an official escort uptown. A car with a siren and driver with credentials to ease him past roadblocks and through bottleneck traffic. But being chauffeured around had never been Haddox's style—so he walked west, past the concrete blockades and the crush of rubberneckers and cops. Through snarled traffic and men in uniform who carried ballistic shields and had suspicious eyes. He passed through Rockefeller Center, where this year's tree awaited its lighting. Next was Radio City Music Hall. He went by the Time-Life building and Bobby Van's Grill and Barclay's with its three-line neon-blue ticker. Reaching Broadway, he opted for the surest way of getting around Manhattan in a traffic jam: the subway. Even if it was crowded tighter than a sardine can.

Haddox took the 1 train uptown and began his search for the elusive Luis J. Ramos by spreading Franklins through the remittance houses clustered on Broadway in Lower Harlem. He asked for the Luis Ramos who sent money each week to Oaxaca.

There were lots of Mexican men doing similar things. But Luis had been regular. A man of habit. Showing up every Friday after finishing work at four o'clock.

It was a habit he hadn't broken—until just before Thanksgiving. He had sent no money since mid-November. He hadn't been seen working his usual jobs—cleaning windows at Trump Tower or Gladstone Properties.

He could've gotten sick.

An injury or argument could've put him out of work.

It was now 4:47 p.m. Haddox canvassed the men smoking outside the bodegas. Men who wore exhausted faces and stained clothes after a hard day's work. Haddox told them who he was looking for. Not a single man asked why. Their sole interest was in the hundred dollars that was promised the man who gave Haddox Ramos's location.

That man was named Jesus. His middle kid had recently taken a job delivering Chinese food at the Happy Panda. Jesus's son got bored when it wasn't busy. He liked it better when orders came flying in, just so he'd have something to do. Because he was bored, the boy had noticed the man who moved into the restaurant's basement shortly after Thanksgiving. He also noticed the woman and little girl who later joined the man. Neither of them spoke any English. In fact, they never spoke a word of Spanish, either. But the girl had plump red cheeks and big round eyes that stared.

The Happy Panda was busy with kids out of school. A gang of seven bunched at a table in one corner, joking around, hanging out, ordering lo mein and Szechuan beef. Three clustered at the checkout register, two boys horsing around, playing keep-away with the girl's backpack.

Haddox headed for the dingy bathroom in the rear, but cut to the stairs before he reached it. The stairs were narrow, decrepit, and sagging in the middle from decades of shoes tracking down grime, grease, and supplies.

Haddox poked his head into the room opposite the stairs. It contained only utilities—the hot water heater, oil tank, and boiler. Another room—more of a closet, really—held reams of napkins and paper products. He found what he sought in the cramped rear basement room behind the stairs. A single sixty-watt lightbulb dangled from the ceiling. The walls were soot-stained and the room stank of damp and grease. Someone had put linoleum on the floor decades ago; it was now yellowed and cracked with age. There was a metal table in the center, surrounded by three folding chairs. Two makeshift beds had been created by placing blankets on top of boxes. Only the girl's corner was halfway habitable: Pink blankets, a teddy bear, and a row of cheap dolls were the sole bright spot in the dank living space.

Haddox stepped inside.

Three people looked up in surprise when he approached. Luis Ramos was a compact man with hard, suspicious eyes, wearing a rumpled denim shirt and jeans. His wife was very slim and long-limbed, almost disappearing inside the oversized yellow shirt she wore with her jeans. Her hair was glorious, wavy, reaching just past her shoulders. The little girl was a pint-sized copy of her mother, except she still had the round baby fat.

Each of them fixed Haddox with a stare—one terrified, one distrustful, one openly paranoid.

The woman reached for her daughter instinctively. Haddox noticed Luis's right hand slide into the pocket of his jeans.

*A knife?*

"Take it easy, mate." Haddox spread his arms wide. "I'm only here to talk. My name's Corey Haddox."

Luis set his jaw in a square line, as if his life was full of problems he was tired of having to tolerate. "You with Imigration?"

"No. No relation to them at all." He laid his Irish accent on thick. The less American he sounded, the more he would reassure Ramos.

It didn't work. "You a cop?" Ramos asked.

"Definitely not."

"What do you want?"

"I have no interest in your family. I'm just looking for you. Assuming you're Luis J. Ramos, who occasionally finds work downtown as a window washer."

"What if I am?"

"I just have a few questions for you. I need you to come with me to answer them."

Haddox followed Ramos up the rickety staircase. Through the Chinese restaurant. Noticed that Ramos seemed to be moving with deliberate slowness. One foot went very slowly in front of the other. Left, right, left again.

Then he reached Broadway, where the sidewalks were packed with people and the road was jammed with traffic. And Ramos took off, headed uptown—running like a bat out of hell.

Haddox raced after him, shoving his way through a cluster of men drinking out of brown paper bags. Losing a step out of the gate.

Luis must have practiced his escape route, preparing for a day like today. He was small, quick, and damn fast. In contrast, Haddox felt like he was all awkward limbs.

Haddox crossed Broadway across oncoming traffic. Ignored the honking cars. Already a good two blocks behind Luis.

Luis was simply too fast. Too at ease in the neighborhood.

And in less than three minutes, Haddox had lost him.

Returning to the room below the Chinese restaurant would be a waste of time. Ramos's wife and daughter would be long gone.

Haddox had underestimated Luis J. Ramos—and screwed up.

# Chapter 39

*I imagine all kinds of things.*

*I imagine Eve Rossi below, shuttling between the steps of the Cathedral and her temporary office under Atlas's globe.*

*"She can get headlines," I was told. And important messages need to be heard.*

*I imagine the woman I took hostage with the boy, unsure whether I plan to kill her or let her go. Wondering when—or if—she'll see her kid again.*

*I imagine eating a cannoli from Caffè Palermo, stuffed with pastry cream, because I am hungry.*

*Yes, I imagine things—future, present, past.*

*When I was a kid, there was a crazy old woman who liked sitting on her walker in front of the bakery on Queens Boulevard, her grocery cart beside her. Now we'd say she suffered from dementia. Back then we just called her batty.*

*Other kids made fun of her, but I liked her all right: She kept cookies in her pocket for passing dogs. My cocker spaniel Tosca was a fan.*

*The day it happened was a hot, sticky July day—the kind where heat blasts from the sidewalk and swallows you whole. Ma had sent me to the bakery to pick up bread. When I got there, I saw the walker and the grocery cart. But no sign of the crazy lady.*

*They found her next to the dumpster. My mother and aunts whispered about it whenever they thought I wasn't listening. She had a name: Mrs. Brescia. She had been beaten and robbed. According to Ma, if the old lady had been healthy, she would've recovered. She just wasn't strong enough. The Kinser brothers—or, as the neighbors called them, "that boisterous bunch of hooligans"—were responsible. But that wasn't what kept everyone's tongue wagging.*

*It was because the attack on that batty old crone happened on Queens Boulevard at about half past nine in the morning. Broad daylight. In front of six witnesses.*

*Not one of them tried to help.*

*Not one of them bothered to call the police.*

*No, not until it was far too late.*

NEWS NEWS NEWS NEWS NEWS

# HOUR 9

4:58 p.m.

Because of the sensitive, ongoing nature of the crisis at Saint Patrick's Cathedral, we have agreed to a request from the city to cease broadcasting live images from the site.

We do, however, have a guest calling in—John Roberts, an architect who is not involved with the restoration project ongoing at Saint Patrick's, but whose expertise can maybe help us understand it.

John, what can you tell us about the project—and how the restoration may play into the terrifying events unfolding at the Cathedral today?

*ROBERTS:* Well, visitors to the Cathedral in recent years will have noticed that a sizable portion of the building has been covered in scaffolding—both interior and exterior. That scaffolding has facilitated everything from roof repair to stone restoration to stained-glass cleaning. The interior scaffolding structure remains extensive. The exterior scaffolding is in the early stages of removal—resulting in gaps that may not have previously existed.

How does this landscape impact the hostage crisis?

*ROBERTS:* These gaps can give a shooter opportunities—and protection. Gaps add an element of unpredictability, I'd say. For the man or men holding these innocent victims hostage—as well as authorities trying to resolve this crisis.

# Chapter 40

Cassidy Jones was radiant, dressed to the nines for her presumed audition at Rockefeller Center. The white dress and matching ivory puffed jacket accentuated her resemblance to Marilyn Monroe. As she hustled inside the MRU, she flashed a dazzling smile toward the group of officers and medics who had stopped what they were doing to look up. Then she saw Haddox and her smile was all for him.

He returned it with a grin. It only seemed polite.

"I can't take my eyes off her, which makes me feel like some kind of pervert," Eli grumbled. "I mean, what—she doesn't look a day over sixteen. But I always had a thing for Marilyn."

"You, Elton John, and half the gay planet. Why is that, anyway?"

"You've got me." Eli shrugged. "But my sister always said she knew I was gay when at age twelve I plastered posters of Marilyn all over my room."

"Well, you can relax a little watching *this* Marilyn. She's twenty-one and fully legal. As verified by the New York State DMV, Department of State, and her Actors' Equity application."

"What do you think the guy inside wants with her?"

"Maybe he's looking to satisfy his Marilyn fetish. To change topics, you were jokin' me about that number, right?"

"What number?"

Eli looked so confused, Haddox figured he must still be dreaming of *The Seven Year Itch*. "You gave me a cell number to run. Said it was personal?"

"Ri-ight." Eli stretched the word in two long syllables.

"Well, I took a few minutes, did some digging. The phone's battery is dead—or maybe it's been removed. So I can only track its movements and calls up until the time it disappeared from the grid. It last emitted a signal yesterday. At precisely 7:49 p.m. When it toggled with a base station in Times Square. Heart of the theater district, actually."

"So how specific a location can you get?"

"Given the number of base stations in Times Square, pretty specific. Let's just say that it looks as though that phone showed up for the evening performance of *Kinky Boots*. Probably had a fantastic time."

"*Kinky Boots*?" Eli repeated.

"You said it was a young lass, right? There's no cause for worry. She was busy and didn't tell everybody what she had planned. Then she used her phone too much and let the battery drain. She was out having fun. We should all be so lucky."

"Guess you're right."

Haddox couldn't resist teasing. "Fess up, mate. It's not really her phone, is it? I'm guessing you don't trust your new boyfriend. Is this your way of checking up on his doings?"

Eli flushed. "Hey, I'm not the one who got left high and dry in Rome. At least I know when I got a good thing going. Besides, she's too good for you."

"Easy, Casanova."

Eli shook his head as he stomped away, pulling out his cell and dialing as he went.

Eli was a feckin' gobshite and Haddox planned to tell him as much. First, Haddox needed to tell Eve news she wouldn't want to hear.

He poked his head into the primary MRU and saw Eve. She had somehow found a black sweater and draped a burgundy wool scarf around her neck. Her sweater was form-fitting, and it would have been open at the top—except for the scarf. Her hair was a tangle of curls, pulled back in a low ponytail. Even tired and stressed, she still looked grand. "I have good news and bad news," he announced. "Which do you want first?"

No response. She was staring out the small window at the Cathedral itself.

Haddox walked over and looked, too. While the surrounding buildings had been blacked out, the floodlights of Saint Patrick's bathed its towering spires in soft white as they stretched toward pea-soup clouds. The effect was otherworldly. "It's a spectacular piece of architecture, isn't it? We've got a Saint Patrick's in Dublin. It's stately—but it doesn't hold a candle to your Saint Patrick's here. I keep imagining the people who were involved in building it. Different generations working in fits and starts over the years. That's always the way, isn't it? The money runs out."

Eve nodded. "Which was why it took twenty-one years between laying the cornerstone and celebrating its grand opening. Plus, the Civil War didn't help."

"Wars never do." Haddox stepped beside her to look. "Doesn't stop people from fighting them."

"I keep wondering: Why today? Why here? Why choose *this* building as the setting for so much bloodshed? Why is it special to him?"

Haddox squinted, again admiring the twin spires as they rose up—over the scaffolding, over Fifth Avenue, over the small group of forensic techs in full body armor who were securing evidence from the steps. The scene sparked a barrage of memories: Going with his mother to Sunday Mass, a wiggly boy in a stiff blue suit and fancy dress shoes. The way the priest's chalice would glisten when the morning light danced through stained-glass windows. How he'd played darts in the rear churchyard with Kiernan Donohue, using the trunk of an old yew tree.

And other memories, too: the countless times Mass had been interrupted by bomb threats—and the eerie sensation of free fall, coming out of Church to find himself on the wrong side of the police barricade. This was *his* Church—and it had shaped the life he'd chosen to live. First as an influence. Later, as something to rebel against.

As a child, he'd loved its mystery and ceremony. As an adult, he'd hated its hypocrisy. Disliked the priests who thought they knew all the answers. Never married, but plenty to say about marriage. Not family men, but they'd preach 'til they were blue in the face about the importance of family. Didn't they realize most families were completely feckin' nuts? His own included—which boasted alcoholics and gamblers, wife-beaters, killers, and cheats. Since the Church didn't answer the questions that really mattered, he had satisfied his curiosity elsewhere—thanks to Internet access and the siren call of technology. The community he'd found there was almost family. *His* version of it, anyway.

"I dunno why he chose Saint Pat's." Haddox returned to the present. "It's a major landmark, but it has religious significance as well. Maybe that's what this is about. I'm sure being Irish skews my perspective, but seems to me that most of the violence we humans have inflicted on each other has been done in the name of religion." He smiled thinly. "Not to be overly reductive of several hundred years of human history, of course."

"His three killings were deliberate, methodical crimes. He was in control of his targets—so completely he knew they wouldn't run. He acted like a showman, managing the timing of their deaths for maximum effect. And he adapted: I believe that he was aware when we discovered his sniper position, and that was when he changed his method of killing."

"Yet the hostages are random individuals. He couldn't have known who would show up for Mass this morning."

"We have preliminary ID on a handful of those held inside. To your point, they appear to be strangers. Completely unconnected."

"What about the cop?"

"A handful of agents are on it. He's the wild card in all this." She turned away from the window, frowning. He wondered when she'd last eaten. "These people may have been taken hostage at random, but I'm worried. Do they represent something—or someone—he despises? And the witnesses are the same. He's given us names—but I can't help but think each one symbolizes something to him. Even though they seem to have nothing in common." She sighed and drew up her shoulders. "I'll take the good news first."

"We've located and spoken with all five of the witnesses."

"You're right; that is good news."

"Even better, four of them are on-site already. Safe and secure."

"And the fifth?"

"That's the bad news. I tracked Ramos to the basement of a Chinese restaurant in Harlem. Just when I thought he was onboard, he took off like a jackrabbit into the crowds. We're not gonna see him again anytime soon."

"Damn. We were so close. How am I going to spin that to the Hostage Taker?" Eve wondered aloud. "Tell the truth—or fake it?"

"Depends on how well he really knows these people. Maybe you'll get lucky."

"I don't believe in luck. I believe in patterns and predictability. Order and planning."

"But every once in a while, you need to turn to karma and kismet. Fate and divine intervention. It's the only way to explain certain mysteries in life. Like the healing waters of Lourdes. Or the 1969 New York Mets. Or"—he shook his head—"how I ended up meeting you—and getting roped into working for the feckin' Feds."

# Chapter 41

Fifth Avenue had grown eerily quiet. Cops and Feds were waiting in anticipation of their next move. Only the soft strains of "I'll Be Home for Christmas," drifting from the deserted ice rink at Rockefeller Plaza, broke the hushed spell.

A priest intercepted Eve before she had a chance to walk over to the secure unit where the four witnesses were waiting. He was gaunt, with sharp, high cheekbones, keen blue eyes, and an awkward gait. He clunked along like the Tin Woodman from *The Wizard of Oz.*

"Hello there." The words were friendly. His smile wasn't.

"Are you the priest I requested?" Eve asked him.

"I'm here to represent the interests of the Church. My name is Monsignor William Geve."

"Special Agent Eve Rossi," she answered, offering her hand. "You've previously served at Saint Patrick's?"

"No—I'm a senior director of New York City Catholic Charities."

Eve frowned. "I was hoping they would send someone active in the ministry. Familiar with the Cathedral. Listen, I don't have a lot of time—"

He cut her off. "I *was* a parish priest serving a congregation. I created a program to combat homelessness; it thrived and I seemed to do some good. So the powers-that-be decided charity development was my true calling. I was given a fancier title and more charity organizations to run. But at root, I'm a pastor, and my heart belongs to that Grand Lady. Even covered in scaffolding, she is magnificent, is she not?"

"So you don't normally support His Eminence, the Archbishop?"

"The Cardinal and his staff are traveling, Agent Rossi," the Monsignor replied coldly. "Has no one told you that? They left the Vatican yesterday; by now they are en route to the refugee camps outside Syria, where their ministry will occupy them for the next fourteen days."

"The key is that I need help from someone who's familiar with the Cathedral. Someone with intimate knowledge of its every nook and cranny."

"Why didn't you say so?" The Monsignor's smile still struck her as cold. False. "Did I not mention that long ago, I served there?"

"Father, I don't mean to be disrespectful, but can you help me or not? Time is of the essence."

"Many of us have grown to feel a special bond with Saint Patrick's; after all, it's no ordinary Church. Never has been. When James Renwick was commissioned to build it, his instructions were to make it larger than any other Cathedral. It needed to tower over the city it served, to show the world that everything else was small and insignificant, compared to God."

"That didn't last," Eve reminded him.

"Few things on this earth do, Agent Rossi. But it still manages to dominate the city, doesn't it? Even with so many skyscrapers dwarfing it. It's my job to ensure that it weathers whatever Armageddon your Hostage Taker intends—or whatever onslaught you direct your tactical teams to prepare."

Eve had met bureaucrats like Geve before—and despite the priest's collar and title, that was clearly the role that he was here to play. She understood his position too well: He was there to protect the Church's reputation—and the Church's physical architecture. The lives at stake weren't his concern.

"If you know the Church so well, maybe you can answer my question. If I need to get inside Saint Patrick's—but without walking through one of the main doors—how would I do it?"

"I wouldn't," he answered coldly. "Any untraditional entry is certain to destroy something of architectural significance."

"We have no choice. Every door to the Cathedral has been booby-trapped. Go through a traditional entryway, the Cathedral will go up in flames and hostages will die."

The Monsignor almost said something but changed his mind. Instead, he offered, "You could take the underground passage connecting the Rectory and the Cathedral. It goes right through the Crypt—then you can head up around the altar to the high pulpit."

"That would be a great idea if the entrance to the Crypt weren't also booby-trapped. I'm asking you if there's something else. More secret—something few people know about."

"You're hoping for a secret tunnel, like runs under Grand Central or the Public Library." His voice was suave.

Eve's heart sank. He was going to be of no help. "Those are documented. Those we know about."

"There's a whole labyrinth of tunnels running under Old Saint Patrick's downtown. People say the stonemasons who built its replacement—this Saint Patrick's here on Fifth—didn't want to be outdone by their predecessors."

"Do you personally know of a secret passageway?"

"If I did, why would I tell you? That would just allow you to send a tactical assault team in. And irreplaceable Church treasures could be destroyed."

"We always work to minimize the risk. Are lives less important than Church treasures, Monsignor?"

His lips tightened. "Do you know what a Cathedral is, Agent Rossi? We call it a prayer, set in stone."

Eve watched the Monsignor turn on his heel and disappear into the crowd of cops and Feds. She thought: *He'd be singing a different tune if someone he loved were inside.*

# Chapter 42

"Why kill the priest?" Eve wondered aloud. "Or the NYPD negotiator? Or Cristina Silva?" Three seemingly unconnected individuals—each in the wrong place at the wrong time. Had they truly been killed only to make the point that the Hostage Taker was willing to take a life?

Or was there something more? A deeper, hidden message?

Only one hostage—a young boy—had been freed. Why? Was it a sign of empathy?

She'd been told she could tell things about people. That she could instinctively understand the motive behind the act. Read the details and find the pattern. An intuitive, almost magical process—like reading tea leaves in a cup or divining the meaning of a drawn tarot card.

Except no magic was happening. Not today. Not for her.

The Hostage Taker had now been in charge for too long. Twenty hours, fifty-two minutes—if Eve counted from the time the Cathedral closed last night. Ten hours, twenty-eight minutes—if she counted from the moment he murdered Cristina Silva, his first hostage, that morning.

The phone rang. She picked it up on the third trill.

"I'm disappointed. I didn't think I'd have to call you again."

Eve glanced at the computer to confirm they were being recorded. Then she listened intently to his voice. She heard exhaustion, confidence, and rage. A terrifying combination. "I'm glad you did call. We need to talk."

"About how you betrayed me? Sending four agents up the backside of the building to take me out? I thought we had an understanding."

"Harming you wasn't their goal. They were only gathering information."

"Are you denying they would've been happy to take a shot, given the chance?" He didn't wait for her answer. "Didn't think so."

"You're the sharpshooter. Why didn't you take them out?"

"Maybe I like pretty architecture. Maybe I didn't want to shatter that stained-glass window they were climbing behind."

"A generous impulse. What about the priest? Do you have something against men of the cloth?"

"Everyone has to pay for their sins."

"That's what this is about: paying for sins?"

"Somebody has to."

"Or is it just that you have something against the Catholic Church?"

"Have you ever been afraid, Eve?"

"Of course. Everyone has."

"What of?"

"The dark. The shadows. The monsters I once imagined lived under my bed."

"You want to know what I was once afraid of? I was afraid of my teacher. I was eleven when I got caught drinking the altar wine before CCD class. That's Catholic Christian Doctrine, which I had every Tuesday night. I thought he was going to give me detention. That was the usual punishment for boys who stepped out of line. So I didn't think much of it when he took me to a different classroom. Not until he closed the door behind him—and locked it shut. I'll never forget what happened next. He sat down, gave me this weird smile, and you know what he said to me? 'This is what God wants.'" His voice dripped sarcasm. "*This* is what God wants."

"I'm sorry." Eve reminded herself that it could be nothing but a trick. A lie designed to win her sympathy and distract her from what needed to be done. Except her every instinct told her: What she'd just heard was the truth.

She'd initiated this dance with various Hostage Takers more times than she wanted to count. Time after time, she and her target spun their lies into a web designed to ensnare the other—and yield the upper hand. But something strange always happened: As often as they lied about the crisis at hand, they confessed the truth about their doubts and fears.

"Now that you're grown up, Eve, what are you afraid of?"

"Myself."

"Is that why you stayed overseas so long?"

"You did your research on me. Maybe you can tell me something more about you? Even it up a bit?"

"Stay focused, Eve. Why didn't you come home? You weren't sightseeing."

It always surprised her how easily she could share her intimate thoughts with an enemy, thoughts she wouldn't share with her closest friends. "I decided to search for a story," she answered evenly. "One that would explain things I don't understand about my stepfather's life—or his death. There are gaps in his history, involving an old family friend. He was important to Zev. He might be important to me."

"What's the mystery?"

"Everything. Nothing," she said evasively. "Right now, I can't separate the truth from the myths and legends surrounding it."

"I've always liked a good story. Tell me this one."

"Maybe when this is all over. Which it could be—right now—if you want to come on out."

He laughed softly. "I propose a trade. Tell me how your story starts—and in return, I'll tell you something useful."

*Why do we share these things with each other?* Eve wondered. To connect and establish some bond of trust, of course. That's what she'd been taught to do. But it was also something else. Maybe it was the appeal of an interested listener. Maybe this was just her own twisted therapy session. "I think my story begins with six numbers. 174531. Tattooed onto a man's left forearm, next to a short scar. I can find nothing before it. But I think 174531 explains everything about his life afterward."

"It would be great if all our stories had a clear beginning. A spot we could point to and say, 'Yes, because of this, I understand—' " The Hostage Taker broke off. "The priest that's dead? He was a bad priest. I heard his confession, not two hours ago. So he fuckin' deserved what he got."

"And the other victims? Did they deserve it?"

"Enough." His voice was pure steel.

"Did you make all your hostages confess?"

"I need to know what they're guilty of. How are my witnesses?"

"Bewildered. Wondering why they're here."

"As long as they're present and accounted for." His tone was clipped.

"Why do you need them?"

"That's personal."

"I won't jeopardize their safety," Eve warned.

"You don't have to."

"Maybe just a show of good faith, then?" Eve wanted to test whether their moment of bonding could yield a concession—and yet she had to tread softly. "Release one hostage," she suggested. "Just one. Maybe the boy's mother."

There. She'd once again broken one of the fundamental rules of hostage negotiation. The one that forbade the negotiator to draw attention to the hostages. The theory was that you should always keep the Hostage Taker's attention directed somewhere else—and avoid suggesting that his hostages had value.

Except he'd already shown a soft spot for the boy.

"Why the mother?" His voice was rough.

"The boy needs his mother." She lowered her voice to a conspiratorial whisper. "I don't know much about you. I still don't know your name. Where you're from. Or even why you're doing this. But I know one thing: You're a parent. And that kid you released before? He's eleven. Just like you were, when your Catholic school teacher hurt you."

In the silence that followed—the breath of his hesitation—Eve imagined she could hear his emotions jostling together. "You know nothing about me," he finally growled. "Nothing at all."

"Just the mother," Eve pressed. "Just one hostage."

*Click*. The line went dead.

And Eve was left alone in the silence, wondering how close she had come.

# Chapter 43

*I didn't think about Mrs. Brescia again for more than twenty years. Not until I was back in Afghanistan.*

*It should have been a lucky tour. I'd been deployed with Stacy, who was fluent in both Pashto and Dari, and would be working as an interpreter out of my FOB—forward operating base. I was a combat engineer who'd gone through the sapper course at Camp Pendleton—arguably the best training available, stateside. I'd learned to defuse the IEDs that plagued the military operation over there.*

*We had no illusions: We were going to hell in a sandstorm. A place with a name most Americans couldn't spell. Located in a no-man's-land most couldn't find on a map.*

*Stacy had been on four past tours, and I'd done three, so I figured we knew just what to expect. I remembered how once we left base for the FOB, it would be months before I felt clean and full and rested. How I would die of boredom most of my days—and be constantly on edge the rest of them.*

*Because we'd be on patrol through bazaars swarming with locals wearing robes big enough to conceal suicide vests.*

*Because most places we went, we'd be greeted with the thumbs-down signal.*

*Because there were too many Afghan soldiers who played both sides of the game. One day, they'd pretend to be our ally. The next, they'd try to shoot us.*

*Mostly because the roads were full of buried IEDs.*

*What I also remembered from those tours was how we all carried pictures of our loved ones in our wallets. After an extended trip out-*

*side the wire, we'd come back to base, strip out of our gear, and take out those pictures. And just stare—wishing we were home.*

*I knew Afghanistan was going to be hard.*

*I thought having Stacy with me would make it easier.*

*I had never been more wrong.*

# Chapter 44

The team agent in charge was having a word with Henry Ma. They had just walked the circumference of the Cathedral, encompassing an entire city block, checking out all four sides. The streets on that block—Fifth Avenue and Madison, Fifty-first, and Fiftieth—were jammed with emergency vehicles. Fire trucks filled the center span; police, ambulance, and unmarked government sedans filled the side lanes, spilling onto the sidewalks. A television crew was trying to sneak around the police barrier on Madison. Uniformed officers converged, blocking their path and confiscating their cameras. When one reporter ducked through, he was immediately tackled and pinned to the ground. His chest landed in a leftover puddle.

The agent allowed his gaze to follow the steep lines of the roof. "I've been wondering since first thing this morning how to do it. How to get inside, once the time comes to breach the Church."

"My negotiator is convinced this building is as impenetrable as a medieval castle." Henry angled his head. "What do you think?"

The lead man gave a slow nod before continuing. "I couldn't figure it out for the longest time myself. The only visible vulnerabilities are the windows near the roofline and certain areas of crumbling stone that are in the process of repair. Both access points require an assault from above. Breach the roof and drop in from above. And while it would work, given enough armor and firepower, good people would die. The Hostage Taker would see us coming. He'd have the opportunity to detonate all the explosives anchored to the foundation."

"So you do not recommend such an approach."

"No, sir. Absolutely not."

They had circled back to the front of Saint Patrick's. Cops and Feds and firemen still swarmed. But now they were all working behind bulletproof glass barriers. Newly erected to offer protection from the sniper or snipers inside.

The agent focused his attention on the central bronze doors. "Those doors aren't just wired with explosives. Each one is sixteen and a half feet high. Each weighs about nine thousand two hundred pounds. There's a lever lock on the bottom. And both the Church and the Landmarks people will erupt in a shitstorm if the saints on the front of them are disfigured in any way."

"If it's our only option, I can handle it."

"There may be a better approach. Three hostages have come out those doors. And what's happened every time the doors open? He disarms the explosive charge so the hostage can walk outside and speak to your negotiator. Best I can tell, we have one small window of opportunity to act while he rearms the explosives and gets himself or his associates in position."

"So assuming he sends another hostage out?"

"We have an eight-second window to breach."

"Risk to the hostage?"

"High. But what is it your casebooks say? The hostage is already as good as gone. Better to deploy our resources toward those inside—the ones we still have a chance of saving—and end this once and for all."

Henry considered this. "The faster this crisis is over, the better. I don't just have the FBI director breathing down my neck. I have the mayor's office. The Landmarks Commission. The Chamber of Commerce people. The police commissioner. I've fielded three calls from the White House. And don't get me started on officials from the Church. Everyone is upset, wanting answers. Most of all, wanting this to be over, so Christmas season in Manhattan can get back to normal. But everybody's worried about the hostages, and I can't risk a bloodbath."

"Either way, you might not be able to avoid it. My guess is the guy inside isn't done yet."

CLASSIFIED

**VIDOCQ FILE #W19767588**

**Current status: ACTIVE**

**Henry Ma**

Age: 56
Race/Ethnicity: Asian (Chinese American)
Height: 5'9"
Weight: 196 lbs.
Eyes: Brown
Hair: Black

**Current Address:** 152 Hester Street (Chinatown).
**Criminal Record:** None.
**Expertise:** Behavioral analyst.
**Education:** Georgetown University, B.S.

**Personal**

**Family:** Daughter Julie, age fifteen. His large extended family—including nine cousins—still resides in Hunan, China.
**Spouse/Significant Other:** Separated from wife, Caroline, after twenty-seven years of marriage.
**Religion:** Active member, First Chinese Presbyterian Church.
**Interests:** Deep knowledge of modern Chinese history. Model train enthusiast.

**Profile**

**Strengths:** A political animal always seeking out the next opportunity or promotion. Succeeds because his ambition is backed up by his ability: He's adept at solving complex scenarios, always thinking multiple steps ahead. Can be relied on to execute, even in the most difficult situations.

**Weaknesses:** Inspires little loyalty in those he supervises because he shows them none. He treats them as pawns in the larger game that he plays—and should he find himself back in the field, he will discover few allies willing to support him.

**Background:** Entered duty as a special agent with the FBI in 1981. After completing training at the FBI Academy in Quantico, Virginia, he was assigned to the Los Angeles division, where he investigated organized crime, drugs, money laundering, and gang matters. In 2001, he returned to FBI HQ as assistant special agent in charge of the FBI Critical Incident Response Group, National Center for the Analysis of Violent Crime. Henry joined the New York division in 2006, serving as head of the Vidocq Unit until his promotion in 2008 to assistant director in charge.

**Assessment prepared and updated by Special Agent in Charge Paul Bruin. For internal use only.*

# Chapter 45

Frank García walked briskly down Seventh Avenue, having decided he would cut east only when he reached Fifty-first Street. He didn't like crowds—so he usually had a strategy to avoid them. He also didn't like being cooped up, told what to do, and forced to talk about his feelings—so he was happier today than he had been in weeks. His ex-wife had certainly gotten her revenge. Teresa had convinced some judge to mandate his participation in a PTSD treatment program for vets as a condition of continued custody visits with Frankie Junior.

Frank got it: Four tours overseas had changed him. His already short fuse had become hair-trigger. His generally wary nature was now nakedly suspicious. His brain sometimes churned with memories he wanted to forget.

None of this made him an unfit parent.

Men had gone to war for centuries. Afterward, soldiers came home—manned up—and buried their wounds so deep they couldn't be touched. No one needed a shrink or the "talking cure." They sure as hell didn't need medication. Or a treatment plan. Or a schedule so tedious it was clearly designed to bore them to death. The irony hadn't escaped him that Eve—who could psychobabble with the best of them, and who actually seemed to believe some of that shit—was responsible for his newfound freedom.

García breathed in the mix of smoke and exhaust from the hundreds of cars that were stalled. Traffic was backed up for miles. He noted the familiar: His favorite deli. A bar he knew all too well. A gentleman's club he'd frequented years ago. Then focused on the new additions choking out the seedy establishments that were his comfort zone: A French bakery. Two banks. A wine bar. All catering to the thousands of tourists that roamed the streets surrounding Manhattan's most popular destinations—Times Square and Rockefeller Center.

Cops stood at every street corner. Security, in theory. Except the uniforms didn't know what the hell was going on, either. Their main job was to make sure no traffic went east.

The real law enforcement presence began at the rear side of Rockefeller Center. The cop standing by the concrete blockade on West Fifty-first Street gave García a sour look.

"I'm on your list," he said, producing his ID.

The officer glanced at García's scruffy jeans and mud-stained boots. "Didn't expect to come in today, huh?" Then he compared García's mug with the official photo and frowned. "You look older now."

"No shit. Happens to all of us, pal."

The officer chuckled. "You can say that again. Go on ahead."

García walked on, passing by more banks. The entrance to the ice-skating rink. He glanced at the Christmas tree, all set for lighting. The only thing missing was the tourists. Normally, one could hardly walk in this area during the holiday season. Now all he saw were men and women in uniform—NYPD and FDNY—standing around, waiting, jumpy. Frank got a chill and made the sign of the cross. It was a habit he'd developed overseas to protect himself.

He reached Fifth Avenue. Showed his credentials again to four different cops. Saw the bulletproof fortifications that had been put in place in front of the Cathedral. Ignored them—and went up the short flight of stone steps to the massive bronze doors in front. Considered the various sculptures of the saints. Everyone paid attention to Saint Joseph and Saint Patrick on the top row. But he'd always preferred Mother Cabrini in the middle row. *Mother of the Immigrant.* He crossed himself again and cast a quick prayer to her now.

Then he knelt by the door.

It was as though that one action grabbed everybody's attention. Cops started waving their arms. Emergency personnel shouted for him to take cover.

Frank ignored them all. He'd said his prayers. He was wearing his lucky red socks and bandana. He believed this wasn't his time yet.

Eve had said the explosive technique was an HBIED. García had seen too many of them. Sometimes, doors or lights switches were rigged with wires leading to an initiator switch. Sometimes the makeshift bombs were embedded in the floor. Still other times, insurgents built holes in the load-bearing walls and packed them with explosives—so if the explosion didn't get you, the structural collapse would.

Hostages were coming and going through this door, however. That meant it had to be rigged.

Which was good. Because when IEDs were buried, the only safe way to clear them was to level the structure.

Someone with a bullhorn shouted for him to leave the door. "Take cover, for Christ's sake!"

He ignored that, too. Checked out the small doors on either side of the main entrance. In his own time, he turned the corner and continued his inspection, walking down Fifty-first Street.

Taking in the side access doors. Windows of jeweled stained glass up high, shrouded in scaffolding. Past the Parish House. Then the Cardinal's Residence. Then back toward Fifth Avenue via Fiftieth.

Eve had said their experts had discovered few vulnerabilities to exploit.

García didn't understand why they'd had so much trouble. Maybe that was because after four tours of duty in Iraq and Afghanistan, he was good at finding openings where they didn't exist. Not much ever surprised him. And the issue at Saint Patrick's was really no different from what he'd encountered half a dozen times in Fallujah.

A madman was inside a house with weapons. He'd booby-trapped the place with IEDs. There were civilians around that Frank was forbidden to hurt. Not to mention religious treasures he was forbidden to destroy. Despite these impossible parameters, he had to complete his mission.

It was just a matter of being creative. Outsmarting the dirty bastards.

He glanced down at the pavement under his feet.

Yes. He had no doubt that his idea would work.

# HOUR 10

5:42 p.m.

As we continue to follow this developing situation at Saint Patrick's, we have a caller on the line, Jorge Valdes, a sous chef at Café Bonne Nuit, who believes his coworker is among the hostages being held. Mr. Valdes, what can you tell us?

*VALDES:* First of all, I don't *think* my friend, Ethan Raynor, is inside the Church. I *know* he is. He'd made a Mass request for his father, who died in October. And this morning's Mass was going to be said for Raynor Senior. So Ethan wouldn't have forgotten. He wouldn't have overslept. He wouldn't have been deterred by the bad weather. He definitely wouldn't have skipped work after. He's responsible, loyal, and generous to a fault.

We're all worried about Ethan. We've been calling the number the city gave us. They haven't been able to tell us anything. They say they're doing everything they can. But they aren't.

What are you asking for, Mr. Valdes?

*VALDES:* I want the kind of response we got on 9/11 and with Hurricane Sandy. So what if every single first responder in New York is working this? Bring in responders from Baltimore and Boston, Philadelphia and Pittsburgh. Bring in all the help we can get—so we can save these hostages and send them home.

Thank you, Mr. Valdes. Our thoughts will be with you. It isn't easy for any of us to watch, helpless to act, as this tragedy unfolds before our eyes . . .

# Chapter 46

Three women and one man stood in a semicircle facing Eve in the temporary holding unit. Its warm overhead lights were the color of honey. So were the walls, painted a light hue with a slight pink overtone that a consultant claimed had a calming effect. Because most people inside this holding unit—criminal or not—tended to be on edge.

These four were no exception.

It didn't help that the air was cold and drafty, and the tables and chairs were made of cheap plastic that attracted the chill and held it.

Four chairs.

Four people.

None of them sitting down.

The man was tapping his foot. He looked Eve up and down, evaluating. "Mind telling us what's going on here?"

Eve glanced at her notes quickly. *Blair Vanderwert.* The realtor. He was wearing a well-cut pressed suit and an immaculate white shirt. His tie was navy and red, and his dark blond hair was practically glued in place with gel.

"Special Agent Eve Rossi. Thank you for coming." She shook each of their hands in turn. Blair's was warm and dry. The women's were each icy cold.

"Special Agent?" The woman who spoke up had a low, husky voice. She was wearing a dumbfounded expression and a white summer dress; she gave the impression of a woman who'd ended up in Milwaukee when she'd expected Miami. *Cassidy Jones.* "What does the FBI want with *us*?"

"Yeah," the realtor chimed in. "I mean, I thought I had a professional appointment. Then the Feds brought me in. But out there, it's swarming with cops. What the hell is going on?"

A shadow filled the doorway as the door opened. Haddox had changed his shirt. The new one matched his deep blue eyes and had no blood on it. He also smelled faintly of aftershave. Eve found that she liked it.

"Have you been told what's happened at Saint Patrick's this morning?" Eve asked.

A petite, dark woman removed her earbuds. Wearing a little black dress and ballet flats. Hair pulled back. *Alina Matrowski.* "This place is crawling with police and EMS and firemen. The news said there've been reports of a shooting. You have Midtown completely buttoned down under tight security, like this is the next 9/11, yet you bring us right into the middle of it all?"

"We're not idiots." Another woman with a colorful red-and-green cloth on her head glared at them. *Sinya Willis.* Her accent was clipped. Caribbean. Jamaican.

"Before I explain, I have a question that might sound odd: Do any of you know each other?"

Blair said no immediately—with an almost imperceptible tone of disdain. The women shook their heads, with Cassidy saying, "You're talking about before we met a few minutes ago, right?"

"Have any of you *seen* each other before? Meaning you might recognize each other's face, even if you never met?"

There was a chorus of no's.

"I'm positive I've never seen a single one of these people before," Sinya added emphatically.

"Do any of you recognize this voice?" Eve pressed a button—and for thirteen seconds, the Hostage Taker's words filled the room.

All four witnesses stared at her, blank-faced.

"What about this man? Do any of you recognize him?" Haddox stepped forward, clicked on the keyboard near Eve, and a facial composite of Luis Ramos—made by the staff sketch artist after talking with Haddox—flashed on the screen.

"Never," Alina said, her brow furrowed. The others agreed.

"Is he the guy who shot people?" Cassidy asked.

"No," Haddox said. "His name came up. Just like each of yours."

It was exactly as Eve suspected. This would not be a search that moved forward in a straight line. It would go backward and sideways and at diagonals, probing their social connections and everyday habits. Figuring out if any of them shared the same dentist, shopped at the same grocer, prayed in the same church, or went to the same dog park.

"The reason all of you are here is because you're connected somehow," Eve informed them. "And we need to figure out how."

"What do you mean, *connected*?" Blair demanded. "Like how all of humankind is connected? Like that Six Degrees of Separation with Kevin Bacon game?"

"What are you talking about?" Alina interrupted.

Cassidy turned to her. "You know the actor Kevin Bacon? There's a game you can play: Link any actor to him through no more than six connections. You can even search any actor's 'Bacon number' on Google."

"Huh." Alina fingered her ear buds.

"Why do you think we're connected? And why do you care, if we are?" Cassidy wanted to know.

"We believe you are each somehow connected to the shooter at Saint Patrick's Cathedral this morning. He's armed—and he's killed innocent people," Eve answered bluntly. "We don't know who he is. But we have reason to believe all of you know him."

"Nonsense," Blair said. The others chimed in with a round of denials: *I definitely don't know any murderer. Don't know anyone who'd do something crazy like this.*

"Maybe you don't know him well. Maybe he is a teller at a bank where you all deposit your checks. Maybe he's the movie ticket usher where you all went to the movies. Maybe he sold you all a pair of shoes."

More denials. *I don't think I shop where he shops. I don't like movies. I only buy shoes online.*

"None of you are Catholic?" Eve asked. "None of you regularly attend Mass—at Saint Patrick's or elsewhere?"

Another round of denials.

"I think your information is wrong," Sinya insisted.

"Unfortunately, it's not," Eve said. "The shooter inside has taken hostages. He has issued only one demand: For you to come here as a 'witness.' He asked for each of you by name."

This time, no one spoke. They were speechless. Stunned.

"What does this guy want from us?" Alina finally ventured.

"Apparently, nothing more than your presence here as a witness."

"To what?" Blair asked. "Why would this nutjob want us?"

"We don't know," Eve admitted. "But you should be aware: We will do nothing that in any way jeopardizes your safety."

"Are we safe here?" Cassidy cast a nervous glance around the holding unit.

"Safe as houses," Haddox said. "Safer than you've ever been in this city." He rapped on the window of the unit. "Bulletproof. Bombproof. Fireproof. And hundreds of New York's Finest to protect you outside."

"So we're asking you to stay here. To answer our questions and help us figure this out."

"What do we get out of this?" Blair asked.

Eve didn't smile. "The satisfaction of knowing that you're helping. Saving lives, by sharing what you know. And when it's over, you'll be the center of attention—if you want. Each of you will get your fifteen minutes of fame—because every news outlet in the world will be clamoring to talk with you."

"Even NBC?" Cassidy cast a glance toward Rockefeller Center.

"Especially NBC," Eve reassured her. "What's really important is that each of you is our only connection to knowing the Hostage Taker inside. You may have met him without being really aware of who he is. If you can work with me—and help me figure out how you might have each crossed paths with him—I think I can identify him. Maybe even figure out what he's doing in there." She nodded toward the Cathedral.

"What *do* you know about him?" Sinya crossed her arms across her chest.

"Not much," Eve admitted. "I've developed a profile. My best guess is that he's middle-aged. He has an above average IQ, developed social skills, and substantial organizational skills. He has a security background: Military. Police. Maybe even prison guard. He knows this Cathedral intimately—which leads me to guess that he's Catholic, from the local area, and has spent significant time in the building over the years. He doesn't just want to kill the victims he's taken. He wants to destroy them on a public stage, with not just the world watching." She looked from person to person. "With each of *you* watching. *Witnessing,* he calls it. That suggests a religious fixation."

They stared at Eve. But there were no questions, so she continued. "He lives alone or with an elderly parent. No one has reported him missing—or called with specific concerns—which means he is able to plot and execute his plans without interference from a spouse or partner. He may have been married in the past. I believe he has a child—or had one."

Still no questions.

"He understands forensic procedure. What cops do. What negotiators do. How technology works. He has concealed himself by using multiple burner phones: some stolen from his victims and others prepaid. Ostensibly, his victims were random visitors to Saint Patrick's Cathedral. Yet there are reasons why he might have wanted each of them dead. We don't know who remains inside and how they play into his plans. Mainly, we're unsure why he mentioned each of you by name. It appears you do not know each other. You never went to school together. You don't share common friends. You don't live in the same apartment building or even the same neighborhood. But *something* connects you—and makes you important to the guy inside that Cathedral."

They all kept staring at her. No one made a comment.

"We have questionnaires for all of you," Eve said.

"I've designed a program that will cross-reference your answers and identify any patterns or similarities," Haddox explained. "To make this as painless as possible."

"Let me get this straight," Sinya demanded. "You just need information from us? Then we get to go home."

"That's what I'm hoping," Eve replied.

She fixed Eve with a fierce stare. "Well, why didn't you just say so?"

# Chapter 47

Haddox looked at the clock. Seventy-eight minutes until deadline.

Still no ID for the guy inside—or the hostages he was holding.

Still no connection among the witnesses.

Still no line on the Hostage Taker's motive or end game.

He didn't have much. But he had the voice recording taken from Eve's conversations with the Hostage Taker. Might as well try voice biometrics. *His* brand of it.

Other Feds had already run the recording through the FBI Biometric Center of Excellence database. It hadn't yielded a hit. In the years since 9/11, the Feds had developed an extensive database for law enforcement to use. It included biometric data ranging from palm prints and iris scans—to voice and facial recognition—to scars, marks and tattoos. His absence from that database only meant the Hostage Taker hadn't yet been arrested—or left behind bio-data at a crime scene that was part of the Next Generation Identification system, or NGI.

Haddox wasn't surprised. The NGI was rife with errors and far from perfect. Recently, a poor bloke in Massachusetts had his driver's license revoked because the government's facial-recognition system screwed up and said the man wasn't himself.

So to be thorough, Haddox ran another standard industry program. It also came up empty. No surprise there, either. The telecommunications industry might estimate that fifty million customers had enrolled their voiceprints for authentication. Trading their voice fingerprint for faster customer service, or to replace a passcode, or for a bank to process a payment.

But Haddox agreed with Eve: Their Hostage Taker had a background in security. This guy wasn't the type to trade privacy for convenience.

Fingers flying, Haddox brainstormed.

He'd known a hacker in London who was on the cutting edge of this technology. The fellow had invented a creative fix—or so Haddox thought—for the failings of most software systems. Namely, the fact that a regular guy might speak in one accent—say, his educated London one—when he was being questioned at the police station. But he might revert back to his East London Cockney when he was with his mates at the local pub.

Haddox remembered a good bit of what the British hacker had done.

Plus, he had pretty decent instincts of his own.

García never made a big deal about goodbyes—so he was equally low-key about greetings. He walked into the MRU, acknowledged Eve and the team with a brief nod, and got right down to business. "I know how to get inside that Cathedral. Whenever you're ready."

"Welcome back, Frankie." Mace didn't look up. The center table in the MRU had just been transformed into a smorgasbord of hot deli sandwiches, salads, and coffee. He couldn't decide between the steak, pepper, and onion—or the chicken with melted cheese.

"You know, I'm so happy to be away from the white coats, even Julius Mason can't get under my skin today. But don't test me, Mace. You never know when my happy juice is gonna wear out. In case you forgot, I don't like being called Frankie."

"So talk to me. How do we get in?" Haddox asked, ignoring their banter.

"Pull up the blueprints and I'll show you."

Haddox pressed a series of buttons on the computer. A partial schematic projected onto the white board. "They're incomplete," he explained. "The result of the Cathedral being constructed in so many different phases over such a long period of time. There aren't many surviving building documents—certainly no sketches, schematics, or blueprints from the early days. That's hampered the restoration effort considerably—and now it's slowing us down, too."

"There are rumors of a secret tunnel offering access to the Cathedral." Eve frowned at the screen. "People are convinced it's there. But just like the missing cornerstone, no one claims to know exactly where it is. There's a Church representative here who may have an idea of where to try. But he's not exactly cooperating."

"Don't need him. I know exactly where to find it," García said matter-of-factly. He noticed their looks of consternation—and took a moment to savor having the information advantage.

"Since when did you become a construction expert?" Mace challenged. "Able to locate a passageway nobody's been able to find for a century. You don't know shit about this."

"You don't know shit about me," García retorted. He stalked to the window that faced the front of Saint Patrick's. The world outside was dark, but spotlights designed to illuminate any movement the Hostage Taker might make were focused on its layers of scaffolding. It transformed the Church into a hulking iron structure—but García knew that underneath, it remained pure white marble stone and spires. An American Cathedral, built in the old traditions.

His mind jumped over an ocean and past a handful of countries. "You know how I spent my thirteenth wedding anniversary?" he asked them.

"If the answer involves anythin' other than your wife, I understand how you ended up alone," Haddox answered.

"Thirteen's his unlucky number," Mace added. "So this story can't be good."

García glared at them both. "It was when things were starting to go bad with Teresa. So my buddy Tony decided we should go out drinking in Hell's Kitchen. He'd just started a new job, so he was flush with cash."

"Is this going anywhere useful?" Mace's patience was running thin.

"Put a cork in it, Mace." Eve nodded at García to continue.

"We'd downed too many shots of tequila when he decided he wanted to show me something. Tony called it the Bat Cave, 'cause it looked like something straight out of Gotham." García paused long enough that they got the impression he was on a crazy tangent. "It was kind of like entering a different world, going inside this massive tunnel that runs through the heart of this city's bedrock."

"What *are* you talking about?" Mace couldn't help himself.

"You've heard of the East Side Access project?"

"You mean the Long Island Railroad extension?" Eli asked.

"Yeah. Almost six miles of brand-new tunnels being built under this city. Tony snuck me inside the main tunnel extension serving Grand Central. Runs from the Sixty-third Street Tunnel right down Park Avenue."

"Park is a whole 'nother block behind the rear of the Cathedral. How's that help us?"

"It's close enough that the Church was pretty worried about the tunnel work causing damage to Saint Patrick's—even an entire collapse," García answered.

"I repeat: How's that help us?"

"Sometimes when they're drilling through bedrock with these monster machines, they create openings in the rock that maybe they don't fully intend. Not big enough for a subway car . . . but plenty big enough for an average sort of guy. Tony took me into one of them. Guess where it went?"

"We're all ears, Frankie." Mace took a bite of the steak-and-pepper sandwich he'd chosen.

García frowned. "Not gonna ask again: Don't call me that. He took me down a passage that went right to the air vent for the new East Side tunnel—the one that's right on Fiftieth and Madison. Not far from the Lady Chapel in the rear of the Cathedral. And here's the best part: It just kept right on going."

"How far?" Eve's eyes went wide open.

"What do you know about the Lady Chapel?"

"I know it was an addition to the Cathedral by"—Eve paused to check her notes—"Charles Mathews. Not part of Renwick's original plan. Work began in 1900 and finished in 1906. And—the last major renovation was in 1931, when the organ was added and the sanctuary was enlarged."

"It was built in the same old-school style as the main Cathedral," García said. "The exterior wall is white marble. But it's backed with brick and stone, with plenty of hollow spaces built in to prevent dampness and aid ventilation. A few of those are wider than others. Again, not *big* . . . but large enough for an average-sized man—"

"Such as yourself," Haddox interrupted.

"I ain't average," García objected. "Tony found the way in. Said you followed the passage between the walls. Then there was a hidden panel."

"But you were with him?" Eve asked, confused.

"Not the whole way." García looked down. There was no good way to explain the problem. The claustrophobia. What it had felt like, being trapped in Fallujah.

He had wanted to follow Tony through the narrow walls. But the farther they walked, the tighter the walls had closed in. Soon he had been struggling just to breathe. Fighting the heat that threatened to overpower him. Bombarded with the images he wanted to forget. Crumbled concrete. The stench of burnt flesh. The body parts everywhere.

"But you trust this guy? You don't think he was just pulling your leg?" Eli found his way to the food. He loaded up on salads, knishes, and a turkey-avocado sandwich.

García looked Eli square in the eye. "He says he snuck all the way in and lit a candle for me in Saint Patrick's Cathedral. It was the night of my thirteenth wedding anniversary. Tony wouldn't lie to me."

"So do we need to bring in Tony?" Eli glanced at Eve.

"Not an option, unless you brought someone who can wake the dead into Vidocq. But if he found the route, I can find it, too. I'll use the same principles: Get us inside the walls, find the access panel door, and avoid the booby-traps this asshole has set for us."

There was a dry cough from the doorway. Monsignor Geve had decided to rejoin them. "Try not to take offense," the Church representative said. "But what you've just described is impossible."

"Excuse me?" García locked his gaze.

The Monsignor's lips pinched in disapproval. "You're discussing an assault entry into a national treasure that's afforded the *strictest* landmark protection."

"I thought we were discussing a rescue operation," Eve interposed coolly. "There are at least five hostages. Likely more."

Geve kept his eyes on García. "You mention the Lady Chapel in particular. You say it would be your point of entry to the Cathedral. It's of particular importance."

"If we do it right, everything's going to be fine, padre," García said flatly.

"Wait." Monsignor Geve held up a hand. "There are seventy-one stained-glass windows within Saint Patrick's. All of them masterpieces. You cannot risk the use of gunfire in the Cathedral."

"We cannot risk the continued massacre of innocent victims, Monsignor." Eve straightened, crossing her arms.

"What does he want? Can't you just give him what he wants?" His tone scarcely concealed his irritation.

"Unless the Church knows how to read minds, not an option," Eve replied, her own irritation rising to the surface. "He still hasn't told us what he's after."

"Maybe instead of tunnels and walls, you should be thinking about that."

"Maybe you should be thinking about letting us do our job." At six-foot-seven, Mace towered over the Monsignor.

"The Rose Window is just one example of the priceless treasures in the Cathedral," the priest persisted. "Charles Connick's work depicts the faces of angels in the eight petals of the rose. I'm here to make sure you protect it—and other treasures like it."

"I'm not saying Saint Patrick's isn't an awesome place to pray," García shot back, "but any Church—including this one—is for people. Right now, there're people stuck inside whose lives are in big danger. What's more important to you: Saving this building? Or saving the hostages with the bad luck to be stuck inside?"

The Monsignor was trembling with anger. He was about to argue more, but then he changed his mind. "You people don't understand. There must be another way."

NEWS NEWS NEWS NEWS NEWS

# HOUR 11

6:18 p.m.

We continue to monitor ongoing developments at Saint Patrick's Cathedral. Meanwhile, we have Cliff Raymond on the line, a security expert at Broadwell International and former FBI agent.

Mr. Raymond, tell us: How could something like this have happened?

*RAYMOND:* Well, no one wants to hear this, but the unfortunate answer is that it's easier than you'd think. Saint Patrick's is what we call a *soft target* in security speak. As both a religious institution and a cultural landmark, it welcomes everyone—which, as we approach Christmas Eve, means about twenty-five thousand people a day. Saint Patrick's has a full security detail—one of the best employed by a soft target. But the Cathedral's primary job is to welcome everyone who visits—especially at Christmastime.

# Chapter 48

Forty-two minutes 'til deadline.

Eve organized the responses to the four questionnaires they had given the witnesses. Haddox was pursuing the same data quest through the more scientific filter of his computer program. Eve, on the other hand, divided the lives of each witness into four large quadrants on her computer screen. Inside each quadrant was a series of statements, time lines, phone numbers, addresses, and acquaintance lists. She tugged on a curl by her left temple. A bad habit that always helped her to concentrate.

She was staring at the minutiae of four lives, tasked with building a different sort of picture than she usually created. She'd always had a good mind for finding small details, analyzing them, and weaving together certain patterns. When she was done, her creation resembled a spider's web—with multiple strands coming together to form an intricate whole.

Today, she felt she was staring at four separate webs. And she was searching for the single flyaway strand that would allow her spider to cross from one web to a completely different one. Some shared habit—or perhaps only a single experience—that linked one to another through the most fragile of connections.

They were different ages and from different generations. Cassidy Jones was barely twenty-one years old, and Alina was twenty-nine. Blair Vanderwert was forty-five and Sinya had just turned sixty. Eve tried to imagine their lives, their routines, and the people they would have met.

Cassidy grew up in Atlanta, where she became Miss Georgia Teen

USA as a senior in high school. Following graduation, she moved to New York to become an actress, settling into a community of actors in Astoria, Queens. Cassidy was a party girl. Her days might be spent in and around Astoria, where she worked at the Utopia Diner. But she came into Manhattan most days, too—for auditions as needed, and for the bars and dance clubs at night. Her list of friends and recent boyfriends was a daunting one.

Alina could not have been more different. She was quiet and hard-working, devoting hours of practice each day to her piano. She lived uptown in Washington Heights, in a tiny studio apartment overlooking the George Washington Bridge and the Palisades. She had cobbled together a career of playing chamber music and teaching students. But her work took her primarily to areas in and around Lincoln Center and Midtown West, where she was affiliated with one of the local private schools. She had a handful of close friends and no boyfriend.

Blair Vanderwert had lived his entire life on Manhattan's Upper East Side. He'd graduated from the Dalton School and Yale before entering his family's real estate business. There was no real distinction between his work life and his social life; they fused at the endless society and charity events that he attended. He was always networking—but among a certain social set that didn't seem to encompass or overlap with the worlds of the other witnesses.

Sinya Willis was a live-in nanny whose main daily contacts were under the age of eight. She resided with the Abrams family. She went to the Baptist Church in her neighborhood every Sunday. She sang in the choir—and those choir practices formed the backbone of her social life. For work, she shuffled the three Abrams kids back and forth to dentist appointments and soccer practice, homework club and playdates.

Haddox had reported that Luis Ramos's life was lived in the shadows of Harlem. Ramos had come downtown to work as a day laborer whenever a contractor needed extra manpower. All cash, no paper trail. No unnecessary friendships. No excursions.

They lived in different worlds, but they were all typical New Yorkers in one respect: They had provincial routines. Eve had always thought it ironic that the largest city in America cultivated small-town habits better than any small town. But that was what happened when virtually every need anyone had could be satisfied within five blocks of home.

*How do you know them?*

She started an imaginary conversation with the Hostage Taker, trying to understand how he would have seen them. Why he would have chosen them. How they were bound together.

Then it occurred to her: How was she ever going to do that, when she still didn't understand the most basic question of all. *Why had he insisted on her?*

A sound behind her startled her. She gasped, whirling.

It was Haddox. "Just a quick question for you. I've got a list of everybody you've worked with at the FBI, including those who were in your training class at Quantico. Were you ever part of an inter-agency joint task force?"

"You have a list of *what*?" That was the problem with Haddox. Normal boundaries meant nothing to him.

"I live in a world of information, luv."

"Can you stop calling me *luv*?"

"Maybe not altogether. Maybe just less often. Are you going to answer my question—or don't you *want* to know why he chose you?"

"I've worked closely with the NYPD in past hostage crises—but nothing sustained."

"That blows that theory, then. Guess he's just a fan." He stepped closer and peered at her computer screen. "We can't figure out why he wants you or what connects them. Seems like he couldn't have chosen a more random group of people. Makes me wonder: Is that the point?"

"I've thought of that. That he's chosen people at random to be witnesses. That he doesn't actually have any past connection with any of them."

"But?"

She shook her head. "This feels too personal to me. Even if he doesn't know them well, they represent something important to him.

I've got another idea that might help. You listened to my last conversation with him?"

"Just ran it through the FBI's biometric database. No hits."

"Good. Pull it off the database again. Skip to the section where he talks about a religious school teacher and an incident when he was eleven years old."

"You think his motive is as basic as his history with the Church?"

"I wonder if we can identify the teacher. It sounded like he was a layperson—but that could've been a lie. Take what we know—our presumption that the Hostage Taker is local, that he is about thirty-five, and any other data we can glean. Then cross-check it against any child abuse cases that fit the timing. Use a Venn diagram–style approach to establish IDs for those who fit within the overlapping circles—and go from there."

"Aye, sure," Haddox agreed. "I'll need to design a scientific approach to make it work."

Eve shot him an exasperated look. "Haddox, it's just data. Sometimes you have to look beyond the bits and bytes. Keep your eye on the human element."

"Without bits and bytes, we have no data patterns to make sense of." Haddox started to turn away, then stopped. "By the way, I've decided: I won't call you *luv* anymore."

"Thank you."

"Even though it suits you. Loosens you up a bit. So you may as well reconsider."

"Reconsider what?"

"Having dinner."

"We still have work to do."

"But if we didn't?"

"You mean after the hostages are saved and the Cathedral is secure?"

"Aye. It's a date."

"I didn't agree." She wasn't smiling.

"You will when you see the brilliant idea I've had. I just need someone to do a little shopping."

"No cigarettes or Irish whiskey. You're on Uncle Sam's dime."

He ignored her—or seemed to. "This Hostage Taker has more secrets than anyone's entitled to. Better get back to unraveling his motive." She heard his steps, returning quickly to his own workstation.

*You're one to complain about hidden motives,* she longed to tell him. She settled for asking herself, *What about your own?*

# Chapter 49

Sixteen minutes until deadline.

Haddox listened to the recording of Eve's conversation with the Hostage Taker and decided that she had been played. The Hostage Taker had spun a tug-at-the-heartstrings tale and gained Eve's sympathy. Completely distracting her from the fact that he'd just that very morning murdered a priest.

No, that wasn't fair. Maybe Eve was playing the Hostage Taker as well. Acting as though she cared.

Either way, Haddox kept coming back to the witnesses. Given that not one of them even went to a Catholic Church, he simply couldn't buy Eve's theory that anger over abuse cases was fueling this Hostage Taker. It felt too pat.

And finding the single common thread linking the witnesses wasn't working through the usual means. The human brain simply wasn't capable of connecting the thousands of potential connections among five separate individuals. But his advanced diagnostics program was perfectly designed to uncover the answer.

Sinya Willis was a rabid Mets fan. So was Cassidy's latest boyfriend. Both regularly attended games. But Blair Vanderwert followed only the Yankees, and neither Alina Matrowski nor Luis Ramos was known to have an interest in baseball.

Alina and Blair were both avid runners, active in New York Road Runners races and events. They had probably run together, time and again, without realizing it. But his practice runs took him down the FDR, while her preferred jogging paths were on the banks of the Hudson River. Cassidy practiced Pilates, Sinya found chasing three boys to be exercise enough, and Luis worked shifts so long he only slept between them.

All but Luis and Sinya had served jury duty downtown. Blair and Alina had even been summoned during the same week two years ago. Blair had been chosen as an alternate in a civil case to determine liability for fire damage to a building. Alina had been dismissed after three days.

They had granted Haddox permission to run a cross-search through their credit card and banking records. Sinya and Alina frequently shopped at the Harlem Fairway. Blair and Cassidy frequented the same indie multiplex on East Houston on the Lower East Side. Everyone but Alina had eaten at least once at the Madison Square Park Shake Shack. Everyone but Blair had visited the TD Bank branch in Times Square. But no one habit, activity, or transaction had yet been found to link all five witnesses.

When something wasn't working, Haddox's solution was to try a different strategy. Tackle a different issue. So he turned his attention to the flip side of the problem: the Hostage Taker.

When he ran a skip trace, his starting point was the name—and he used multiple data sources to create a path that inevitably led him to the individual he sought.

Here he had the opposite problem. The living, breathing person he wanted was less than a hundred feet away from him. What he was missing was everything else. A name. An identity.

He clicked away on his keyboard, fingers racing at his usual 120 words per minute. He pulled up the transcripts of Eve's conversations with the Hostage Taker—which included both text and audio. He cobbled together a kludge, inelegant and clumsy but designed to do what was necessary.

Haddox knew there were many flaws inherent to biometric technology—and especially voice biometric technology. He had already hit a brick wall using the FBI's database. So he didn't design his search to generate a specific ID. That would just be a recipe for crashing and burning. The technology wasn't there yet—and those who pretended it was made embarrassing mistakes. Like when incomplete biometrics led law enforcement to falsely identify Richard Jewell as the Atlanta Olympics Bomber. Or when Brandon Mayfield was falsely accused of orchestrating the Madrid train bombings.

Instead, Haddox's kludge would search for patterns and produce the most general of biometric profiles. A counterpart to Eve's working psychological profile, based on the data that could be gleaned from her three brief conversations with the Hostage Taker.

Eve had been convinced the Hostage Taker was a local man, given his comfort level with the Cathedral. So Haddox linked his program to a database run by a linguist at the University of Pennsylvania. That would allow for analysis of consonants and vowels, and generate possible regions where speakers used them in similar ways.

He then connected to a linguist at the University of Virginia who did similar work, but focusing on word choice and phrasing rather than vowels and diphthongs.

Eve believed the Hostage Taker had some background in law enforcement or security. A third linguist—this one at the University of Colorado—specialized in research on military and police slang.

He used an old trick to minimize the static background of the audio.

He let everything run. If he got lucky, these multiple data points—voice details, speech patterns, and key language choices—would work together and yield something they could use.

Eight minutes until deadline. Seven o'clock. At the exact moment the world had expected to celebrate the lighting of the Rockefeller tree, a madman would be demanding his witnesses.

Haddox stole a glance at Saint Patrick's. Though the rest of Fifth Avenue had gone dark, the Cathedral was bathed in light. Its own floodlights, plus the spotlights brought in by the Feds that fully illuminated its exterior, transformed the Church into a shining beacon of light.

It inspired him to do one more thing. He sent up a prayer to Saint Jude—the patron saint of lost causes and desperate cases.

# Chapter 50

Four minutes until deadline.

Mace had followed García into the equipment supply van, set up for the tactical teams readying themselves to breach the Cathedral. An operation certain to occur if Eve was unable to bring the situation to closure. Mace normally hated shopping, but this was different. He scooped up a laser-guided automatic weapon. Checked out its sight line, felt its weight in his hand. Even if he no longer made a living selling this shit, he still got a kick from checking it all out. Special operators always got the cutting-edge technology. Stuff that came straight out of the lab and had never been battle-tested. From there, it would eventually filter down to the regular guys in uniform and then make its way onto the street.

Since Mace never wanted to be surprised when new goods hit the dealers, he told himself this was important learning. He was furthering his education. But who was he kidding? He was bored out of his skull. He needed a diversion to keep from going stir-crazy.

A compact man with round wire glasses, pocket protector, and a name tag that read BURNS was showing García a handheld device. "This is a directed-energy weapon with dual capabilities. Use it to inflict pain when you're dealing with a noncombatant you just need to neutralize. It makes your target feel like his skin is on fire."

"Is it?" García raised an eyebrow.

"Not literally. Then see this switch?" Burns indicated a device on the underside of the handheld gun. "It lets you change your force level from nonlethal to lethal."

García scowled. "Still a little bulky. Not exactly handheld."

"Looks like a lightsaber. Straight out of *Star Wars,*" Mace chimed in.

Burns shrugged. "It's a lot of technology in a small package. Comes in handy with an operation like this, where you've got civilians who could interfere with your ultimate target." He handed García a pair of sporting sunglasses. "This is another device you might find useful."

García held the black glasses up to the light. "I'm going to be underground. Probably need a flashlight more than these."

They had dark lenses, but red plastic ran the length of their top. A designer might have said it looked stylish, but Mace guessed it concealed some functional purpose.

"They look like ordinary sunglasses," Burns explained. "But they have technology embedded that will let you receive data. Photographs. Video. Location specifics."

"Kind of like Google Glass?" Mace said with a grin.

"Way cooler than that," Burns replied seriously as García put them on. "Let me show you what they can do."

Mace's phone buzzed in his pocket. He answered it and said, "This better be important, 'cause otherwise I've got a chance to try a real-life lightsaber."

Vernon Brown's friend Snoopy said, "Got something to write with?"

"Not handy."

"Then listen up. You know I've been investigatin' why my man Vern's sitting in the clink."

"Yeah."

"I spoke with a couple guys outta Midtown West. Jeff Simmons and T. J. Pierce. They're assigned to tracking sensitive items as they move into and out of the evidence locker. A big haul a few weeks ago has been keeping them real busy. First they had to secure it, meaning load it up and safely transfer it from some ratty crime scene to the evidence locker. Then they spent a solid month shuttling pieces of it back and forth to the forensics lab so everybody could learn about it. They weren't happy when it all disappeared. Reflected badly on them, you know? Now they're the subject of an investigation and stuck on desk duty. Bored out of their skulls."

"So did they steal it?"

"Don't think so," Snoopy said. "Word on the street is that nothing like the stash that's missing came up for sale. And neither Simmons or Pierce have anything to show for it. There's no extra zeros in their bank account or new cars in their driveway."

"What's your point, then?"

"They can't prove it. But they've got a theory."

"I'm all ears."

"Here's the deal. I'm gonna give you the info—and if it works out, you're gonna pay me back by makin' sure Vern gets sprung. That he knows old Snoopy's the one responsible for his freedom. And the high-ups need to give him a big, fat apology."

"Sounds like a tall order."

"Not for you," Snoopy said as he gave Mace the names.

Haddox's down-and-dirty algorithm turned up one result almost immediately. It identified the Hostage Taker as a Brooklyn native. When he was calm and in control, his articulation was careful. When his temper rose, he reverted to a communication style found primarily in Brooklyn. In other words, he punched his initial consonants. Jumbled his words together. And left off his *r*'s and *g*'s. There was also a slight—so slight as to be almost imperceptible—substitution of *d* for *th*.

*Brooklyn,* Haddox thought. *A borough of only 2.6 million people. And that's assuming he was Brooklyn born and bred and never moved away.*

Brooklyn contained microcosms of different communities—Italians, Greeks, Jews, Irish, African Americans, Germans, and Russians. Now Haddox's kludge would search for slight variations that might indicate one of those particular groups.

The final linguistic analysis centered on one phrase. The term *house mouse.* It was what the Hostage Taker had called Annie Martinez, the NYPD negotiator he had killed. It wasn't part of the recording—but Eve had remembered.

As Haddox discovered, it was a common term in three different communities. Haddox put the first—the S&M practitioners—aside for now. Not that the Hostage Taker hadn't inflicted plenty of pain, but it didn't feel like his primary motive. Next was the Marines. *House mouse* was their term for the drill instructor's gofer. That felt better to Haddox. Annie Martinez had been killed because she wasn't important enough. Because she wasn't *Eve*—the negotiator the Hostage Taker had demanded.

The third community where the phrase was commonly used was the police. Cops used it to describe a homebody. Someone who did more filing than fieldwork. Haddox liked this scenario because they knew the Hostage Taker understood police protocol and procedures so well. *He knows the playbook,* Eve had said.

*So which is it?* Haddox wondered.

The more he could triangulate the data, the better his odds of success. So he added a search function that would pick up sex-abuse cases. Anything in the local area, happening in the right years. Then he waited.

García was having bad dreams already, and it wasn't even close to bedtime. Haddox had downloaded a few files to the special optics glasses. Just to be sure things were working. Now García had access to the partial schematics of Saint Patrick's Cathedral, marked with the possible location of hostages. He also had photos and plenty of data about the explosives that were rigged throughout the Church.

García didn't like these high-tech glasses. He wanted to stay focused on what was real and immediate. He didn't need extra images filling his head. Wasn't that the problem in the first place?

He took the glasses off. Stuck them on his belt. Maybe he'd try again later, if he ran into an issue.

He'd gone into plenty of houses like this before. His mission had been pretty much the same: Take out the insurgents. Rescue the civilians. Then get the hell out.

The only difference—and it was a big one: When he'd been on overseas duty, no one cared if the house blew. Not once all innocent civilians were safe.

He didn't have a good feeling about this. It had the potential to be a major bloodbath. And there might not be a damn thing he could do to stop it.

Eli was waiting. He'd commandeered two machines, and had his favorite databases open and running. Mace strolled right up to him and handed him the names.

"Check these guys out for me, will ya?" He turned, thought of something, turned back. "Want some more coffee?"

"Do bees sting? Do bears shit in the woods?" Eli grinned. "Except I can't believe Julius Mason is offering to fetch me a cup of coffee."

"Don't get used to it. I only do favors when I need something bad." He noticed that Eli had changed shirts. The new one was a bright green New York Jets jersey. He must've had someone grab it for him from one of the tourist traps on Broadway.

"What am I looking for, exactly?" Eli typed the first name into the database.

"The usual. Any big purchases. Any sudden infusions into their bank account. Basically anything to indicate they might have stolen a whole lotta explosives and sold 'em for a tidy profit."

"What if they didn't sell it—but used it themselves?"

"Then we'd have a pretty good line on the man inside. Say, you feelin' okay?"

Eli suddenly looked as green as his new jersey. Eli shook his head. "Think I ate something that didn't agree with me."

"You didn't have a hot dog from the vendor on Sixth, did you? They get me every time."

Despite Haddox's misgivings, it turned out that his bad apple search—combined with his other parameters—provided the necessary magic to narrow the field. At first, he thought his data points were too obscure. But once he combined the right age with the right time period with the right borough, only four sex abuse cases fit his parameters. It would have been impossible to miss one case in particular. That of John Timothy Nielsen.

The list of those who claimed to have been victimized by Nielsen was not small. Once the first victim was brave enough to come forward, more than fifteen boys—many of them grown men by the time of Nielsen's arrest and subsequent trial—came forward with additional accusations. Haddox's search cross-referenced their names against the results of his broader search.

A Brooklyn native.
Once an altar boy in a Parish in Bensonhurst, Brooklyn.
Who ended up a Marine or part of the Thin Blue Line.
With an estimated eighty-one percent chance of being Irish. Or an estimated seventy-six percent chance of being Italian.

Within moments he had generated a couple of names.

Paulie Corsillo, son of a Marine, had joined up at age eighteen. Paulie barely waited forty-eight hours after graduating from Saint Xavier's, the local Catholic boys school. His parents had been proud. Following the family tradition, they bragged. A jarhead, just like his old man. A captain who'd served in the Far East and the Middle East before coming home to Brooklyn.

Paulie had done three tours in Iraq and two in Afghanistan. He was decorated, having received two special commendations and one Purple Heart. He had trained as a sniper, but had just barely missed making the cut. So he worked as a sapper, defusing hundreds of bombs. Roadside IEDs. House Borne IEDs. It was painstaking work. Requiring a certain kind of temperament. A temperament Paulie had—right up until the day he didn't.

He wasn't held captive by the Taliban for long. It was only nine days—after which a prisoner exchange was brokered. The Americans didn't participate, naturally. Americans always balked at negotiating with terrorists. But a third party brokered the deal, and Paulie was sent home permanently. Nine days with the Taliban had apparently triggered serious anger issues on his part, and the Marines didn't need that kind of liability. Between the Abu Ghraib torture scandal and the Mahmudiyah killings, things were bad enough for the American military.

When he returned home, Paulie refused any kind of therapy. He insisted his only issue was that he hated the Talibs for what they had done to him. In his mind, they deserved every ounce of loathing he could muster. Soon he figured out he hated someone else, too. Someone much closer to home. Someone who'd done things to him that were equally terrible and just as perverted.

When the original complaint was filed against John Timothy Nielsen, it was Paulie Corsillo who spearheaded the action. He wanted to make Nielsen suffer and pay. To make sure no other boy was abused the way he had been. It was only right.

Haddox liked Paulie as a candidate for being the Hostage Taker. The military background and deep knowledge of explosives made perfect sense. His anger issues were well documented. No doubt his captivity with the Taliban had left a less visible, but no less permanent, scar than the shrapnel damage that led to his Purple Heart. And his motive was perfect: a vendetta against the Church, which he believed had failed him.

Sean Sullivan was also in his early forties, just like Paulie. They'd been born at the same Brooklyn hospital: Kings County between Clarkson and Winthrop. Been baptized in the same parish in Bensonhurst. Even served as altar boys at the same time. Their paths differed in three important respects.

First, Sean's family was Irish—and thus a world away, culturally, from Paulie's Italian clan.

Second, Sean's family was a family of cops and firemen. When a Sullivan boy turned eighteen, he chose the NYPD or the FDNY. He'd have no more have enlisted with the Army, Navy, or Marines than he'd have drilled a hole in his head. Even after 9/11 happened—and Sean did like a lot of young men and enlisted in the Marine Reserves—he saw himself as a cop through and through. When the time came to serve his tour of duty overseas, he didn't do it for honor or country or apple pie. He did it for the boys in blue.

Third, Sean and Paulie's paths diverged significantly when Sean's parents separated—and his mother decided to leave the neighborhood for suburban Long Island. Sean moved when he was twelve; his return visits to the old Brooklyn neighborhood became sporadic.

It's likely his family never knew what he claimed to have suffered at the hands of Mr. Nielsen. From the sealed complaint in the DA's files, Sean was one of the luckier ones: His forced relations with the teacher lasted only three months. He had testified on the QT, using an assumed name. He wanted only to corroborate what others said. To make sure justice was meted out to this priest. But no more. No headlines, no public vendetta. All Sean wanted was to return to his own life on the Island.

Never mind how that life was falling apart. His wife was divorcing him. By all accounts, he had a rocky relationship with his thirteen-year-old daughter. He had filed for bankruptcy. He was on suspension from the NYPD, the subject of an Internal Affairs investigation.

That last part fit, but not what Sean was accused of stealing. Drugs and money. Easy to pocket. Even easier to deal on the streets.

One more thing: Sean had trained to serve in one of the NYPD's elite counterterrorism units. That training had taken him to Afghanistan, Egypt, and Pakistan, where he and other team members had liaised with numerous military operations. He'd have learned about explosives and received sniper training. But was his learning sophisticated enough?

Sean had plenty of issues. But he lacked the clear sense of anger—and motive—that Paulie had.

Yet one fact troubled Haddox. Angus MacDonald—the one true witness they had at this site—claimed to have seen a cop entering the Cathedral.

Angus's description was vague. It centered on a raincoat and a certain bearing to a man's walk. Plus, the timing was all wrong—because the hostage crisis was well under way by the time the cop allegedly entered the Cathedral.

It was equally likely one of New York City's forty thousand Finest had wandered into early-morning Mass and found himself entangled in a situation he hadn't bargained for.

Haddox decided: He would present all these facts to Eve. She was the expert. Let her decide what she thought.

Assuming the Hostage Taker wasn't talking a load of lies and blarney, Haddox was convinced: The man causing so many problems inside Saint Patrick's Cathedral was Paulie Corsillo.

The profile fit. More important, the data fit. And in Haddox's experience, the data never lied.

Eli ran the database search Mace had requested, but he needed time to think about the results. Especially now that Haddox had forwarded the two names he had uncovered.

This was all shaping up in a way that made Eli uncomfortable. He honestly wasn't sure what it meant. It didn't help that John kept calling him on the job. He'd now ignored two voicemails and five texts. He wasn't feeling very well.

Eli breathed in and out, tried counting slowly to sixty, but the urgency couldn't be ignored. He stepped away from his computer. Lurched out the door of the MRU. Half ran, half walked toward an area ten yards behind Atlas, where a big gray Rubbermaid trash can had been brought to handle the trash generated by a few hundred agents and officers.

He leaned over and emptied the contents of his stomach.

When he finished, an NYPD tech officer was standing beside him, offering a tissue.

"Thanks," he mumbled sheepishly. "Sorry."

She shrugged. "Happens at pretty much every crime scene I've ever attended. Not a big deal." She pointed. "There's a water station over there. Might help you feel better."

Eli nodded miserably. Nothing was going to make him feel better.

NEWS NEWS NEWS NEWS NEWS

# APPROACHING DEADLINE HOUR

6:59 p.m.

We continue to talk with Cliff Raymond, internationally renowned security expert and former FBI agent. Mr. Raymond, we know the FBI has the lead here and must have a top-notch negotiator on the job. What can you tell us about what's happening?

*RAYMOND:* Here's a remarkable statistic for you—about ninety-five percent of all hostage crises are successfully resolved through negotiation strategies. Hostage negotiation is basic psychology, and most negotiators are among the most skilled practical psychologists you could ever meet.

But hypothetically speaking, what happens if talk fails?

*RAYMOND:* Well, from the earliest hours of this incident, I can guarantee you that a SWAT team has been on standby outside the Cathedral. If a tactical rescue is authorized, their first priority will be to isolate and contain the Hostage Taker or Takers. They will do so with every effort made to preserve life and—especially in the case of Saint Patrick's—mitigate property damage.

We also have a representative from the Catholic Church on the line—Monsignor Bill Geve.

NEWS NEWS NEWS NEWS NEWS

What can you tell us about the Church's concerns, Monsignor?

*MONSIGNOR GEVE:* It's because I'm so concerned that I'm calling in to you today. Saint Patrick's Cathedral is the most important Catholic landmark in North America, if not the Western Hemisphere. And I am not satisfied that the FBI will do what is necessary to protect it. So I'm asking all your listeners—if Saint Patrick's is important to you as a Catholic . . . as a New Yorker . . . or just as a concerned citizen—please call the mayor's office and let him know!

# Chapter 51

Eve watched the clock tick seven. Then she waited for the call that was sure to come. It was deadline hour, and the Hostage Taker would want his witnesses.

The Hostage Taker. *Paulie.* No reason she couldn't start calling him that.

When Haddox presented his findings to her, she found herself in complete agreement: It had to be the Marine. Paulie Corsillo. She felt she recognized his signature in all the events of this day. The careful planning. The knowledge of explosives. The sniper training. The way he'd buttoned up Saint Patrick's like it was an ordinary HBIED. The fact that he had significant, unresolved anger against the Church.

He was also missing.

Corsillo worked part-time as a building super. But no one had seen him for four days—and the tenant complaints were mounting. That had been a pattern in recent months.

She stared at the Hostage Taker's cellphone, sitting on her desk. A cheap little Nokia throwaway. Silent, like the proverbial pot of water that never boils when it's watched.

What would Corsillo want with these witnesses—the four individuals she'd sworn to protect?

Would he recognize the fifth as an agency plant—a substitute for Luis Ramos, who'd vanished?

The cellphone sat silent.

Eve glanced at her watch. *7:02 p.m.* It wasn't like him to be late. She supposed his earlier punctuality was a Marines thing. Something that got drilled into them during basic training, just like making hospital corners or running a five-minute mile. Kind of like how at Quantico, she'd learned to shoot a Glock 23 and decipher basic forensic analysis—whether she liked it or not.

She felt rather than heard the gasp of surprise when the immense bronze door to Saint Patrick's opened—and another figure stepped outside. She grabbed the phone that wasn't ringing, shoved it into her pocket, and raced out of the MRU toward the Cathedral steps. If anyone followed her, she neither noticed nor cared.

The man on the step was maybe mid-thirties, maybe mid-forties. He had a dark-brown buzz cut, a thick five-o'clock shadow on his face, and his blue suit looked cheap. No coat. But he wasn't shivering in the cold. In fact, he was sweating. Profusely.

He paused at the top of the steps and looked around. He was blinking, hard—the aftereffect of a blindfold? Finally, his gaze locked on Eve's and he said, "My name is Ethan Raynor."

Eve frowned. This was different—and change from the pattern wasn't a good thing. No names had been given before.

She turned away from Raynor long enough to pin a wire on her collar and give a crisp order: "I need everything we have on him." Then she turned back. "My name is Eve Rossi. I'm a special agent with the FBI. I'd like to help you, Mr. Raynor."

He wore a pair of dirty, beaten-up sneakers. Blue-and-gray Nikes, easily two sizes too big. Not his own.

This man was a hostage; she was certain of it. Not just because his name was among those reported missing, presumed to be held inside, but because his body language betrayed both fear and bewilderment.

She took a step closer. She thought she saw the telltale red marks on his wrists. The sign of having been recently bound.

She squinted, trying to see what he was holding in his right hand. There was something—some small device—between his fingers and the palm of his hand. "Someone try to find out what what he's holding. It may be a pressure switch, so this is important: *Hold all fire,*" she said into her piece.

"I've been instructed to tell you," Ethan said. "Your time is up."

Haddox's voice was in Eve's ear. *Assuming he's who he says he is, this kid is from Chicago. He's come to New York to work as a chef. He handles vegetable prep at the Café Bonne Nuit in Midtown. No girlfriend—or boyfriend—but based on comments from his Facebook page, he's well liked. There's only one odd thing: He was in the news, maybe ten years ago. He was the boyfriend of a girl who disappeared. A young coed he'd been seein' for a couple years. He claims he didn't walk her home after a party one night. No one ever found her—and suspicion fell pretty heavily on him.*

To Ethan, Eve said, "He gave me a deadline. I've met it. So why isn't he calling me directly? Why is he talking through you?"

Ethan ignored her questions. "He wants to remind you that nothing is negotiable. That I will die—that he will detonate all his munitions—if his demands aren't met. You must do exactly as he asks."

This time it was Mace's voice in her ear. *That switch in his hand looks legit, Eve. Time to be super-careful.*

"I need to talk with him directly," Eve told him. "Can you tell him that?"

But Ethan gave no sign of wearing a wire. His speech seemed prerehearsed. "You are to bring each witness forward. One by one. For identification confirmation."

Eve's eyes raked the scaffolding high above. *How was he going to confirm these IDs? Through his sniper's lens?* "His witnesses are here," she told Ethan. "But I must guarantee their safety."

Eve looked around. She had no advantage, anywhere. Never mind the threat of the switch in Ethan's right hand. There were too many civilians. Too many cameras. Too many saints and stained-glass windows to worry about.

She closed her eyes. Remembered the Hostage Taker's voice. Struggled to put her finger on their past connection. Tried to *know* him.

She took four steps backward and grabbed the bullhorn with her right hand. Maybe it would be a one-sided conversation. But like it or not, he was going to listen to her.

"I know who you are," she shouted. "Your name. Your background. Your motive. I'm going to announce this information to the media—unless you contact me directly, right now." She held up the cellphone with her left hand.

Waited one second. Two. Three. Four.

Nine seconds in, the cellphone bleated.

"What the hell are you doing?" His voice was low, angry, strained. "There's too much at stake here for you to ad-lib the playbook."

"I know exactly what I'm doing," she lied. "Tell me—"

The phrase *Should I call you Paulie?* was halfway out of her mouth when she looked again at Ethan Raynor—and thought of Luke Miller instead.

*The boy who'd been let go.*

Her gut clenched. She reminded herself of all the evidence. How it was solid and convincing. How Paulie Corsillo had documented sniper training and explosives experience. Then she thought: *The Hostage Taker let the boy go.*

Paulie Corsillo was childless. Alone.

Sean Sullivan was a father—with a thirteen-year-old kid.

"Time's up, Eve. Either bring one of my witnesses out now—or Ethan Raynor is going to die."

"All right. Let's talk about how we're going to handle these witnesses." She took a deep breath. "Do you mind if I use your first name, Sean? Or do you prefer Captain Sullivan?"

Inside the MRU, Eli listened to Eve's conversation. He recognized that things had taken a turn he would never have anticipated. What he didn't understand was what it all meant.

He did know one thing that he resolved to tell Mace. NYPD Captain Sean Sullivan was stationed at the Midtown West Precinct. The same place where the stolen goods Mace was tracking had disappeared.

Eli saw clusters of cops and Feds converging on the holding unit where the witnesses were being held. Trying to decide if any were going to be permitted to go outside the secure area. Figuring out if it was possible to protect them, if they did.

They'd known for the past eight hours that there was likely a cop inside the Cathedral. They'd worried that he was disabled—but assumed he was a friend.

The cop was no ally.

And Eli had a secret others now needed to know.

García crouched low as he made his way down the narrow passageway. He was surrounded by Manhattan bedrock.

Wide in some spaces, giving him room to breathe. So narrow in others that his tight mental control threatened to vanish.

*Breathe in. Exhale out.*

His footsteps made loud echoes, but he didn't hear them.

He was too busy maintaining focus.

The reality in front of him was dank and stale and crushingly narrow.

His mind's eye manufactured an image that was sunny and expansive. Wide skies. Vast beaches. Waves that stretched for miles.

García crept forward. His own demons were chasing him—and the only way out was to make it to that imaginary beach, hidden behind the secret door accessing the Cathedral.

Sirens filled the air. Choppers—from different media outlets—made wide circles overhead. Kept back only by the FBI chopper that held the perimeter. Rumors were spreading that the mayor was en route.

With all eyes on her, Eve steeled herself for Sean Sullivan's response. For whatever would come next. A tornado of fury? Or just a calculated request?

Seconds ticked by.

She was half surprised that the world didn't end. That time marched on. The Cathedral stood. The hostage lived.

Then she heard Sean's voice cut through the chaos.

NEWS NEWS NEWS NEWS NEWS

PART FOUR

# DEADLINE HOUR UNTIL HOUR 14

7 p.m. to 9 p.m.

We are continuing with our live coverage of the unfolding crisis at Saint Patrick's Cathedral.

The time is a quarter past seven. In normal circumstances, the Tree Lighting ceremony at Rockefeller Center would be well under way.

Let's listen in as Father Michael Ryan, who blessed the tree before it was cut down and brought to Rockefeller Center, leads a group of concerned friends and family in prayer, just beyond the police barricade that's been established on Sixth Avenue and Fifty-first.

*FATHER RYAN:* We unite ourselves in prayer tonight for the victims who are suffering at the hands of those who have overtaken our beloved Saint Patrick's. Violence cannot be conquered by violence. Lord, send us the gift of peace. Restore to us our brothers and sisters who are being held captive in your house against their will.

# Chapter 52

"How did you find me?" Sean Sullivan demanded.

Eve focused on tuning out the background noise. Behind her, there was a commotion at Rockefeller Plaza. A news crew had broken past the police barricade. Officers with bullhorns were shouting at them to stay behind the perimeter; meanwhile a half-dozen SWAT team members had converged to stop them. A woman screamed as her camera was confiscated.

Above her head, a chopper circled.

At first Eve wondered what had become of the media blackout Henry had ordered.

Then she realized: The choppers overhead were FBI.

"How did *you* find *me*?" Eve answered Sean. "More important, why did you want me? There are plenty of other negotiators."

"You're a smart girl. I'm hoping you'll figure out that answer soon."

"Should be easy, now I know who you are."

"Do you, Eve Rossi? Seems to me that all you know is a name. Maybe my date of birth. I'm sure right now, as we speak, your experts are pawing through my background. Figuring out where I went to school. What my teachers said. You'll interview my commanding officers in both the police and the Marines. You'll comb through my divorce papers. You'll search for signs of a breakdown. For anything that will explain *this*. Explain *me*."

"It's what I do. I observe people; I catalog their behavior; I learn from their life experiences. It's how I understand people—and I'm going to understand you, Sean."

"Problem is: You're going to find the obvious answers. And the answers are going to be wrong."

"I wouldn't be so sure." Before, Eve had recognized the half-truth in what Sean had said. Now she recognized the lie. He hadn't wanted to be identified so soon. So he was strategizing, playing her, trying to minimize the damage.

"Look, Eve: What I've done for a living isn't so different from you. I've conducted hundreds of interviews. And something I learned: Most people notice the obvious, then make the wrong assumption."

"I'm not most people."

"Hear me out." The note of desperation in his voice was new. Her heart quickened. "Let's say you're walking past a church. You see a man wearing filthy jeans. No shoes. There's a vacant look in his eye. A shopping cart a few feet away from him. What do you immediately assume? That he's homeless. Probably an addict. Maybe even mentally ill."

Up until now, Sean's communications had fallen into two categories: instructions and threats. For the first time, she had the sense he was about to say something that mattered. Her hopes soared. "Sounds like a valid assumption, most of the time."

"Exactly. *Most* of the time. But what if he's not homeless? What if he's a middle-class man with a family who worries about him? What if he got lost on the way to his doctor's office or the grocery store because he's suffering from dementia? What if the shopping cart just happened to be there, left by some other guy?"

"I'd look at any small clues that might tell a different story. Maybe he was wearing a nice watch or a wedding ring. Maybe his dirty jeans were new." Sometimes communication was less about exchanging words than matching emotions. In this case, hope for hope. What-if for what-if.

"Sure, but not everybody notices small details like that. We're all subject to bias. Happened to me. I made a wrong assumption. I learned my lesson: The obvious solution is usually right, but not always. Definitely not now."

Sometimes the best approach was the direct one. "Are you saying that what you're doing here today has nothing to do with the Church?"

She allowed herself to hope—to *believe*—that he'd answer the question. Because they'd now experienced a moment of understanding. Because the day had disappeared and she was tired. Tired of being kept in the dark. Tired of struggling to make sense of what defied all logic.

He must have heard it in her voice. "I like talking with you, Eve, but I'm tired, too. And we're wasting time. We have only two hours, forty-five minutes until the next stage of my operation. Starting *now.*"

"Okay, I'm listening." Eve set her stopwatch as a precaution.

"You have my witnesses on-site."

"I need to know what you want with them."

"They're here to witness God's truth."

"You're making no sense. You and I both know that." *And if your motive isn't religious, then why the hell do you use phrases like this?*

"How is Cassidy Jones?" he asked abruptly.

"She's not happy to be here. She'd rather be home."

"Working at that dead-end job?" he scoffed. "What about Vanderwert? I'll bet he's fit to be tied, being stuck here. He probably finds it worse than jury duty. Maybe I should see him first."

"See him now, if you want. I'll ask him to wave from the holding unit window."

"That won't convince me that he's here."

"He can send a smoke signal."

"Get with the twenty-first century, Eve." His slashing reply signaled his mood was shifting. Eve knew she was walking on emotional quicksand.

"I won't risk his safety."

"C'mon. I know you've installed a bulletproof shield around the perimeter."

"So you're saying you'd like the witness to stand behind the shield?" *No way was she doing that.*

"Right in front of Atlas. Where I can see him."

"We can set up a Skype connection. Is that twenty-first-century enough for you?"

"Sarcasm doesn't become you, Eve."

"Help me understand something, Sean. Why do you need these witnesses?"

"Why do people need anything—air to breathe, food to eat, water to drink?"

"Enough one-upmanship. A simple answer would be nice for a change."

"I knew you'd have a term for it. That's what psychologists do: They train you to put a fancy name on everything. Because if you can name it, you can understand it, right?"

He was trying to annoy her, to distract her from the dilemma at hand.

"Put Blair Vanderwert in front of Atlas," he said. "You have four minutes—or Ethan Raynor will die, right in front of your eyes."

"If I do as you ask, will you let me take Mr. Raynor into my custody?"

"I have to go, Eve. Always a pleasure chatting with you."

The line went dead.

Eve hit *redial last call.* Her rings went unanswered.

He had been right about one thing. She was a psychologist by training—and that experience defined who she was. It gave her an eye for detail, an understanding of human behavior, and the ability to make reasonable leaps of logic.

But it wasn't doing a damn thing to help her understand Sean Sullivan.

She looked up—beyond the scaffolding, above Saint Patrick's spires—into the black void of the night sky. A big, wet snowflake fell on her nose. Followed by one on her forehead and another on her cheek. Suddenly snow was swirling all around her, coming down almost like confetti from the Cathedral itself.

# Chapter 53

*It was during the third month of Stacy's deployment that it happened. It was getting toward winter, and the rains had started. I've always liked rainy days—but I have never loved rain as much as I did in Afghanistan.*

*It tamped down the sand so we got fewer of those damn sandstorms.*

*It freed us from the perpetual trap of dirt and grime.*

*Stacy had gone with a small team on an adventure beyond the wire. They were investigating a village that may have been harboring a group of insurgents responsible for planting a round of IEDs on the road. They went house to house, searching.*

*Asking questions.*

*Gathering intelligence.*

*They were told to look for a man at the bazaar. And that's where Stacy became separated from the rest of the group.*

*What I wanted to know then . . . what I want to know now . . . is how does a group of Marines—a group of tough, battle-hardened, take-no-shit Marines—manage to lose their interpreter in enemy territory?*

# Chapter 54

It was snowing.

Not the dazzling display of illuminated snowflakes that normally lit the façade of Saks, but the real thing. Beautiful, thick, white flakes that made Saint Patrick's look like something out of a fairy tale. And maybe it was—complete with a villain inside.

Outside, there was chaos. Shouts, and people running in all directions. Henry Ma was barking orders and federal agents and NYPD were getting into position. EMS had pulled back.

The buildings nearby remained dark. Empty. The goal was to see the sniper coming. Not give him an additional target.

For their plan to succeed, now the lights of Saint Patrick's needed to be extinguished as well. Eve gave the command—and watched as the spotlights illuminating the Cathedral went black.

Inside the holding unit, Sean Sullivan's photograph had been passed among the witnesses. They were shown two copies—one of him in full uniform, the other in casual clothes. Just to cover all bases, Eve made sure they were also shown photos of Paulie Corsillo. She had also sent the photos over to the hotel where Luke Miller—the only hostage to walk away so far—was being kept safe.

It didn't matter. Not one of the witnesses remembered seeing either man before. And Luke was unsure.

"Are you ready?" Eve asked, Haddox behind her.

Her answer was the dance of his fingers on the keyboard and the hum of a video camera come to life. Haddox was in his element. Doing what he loved most.

Finally he said, "Showtime!"

"Blair, will you come over here?" Eve pointed to where the video camera was focused against a white wall. "The Hostage Taker is asking to meet you—"

He didn't let her finish. He started babbling, voicing a dozen different concerns, but she made out *You promised I'd be safe.*

"—so we're setting up a virtual connection," she explained, shouting him down. "My associate here is going to project a walking and talking image of you outside this building. Do you want to take a moment to compose yourself? There's water in the interview room."

Eli waited until the realtor was out of earshot. "I dunno, Eve. Somehow I don't think a projection is going to satisfy this guy. He went to all this trouble. He's gonna want the real thing—"

"This is as close to the real thing as we can get," Haddox cut in. "Remember how a few years ago everyone was talking about how computer technology more or less resurrected Tupac Shakur from the dead to perform with Snoop Dogg and Dr. Dre at a music festival? Everybody called it a hologram—but it was actually a two-D projection against a transparent screen."

"Sure," Eli said. "Even people who don't follow the music scene were talking about it. Some people thought it was totally awesome. Others said it was creepy."

"Either way, it should work for us. The technique is a basic illusion based on Pepper's ghost—a centuries-old theater trick. Onstage, the actor hides in a recessed area, faces a mirror, and his image is projected by a sheet of glass suspended above the stage. The rest is just lighting."

"Okay, so how do you do that here?" Eli wanted to know.

"I use 3-D computer graphics to produce a reflection that is similar to a hologram. Remember my shopping list? Well, I now have everything we need—a video cam, a high-def projector, and a flat translucent screen." He shot Eve a boyish smile. "I know; I surprise even myself sometimes."

"You can do this live?" Eve asked Haddox.

"Have a little faith. I can do it live, prerecorded, upside-down—however you like it."

"Do it. It's certainly the only viable option we have. I won't put innocent civilians in harm's way."

"What if he makes good on his threats?" Eli fretted.

"I believe this isn't really about killing hostages or destroying the Cathedral. If we meet him halfway, I think I can convince him to compromise."

"How can you say this isn't about killing hostages, when so many have died?" Alina gave Eve an icy stare.

"Because he killed them as a means to an end. He's not afraid to murder when he feels he must. He may even enjoy it—or see it as some kind of perverted act of justice. But it isn't what he *wants*."

"What do you think he really wants?" A muscle twitched in Blair's jaw as he rejoined them.

"He wants you," Eve answered. "Each one of you—for some reason I still don't understand."

She glanced at her stopwatch: *Fifty, forty-nine, forty-eight, forty-seven seconds to go.* "It's possible he will want to talk with you," Eve told Blair. "If he does, we're right here. We'll be recording the conversation and coaching you what to say. You won't be alone, not for one second."

"Now," she told Haddox.

And a full-sized image of Blair Vanderwert appeared right next to the statue of Atlas across from the steps of Saint Patrick's Cathedral.

The image appeared to stare directly at Ethan Raynor.

And despite the tremor of surprise that Eve detected, Ethan Raynor stared right back.

# Chapter 55

García continued his journey inside the rocky, cavernous construction site that would one day house New York's newest subway extension. It was an eerie underworld that included a 160-foot cavern, dripping stone walls, and watery gravel pits.

Right out of a *Batman* flick.

To García, it was hell.

He had been underground for nineteen minutes. Which was already eighteen minutes too long.

His current location was eight stories below ground. Which was eight stories too many.

And seven stories below where he'd abandoned Tony the first time around.

He had followed Tony's directions. First, he located the two wide metal ventilation pipes that led aboveground. Set on the wall between them was a circular hole covered with an intake screen. It was designed to look like any other vent—an ordinary air shaft allowing for efficient air movement. But according to Tony, it was the mouth of the secret subterranean tunnel that eventually led right inside Saint Patrick's Cathedral.

At first he was able to walk—albeit in a slightly stooped position. There was even a safety rail that lasted about fifteen feet. Someone had installed it to protect those navigating the rocky, wet terrain.

By the time he had gone twenty-five feet, he was in uncharted, cramped territory. Someone had tunneled out a narrow chunk of bedrock that Tony claimed was passable.

*Passable* didn't look pleasant. He remembered what he'd been

# García's Underground Journey

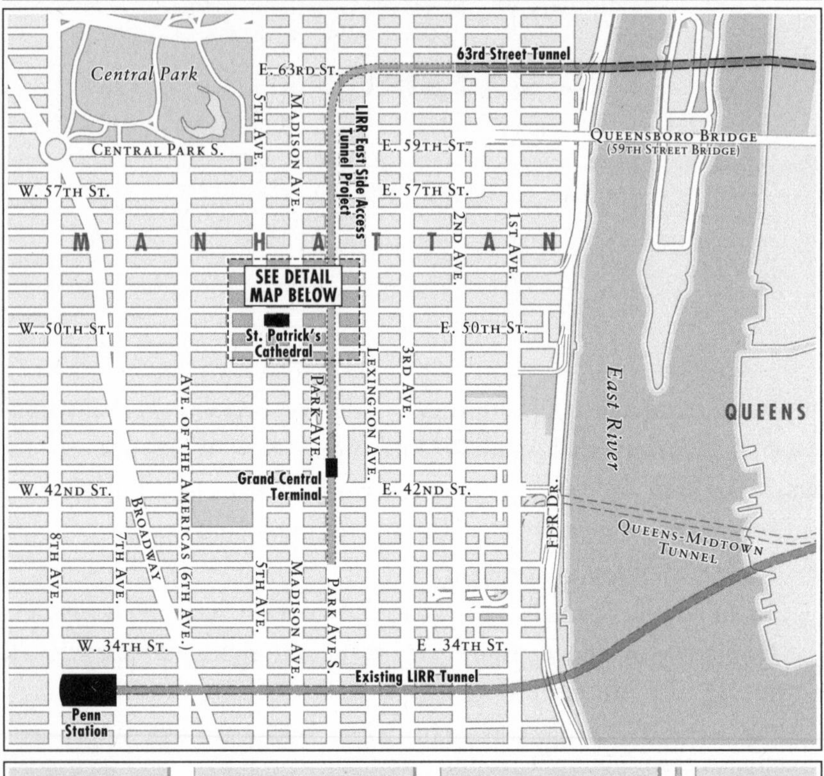


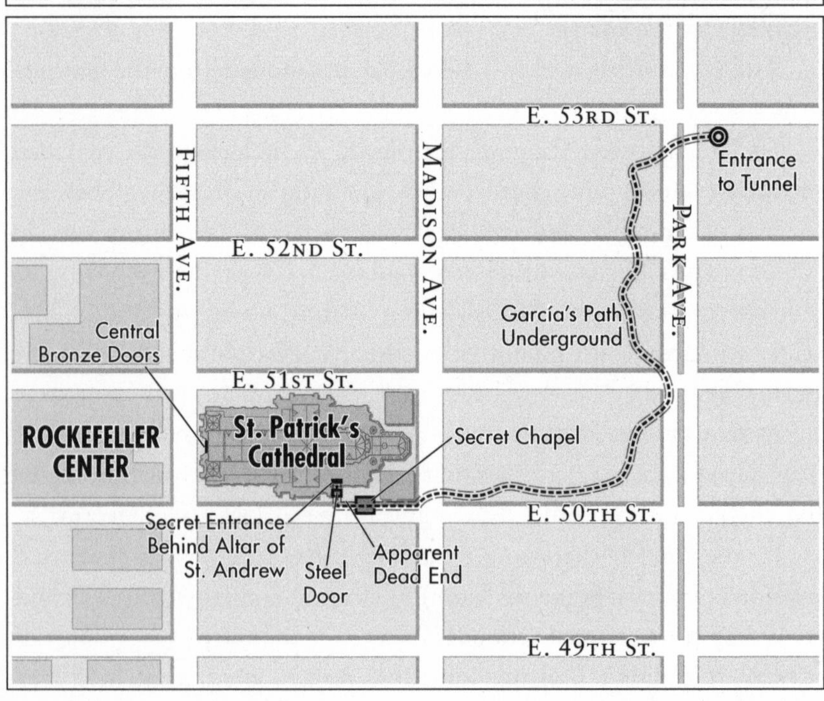

told about the tunnel's construction. This was done as an inside job, by masons who didn't feel the need to drill beyond the bare minimum. So the space was narrow. García had to drop to his hands and knees. Even then, his shoulders regularly brushed against the jagged roof of the passageway.

He shone his flashlight beam straight ahead—and cursed. It was like looking into a bottomless well.

He went on and on. One foot—or, rather, one hand and knee—at a time. Another twenty-five feet. Then fifty. Seventy-five. A hundred.

Ironically, it was when he felt he must be getting close that García felt the walls collapsing in on him. He squeezed his eyes shut. Focused on taking deep breaths. *In. Out.* Reminded himself that he had enough air. More than plenty.

But the air had changed. Where it had been cold and damp, now it was still and dry.

In his mind's eye, he focused on his tranquil image: The endless stretch of sky and beach that some shrink had suggested he use when he needed to calm down.

*In. Out.*

He fought his growing panic.

Without success. He was losing it. He felt the tunnel ceiling start to come down. The walls edged closer. Even the floor seemed to rise up. He smelled smoke. Heard rumbling. All his senses started working in overdrive.

He was suffocating. Gasping for air that wasn't there.

His palms were sweating. The taste of bile was in his mouth.

His brain tried to stay in the moment. But every overstimulated sense in his body was working to convince him that he was trapped—again—in the rubble of Fallujah. His mind couldn't stay in control. Raw instinct took over.

There was a buzzing in his ear. Coming at regular intervals. Every three seconds.

He had to get out. If he didn't, he was going to die down here.

A buzzing in his ear.

He ignored it as best he could. He was running out of time. He was hyperventilating.

His mind could not fully process what was happening. But some half-remembered muscle memory must have led his right hand to click the button and answer the call—because within seconds, Mace's voice was booming in his ear.

*Mace?*

Mace saying, "Hey, Frankie, whassup?"

He recognized the disconnect. Mace was in New York, not Fallujah.

"Frankie, you with me?"

García focused on the voice. "Mace?" The name caught in his throat, came out strangled.

"Take a deep breath, Frankie."

García did. Was surprised that he actually could.

"You with me now?"

"Yeah."

*In. Out.* He was still hyperventilating, but only in spurts. Miraculously, his breathing was working again.

"Great, now listen up. You can do this. You're almost there. Know how I know?"

García had no idea. *In. Out.* Just breathing deep.

"Those fancy sunglasses of yours have a GPS chip. So I can track your every movement." Mace chuckled. "Just what I always wanted to do, Frankie. Hang out with you even when we're not together. You never know, we could be Facebook friends."

"Fuck you," García growled. "And stop calling me Frankie." He didn't feel the walls closing in anymore. He felt the sullen tension he always felt around Mace. The guy he got along with least in the world. They were worse than oil and water. More like truth and lies. Fire and gas.

He reveled in that feeling—because it was familiar. It calmed him almost as much as being aboveground and breathing in a huge gulp of New York City pollution.

García started moving again. "How come you're calling me?"

"Just checking in. Making sure you're okay."

"In other words, Eve knew something was wrong and told you to dial in. How come she didn't do it herself?"

"I know, I know—this is Eve's typical play. But give me some credit. Eve is kinda tied up right now, and it was me who noticed you starting to have a full-fledged freak-out."

"It has a name. Post-traumatic stress disorder. PTSD. Which you might know, if you'd ever worried about anything other than yourself."

"Easy, Frankie. We're all friends here—or what passes for it in Vidocq, anyway. Those fancy glasses of yours have two-way video stream. Do me a favor, put 'em on. You keep 'em on your belt, I can see where you're going—but not as well as I want."

Frankie obliged. But not without giving Mace the middle finger the moment he'd done it.

Mace chuckled. "Looks like you're feelin' better already."

"Don't know how I even have a signal down here."

"Military technology. It's the best. Now, normally I don't like hearin' your annoying voice, but today's the exception. I'm gonna stay with you like white on rice, all the way in."

"Don't want you," García grumbled again. "How much farther do I have to go?"

"Frankie, baby, I'm like death and taxes—unavoidable. Let's just do this. You're real close now. And once you're in that Cathedral, you can turn those PTSD sensors of yours full on. In fact, we need you to. They'll help you stay safe."

García had heard that before.

"But right here, right now? We don't want your superpowers messin' things up. So one deep breath at a time. One step at a time."

"Since when did you learn to talk like a hairdresser? All this understanding crap ain't your style."

"Eve's fault," Mace retorted.

"What—she gave you lessons in psychobabble bullshit?" *One deep breath.*

"Naw. She left me Bach—that German shepherd used to belong to her stepfather."

"You're making no sense, man." *One step forward.*

"It was a CIA dog—already had attack training, not to mention plenty of other cool skills. Plus, it's young. Got way too much energy pent up to settle down like some couch potato. I had to teach it *something* it couldn't already do."

"I'm afraid to ask." *Deep breath.*

"Therapy training. Specific to PTSD, actually. I guess I picked up a thing or two along the way."

*Another step forward.* "I nailed it, then. It's like you took Hairdresser 101."

"Change that to Bartending 101, and I won't beat the shit out of you once you're out of that tunnel."

*Another deep breath.* "How much longer?"

"You're getting there, Frankie. Just keep movin'."

# Chapter 56

Light snow was still swirling to the ground. Fifth Avenue was still dark. But there was one beacon of light: Blair Vanderwert's projected image. It stood awkwardly next to the statue of Atlas. An illuminated hologram that lit up the night.

Eve hurried to position herself beside it. Beside *him*.

Haddox's idea had been genius. Because apart from the neon glow, the image of Vanderwert was perfectly lifelike. Exactly the right height, with the right dimensions and the right expression. He seemed almost real, standing on the plaza with snowflakes falling all around him. No, make that *through* him.

Ethan Raynor shifted nervously on the steps.

Eve walked toward him; she didn't stop until she was halfway between the hostage and the hologram. Then she positioned herself so she was facing up Fifth Avenue, situated to see them both.

The commotion around her had faded. Cellphones still chirped and radios crackled, but the uniforms around the perimeter had stopped what they were doing. They stared at the hologram. Nobody spoke. The only sound Eve heard was that of her own quick breaths—and Ethan's heavy rasping, as mere feet away, he inhaled every gulp of air as though it were his last.

They stood there together . . . twenty-six seconds to go. Then twenty-five, twenty-four, twenty-three . . .

Finally, just before her stopwatch ticked the three-second mark, the cellphone in her hand rang.

"What the fuck do you think this is? Some Hollywood movie where you send me a message from Princess Leia and think it's okay?"

"I think this is me getting with the twenty-first century, exactly as you asked. Not to mention, it's clever. I've managed to offer you Blair Vanderwert—while keeping him under my protection."

"Where is he?" Sean demanded.

"Inside the holding unit, of course. I wouldn't lie to you, Sean."

"Of course you would, if you thought you could get away with it. Prove it."

"You can see him. Talk to him, if you want. I'll give you the number."

"Do you think I'm here to negotiate? If you don't want that hostage bleeding to death in front of you, I want Vanderwert out here. Now."

"He *is* here, ready to talk. I'm not playing games with you, Sean. You wanted these witnesses brought here. I did that. You demanded visual ID. I arranged for it. You want to speak with them? I'll tell you the number to dial."

"I'll blow up the Cathedral. It's not an idle threat."

"Except then you'll never get what you want." She paused before she continued. "What *do* you want, Sean? When you're ready to talk about that, let me know."

She pressed the button on the handset, abruptly ending the call. Turned and started to walk back to the holding unit.

Henry Ma yelled from the perimeter's edge, asking what the hell she was thinking.

"Trust me, I know what I'm doing," she said serenely as she passed him.

"You hung up on him!"

"I did."

"He's going to kill that man on the steps!"

"I don't think he will," Eve said evenly. "Not now."

"If anything happens, it's all on you."

She turned and looked him square in the eye. "You think I don't know that? Whatever happens here today, good or bad, I've got to live with it. Yes, I'm taking a risk. But if I don't play to win, I'm certainly going to lose."

Henry wasn't listening. "He'll kill that hostage. Just like the others before. And when you walk away like that, it sends one message loud and clear: That you don't care. That the FBI has abandoned those hostages inside."

Eve started counting. *One, two . . .*

On the count of *three,* the cellphone rang. She reached for it and answered. "What do you want?"

"WHAT THE FUCK ARE YOU DOING?"

Eve hung up. Counted again. *One, two, three . . .*

She barely made it past *three.*

The cell rang again.

Henry put out his hand for the cellphone. "Give that to me, Eve. Clearly you weren't ready for this. It's too soon."

She ignored him. Answered the call.

"IF YOU HANG UP ON ME AGAIN, I'LL—"

Eve clicked off the line.

*One, two, three, four . . .*

He called back on the count of *five.*

"THIS IS YOUR FINAL WARN—"

Eve pressed the end key. With a glance at Henry, she said, "I'm handling this." She forced a note of confidence into her voice that she didn't feel. She still didn't know nearly enough about this Hostage Taker. But she knew enough to realize that she had refocused his attention. He was absolutely enraged—but his fury was now directed at her.

Not at the hostage on the steps.

Not at the witnesses in the holding unit.

Eve counted again. This time the Hostage Taker called back on the count of *eight.*

That was progress. Because it meant he was taking time to collect his thoughts between calls. Eventually he would say something real. Maybe even now.

His voice was restrained when she heard him again. "If you continue treating me with disrespect—"

"What do you want, Sean?"

"Right now, I want that number."

Eve rattled off the special number. It began with 646.

This time, it was the Hostage Taker who ended the call.

Eve didn't move, but she clicked the button on her headset that would patch her into the Hostage Taker's call to Blair Vanderwert.

# Chapter 57

Eli was at his computer, tracing the details of Sean Sullivan's fiscal life. He was Haddox's technological equal when it came to following the ins, outs, and potential hiding spots for the U.S. dollar. Or any other currency, for that matter. His grandmother had always said *People spend their money how they want to spend their money.* She punctuated the statement with a huge shrug and an eye roll—as if to say she might not agree with their choice, but who was she to judge?

So what if the Kaufmans never managed to save a dollar in the bank but kept a Cadillac on the curb? Why should she care if the Mandels sent their three sons to private school uptown, not the highly regarded public down the block? And if miserly Mrs. Green played the penny stocks, made a small fortune, and couldn't bring herself to spend a dime of it, then that was her own business. We were all different people who valued different things. This was the science of the mind that Eli understood—where such small details and individual choices spoke volumes about personality, behavior, and values.

In other words, people might lie—but their money never did.

So what did Sean Sullivan's financial choices say about him?

He had joined the NYPD right after graduating from Saint John's. Over his twenty-plus-year career with New York's Finest, he'd earned promotions and raises at a rapid clip, suggesting that as a young man, Sean was a go-getter, just plain lucky, or both. He'd joined the U.S. Marine Corps Reserve and been deployed to join the War on Terror. He'd learned weapons expertise and interrogation techniques. His deployments had been his undoing. They had destroyed his first, brief "starter marriage" and then wrecked his second marriage to Meaghan.

Which maybe wasn't a bad thing—since financially, Meaghan had been his undoing. First when he married her, spending much more than he could comfortably afford on a fifteen-thousand-dollar engagement ring and a sixty-thousand-dollar wedding. Again when he divorced her and she took half of everything he owned.

Now he had thirty-four thousand dollars in credit card debt, was more than two months in arrears on his apartment rent, about to bounce his next alimony check, and his car had been repossessed. That was the big picture. It wasn't pretty.

Eli ripped open a bag of chips, popped a handful in his mouth as he stretched his aching back. Several vertebrae cracked. The sound was ugly, but it relieved his tension. He resettled in front of the computer, opening a new screen filled with credit card and bank debit data.

He scanned the details. Sean Sullivan had spent most of his money on groceries and beer. He wrote checks to Con Ed and had paid his rent on time until he started struggling nine weeks ago. Every other Friday there was a charge at the Peking Kitchen, followed by Dusty's Alehouse. Eli guessed it was a regular guy's night out. A tradition no different than poker night. Sean must've participated whenever Meaghan had their daughter. Because other weekends his spending looked very different. Movies. Broadway shows. Lunches at Serendipity 3 and ice-skating in Wollman Rink. A typical dad trying to do fun things with his daughter.

He didn't make any charitable contributions. There was nothing left over at the end of the month.

There were two incident reports in Sean's history. Both had resulted in cash outlays for attorney's fees.

In the first, Sean Sullivan had been named the subject of an Internal Affairs investigation into evidence-locker theft. Cash and ecstasy, taken from a series of busts his precinct had been responsible for.

Eli checked Sean's bank account again. It was basic checking at Citibank. It had plenty of debits. But only a handful of deposits—all payroll ACH transfers initiated by the NYPD. If Sean had taken the money or sold the drugs, he'd put the proceeds under his mattress and left it there. His financial life showed no sign of a sudden infusion of cash.

Eli flipped to a new screen, searching for the investigation's outcome. As of yet, there wasn't one. He made a note of Sean's police union representative. It would be worth giving the guy a call.

The second incident involved a complaint from his ex-wife, Meaghan, who had accused him of harassment and making threatening phone calls. She alleged that he broke into the home of the first man she dated seriously after the divorce. He rifled through the man's emails and credit card bills, bookshelves and medicine chest. Then he'd dialed Meaghan and informed her that her new man liked girlie magazines and needed Viagra.

No outcome there, either. The date was five months ago. It appeared to have been a onetime incident that never repeated. More the result of poor judgment and too much alcohol than a bad pattern of behavior.

Eli felt a tap on his shoulder. Looked up, blinking into the lights.

Haddox was standing behind him, a grim expression on his face. "Hey, mate—we need to talk."

"Those words are usually reserved for someone breaking up with me. Didn't know there was a thing between us," Eli said.

"You've been looking into the financial part of Sean Sullivan's life. I've been learning the rest of it. Picking out the details of his background that might be relevant for Eve to know about. I've been studying his religious background and talking to his friends, learning as much as I can about his feelings toward the Church. About the sex abuse he suffered as a child. Not fun reading."

Eli wasn't sure where Haddox was going with this. "Sullivan's also got major money issues. Running through them is no picnic, either."

"Sullivan's got a long case history." Haddox pulled a pack of cigarettes from his pocket, shot a dismissive glance at the NO SMOKING sign before he lit up. "I've been looking, but I can't find a connection to Eve in his past, anywhere. There's nothing remarkable in his arrest records. Only Luis Ramos has ever had a brush with the law, and it didn't involve Sullivan. But I did find one thing *really* interesting. Know what it involved?"

"A connection with the witnesses?" Eli asked, hopeful.

"Sullivan's family."

Eli froze. The truth hit him like a ton of bricks. He suddenly knew what Haddox was going to say, but he couldn't manage to intercept it.

"That mobile phone number you gave me to track? The one whose last known whereabouts, best I could tell, were at the Hirschfeld Theater on West Forty-fifth Street enjoying a performance of *Kinky Boots*?"

"Yeah." Eli blinked again, struggling to focus. He had no desire to lie to Haddox. He equally had no desire to have this conversation.

"Were you ever planning to tell me that Georgianna Murphy is the daughter of Sean Sullivan—the man holding all the hostages inside Saint Patrick's Cathedral?"

# Chapter 58

*We'd always heard that interpreters carried an extra risk of danger in case of capture. They'd be treated the roughest—tortured in ways an ordinary soldier never was—because the Afghans considered them traitors.*

*Even if, like Stacy, they'd grown up in Sacramento, California. And had no personal connection to the area by family or culture—just a gift for languages discovered while in college.*

*It happened in broad daylight, in the middle of the village square near the bazaar.*

*One minute everything was normal: A jittery walk through a crowded market. Looking for someone suspicious among reports of a suicide bomber.*

*Everyone's attention was consumed by those men and women in long robes who might be concealing Christ-only-knew-what underneath. And all the villagers were jumpy and distracted. It was only natural when a unit of Marines with twitchy, nervous fingers was passing through their midst.*

*They entered the bazaar a unit of six plus an interpreter.*

*They exited a unit of six minus an interpreter.*

*I had to imagine what happened in the chaos of the moment—and I did. I helped my imagination along with plenty of solid evidence.*

*I took months to piece it together.*

*I understood what it's like walking among people who want to kill me. I am familiar with the chaos that follows the firing of submachine guns. I understand the politics when Marines put civilians at risk. I even know why those jarheads with Stacy froze in the chaos—and didn't act. They were twentysomething-year-old kids who just wanted the same thing we all did: to get back home safe.*

*I understand it. I just don't accept excuses.*

*Didn't then.*

*Don't now.*

*Why couldn't just one soldier go above and beyond the call of duty? Make a sacrifice to merit a commendation in his bureaucratic file? Just enough to busy some politician with a medal ceremony, and add a shiny gold badge to his uniform sleeve.*

*Sure, I was to blame. I'd encouraged Stacy to apply for the damn tour. I stupidly thought we were safer together than apart.*

*But why didn't someone who was actually there step up? How hard was it to say, LISTEN, YOU COCKSUCKING RAGHEADS, GIVE US BACK WHAT'S OURS OR WE'LL RAPE YOUR PRECIOUS WIVES AND DAUGHTERS BEFORE WE BLOW THEM TO BITS?*

*Because goddamn it, we're Marines.*

*That's when I thought again about batty old Mrs. Brescia's murder on Queens Boulevard. And decided most people are fucking sheep.*

# Chapter 59

Eve had only enough time to give Blair Vanderwert a few hasty words of advice before he had to answer the Hostage Taker's call. She stared at the projection of the realtor's image. He was sweating and had a stricken expression on his face.

"I don't want to do this," Blair said into her earpiece.

"I know," Eve replied evenly. "But your conversation with him may be our first real clue to what he's after. I'll be right on the call with you. And if you're unsure what to say, all you have to do is echo him. Do you know what I mean by that?"

Blair's image shook its head. "I have no clue."

"It's a negotiation technique. It shows him you're listening, but mainly just keeps him talking. So if he says, *I love summer at the lake,* and you don't know how to respond, just mirror the thought. Come back with *Summer's great,* or *The lake's nice.* Don't introduce anything new, like how you prefer winter or always get bitten up by mosquitoes at lakes. The goal is to follow whatever direction he takes."

"I don't think I can do this."

"'Course you can. Tell me: What's the highest listing you've sold this quarter?"

"In October, my client went to contract on a twenty-three-million-dollar townhouse on East Seventy-eighth."

"If you can negotiate that, then you'll do fine here."

There was a buzzing in Eve's ear.

"Go ahead and answer," she directed Vanderwert. "It's just like call waiting. Except it'll generate a three-way connection, so I can stay right with you."

She heard Blair take a raspy breath; then a *click* established the connection.

"Am I speaking with Blair Vanderwert?" Sean was using his best manners—and his best speaking voice. Eve thought that was a positive sign.

"This is he," Blair answered.

"The realtor?"

"Yeah."

"Know any good realtor jokes?"

"Uh . . ."

"I've got one. My realtor just sold me a two-story house. One story before I bought it. A different story after."

"That's a good one," Blair managed.

"First, I need to check your ID. Is that image really you?"

"I-I think so," Blair stammered.

"Kick your left leg up high, like you're a Radio City Rockette."

"Seriously?" Blair gave a halfhearted kick.

"Try again—and if you don't do a better job, that hostage on the steps is going to get a bullet. And Eve won't be able to stop it. You *are* still on the call, right, Eve?"

"Of course; I wouldn't leave you all by yourself."

"Meaning you don't trust me alone with Blair."

"Do you really want him to dance, or do you have something to ask him?"

"KICK!"

This time, the realtor kicked his left leg so high he nearly lost his balance. The image teetered and wobbled, then, finally, righted itself.

A cold gust of wind briefly turned falling snowflakes into a whirling tornado. For a moment, the neon projection dimmed. Vanderwert faded into a ghostly shadow of himself.

"Thank you. Now, one more test to make certain you're who you say you are. Do you remember the closing you handled on July ninth?"

"In general, I remember my July closings. But you'd have to give me specifics to jog my memory. That's around the Fourth of July. I had several clients close deals around then." Vanderwert's projected image brightened again.

"This was the Chung family. Family of four. Husband is a banker with Paribas; wife stays home with their two girls."

"I-I remember," Blair managed. "They bought on Park and Eighty-ninth."

"Who was the lawyer who handled their closing?"

"It was Toby Blaine. He's the attorney I always recommend when the buyer is experienced and doesn't need a lot of handholding."

"And they had an issue at closing. What was it?"

"The bank wire took forever to come through. We all sat there forever, waiting for the money to hit the account."

From deep inside Rockefeller Plaza, music was playing again. "Silver Bells." A couple of cops added their talents to the recording, offering plenty of spirit as they yowled off-key. Their noise would distract unwelcome onlookers—but Eve strained to hear the conversation she desperately needed to follow.

"Good. So let's get down to business. Before you can truly witness the event to come, you must confess."

"Excuse me?"

"You know what a witness is, Blair?"

"In court. Where someone testifies about something they've seen or heard."

"Excellent. That's what will be required of you today. But to do it well, you need a clear head and a focused mind."

"Sure, my mind is focused."

He was echoing. Just continuing the conversation—conveying interest but no judgment—which was exactly what was needed. Eve allowed herself a quick sigh of relief.

"You don't understand, Blair. You confess in order to *have* a focused mind."

"You mean like in Church?"

"Less formal, but similar."

Blair hesitated. "But I'm not Catholic. And I'm pretty sure you're not a priest."

So much for echoing. Eve's heart sank.

"Is this really necessary?" Blair challenged. Eve realized the question was for her.

"How about I go first?" she answered.

"Sorry, Eve," Sean interposed. "You've got a role to play here, but you're no witness. C'mon, Vandy. It's not so hard. Just tell me: What are you guilty of?"

"Umm . . . I regret not visiting my mother more before she died."

"Yes, sins of omission are often the worst. Why didn't you?"

"Why didn't I?"

"Visit her more."

"I was busy. She was sick. It scared me."

"Good. What else?"

"I waste money. Last year, I threw out a six-hundred-dollar pair of shoes because I stepped in dog crap and wanted to vomit every time I thought about cleaning them."

"C'mon. You can do better than that. What are you *really* guilty of?"

"I don't know what you want," Blair responded, exasperated. "Do I make mistakes? Sure. Everybody makes mistakes. But I'm not a bad person. I don't steal. I don't kill."

Eve winced. Forget echoing. That last comment was going to take the conversation in the wrong direction. She was losing control.

"So what does that make me, Blair? A bad person? Since I *am* responsible for people dying."

"As am I," Eve broke in. "Maybe I didn't intend it, but people have died or been hurt because I made a mistake. Too many people."

There was a pause. Sean seemed to be processing the information.

Eve wondered: Had she said enough to deflect Sean's attention? Her heart was racing.

"Eve, I don't really care about the times you've screwed up," Sean said. "You're dealing with assholes most of the time; it's bound to happen. I want you to tell me something you're scared to tell. Tell me more of your story—the one about the man with the tattoo?"

Eve shivered as a gust of wind caught the edge of her jacket. She blinked the flurry of snow out of her eyes. And reminded herself: *The content of these stories is never the important thing. What is important is to distract—to further the connection, build the illusion of trust.*

"The man who wears that number on his arm has only been captured once in his life—by the Germans. Bureaucrats at heart, they kept complete files. It took some digging, but I was able to find his records."

"You personally?" Sean sounded intrigued.

"With a translator, of course."

"The FBI helped?"

"No. This was personal—and I was on leave. I got help from a German tour guide, a young woman who spoke eight languages." She was on tenterhooks, aware of the rhythm of her blood, pumping through her heart.

"Europeans are impressive that way. What did you learn?"

"I learned that the number had been tattooed onto the man's arm when he was still a boy, not yet turned thirteen. Based on the records, I found the name he was born with. I found the names of his mother and sister, both now dead. Then I went to France. I found the family home, the place he went to school; I even talked with people who remembered him. They were used to questions; plenty of others had passed through their town before, asking the same ones. But none of the questions led to the right answers, and I think I've figured out why. The boy died in the camps. An entirely different man was born there. The boy and that man have just one thing in common: the blue number tattooed on their forearm."

"Why do you care so much about this man with the number on his arm?"

"That's another part of the story, for another time." Eve said it lightly.

"Guess we've wasted enough time on stories. Let's put the next witness on the line, shall we? I'm ready to talk with Cassidy Jones."

# Chapter 60

Haddox lit another cigarette and drew on it slowly, staring at Eli as he exhaled. Really studying him for the first time since he'd arrived almost nine hours ago from Boston. Eli had put on even more weight in the past three months and was now pushing the boundary between big-boned and obese. His hair had grown longer. His shirt was still perpetually stained, his glasses were still held together with tape and safety pins, and he still could barely manage to keep his shite together. But there was something new: Eli seemed content. Maybe not happy, but fulfilled in a way he hadn't been before. Haddox was puzzled. What had changed in his life?

"You're not supposed to smoke here," Eli scolded, a little shrilly. "Maybe this unit is only a fancy sardine can on wheels, but it's still technically a government building."

"Do you really want to go there, mate? Besides, a good smoke helps me think."

Then he remembered Eve asking: *Killing brain cells helps you think?* He shook his head, banishing the memory. There was a simple explanation for why he couldn't get her out of his head. The Irish loved a good story—and every story needed three acts. First, you introduced your characters. Next, you explored their conflicts. And finally, you resolved their issues. Problem was: He and Goldilocks's story had no proper ending. Not even a good-bye and good luck. *So am I here for closure—or because I owe Eve for saving my sorry ass?*

He blew smoke into Eli's face. "Your little secret's given me something serious to think about."

Eli grimaced. "I told you, it's not a secret. It's just personal business that I don't particularly want to share with the world."

"How do you know Sean Sullivan?"

"I don't. I met his ex-wife at a Christmas party."

"When?"

"Last night."

"Tell me about it."

"There's not much to tell. She told me nothing that you don't already know." Eli began ticking off the relevant facts on his fingers. "He went to Saint John's; that's where he met Meaghan. He's with the NYPD, but currently on suspension; Internal Affairs suspects him of pilfering money and drugs from the evidence locker. Meaghan doesn't care about any of that."

"No?"

"She only cares about whether he's too messed up to take care of their thirteen-year-old daughter. They have joint custody."

"And if Sullivan's a thief, that means he can't take care of his child? If that were true, half my friends in Dublin would have grown up without parents."

"It's more complicated than that."

"It always is." Haddox mentally reviewed the details of Sean's file. "He's not an addict. No one suspected he stole the drugs for personal use."

"No," Eli agreed thoughtfully. "But I think he had problems that broke up their marriage all the same."

"You still haven't explained how you got that mobile number—and why you were interested in it."

"Because Meaghan was freaking out. As you know, the number belongs to her daughter, Georgianna Murphy. Georgie hasn't returned calls, and she's usually glued to her phone. And she didn't make it to school today. In fact, she disappeared day before yesterday. Sometime between noon and two p.m."

"Why is Sean Sullivan's daughter named *Murphy*?"

"It was part of the divorce settlement. Georgie took her mother's name."

"So Georgie's phone saw *Kinky Boots* last night? And then it went dead."

"That's what you told me. So I told my friend not to worry."

"Sounds like you spoke too soon. And keeping this secret? You're either an idiot or living in complete denial."

"Believe me," Eli said miserably, "I know."

Haddox let his gaze wander out the window toward the Cathedral. Thanks to the dark and the swirling flakes, he could barely make out its gothic lines—but they were stunning. Literally sugarcoated with snow. "The lass is an added complication we don't need. Would Sullivan really keep his own daughter in there? We need to figure out if anyone saw her since she disappeared from school."

For the first time, Eli looked hopeful. "Sounds like a good idea."

"And one last thing."

"You name it."

"*You* have to tell Eve."

# Chapter 61

Henry Ma's eyes lifted from the message he was reading on his phone and acknowledged the Omega Team leader.

"Think he's got a chance?" The officer nodded to Ethan Raynor, still standing, miserable and shivering, on the steps.

"He killed the others," Henry said bluntly. "Sent them out, then shot them, or blew them up unawares."

A horn blasted somewhere north of them.

"A coward's way. Just give me five minutes alone with him." The officer shook his head. He'd removed his headgear, exposing his thinning crew cut.

"My negotiator is holding steady for now. But she's going to have a big problem soon. She's missing a witness."

"Missing, sir?"

"They found him, then he disappeared down the rabbit hole. The Hostage Taker is going to blow when he figures it out—and I'm not sure my negotiator can contain him."

"In my experience, sir, there's some people you just can't reason with. Talk all you want, but talk won't solve your problem. A semiautomatic twelve-gauge will. I take it you want to proceed with plans for a breach."

Henry's lips twitched. "You know I used to be a criminal profiler before I became a desk jockey. I have my own thoughts as to this Hostage Taker."

"What's your assessment, sir?"

"He's doing a lot of this for show. Killing hostages in public. Demanding these witnesses as opposed to making more normal requests, such as money or political leverage. I think he's a religious zealot who's going to kill all his hostages eventually."

"So what are your orders, sir?"

"You mentioned an eight-second window, when the bronze doors would be unarmed. Next time that door opens, I want you and your team to be ready to breach."

The team leader nodded. "There won't be much time. It's a small, unpredictable window of opportunity. Am I to understand this is your official authorization to move in and secure the premises?"

Henry nodded. "When the opportunity presents itself, you're authorized to do whatever you deem necessary to secure the situation."

"Yes, sir. Is your negotiator in the loop?"

"That's none of your concern."

"Yes, sir. Anything else?"

The question was almost drowned out by the approach of a chopper in the air overhead. One of their own. Keeping a close eye on the situation from above.

"I'm counting on you. This whole city—this country, even. We need you to save those hostages and save Saint Patrick's."

García continued making his way through difficult terrain, but there were signs he was getting close. He was still surrounded by stone—the bedrock on which the island of Manhattan had been built. But the passage had become taller if not wider. He was able to half-stand. Another fifty feet. Seventy-five. A hundred. García crept along sideways and shuffled his way through the narrow passageway.

The panic inside him was swelling once again, but so far he was keeping it at bay.

Not because Mace was still on the line with him, jabbering about everything from his last girlfriend to his first ball game to his newest dog to how the weapons trade in New York City was changing because of Iraq and Syria and even Gaza. If he succeeded in making it inside, he had no doubt Mace would take all the credit.

But the real reason? He'd reached a point in the rock where he heard water. Not rushing water, like a waterfall. Not crashing water, like ocean waves. Just the steady hum of water flowing, almost like a babbling brook.

It was calm and soothing. Kind of like those overpriced Zen spas Teresa had taken such a liking to after he came home, when too much time around him stressed her out.

The water babbled.

Mace babbled, too—something about an opponent with a sweet left hook.

And from somewhere else—perhaps inside the Cathedral—he thought he heard voices.

García crept toward them as fast as he could.

The Omega Team leader stood twenty feet to the left of the bronze door, in the shadows of the scaffolding that surrounded Saint Patrick's. With the floodlights unlit, the Cathedral was shrouded in darkness. The team leader hoped it would provide enough cover. He felt visible and exposed—but he knew that was just a state of mind. He hoped that the Hostage Taker hadn't positioned cameras that would track the movements of his team. The fact that reconnaissance had identified none didn't reassure him.

Immediately behind him, the fifty-one-story Olympic Tower was dark. He knew sharpshooters were positioned behind its glass windows.

On the opposite side, on the roof of Saks Fifth Avenue, another crew was ready for action.

Tandem units Alpha, Beta, and Theta were well camouflaged. Hiding in the shadows, armed to the teeth.

Alpha was prepared to secure the hostage Ethan Raynor.

The signal would be the instant he took a step forward. That movement was to initiate their assault plan.

Beta and Theta would commence action the moment the bronze doors opened once again.

For now, they stayed put. And watched.

Alpha Team had the visual. Beta, Theta, and team leader followed a grainy live feed on their wristbands.

They saw Ethan Raynor stand a little straighter and tilt his head to the left, toward downtown. Almost like he was anticipating instructions.

Team Alpha tensed for action. Waiting on the fourth level of the scaffolding, they threw the rope and rappelled down the left front side of the Cathedral. Then they began crawling toward the bronze door. Alpha leader kept his eyes on Raynor as he moved toward him. Waiting for the exposed hostage to take a step forward. Ready to drop and secure.

Instead, just as the bronze door opened, Raynor turned abruptly on his heel.

He disappeared inside. Another figure stepped outside.

The door closed again.

Ethan Raynor was inside. A middle-aged woman stood outside.

Exactly four and a half seconds had elapsed, and a hostage switch had been accomplished.

Right under Omega Team's nose.

Three seconds later, Henry Ma's voice shrilled in the team leader's ear. "What the hell just happened? I thought your boys were ready."

The team leader didn't show anger, even if inside he felt like a volcano ready to explode. Any show of emotion had been drilled out of him through extensive training, when he learned the only approach in dealing with superior officers was to stick to the facts. He did that now.

"We didn't have the angle, sir. To intervene, we needed the hostage to step forward, just beyond the scaffolding. And two hostages simultaneously passing through the bronze door—not just one—limited our access and impacted the eight seconds we have to make breach."

"Damn it. It's like this Sullivan *wants* to frustrate us at every step!"

"Yes, sir. This is the first hostage to come out, then go back in, right?"

"That's right. Why?"

"Seems like he's making a point of being unpredictable."

# Chapter 62

Cassidy Jones was blond, beautiful, and not exactly unhappy to be the center of attention for the next ten minutes. Even if the price of fame was a conversation with a madman.

Eve watched as Cassidy's projected image preened in front of Atlas, striking her best Marilyn Monroe pose. She guessed no one had told Cassidy there was a media blackout in effect and all cameras were on the other side of the blockade fifteen blocks away.

Then again, Haddox was watching. Eve had seen the way Cassidy looked at him. Perhaps Haddox was audience enough for her.

Eve's phone trilled. Sean Sullivan was dialing in.

"How's my favorite waitress?" he asked. Eve thought he sounded surprisingly upbeat.

Cassidy's face was first crestfallen, then angry. "I'm an *actress*."

"Really? You've served drinks at a diner within the last twenty-four hours, but when's the last time you acted a part?"

"I have an agent at William Morris," she retorted, indignant now. "That's better than a lot of working actors can say."

Sullivan laughed softly. "Sure, 'cause that's what they'll write in your obituary when they list your accomplishments. Landed agent at William Morris."

Eve could see that Cassidy's cheeks were burning a brilliant red.

"But today it's not your accomplishments I want to talk about. It's your sins," Sullivan continued.

"Don't have any," she answered pertly.

"That's not what the priests always told me. Everyone has sinned."

"Then Jesus has died for us, so it's all good."

"Not very religious, are you?"

"No. Are you?"

Eve hadn't bothered to make suggestions for what Cassidy should say. It wouldn't have mattered. Cassidy was headstrong and young; she wouldn't have listened anyway.

"A couple days ago, I'd have said no. But spending time in this Cathedral, contemplating my own mortality? Maybe I'm reevaluating things."

"Is that why I'm here: to help with your reevaluation?"

"No. But are you aware that right now, at this very moment, a hostage is standing on the steps of Saint Patrick's?"

"Um . . . I can't see anything from in here."

"Tell her, Eve."

"The hostage is middle-aged—heavy-set, with a medium-build. She has a plain gold wedding band on her finger and a bracelet made of string on her right wrist. It looks like the kind of thing a boy might make in art class for his mom. I think she's Luke's mother, Penelope Miller."

"Correct," Sean said. "And you're here to save her life, Cassidy. Now, Eve, tell Cassidy what happened after Blair confessed to my satisfaction?"

"The previous hostage out front—his name was Ethan Raynor—returned inside. But, Sean, I thought our deal was that once I brought you the witnesses you wanted, you'd let the hostages go."

"Wishful thinking. Your actions have allowed the hostages to *live*."

"You released Penelope Miller's son. You could let Penelope go."

"Let's see how Cassidy does."

"I don't know what you want." The preen was gone. Cassidy was standing there, in a white dress too thin for the winter weather, looking terribly young.

"I want to know: What are you guilty of?"

Cassidy looked down, mute.

"Consider your failings. The things you're sorry for. Where you'd have done something differently."

"Ummm . . ."

"Think! That woman's life is in your hands," Sullivan thundered.

"I was mean to a girl in high school," Cassidy said in a rush. "She was pretty and a good dancer and I was jealous. I made sure none of my friends ever sat with her at lunch or invited her to our parties."

"That's a start," Sullivan jeered. "But I want more. For the woman opposite you to live, I need to know your deepest regret."

Cassidy was silent.

"Or are you going to have to live with the fact that you're responsible for a little boy losing his mother? I wonder if they'll bury her with his art project still wrapped around her wrist?"

"I cheated on my boyfriend by sleeping with my agent," she blurted out.

"You mean your savior at William Morris?" Sullivan sounded almost amused.

"NO. This was before I signed with him. I was new here, and I met this small-time guy with what I thought was a legitimate agency but was really a scam. He promised he could get me a role in a major motion picture. He said Sandra Bullock had already signed on, but I would be perfect for the supporting female lead. He was a liar!" Cassidy's voice wobbled.

"Now we're getting somewhere. So you were a cheat. Did you ever tell your boyfriend?"

"No. But I wrote to the advice column at *Cosmo*, and they said if I loved my boyfriend, I shouldn't hurt him by telling him," Cassidy managed to say. Tears were now rolling down her cheeks.

"Dispensation by *Cosmo*. You've got to love it." Sullivan chuckled. "What else are you guilty of, Cassidy, honey? What are your sins of omission?"

"I guess not going to Church every week with Aunt Dani and Uncle Rob. My mother wanted me to, but I haven't managed it once."

"Why not?"

"Because I like sleeping in, I don't like Church, and I've got nothing in common with Aunt Dani or Uncle Rob."

Sean heaved a disappointed sigh. "All right, Eve. We're done with this one. Let's see Alina Matrowski."

"One question before I do, Sean. Last time we talked, I shared a story with you. Now it's your turn. People reported seeing a cop entering the Cathedral this morning just before seven. Was that cop you?"

"I'm still asking the questions, Eve. And because you asked that one, any chance of Penelope Miller joining her son just went up in smoke."

NEWS NEWS NEWS NEWS NEWS

# HOUR 13

8:07 p.m.

She was there today because her AA leader asked her to be.

We are learning more tonight about Cristina Silva, the very first victim of this hostage crisis still in progress at Saint Patrick's Cathedral, here in the heart of our city. She was a young woman struggling hard to overcome a life shattered by tragedy, which led to her descent into alcoholism. But family members tell us tonight that Cristina had been clean for the past two years. She credited Alcoholics Anonymous with keeping her sober, and apparently her reason for visiting Saint Patrick's this morning was to work on the eleventh step . . .

# Chapter 63

Haddox and Eli decided to divide and conquer, playing to their respective strengths. Haddox focused on cellphone, text messages, and Instagram postings. Eli focused on a teen checking account, a debit card, and certain expenditures on Meaghan Murphy's Visa card. Between the two of them, they swiftly uncovered some important facts about Georgianna Murphy, Sean Sullivan's daughter.

- Georgie was thirteen years old. As of three and a half weeks ago, she no longer wore braces on her teeth.
- Her best friend was Sophie Ames. Six and three-quarters months ago, Sophie and Georgie convinced themselves their future was on the Broadway stage.
- Georgie's teachers were very worried that she was routinely cutting class. Apparently, she and Sophie decided that hanging out in Times Square near the Broadway "action" was a better use of their time than afternoon math class.
- No surprise, her grades were slipping.
- Georgianna had crushes on movie stars, but not real teenage boys.
- She had a five-and-a-half-inch scar on her left knee—the result of a childhood fall.
- Friends and teachers agreed: Georgie was not the type to run away from home.
- Teachers also agreed: Her parents' divorce may have triggered a bout of depression.
- She was last seen at school wearing a red blouse, faded jeans, and a glittery gold scarf.

Eve poked her head into the MRU, catching Haddox's eye. "Anything I should know?"

"Before you die, you ought to see the sunrise on Kauai. Enjoy a steaming cup of beef pho at a night market in Hanoi. And drink a well-poured pint of Guinness."

"Anything *else* I should know?"

"I've just tracked down some information that's going to help you with Captain Sullivan."

Her eyes lit up, and she stepped all the way into the room. "I'm all ears."

Haddox kicked the chair opposite him out from under its desk, indicating that she should sit. "I'd suggest you save what I'm about to tell you for when you really need it. Like when Sullivan figures out Luis Ramos is a no-show."

"Advice noted."

"Sean Sullivan has a thirteen-year-old daughter. Georgie."

"I know." Eve shot him a where-is-this-going? look.

"What you *don't* know is that Georgie is missing. And has been since the middle of the school day yesterday."

"So where is she? Do you know?"

"I can think of two good possibilities. Either Sean Sullivan's got her inside that Cathedral with him—in which case, assuming he bears any measure of love for his own lass, I think his threat to explode the place to smithereens is an idle one."

"I agree. What's the other possibility?"

"That he's got her squirreled away somewhere else to protect her. Either way, maybe you can use her as leverage."

"Nice job. How'd you discover that Georgie was missing?"

"C'mon, luv. Finding information is what I do best."

"I thought you were going to stop calling me that."

"Fits you too well. Now, want to call Eli over? He's got a secret he's dying to tell you."

When Eli finished explaining to Eve how his unofficial search for Georgianna Murphy had collided with the very hostage crisis she was working to end, he mumbled an apology and slunk away with a hang-dog look on his face.

He couldn't go far. The MRU wasn't that big. But he took the farthest chair at the farthest table—as though he couldn't bear being near Eve, now that he had disappointed her.

Haddox pulled the last cigarette from his packet, rolled it between his fingers as he reached for his matches.

Eve didn't talk right away. She looked out the window, watching the snowflakes swirl. The best part of snow was how it covered a multitude of sins. Its white frosting camouflaged the dirt and the dog crap on the sidewalk. And transformed garbage cans into cotton-candy cups. When it covered cars and buildings and scaffolding, it changed city grit into a winter wonderland.

But it couldn't sugarcoat what Haddox and Eli had done.

"Can one of you explain to me why—*exactly* why—you didn't bother telling me this earlier?" she demanded.

"You were busy." Haddox opened his book of matches. *Empty.*

"Of *course* I was busy." Eve felt her jaw tightening. "I've been busy since eight-seventeen this morning—the instant I first got word of this hostage-taking. But apparently *you* weren't busy enough—or you wouldn't have had time to run extracurricular searches."

"Just tryin' to help a friend." Haddox opened the table drawers, one after another. Searching for another book of matches.

"We don't keep matchbooks here, because smoking's not allowed," Eve said coldly. "And Eli is *not* your friend. What we have is a business arrangement—except in this business, people live or die based on our decisions. So when I don't get the information I need to make the right decisions—"

"Sorry, luv," Haddox said. "I mean that." He tossed his useless cigarette into the trash.

"What more can we do?" Eli rejoined them, clutching his own brand of liquid courage: a celery soda.

"Focus on doing your job—which includes helping me do mine."

"Not saying this situation isn't deadly serious—I know it is—but part of my job is improvising. Working off the cuff. No rules or restrictions," Haddox pointed out. A muscle in his jaw clenched. "You want someone to say 'Yes, ma'am' and 'Here you go, miz,' we're the wrong guys for that. All of us."

"You know this is different. I get it: You think that unless you make everything into a game, you won't be creative. Or effective. But understand something else. I brought you back onboard because I wanted people loyal to me. So don't fail me again."

The moment she'd said the words, Eve no longer felt angry.

Just focused.

Because the next hostage was coming out of Saint Patrick's.

On the Cathedral steps, Penelope Miller retreated back through the bronze doors. Just as Sullivan had threatened.

At the exact same moment, another priest—Monsignor Tom DeAngelo, who was meant to have conducted the aborted seven-o'clock morning Mass—exited.

Two hostages again swapped places. Their movements were precisely orchestrated, as if they were connected to a remote-control apparatus under Sullivan's direction.

Once again, Omega Team found itself unable to intervene. Because the hostages remained so close to the building and passed through the doors at the exact same moment, no one had a clear line to take action. And if they did, there was no doubt the hostages would be placed in extreme danger.

If Sullivan was going to move the hostages in and out of the Cathedral like a revolving door, they needed a new plan of action.

Only three witnesses left.

Time was of the essence.

# Chapter 64

The phone was ringing. Alina had to be coaxed to the handset, ordered to talk. She clicked on the line; simultaneously, Haddox projected her image outside next to Atlas.

"Is this Alina Matrowski?" Sean asked.

"I don't know you. What do you want with me?" Her accent was heavier than before. Russian. Brusque.

"By now I think you get the point. I want you to tell me: What are you guilty of?"

"Nothing." Her mouth turned down, which gave her a sullen expression. "I'm not Catholic. I'm not Christian. I'm not even religious."

"But you consider yourself a good person."

"Of course!"

"Then today you must confess—or the good Father will die."

Alina drew a sharp breath. "Who is he?"

"Monsignor DeAngelo, one of the substitutes on staff here at Saint Patrick's. He's counting on you."

Alina narrowed her eyes, unsure of what to say next.

"Tell me what you're guilty of."

"When I was maybe ten, maybe eleven, my friends and I made fun of our music teacher. Her name was Miss Budinsky. We always called her Miss Butthead."

"You can do better than that."

She shook her head too vigorously. Beginning to panic. Hair escaped from her ponytail clip. It made her look less severe.

"What else have you done?"

She shrugged.

"It's really important, Alina. A man's life rests in your hands."

"How am I supposed to know what you want? Who are you to want to know my deepest secrets? I'm nothing to you—and you're nothing to me."

From somewhere in the pitch-black—high above the scaffolding, perhaps even from the roof of Saint Patrick's—a shot ricocheted down.

It didn't strike near Eve.

It was nowhere near Monsignor DeAngelo.

But it struck near enough to Atlas and Alina's image that Eve saw the shudder of fear that seized hold.

"I'll keep talking. I'll do exactly what you say," Alina babbled. "Please don't hurt anybody else."

"What are you guilty of, Alina? What have you failed to do?"

"I stole," she whispered miserably. "I never paid."

"Speak up, Alina. So we all can hear you."

"It was my annual recital. I was going to perform Rachmaninoff, which my friend Yura played, too—except even better than me. I wanted something to feel more confident, and I saw it—this black sequined dress at Saks. The price was . . . I don't remember anymore. But it was nothing my family could afford." She rocked back on her heels.

"Go on, Alina."

"I watched the sales clerk. Another woman came into the department, needing a lot of help. So when she wasn't looking, I snuck the dress into my backpack." She took a shuddering breath. "From there, it was easy. A quick trip to the ladies' room to remove the tags and sensors. Then a big smile at the security guard as I walked out of the store."

"What about later?"

"Later? I felt bad."

"No. Later in life."

"Is what I told you not good enough?" The words were anguished, wrenched from deep inside her.

The answer was a cold silence. Then, "I'm ready for Luis Ramos." And he clicked off the line.

# Chapter 65

The Monsignor stood on the steps of Saint Patrick's, shivering. He wore a simple black cassock with vestments. Gold ones—the color usually worn for celebrating Mass at Christmastime. Lightweight—not nearly substantial enough to protect him from the cutting wind and blowing snow.

*Waiting.*

No witness appeared.

When Sean dialed in, it was Haddox who picked up the phone.

"Hello, mate." He immediately patched Eve in as he answered.

"Who's this? You don't sound like Luis Ramos. And if you are, where's your *sci-fi* hologram?"

"I'm not. The name's Corey Haddox. Unfortunately, Ramos is indisposed at the moment, so I'm prepping Ms. Willis to go next."

Eve had forgotten what a practiced liar Haddox was. His tone was perfect: unconcerned, without a shadow of stress. In fact, the lie came so naturally that even Eve might have believed him, had she not known otherwise. Actually, that was the thing about Haddox—he made you *want* to believe him.

"Where's Ramos?"

"In the toilet. Poor guy ate a bad taco from some food truck in Harlem. Probably wasn't cooked through."

"Let me talk to him."

"Ms. Willis's computer mapping is almost complete. Try her first, and maybe by then Ramos will feel better."

"Wrong answer."

"There's no right or wrong here. Listen, when I talked with Ramos earlier, I met his daughter. She's a cute lass, maybe five or six. Full of questions. And the main one: Why did I have to take her father away? The lass didn't understand, and I'm not sure I do, either. Why are these witnesses so important, Sean?"

Eve could hear it: Sullivan's breathing had altered. Haddox had hit the mark. And without giving away their hand.

A unit of NYPD officers huddled just beyond the MRU, crouching over a laptop. Behind them, a cluster of plainclothes officers watched. The mayor was now on-site; the officers were part of his security detail. Henry Ma was standing to their left, arguing with Monsignor Geve. Two helicopters made wide circles in the air—drawing as close as they dared.

"You still there, Sean? I'm putting Sinya Willis on the line."

Through the secure line connected to her earpiece, Eve listened to Eli confirm the upload. *Signal strength is optimum at twenty-eight decibels. You are a go.*

Sinya's image was illuminated next to Atlas.

*2.7 seconds passed.*

The Monsignor turned and retreated into the bronze door of Saint Patrick's that had opened to receive him.

*1.85 seconds passed.*

A large woman with short-cropped salt-and-pepper hair and a raised flesh-colored scar drawn from her left eye down to her jawline started to emerge from the door. She wore a thick black down coat. She braced her large feet wide apart. It appeared she was wearing men's shoes.

Omega Team leader was watching through his field goggles. The moment the woman entered his line of sight, he issued the launch order.

*NOW!*

# Chapter 66

The hostage had barely cleared the bronze door when she noticed the two-man tandem that was Team Alpha rushing directly at her. It took her one and three-quarters seconds to register what was happening.

"No!" she screeched. "There's a bomb!"

Team Alpha slowed. Behind them, Beta and Theta came to a complete halt.

Two clusters of Feds, in full body armor with raised weapons and shields, continued to creep toward her.

"No!" she repeated. "Do not come closer! I am wired!"

She adopted a defensive stance, planting her feet a shoulder's width apart. Then she raised her left arm out to her side. "Don't you see? I'm wearing explosives. I have a wireless pressure switch."

Eve noted it, between the woman's fingers and the palm of her hand. The other officers and agents observed it, too. The effect was the same as though the hostage had shouted *freeze!*—and stopped both time and action by merely lifting her finger.

Eve stood, stunned. Not surprised that Henry had ordered the attempt to breach the Cathedral. But shocked that he hadn't seen fit to tell her about it.

*What the hell was he thinking?*

She could have told him this sort of attempt would be a disaster.

"If I am interfered with—and my fingers no longer put pressure on this switch—I will die," the hostage shrilled. "Then he will kill the others."

Eve stared at the woman's face. Despite the cold, it was flushed and beaded with sweat—which accentuated the raised scar on her left cheek.

The woman continued talking. "The man who took us hostage is in complete control. If you attempt to interfere with cellphone signals, the detonators are programmed to activate immediately."

Eve moved her hands away from her sides, where the panicked woman could see them. Then she began inching to the right, taking deliberate, measured steps. She needed the woman to acknowledge her—but she didn't want to move in a way that anyone might perceive as threatening.

The woman's head snapped toward Eve.

Eve froze. "I won't come any closer," she promised. "I'm going to stay here. But I need to get a message to him. Tell him I'm sorry. I didn't know about this, and I need to talk with him."

The woman didn't answer.

*Is she even listening?*

"Please ask him to call me," Eve urged. "I want to apologize."

The woman looked straight ahead. Sweat dripped down her face. It ran the length of her scar, almost like tears.

The wind howled and gusted, and a stray plastic cup, accompanied by a rag of newspaper, scuttled down the sidewalk in front of Eve. It created a lopsided pattern in the light snow that was beginning to stick.

Were the woman's lips moving?

An instant later, Eve's phone trilled.

"Want to tell me what's going on, Eve?"

Eve stepped back—toward the MRU, toward Rockefeller Center. In a position where she could be seen, assuming Sean was watching. "I had no advance notice of this, Sean. I'm sorry."

"You're SORRY?" The word exploded from his mouth. "An assault team attempts to breach my Cathedral, right under your nose, and all you can say is SORRY?"

"I'm your negotiator, Sean. I want to talk, to find some peaceful agreement of terms, to see you walk away from this. To keep more people from getting hurt. But we have a lot of people here, from all different agencies, people who are getting impatient. They don't understand what you want. Why you've brought witnesses here. What you have planned."

"They don't have to. They just have to understand that if they don't mind their manners, people will die. And this building will be destroyed. Eve, I picked you for a reason. Get control of the fucking situation."

"That's like telling the prime minister of England that he needs to have better control over Spain. I'm in charge of *my* team, Sean. If outside interference worries you, then let's settle this now. What will it take to make you walk peacefully out of that Cathedral with no further bloodshed?"

"Don't you understand anything yet, Eve? It's far more complicated than that."

"Then explain it. I'm listening."

"Just keep asking questions. Like in that personal story you were telling me."

"Questions are good, but I like answers, too. Why did you choose me for this? I need to know."

"You're becoming tiresome."

"I keep hoping eventually you'll answer me."

"Here's your answer: You bring headlines, Eve."

"Only if I screw up. What's the real reason?"

"Maybe I like your voice. People told me it was low and sexy and sweet all at once. They were right."

"Who told you that?"

"I haven't forgiven you, Eve."

"Enough of this. I thought you didn't have much time." Eve swung away from both the Cathedral and Sean Sullivan, cursed under her breath, and glanced at the MRU. "Are you ready for Sinya Willis?"

The phone link to the MRU rang exactly fifty-three seconds later.

"Hello? Is this Sinya?"

"Mrs. Willis to you. I turned sixty last month. I deserve some respect."

"I'll be the judge of that. And as long as we're talking about names, I expect you to call me *sir.*"

"I'd call you worse names than that for what you've done today, you bastard. You're a murderer!"

"Well, aren't you feisty? But you got it all wrong. We have to talk about what *you've* done. What are you guilty of, *Mrs.* Willis?"

"Nothing. I'm sixty years old and I've got no regrets."

"Don't lie to me. Everyone has some, and you probably more than most."

"I take care of kids, Mr. Sullivan. That means I make bottles. Change diapers. Cook mac and cheese. Read *Goodnight Moon* more times than you can count. I locate lost toys and bandage hurt knees. I wake up exhausted and I fall into bed bone-tired. I stay busy and I don't have time for moral dilemmas."

"And this has been your life for how long? Thirty years?"

"More than. Ever since I came to this country."

"See that woman on the steps in front of you? Unless you can tell me about your past sins, I'm going to detonate the bomb that she's wearing around her waist, under that coat. You'll be fine in your bulletproof trailer over there. But plenty of people on the street will die. Do you want that on your conscience?"

Sinya tugged her yellow cardigan sweater tighter around her. Then she whispered, "You ain't really going to kill her."

"No? My body count isn't high enough yet?"

"I imagine a life I'll never have. I spend hours looking at listings for homes I'll never buy, in cities I'll never live, imagining what it must be like to live on my own, without tantrums and spit-up."

"Doesn't exactly sound like a sin to me. More like a vice. Like how some women can't stop shopping for pairs of shoes. Although I don't picture our Eve here addicted to shoes. She prefers things built for comfort, not style. Isn't that right, Eve?"

"Sometimes when Mr. and Mrs. Abrams are out, I put the kids to bed early. Much earlier than their normal bedtime. And I escape online."

"You're not confessing anything here."

"The point is that I let them scream. The little one had a nightmare. Must've cried for twenty minutes before I went to him." She set her jaw and crossed her arms. There was no real regret in her demeanor. Just a tough exterior shell that she would protect at all costs, Eve suddenly realized.

"You're really disappointing me, Sinya."

"I regret plenty. It's just none of your business."

"The woman will die—in fifteen seconds—if you don't confess. Counting now: fifteen . . . fourteen . . . thirteen . . . twelve . . ."

Tears were running down her cheeks.

". . . eleven . . . ten . . . nine . . ."

"Stop!" She swiped at her eyes with a balled fist. "Nobody's dying on my account."

Sean stopped his countdown. He waited.

A lot was happening in just those few seconds. Teams of officers in pairs were staking out positions. NYPD. FBI. Interagency cooperation at work. Their radios were crackling. A new plan was being exercised. Eve took it as a sign: Henry's patience—or perhaps it was the mayor's—had nearly run out. Eve was on the verge of losing control. Her heart thudded into her chest.

"Tell me, Sinya. Tell me who's died because of you." His voice was low. Seductive. Trying to convey: *I'll be your confessor. I'll understand.*

"It happened back in Jamaica, before I came here. I was young. Had no experience with children, really—except for my own brothers, sisters, and cousins. But I needed a job—and Mrs. Palmer had three kids: The twins who were four years old and a six-month-old." She looked around hesitantly to see who was listening. There was fear and guilt in her face; tears continued running down her cheeks.

"Go on, Sinya."

"Not too long after I started with the family, Mr. and Mrs. Palmer had a business dinner out. I put the twins in the bathtub, and the baby was in his crib. Suddenly, he started screaming at the top of his lungs. Not his usual *I want out* or *Change me* or *Feed me*. No, he was yelling like something was seriously wrong."

Her tears were streaming, her nose started to run. She ignored it. "I only left the twins in the tub for a few minutes. I checked on the baby. He was fine. He'd rolled over onto his stomach for the very first time and it scared him. I comforted him and put him to bed on his back. Then I returned to the bathroom and the twins." Now her voice was a croak. "The girl was fine. But her brother? Just resting there—under the water."

"Did the child live?" Sean asked.

She shook her head and turned away. She didn't bother wiping her eyes anymore. "Once he was taken to the hospital, I ran. And I kept running. Found a boat to Cuba and took it. I never looked back. I never said a word."

There was silence. But by the time Sinya Willis lifted her head and looked around, the EMS workers were no longer watching. The NYPD officers were back on their phones.

The truth was: They'd seen worse. They'd heard worse. And compared to what they were facing today inside the Cathedral, this was old news—and they just didn't care.

The woman on the steps spoke one last time. "I am going to return inside the Cathedral. You will not interfere with me. You will not interfere with the next hostage who comes out. If you do, we will all die."

But before she turned, she raised her face to the wintry sky, breathing in the light falling snow, as if she wanted to enjoy this final moment of freedom. To savor it completely—while she could.

# Chapter 67

Deep in the tunnels surrounding Saint Patrick's Cathedral, Frank García kept moving.

It wasn't by choice. It was an imperative. If he stopped, even for a second, his hyper-senses would take over. Instinct would rule over all rational thought.

The underground passageway was proving interminable. He half regretted having hung up on Mace. Nothing Tony had said indicated the secret passage was this long. He guessed it was all a matter of perspective.

He already tasted the smoke. It burned his eyes and his lungs. Telling himself it was all in his head—just a distant memory better off forgotten—didn't stop him from choking on it.

The acoustics down here were unsettling. The sound of his boots reverberated back to him in odd echoes. His shoulders scraped the ceiling. His brain scrambled for a strategy to defeat the panic rushing at him.

For no apparent reason, one of his former commanding officers came to mind. Burrows had been a man with a full head of gray hair kept in a tight buzz cut. He was stocky, medium height, and his accent was pure Texas. He'd been to West Point, where he'd become thoroughly disillusioned with bad leadership and reductive thinking. He was famous for breaking their every mission down into his one mantra—KISS. *Keep It Simple, Stupid.*

García reminded himself of that now. What he was doing really wasn't that hard.

*Follow the tunnel to the Cathedral.*

*Get inside.*

*Avoid the booby-traps.*

*Neutralize the Hostage Taker.*

*KISS.*

Simple enough for a guy like him. Couldn't be more than another two hundred, three hundred feet.

*Is it my imagination, or is this passageway actually growing larger?* He still smelled and tasted the smoke that triggered his panic attacks, but he also recognized the taste of fresh air.

*In. Out.* He steadied his breathing.

Until the moment he came not upon a door. But an entire room. A chapel of sorts.

Smaller. Much simpler, with no ornate stonework or decorations. Polished stone. Deep red and royal-blue tapestries. A small altar with a dozen candles on it—unlit.

Big enough that a person six feet tall would be comfortable standing in it. At five-foot-ten, García actually had room to breathe. Which he did—greedily. And relished the fact that he tasted air that was cool, damp, and without a hint of smoke.

Probably not religious—but it felt holy to him, so he crossed himself all the same.

What had Tony told him? That many of the stonemasons involved in building Saint Patrick's had also been Freemasons. And the Freemasons were obsessed with secrecy. Noted for ciphers, communicating with invisible ink—and building unbelievable tunnel systems underground, complete with hidden rooms, to ensure members would be protected from the outside world.

García lifted his face up toward the ceiling—embraced the sensation of air and space—and smiled.

# Chapter 68

Another hostage emerged onto the steps of Saint Patrick's: a woman with clipped dark hair. Asian—probably Japanese. And young—early twenties at the latest. She wore a black T-shirt and jeans. No coat. And a waist pack with wires poking out at odd angles.

*A message,* Eve decided.

This hostage carried no detonator, and Eve instantly understood why: This woman was a bundle of nerves, swaying and trembling. Unable to exercise any measure of control.

The woman said nothing.

There was no reason to. Her appearance said it all.

Eve's handset was rigged to take Sean's call directly. She stood next to Atlas, in the same area where the witnesses had previously appeared.

Sean didn't bother with hello. He asked, "Where's Luis Ramos? Don't tell me he's still puking his guts out?"

"He's very ill," Eve replied. "You've spoken with the other four. Upset them. Humiliated them. Let's move on to whatever's next."

"What's next is the fact that none of them has truly confessed their sins. So I want to see them again—this time, together."

"You've done enough today, Sean."

"I require Ramos."

"He's not able."

"Wrong answer."

"Enough with the witnesses. What do you *really* want?"

"To talk with Ramos." Sean's breathing was coming faster. His voice was pitched higher.

"Why?"

"What kind of trick are you trying to pull on me, Agent? Just put the damn witness on the line."

"Seems to me that you're looking for something from people who'll never give it to you. They don't understand—so they can't begin to help you."

"Put Ramos on the phone. ASAP."

Haddox's voice came into Eve's ear: *We have a Hispanic agent here with acting experience from college. He's ready to go.*

"Calm down, Sean; there's no need to yell."

"Don't fuck with me, Eve. Put Ramos on the line or the hostage dies."

Eve had exhausted all attempts to reason with him. Maybe it was time to figure out what was the truth. Whether Sean Sullivan really knew the witnesses he claimed to want—or if they were only here because they represented something to him.

"I'll get him. Just give me a moment."

"Put Ramos on RIGHT NOW, or I'll blow this hostage into so many pieces you'll still be digging her out of Fifth Avenue come Easter."

"Go ahead," she directed Haddox. Then she stepped to the right, and the projected image appeared next to her. Life-size, towering five inches above her. Dark hair. Sturdy build. The hint of a five-o'clock shadow on his chin. Wearing a red-checkered shirt and dark jeans. She supposed he could pass for a day laborer. She wished he looked a bit more weather-worn. "Patch him in."

"Are you there, Luis?" she asked after a moment.

*"Sí."*

"Do you feel any better?" It wasn't a question. It was a reminder to the Ramos substitute of his role.

*"Sí."*

"Luis Ramos?" Sean interjected.

*"Sí."*

"Speak English."

"What do you want?"

"I want you to confess your sins."

"I'm an illegal. To your government, it's a sin—and for that, they wish to deport me."

Eve heard a sound that might have been the grinding of teeth. "What are you guilty of, Luis?"

"Nothin'."

"Where were you working last July?"

"Midtown. Downtown. Harlem. Wherever I got work."

"I don't think so." Sean said it coldly. "Tell me the last time you sent money home."

"Friday before Thanksgiving."

Sean exploded. "Wrong answer. Where the fuck is the real Luis Ramos? You're outta time."

"This is Luis Ramos," Eve intervened calmly. "But there are plenty of men named Luis Ramos in this city. Did you mean a different Ramos?"

"YOU THINK I'M SOME STUPID IDIOT?"

"Calm down, Sean. What's the problem?"

"The problem is that you've got some fucking Fed pretending to be Luis Ramos."

"Why do you think that?"

"Because of the jeans. The shoes. You thought I wouldn't notice? Even after I told you the story of the homeless man?"

"Notice what?"

"The real Luis Ramos doesn't wear brand-new denims. He wears old jeans, broken in, washed a thousand times by the man who eventually got tired of them and dumped them in a Goodwill box. And look at those shoes. The real Ramos wears beat-up sneakers."

"I can ask my agent. It's possible we cleaned him up for today," Eve said.

The hostage on the steps began counting down. *Sixty. Fifty-nine. Fifty-eight. Fifty-seven.* Her face was blank with terror.

"Okay. Stop. He refused to come," Eve said, telling him the truth starkly. She explained how Luis had run away. How he had been scared, given his immigration problems. Especially given his wife and young daughter. "You of all people should understand that. You have a daughter, too."

*Forty-three. Forty-two. Forty-one.*

"You've made a few mistakes, Eve." His tone was cold, unyielding.

"Is your daughter with you inside, Sean? Or have you hidden Georgianna somewhere else?"

But he was breathing faster now. "First the assault team. Then the missing witness. Mistakes always have consequences."

*Thirty-two. Thirty-one.*

"No," she said firmly. "No, Sean. Mistakes happen, but then we fix them. There's nothing that's happened today—nothing you've done—that can't be made better."

*Twenty-five. Twenty-four. Twenty-three.*

"There's no way out. I have no choice—none at all." He was losing his composure.

*Fifteen. Fourteen.*

"Talk to me, Sean. Do it for Georgie. How do we fix this situation? What will it take for you to give up and come out? To let those people go?"

*Nine.*

"I'm not sure we ever—"

There was a blinding flash of light. Then a rumble of sound.

Eve heard nothing but an eerie quiet.

It was the sound of the world closing in all around her.

# Chapter 69

*I look at the carnage below . . . and I remember.*

*They called for reinforcements after Stacy was taken. Of course I joined them—although the commanding officer mumbled something about conflict of interest and I had to promise to keep my head on straight.*

*Five hours and seventeen minutes later we received a report. A body had been found.*

*They were pretty sure it was an American. If not a soldier, then someone who worked for the U.S. Army.*

*One of the things I had first noticed in Afghanistan was how the locals didn't wear socks. Villagers wore sandals. Afghan soldiers wore unlaced boots without them. That's how everyone knew: This victim was not an Afghan. There were remnants of wool, stuck between each toe, wool that used to be socks.*

*The victim had been shot.*

*Then burnt.*

*Then driven through the city.*

*Then hacked to pieces by both adults and children in front of a cheering crowd before—finally—being hung from a bridge in a burlap sack.*

*After the autopsy results finally came through, the corpsmen—our medical personnel—assured me that Stacy had not suffered for long. That the torture had come well after the gunshot.*

*I knew they said this to everybody who lost a loved one.*

*I hoped—just this once—they weren't lying.*

. . .

Three weeks later, *I was helping to clear the road of IEDs before a unit made up of a group of young twentysomething Marines passed through. The same guys Stacy had assisted.*

*Things happen in war zones. Sometimes in the chaos, we have friendly fire. Sometimes in our state of exhaustion, we miss spotting an IED. Tricky little buggers can be hard to find, after all.*

*Oops! My bad.*

*The way I saw it, if Stacy didn't get to go home safe, then why should they?*

*Why should any of us?*

*There's no safety or security left.*

*Not in our homes.*

*Not in our workplaces or cities.*

*Not even in this house of God.*

# Chapter 70

Aiko Tanaka was no more. She was the trace of blood that smeared a swath on the protective plastic that surrounded the perimeter. She was a fragment that rested against Saint Elizabeth Seton on the lower corner of the bronze door. She was no longer bone and flesh, but evidence in a crime scene.

Eve tried to take a step forward, but her knees buckled and she almost fell. Cops and Feds swarmed around her. A forensics team in full body armor swept in to secure the scene.

Eve's body shook. Her head pounded. She was barely conscious of Haddox putting his arm around her, turning her away from the chaos on the steps, guiding her back to the MRU. All the while saying words she could not hear, but found to be comforting all the same.

When García felt he had enough air, he forced himself to leave the room—the secret chamber where he'd been able to stand and breathe freely—and reenter the tight, narrow passage. Crouched low again, he felt his back begin to throb.

This time, he didn't have to go far. He came to a wall.

It was rough stone. He felt its jagged surface with his fingertips. No apparent opening.

García studied it, looking for something out of the ordinary. A recessed area. A stone that protruded slightly more than the rest. A break in the pattern of the way stones were laid. Anything that didn't quite belong.

He searched for four minutes and twenty-six seconds. It felt like forever.

Then he decided to put on the special glasses he had rejected earlier. Just to see if they changed his perspective.

They immediately sharpened his vision. Made brighter what had before been shadowed in darkness. He revisited the wall again, this time with the aid of technology. Slowly, so as not to miss anything.

That was when he found it—though it was so caked in sediment and dirt that he almost missed it. A thick steel-plate door in the shape of a circle with a handle. It looked just like the entrance to an old-fashioned bank vault.

Except luckily there was no lock.

García dug in his heels as he pulled it open. It was made of concrete behind the steel, about three feet thick. He grunted as he used all of his strength, straining his already tight back. It was one of the heaviest objects he'd handled in months. Its hinges groaned when it finally swung open.

García peered into the opening. He saw nothing but darkness, and for an instant he panicked. Had he just encountered another tunnel? For all he knew, there was a whole maze of them.

Then he focused his flashlight beam.

It was a tiny room, the size of a closet. This time with a small black iron door in the shape of a square. It was about five feet high and four feet wide.

García unhooked its rusty latch and pried it open.

He got down on his knees. Eased his head carefully through the opening. And looked straight up into the dimly lit statue of Saint Andrew atop one of the fifteen altars that lined the periphery of Saint Patrick's Cathedral.

He had never seen a more beautiful sight.

NEWS NEWS NEWS NEWS NEWS

PART FIVE

# HOUR 14

9:03 p.m.

More details are emerging about some of the individuals believed to be held, even now, inside Saint Patrick's Cathedral. One of them is Monsignor Thomas DeAngelo, forty-seven years old, of Philadelphia, Pennsylvania.

Monsignor DeAngelo comes to Saint Patrick's every Christmas to help handle the extra confession load brought by holiday visitors. This year he is also substituting for the Cardinal and his staff, who have been away on a humanitarian mission, stopping by the Vatican before continuing on to Middle Eastern refugee camps.

According to his parishioners at Saint Mary's, Monsignor DeAngelo is a beloved leader. His large following have him in their prayers tonight. He has fought for equality, weathering rebukes from church leaders who objected to his advocacy for gay and lesbian rights—as well as his willingness to allow unordained guests, mostly women, to speak during Mass.

# Chapter 71

García hesitated before entering the sanctuary. It was only natural: He knew the Cathedral was wired to the hilt. Filled with booby-traps designed to reduce the place to embers, ash, and stone ruins in the event of a breach. And García hadn't survived the IEDs of Fallujah, making it home in one piece, only to die in the concrete jungle of Manhattan. At least the odds were low that the Hostage Taker knew about this particular access point.

He checked his belt, making sure his favorite Randall #1 knife was within easy reach.

He listened. He heard no footsteps. No movement. In fact, there was no sound at all except for the creaking of the floor-to-ceiling scaffolding that dominated the center of the Cathedral.

He smelled only the faint scent of candles and the lingering perfume of incense.

So he scooted into the building, bent over so as to fit through the door's three-foot width. His knee joint cracked; the sound dully echoed around the stone walls and granite pillars. He cursed the noise—but mainly was annoyed at how, despite the fact that his body was a prime fighting machine, sometimes it still betrayed its age.

He swiveled, his eyes focusing first on the aisle to his left, then on the Ambulatory to his right. All was dark inside the massive Cathedral. No candles. The chandeliers were unlit.

He looked up. He was under a stained-glass window, which was shrouded by tarps and scaffolding. He crossed himself.

All clear.

"I'm in," he whispered into his headset.

He didn't wait for a reply. He moved into the open. And prayed for the best.

In a low crouch, he inched toward the Ambulatory, closing the access door behind him with a *thud* that was louder than he wanted. The noise echoed through the vast cavern created by soaring Gothic arches, though they eventually swallowed the sound. Iron on the inside, the door was sealed with marble on the outside. It disappeared into the wall that was part of the Altar of Saint Andrew.

Normally his path would be lit with votive candles, but tonight he was grateful for the dark. Some unseen source from above bathed the marble walls with just enough light to cast an otherworldly glow. García was superstitious enough to believe it was a miracle of the Holy Spirit.

Keeping low to the ground and close to the wall, García made his way around the first bend of the Ambulatory.

He passed the altar of Saint Teresa.

Crouched past the Archbishop's Sacristy.

García liked peace and quiet—but this was too quiet. He saw no hostages. He saw no Hostage Taker. The church had the same desperate feel he remembered from patrols in Fallujah—usually right before all hell broke loose and the mission turned to shit.

To his left was the High Altar and Baldachin—the bronze canopied focal point of the Cathedral. This was the point where he knew he was most exposed, so he crept swiftly past it. Past Saint Elizabeth's Altar. Toward his destination, immediately behind the High Altar.

Not the Lady Chapel—the small area dedicated to the Virgin Mary.

But the entrance to the Crypt.

Before he descended the marble stairway that would take him there, he took one final glance down the long nave of the Cathedral. He could see all the way to the great choir loft and pipe organ, with its thousands of pipes soaring to the Rose Window above it.

No hostages were visible. That didn't mean they weren't hidden among the pews, altars, nooks, and crannies of this great Cathedral.

It was tempting to check.

It was smarter to stick to his original plan. He didn't want to save one life, only to jeopardize the larger goal.

So García stayed low to the floor and far to the right and went down the stairs behind the High Altar and Baldachin.

He descended one level and came to a landing with a green, glass-paneled door. It was the burial Crypt—a marble room where the Cathedral's former Archbishops slept for eternity. He left it for now, continuing down to the foot of the stairway, beneath the foundations of the two rear support piers of the Cathedral.

*The Sacristy.*

García had a near-photographic memory for spatial organization. He had only to see a map or a blueprint once to remember its details. So when he saw the two open archways at the rear of the Sacristy, he knew exactly what they were.

The one on his left led to the Rectory. The one on his right led to the Cardinal's Residence.

Two paths in and out.

He went to the left—his default move when all else was equal.

He had his Maglite in his left hand, his knife in his right. Both at the ready. He made his way through the dark void.

Until he found a door—rigged up exactly as he had expected. He studied it with a determined stare—and hoped he remembered how to be creative about disarming it.

The FBI's definition of a hostage-taking is quite simple: Agents are instructed to treat every crisis as a potential homicide.

No matter that it was defeatist.

It was also highly accurate.

Losing another hostage when they couldn't produce the real Luis Ramos didn't lessen Eve's guilt. It steeled her resolve.

And García's message encouraged her. She had a man on the inside. Arguably, her best man: a finely tuned fighting machine.

The moment she received word, she found Henry Ma. The director was still attempting to placate Monsignor Geve—who feared he saw damage to the figure of Elizabeth Seton on the Cathedral's central bronze doors—but wasn't being permitted to inspect it. "I cannot allow you anywhere near an active crime scene," Henry was saying.

She pulled Henry just out of the Monsignor's earshot.

"I need you to stand down," she explained. "Table any and all assault plans until you hear from me again."

"Sorry, Eve," Henry responded in a tone that suggested he wasn't. "Your negotiations have broken down—and time is of the ess—"

She didn't let him finish. "I'm three steps ahead of you. I've got García inside. I need all tactical divisions to stand down until I know exactly what is needed. If you do another end run, the blood and destruction will be on your hands."

She left before he could reply.

Just as the Hostage Taker had demanded, she was back in charge.

# Chapter 72

It was after nine o'clock. The Hostage Taker's timetable was accelerating—and Eve still had no clue as to the end game.

Behind her, she heard the crack of a can of soda opening and smelled the odor of a fresh pizza delivery. Fortification for agents working around the clock. She hadn't eaten in hours. She didn't even turn around. There was no food or sustenance that could distract her from the loss of another hostage.

She focused on her computer screen, staring at the preliminary ID for the latest victim. Aiko Tanaka, age twenty-four. Her Japanese American family lived in Nashua, New Hampshire. A grad student in art history at New York University, which apparently also explained her presence in Saint Patrick's Cathedral first thing that morning. According to her roommate, Aiko had a final paper due—and its topic had been the fusion of the modern into classical Gothic design.

Haddox took the seat beside Eve. He'd just poured two cups of coffee. He pushed one toward Eve. "I notice you take it black now."

"People's tastes change." She sipped the coffee. It was so hot she almost spit it out.

Aiko Tanaka had a sealed juvenile record in her background. It would be invisible to any civilian looking. But no background information was ever hidden from the federal government.

"I remember the first time I met you outside FBI headquarters. You took two sugars. When did you start liking it bitter?"

"The day I was out of sugar—and too busy to get any. Turned out I didn't need it."

"An unnecessary complication?"

"Something like that." She cast him a sideways glance. "Are we still talking about coffee?"

He took a sip from his own cup. "Were we ever?"

"The latest victim had a juvie record. Within the federal computer system, we can access it legitimately. But maybe you can get there faster than me?" She slid the keyboard toward him.

He glanced at the screen to orient himself. Then his fingers sped across the keyboard. If anything, moving faster than his usual 120 words per minute. "Are you okay?"

"Why wouldn't I be?" she bristled.

"Terrible things have happened today. Shootings. Bombs. Lives lost. It's enough to give anyone nightmares."

"I don't have nightmares. I have memories."

"Memories are good. Nice little nostalgic details that stay in the back of your mind until you *want* them around."

"What are you saying, Haddox?"

"I'm saying that every time a gun fires or a bomb explodes, you see him."

"So what if I do?"

"I know you miss Zev. It's normal to remember the dead. Not to see them walking among us."

"You make it sound like I've gone crazy."

"No more crazy than the rest of us." He slid the keyboard back to her. "There's your file."

She tilted the computer screen upward. "Let's see . . . high school senior. Age seventeen. Driving home from a football game with her boyfriend. Car drifted into the guardrail after crossing two lanes. It rolled over. The boyfriend died. Tanaka spent six days in the hospital and was released. Had a few drinks. Perhaps one too many. Fell asleep at the wheel—and was charged with *motor vehicle homicide by reckless operation.*"

"So three hostages dead," Haddox began. "Three hostages with arrest records—and major moral lapses in their pasts. Almost as if he's administering his own form of justice."

"Don't forget about Sergeant Martinez, the NYPD negotiator who preceded me."

"With no brushes with the law that we are aware of. No morality issues."

"Martinez didn't do as he asked. Neither did the SWAT agents."

"So has he taken the Cathedral to play God? Dispensing judgment to those who've sinned?"

"In front of witnesses he's—" Eve stopped.

"Eve?"

She didn't reply.

"What?"

"We searched Sean Sullivan's background thoroughly, right?"

"'Course."

"His testimony in John Timothy Nielsen's trial?"

"With a fine-tooth comb."

"His police and military service? Including all his arrest records?"

"Definitely."

"Would the search you ran pick up any witnesses? Maybe as a victim of a crime? Or, literally, as a witness to one?"

"If they produced a formal witness statement, then sure."

"And if they didn't—or appeared less formally?"

"I see where you're going. I can try changing the search parameters. It might be faster just to ask them."

"Start with Cassidy," Eve suggested. "And Haddox—ask carefully."

# Chapter 73

Eli had ignored three phone calls and seven texts from John. He didn't want to lie—and he certainly couldn't compromise what was now an extremely sensitive federal case. As much as it pained him, that meant he couldn't talk now. Not with Georgianna Murphy still unaccounted for.

They had found her phone. It was live again and easily traced to Allie Horne, an upperclass student at Georgie's school. Allie claimed she had found it near Georgie's locker the day before yesterday. Shortly after lunch. Right around the time Georgie had vanished. Allie planned to give it to the school secretary to put in the lost and found. She swore she just hadn't gotten around to it yet.

"Did you know who the phone belonged to?" Eli had asked.

"Yeah," she admitted sheepishly. "I don't know Georgie—she's two grades below me—but her name was all over it."

"Was there anything else near the phone when you found it?"

"Some papers. No name on them, though. Could've been anybody's." In the background, Eli had heard a Christmas carol and Allie's mother calling her to finish up her homework.

"One more question: Did you see *Kinky Boots* on Broadway last night?"

"Wow. I'm not even going to ask how you figured that out. My dad took me. It was a birthday present."

"Okay. Follow my instructions carefully, Allie. A federal agent is going to swing by to pick the phone up. Don't touch it anymore. Not to dial, text, or anything else. You're in enough trouble right now.

Don't dig a deeper hole," Eli choked the words out. All the saliva in his mouth had turned to dust. He still didn't know whether Georgie was in the Cathedral or not.

*How old is she?* he'd asked John.

*Thirteen.*

*That's old enough to find her way home, isn't it?*

*If you think that, you don't know the first thing about Georgie,* John had warned.

That was the last time they had spoken. And in the silence, Eli missed him.

Mace looked at the blueprints, trying to make sense of where he was headed. They showed his current location—the five-story Rectory on Madison Avenue—behind the Cathedral and separated from it by terraces and gardens. Next door to him was the Cardinal's Residence.

Both buildings were connected to the Cathedral by underground passages leading to the Sacristy and then the Crypt. But these corridors were not marked on the map.

All office staff—who used the underground corridors regularly—had been evacuated. Mace had spoken to a longtime secretary who'd given him confusing directions. Basically, he'd have to go down the Rectory stairs to an elevator, which would then take him all the way to the basement. From there, he'd go down another short staircase and enter a passageway. Follow that, and he'd eventually reach the marble Sacristy. The entrance to the Cathedral. Sealed off and wired for detonation since the crisis began.

The only way through would be from the inside. And that's where García came in. Meanwhile, those agents and officers who would provide tactical support—a mix of FBI, NYPD, and Homeland Security—were beginning to gather in both residences.

Setting up the staging area.

Checking their equipment: Weapons. Communications. Cameras. Location systems. Explosives containment lockers.

Watching them, Mace decided he wasn't going to wait around any longer. García had to have made it to the Sacristy by now. Maybe all that marble and concrete was interfering with their communications. Military technology notwithstanding.

He wasn't worried about the booby-traps. He knew about weapons and explosives. Nothing was going to take him by surprise and blow him to Kingdom Come.

# Chapter 74

*I came home a month after Stacy was killed. I'd been given medical leave—which was what they called it when you suffered psychological trauma, but not so bad that you couldn't go back to work in a few weeks.*

*That was fine with me.*

*I am never one to stay home sick. Excuses are for the weak.*

*Eventually, I figured out how to make it through the day without blaming myself for Stacy's murder. But Muna blamed me enough for both of us. I hadn't been good enough for Stacy before our wedding. I hadn't protected Stacy overseas. I was a failure, through and through.*

*I lasted seventeen days in the same house with my mother-in-law. The same house Stacy and I had once shared. I couldn't live with the bitch.*

*I wasn't like Stacy, who had been able to shrug off every slight and insult the world offered.*

*Still, I knew Stacy would want Muna taken care of.*

*So once a week, I bring her groceries.*

*I pick up and refill her medications.*

*I make sure she has clothes to wear.*

*I'm still terrible at ignoring her insults. But now I close the door to the basement, where I keep her breathing in a five-foot-square cell. And I take satisfaction in the thought: She probably wishes she were dead.*

*Shortly around the same time, I developed blue car syndrome. You know how once you buy a blue car, suddenly you notice blue cars everywhere? After Stacy was murdered, I saw the indifference and apathy all around me.*

*It had probably been there before.*

*Except now—my eyes are open.*

# Chapter 75

García had never officially worked as a sapper, but that didn't matter. Anyone who spent more than a single tour of duty in the Middle East learned how to deal with an IED. Even if the soldier in question wasn't part of the Explosive Ordnance Disposal Unit.

You needed just two skills.

The first was flexibility—for the simple reason that IEDs were by definition *improvised*. Created by different minds and taking all kinds of different forms. Sure, most of them were buried in the roads where convoys of troops traveled. But García had seen them in cars and radios and cellphones. Some were strapped to suicide bombers themselves.

Some had dangerous chemicals inside. Some were hidden in children's toys. It helped to be able to think creatively about all the possible ways the bad guys wanted you dead.

The second skill was the use of all the senses. Sure, robots or water cannons were great if you were in the right circumstances—a nonpopulated area where you didn't care if the device blew up. But where prudence was required, nothing beat the five senses. Sight—to identify what you were dealing with. Smell—to determine whether chemicals were involved. Taste—to identify the type of chemical. Hearing—to make sure one of the motherfuckers wasn't going to come up from behind and shoot. And finally, a soft touch—for disabling the detonator.

García had both these skill sets in spades.

He also had a healthy sense of perspective. People had been defusing bombs for years, since well before World War I. Before there were robots or bomb suits or explosive lockers. Sure, it was better not to do it manually. But there was nothing magical about it. You just needed a method and a clear head.

He stared at the door. On the other side was Mace. He took a soft breath. Paused for a moment to appreciate the challenge he was going to tackle.

And froze.

His eyes had followed the wire.

It led to a spot about seven feet from the door. There, almost obscured in the dark void, García saw the hostage.

He or she was bound in a chair: hands and feet tied, a bandana over her eyes, explosives around her waist, a switch gripped between her fingers and the palm of her right hand. There was a wire leading to the door García needed to disarm.

As if he needed even higher stakes.

There was also something else.

It was just ahead and above him. A small device mounted above the hostage, pointing downward. Every 3.5 seconds, it emitted a blue electronic visual signal.

*A security camera.*

Part of the Cathedral's system—which he *thought* had been disabled? Or a device planted by the Hostage Taker?

He had no idea. But surely Haddox could figure it out.

García stepped back into the shadows.

And since he didn't want the hostage or the camera to hear him speaking, he typed a message into his phone.

# Chapter 76

García's headset vibrated and suddenly Haddox's voice was in his ear. "Just listen, don't talk. I've confirmed that the camera in the Rectory corridor is *not* part of the Cathedral's security system. That means the Hostage Taker installed it—and while I have the capability to disable it by taking down all data service in the vicinity, Eve and I are concerned that could trigger a chain reaction detonating the explosives. At a minimum, it would alert the Hostage Taker to the intrusion. But Eve thinks she can distract Sullivan. Make him look outside. Long enough for you to disarm the door. Free the hostage. Let Mace inside. Then, together, you need to track down and neutralize this bastard."

"What if he checks his camera? What if there's another asshole, whose job is to watch the video? The hostage will blow," García whispered.

"No risk, no reward, right? Guess you'd better move fast once I give the all-clear."

Eli sat across from Cassidy Jones, feeling inadequate for the task at hand. It was true that he had a great eye for details. He could find the patterns that told hidden stories. But he did that by analyzing data, not talking with people. Especially not women. Even if the woman in question was a ringer for his long-ago idol, Marilyn.

He'd tried to break the ice by telling her that. She hadn't appreciated the comparison.

Cassidy drummed her fingers against her knee. Eli felt her stress, her burning desire to get the hell out of there.

No, he definitely wasn't a people person.

But Haddox—who'd originally planned to handle this conversation—had been called to help García. It was all up to him.

"So we've confirmed that you have no arrest record," he told her. "You've never served as a witness in a trial. You've had no dealings that you remember with the police. But I need to ask: Have you ever witnessed a crime—even if it didn't lead to making a formal report?"

"I used to witness Art Dexter steal candy from Mr. Lloyd's shop when we were in middle school. I never told on him—and when Mr. Lloyd went out of business later, I felt really bad. I'm sure the penny candies Art took would've made no difference, but still . . ."

"That was in Atlanta, right?" Eli made the notation in her file. "What about since you came to New York?"

She sat up straighter. "Just a couple Fridays ago, I reported something weird at the movie theater. I was out with a group of my friends, and one of them—Alexis—always has to sit in the center seat. I got stuck at the end of the row, next to a single empty aisle seat. I fought with Alexis about it and asked her to just move over one. Since it was a popular movie, I didn't want some weirdo coming to sit next to me."

"Yeah, I can see that." Except Eli was thinking about all the times he'd gone to the movies alone. And *he'd* been the weirdo in the lone aisle seat.

"What happened was worse. A guy came by and asked if the seat was taken. I said no, and he dropped his gym bag in the seat. Then he left. I assumed he went to get popcorn or use the bathroom or check if there was a better seat elsewhere."

"Then what happened?"

"He never came back. We watched the ads and then the previews, and when the movie started, I poked the bag. There was something hard inside. So we went to security and reported it. I don't know what happened after."

"Did you finish the movie?"

"Only after security said it was safe."

"So there wasn't an actual crime?"

Cassidy studied him with disappointed eyes. "Not officially."

"Sure," Eli said. He highlighted the notes he'd just taken. Pressed *delete.*

"If there'd been a weapon in that bag, I assume they'd have evacuated the whole building. It was still *weird.*"

*This was going nowhere fast.*

"Anything else since you've been in New York?"

She furrowed her brow. "Let me think a minute."

Inside the holding unit, there came a sound of a chair falling over and cans and silverware tumbling to the ground. The witnesses were arguing among themselves, with Blair raging between the desks. Alina Matrowski stepped in front of him, stabbing her finger in his direction. "It's fine if you want to risk your life, but I'll be damned if you risk mine."

Blair responded with a chilly stare. "You saw how that protective barrier worked. Agent Rossi was standing there, and she was fine. Seems to me there's not much risk, but a huge payoff."

"You don't know that. I won't risk an injury. My hands—my fingers—are my livelihood," Alina spat.

"As are my looks," Cassidy piped up. "I don't want to risk it."

"Don't you want to go home?" Sinya Willis fixed her with an icy stare. "I say we all calm down and do what needs to be done."

"And what needs to be done, exactly?" Cassidy asked. She righted the toppled chair. Picked up a Coke can and tossed it into the garbage.

"We need to end this thing." Sinya crossed her arms. "They're saying the Hostage Taker wants to ask us something when we're *together.*"

At the opposite end of the room, Eve and Haddox were discussing strategy.

Haddox seemed amused by the clash of personalities. "They have a point. Switch up the game and we might wrap things up." He made it sound optimistic and perfectly logical, all at once.

"We'll continue to use video feed," Eve said. "Just like before."

"We need to distract him *now.* Physical bodies outside would help do that."

"They're my responsibility."

"So are Mace and García."

"You've already given me my backup plan: his daughter."

"Whom you know nothin' about."

"I'll use her to get under his skin."

"You don't even know: She may be in there, right beside him."

"And if she is, I'll figure it out—just from the way he handles himself talking about her."

"That's just brilliant." Haddox shook his head. "A man's daughter doesn't strike me as the sort of thing you bluff about."

"I have to distract him. Figure out what he *wants* to talk about right now—whether that's witnesses or hostages or priests or his daughter. What do *you* think will grab his attention?"

Haddox pulled a new pack of Marlboros out of his shirt pocket. He leaned against the table with a NO SMOKING sign above it. Pulled out a smoke and rolled it between his fingers. "I think I have the perfect idea. Just about foolproof."

Haddox settled in front of the computer screen; Eve took the chair next to him. He knew exactly what needed to be done. That didn't mean he couldn't also have some fun. He found the site, flexed his hands together, and then let his fingers fly.

He needed something original. Because what's never been seen before has the greatest power to shock.

So he bypassed all the traditional sites.

His search engine of choice was ICREACH. This was the NSA's baby, Big Brother crossed with Google. Perfect for the task at hand. Law enforcement loved it because its 850 billion bits of metadata allowed you to truly know your subject: track their movements, map their friends, and reveal their religious or political beliefs. All you needed was a single piece of data: A phone number. An email address. A Twitter account.

Today Haddox wanted it for one simple reason: It was a repository of forgotten data. Even mining data from apps like Snapchat or Whisper. Places where messages ostensibly self-destructed within moments of being shared.

He devoted four and a half minutes to finding the perfect file. When he uncovered it, he felt like a heartless bastard.

He enlarged it on the screen, angled it toward Eve. "What do you think?"

Her eyes were locked on the screen. "If it doesn't hold his attention, then I don't know what will. I just hate the idea of it."

"Hate it more than the death of another innocent victim?" Haddox waited. "Didn't think so. I'll put it on-screen. Wait thirty seconds. Then green-light Mace and García."

The moment he received the signal from Haddox, García took out his tools and began methodically disarming the detonator.

He worked quickly but cautiously. Found the wires forming the circuit.

Closed his eyes. Said a hasty prayer. Ran a finger over the detonator and tasted it—to be sure there were no chemical components.

There wasn't any magical how-to formula for disarming a detonator. Each one was unique—the product of its maker's imagination. So García spent the better part of three minutes, thirty-one seconds determining what this bomb's maker had done.

García was impressed. It was sophisticated work. And familiar—so probably developed in Afghanistan, if not Iraq.

*He identified the first wire.*

And there wasn't any rhyme or reason to the wire colors, either. It was a matter of sequence, not color.

*He identified the second wire.*

Guys in the field tended to practice with detonators containing only one color wire. It kept their skills sharp.

*He identified the third wire.*

So it actually helped to be a little bit colorblind—which García always was where explosives were concerned.

*He identified the fourth wire—and took out his wire cutters.*

Seventeen minutes later, he had completely finished. He wiped the beads of sweat from his forehead. Swung open the door.

# Chapter 77

A new image was projected onto the screen next to the giant bronze Atlas. The girl was a chestnut-haired teenager wearing black jeans with a sparkle design, a T-shirt that read PEACE OUT, and a crimson scarf. She was sitting on her knees.

Next to her, a series of screen shots—each a confession—began to rotate.

Each bore text that was superimposed on a different photo of her.

Each revealed a code linked to her cellphone number or email account.

*I hate being a teenager. I don't like mean girls, hormones, weird parents—or the way I look in the mirror.*

Eve placed her phone on the table. It didn't ring.

The next was superimposed on a close-up of her wrist. A photo the girl had taken herself.

*I've been clean for ten days. Every time I want to cut, I remember I don't want to have scars when Dad takes me to Miami for New Year's.*

"He's going to call any second," Haddox said.

They both stared at Eve's phone. It didn't ring.

The image rotated again. This one focused on the girl's eyes.

*I drew all over my old scars today. Mrs. Roth was right. It did relieve my urges.*

The phone stayed silent.

A new rotation. Full face.

*I relapsed. It was at school. I faked a smile after. So nobody noticed that I had been crying in pain just ten minutes before.*

The phone didn't ring.

"Dammit, where is he?" Eve muttered.

*I am more scarred inside than my arm is outside.*

The phone trilled.

Sean Sullivan was on the line. Eve braced for his reaction. "Who put you up to this?"

She listened to his breathing. It was rapid, indicating his elevated heart rate.

"What do you mean?"

"Where did you get these photos? Who gave them to you?"

There was no anger in his voice. Just naked panic. Eve had his full attention.

She was giving him only half of hers. Through her earpiece, she was listening to Mace and García's progress. Waiting for word they'd made it past the camera.

"So you've never seen these images?" she asked Sean.

"Is this some kind of damn trick?"

"It's disturbing material, I know. But your daughter shared it herself, online."

"When?"

Eve looked at Haddox. He had been listening to the conversation. Now he held up two fingers.

"Within the last two weeks," she said. "Over multiple Internet postings."

"There's no way anyone could know . . . Meaghan and I never . . ." There was raw pain in the statement.

Eve listened, slightly stunned. She thought: *I hear the ring of truth in his voice. He's not acting. He's worried sick about his daughter.*

Mace crouched his basketball-player frame low and headed down the corridor linking the Rectory to the Cathedral. He spotted Frankie just as he approached the Sacristy entrance.

He'd been as good as his word: The door was disarmed and open.

Problem was: There was a hostage. Still wired to the hilt. Just sitting there with a blindfold covering his eyes—while García spoke to him in a hushed, hurried voice.

Mace had no time or patience for García to pussyfoot around. They had a Cathedral to take back.

He gave a brief nod to García.

"Let's get you out of here," he said to the hostage. He reached forward and tugged the bandana from the hostage's eyes.

Revealing that he was a she. Specifically, a middle-aged woman with gray-streaked hair, now plastered to her face with sweat.

Mace looked down. She wore a wedding band and a funny string bracelet around her wrist. Her eyes were big blue round pools of confusion. She was still gagged—but she managed to make a high-pitched, moaning sound.

García pointed to her right hand, which clutched the pressure switch between her fingers and palm. "I was talking to her so she didn't get startled and let go of that."

"And I took her bandana off so she could see us tryin' to help her." Mace shook his head.

The hostage's moans intensified. Mace ignored them. He told her, "Keep pressing hard on that switch 'til I say I've got it. Nod if you understand."

The woman nodded.

Mace squeezed her fingers between his own. Inched the switch out of her fingers. Set it to *LOCK* position. Then bound it eight times around with a thick rubber band.

"Overkill." García made the word sound like a synonym for *amateur.*

Mace shrugged. "Makes me feel better. What about that?"

García had removed the woman's explosive belt. With fast fingers, he neutralized the wires. Then set the device down by the gate. "Tactical can take it from here."

Mace helped the woman to her feet as García unbound her legs. She wobbled three steps, then collapsed into his arms.

He started to remove her gag. Mace stopped him. "Don't waste time. Tactical can handle that, too."

García glanced nervously at the camera. Prayed Eve was doing a good job keeping the Hostage Taker distracted.

Mace caught the woman's eye and pointed at the passageway.

"Go that way to the end. Take the elevator up. You'll find plenty of help waiting."

Neither he nor García lingered to be sure she made it. They sprinted back up the stairs, toward the High Altar and the main Cathedral.

García was fast, but Mace's strides were impressive.

"When's the last time you were in this place?" García asked when Mace overtook him.

Mace grinned. "I just checked out the map."

García grabbed him by the shoulder. "Then you'd better follow me. You always said book smarts are no match for street smarts."

García crouched low against the wall, not wanting to be a target. Cursing the fact that Mace was behind him—with lumbering footsteps that seemed to echo loudly against the stone. He'd declined additional help from Tactical, telling Eve that he'd rather be nimble. Too many cooks in the kitchen.

She'd insisted that Mace continue. Didn't she realize the damn fool might get them both killed?

The rear of the High Altar was just above. García let his eyes rise to the vaulted ceiling, knowing they were completely vulnerable the moment they reached the altar.

It was the focal point of the Cathedral, crafted entirely of bronze. Its canopy rose almost sixty feet high, with decorated pillars and spires on its gabled roof. *The Redemption of Mankind,* García thought, looking at the statues surrounding him.

He made his way quickly around it. Paused by the window depicting the sacrifice of Abraham.

Eve thought it was just one man calling the shots. She had promised to distract him.

Eve could be wrong.

He turned to Mace. "I'm going up the scaffolding. Cover me."

Then he crossed himself again. This time just for good luck.

# Chapter 78

Mace watched Frank García disappear up the rails of the center scaffold. The guy was small but scrappy, and he moved fast. Mace gave him that much credit.

He took a moment to look around. The building was shaped exactly like a cross. He knew there were hostages scattered throughout, but all he saw from his current perspective was an ocean of wooden pews. And endless marble. He supposed it was what people called beautiful, but it felt cold to him. Too dark. Too deserted.

Something caught his eye in the balcony above the vestibule. He couldn't tell if it was a noise—or a flash of light.

Frankie wanted to be covered. But the way Mace figured it, taking care of the motherfucker responsible for all this was the best coverage of all.

He started walking down the long nave of the Cathedral toward the front. He kept close to the center, where the shadows were deepest.

He felt like he was in a big stone cage.

One where his every footstep echoed.

So far, he saw nothing. No sign of life other than stray flashes of light that he supposed were from official activity outside.

*Black. Yellow. Black again.*

He supposed it was a crazy risk he was taking. But he wasn't the type to stand around. Not when he could get something done.

Then he saw the movement again. Still felt his footsteps echoed too loudly, but he couldn't physically move any quieter.

*How to get upstairs?*

He reached the vestibule by the entrance. Turned into the bell tower. Saw the elevator. No way was he going to be a sitting duck in a box. He looked harder and found stairs.

It took him thirty-three seconds to climb to the top. His eyes scanned the length of the choir loft.

Empty.

Just the massive organ, its pipes reaching up to the stained-glass Rose Window above.

Then a light flashed and he found the source of the movement.

There was a clock at the rear of the Choir Loft. Every 4.3 seconds, a flash of light hit its dial.

The clock chimed ten o'clock.

Somewhere above he heard a noise.

It sounded like the discharge of a weapon. It was followed by a muffled groan.

He looked out across the vast expanse of pews below.

*Nothing.*

García had been heading up the scaffolding. The sounds had come from above.

Mace was at the entrance of the choir loft in a flash. "Frankie?" he whispered.

"García?" Louder this time. "Are you okay?"

*No answer.*

*Shit.* And he was supposed to have had Frankie's back.

Mace had never liked the guy. Certainly had never felt responsible for him. Until now.

García might be a dysfunctional pain in the ass, but he was on *Mace's* team—and Mace didn't like seeing him targeted.

"García!" he called out again.

Tried reaching him on their shared channel. Then by phone. Finally by text.

*Still no answer.*

His chest tightened as he sent a message to Eve: *Shots fired. Possible man down.*

. . .

Eve read Mace's message and shivered as reality shifted. She closed her eyes. Fought the overwhelming sense of helplessness. Then opened her eyes and messaged back: *Tactical support?*

The reply came almost instantaneously. *Give me 13 minutes.*

She shook her head. She knew Mace considered thirteen his lucky number. Frankie was superstitious and would consider it bad juju.

*Careful. Don't be a hero,* she typed. Then caught herself thinking: Wasn't that exactly what she wanted him to be?

Mace took seven steps forward. Peered into the dim stairwell.

No movement. No sound. No sign of anyone there.

He knew that outside there was chaos and shouting, sirens and bullhorns, and the incessant noise from the circling choppers. But ten feet of stone and brick and cement formed a noise-proof barrier. Inside the Cathedral, a dark void had swallowed the Church whole. An eerie quiet prevailed.

He was sure the sound he'd heard was a gunshot.

Growing up on the meanest streets of Hunts Point, cops were always going by with sirens on account of people getting stabbed, windows getting broken, or guns going off. All sounds he wouldn't ever forget.

He thought back to the map he'd seen. Maybe the Church had a fancier name for it, but the large area above was basically like an attic. Even though an attic was the place your aunt in Queens stored her Christmas ornaments and forgotten boxes. Far too ordinary for a grand Cathedral.

He checked his Glock. Zipped his coat a little higher.

Then entered the stairwell and started climbing.

He was feeling the cold. All that stone must trap it inside; it felt like with every step the temperature dropped another degree. And while he wasn't a superstitious kind of guy, there was something about the stale musty air and slight stirring breeze that reminded him of old ghosts.

He continued up the dark stairs. One step, then another. Closer and closer to the top.

His boots were making too much noise. His breathing was becoming more labored—which was either nerves or something bad in the air, 'cause he was in top shape.

He sped up as much as he could, climbing higher and higher until he was almost at the top.

"Frankie?" he whispered. "You there?"

No one answered.

He stopped. Listened.

There it was again. A faint keening sound. It bounced from stone to stone, echoing in the frigid air, until it seemed it came from the Cathedral itself. No, Mace wasn't a superstitious man. But right now, he felt surrounded by ghosts—and one of them was wailing in protest, already mourning a tragedy just about to happen.

Eve worried she had gone too far. She had tried to protect García and Mace by distracting Sullivan. Trying to ensure he paid attention only to her—not whatever video surveillance he may have established. But it was always a risk. They had no real idea what kind of eyes and ears he had set up inside.

She wasn't just responsible for four witnesses and a still unknown number of hostages inside Saint Patrick's Cathedral. Two of her own men had put their lives at risk as well.

*Was García down? Where was Mace?*

It was too quiet. Just her—and the worries that taunted her. Telling her that six people had already died that day. That she'd sacrificed one of her own for nothing. That she'd never succeed. That she'd been wrong about Sean Sullivan and played the wrong hand. Just like she'd been wrong about Rusty Morris. She hadn't been able to establish a connection with the chubby forty-six-year-old mechanic from Yonkers, either. He'd taken fourteen people hostage inside a deli in Queens. She had learned all about him, tried to convince him that she understood his problems, done her best to get inside his mind. But she had failed in talking him down. There had been a tactical assault.

Seven people had died in a blaze of bullets. Two of them were children.

*Was this going to end just as badly?*

She had upset Sean Sullivan—probably more than he let on. When he signed off, he'd said he'd call back in five minutes.

Now nine minutes had passed.

The longest minutes of Eve's life.

# Chapter 79

Mace stepped out of the stairwell and stopped in the absolute black. Listened before resuming course. Keeping his gun close at hand. He pulled out his Maglite and was about to shine it in front of him when he thought better of it.

He couldn't see in the dark.

But no need to make himself a target. Better to avoid light until he knew he was alone.

He pushed the door open in front of him wider. It clicked. He froze and listened.

*Nothing.*

He took a step forward. There was enough light from a distant window to move faster. There was a stale scent of damp in the air—the legacy of the morning's heavy rain and a closed-up room, unaccustomed to use.

*Is anyone here now? Where is García?*

The floor was dusty and mottled with footprints. Some recent. Different shapes and sizes.

Mace went right. Stayed in the shadows against the brick wall. Past the window. He could see writing in the windowpanes, made visible by the lights outside. Messages left by some of the firefighters when visiting the Cathedral for inspections. Before they died on 9/11. It was one of the issues the Church rep had been hassling Henry Ma about. In spite of the massive renovation being undertaken, the Church had refused to clean the panes. They were a treasure—as unique as the Rose Window, the guy had insisted.

Mace kept moving. He wasn't going to find either the Hostage Taker or García hiding in all the dirt.

Mace cracked open another door separating the small room he'd entered from other parts of the attic.

Stopped. Listened. But there was no sound except for the whistle of air from yet another draft.

*Where is the keening coming from? And the gunshot?*

He saw nothing out of the ordinary. The area by the window was empty except for a box. He walked over to it and opened it. There were tools inside—small winches, covered in dust, that might service the bell apparatus. No one had touched them in weeks, if not months.

If two hundred men really did show up to work every day on the Cathedral's multimillion-dollar restoration, they didn't spend much time in the attic.

He moved toward a big window near the front of the attic. Someone had wiped this one's panes clean. In fact, the lower-right pane was cracked, with a small section knocked out entirely. Glass fragments littered the floor.

Mace stared down Fifth Avenue. Snow was falling, blanketing the world below. It was beginning to cover the streetlights and vans. The MRU and other temporary units. The great shoulders of Atlas. He knew it even covered the big unlit tree at Rockefeller Center.

He didn't have much more time.

Braced close to the wall, Mace surveyed the room. He could see only five feet ahead. He needed to check the area to the right. It was dark, framed by treacherous shadows.

One step. Then another.

He found a table with a paper plate littered with food. A half-eaten sandwich. Some chips. A full bottle of water.

Plenty of unfinished business.

*The Hostage Taker's hidey-hole.*

Mace's thirteen minutes were up.

A phone was ringing somewhere, but not for Eve.

She couldn't sit still. She was pacing back and forth, her emotions in a conflicted space between worry and guilt. Her mind trying to focus on strategy.

Haddox was in front of the computer screen, brainstorming a way to get digital eyes inside the Church. Their best shot had been García's GPS-equipped glasses. But—in a careless move—it appeared he had discarded them in the Crypt.

Eli stared at Eve's two phones—one her own, the other used to communicate with the Hostage Taker. Both remained perversely silent. "What are you guilty of?" he muttered. It wasn't a question. Eli's body was trembling and all semblance of confidence was gone out of him. "If I'd said something earlier . . . it's all my fault."

"Nothing's your fault. García would still have gone in," Eve finished for him. "He's not afraid of risk. Besides, the fact he's in trouble, inside that Cathedral, is on me. I arranged his release from the hospital. I authorized his exploration of the tunnels. And if Tactical has to breach now, the fact they have access at all is thanks to García."

"You gotta give the order, Eve." Eli shook his head, miserable. "Who knows what the hell's happening in there! We don't know García's condition. What if Mace is down, too? Minutes count."

"Well, I'm gobsmacked. Eli Cohen worried—about somebody else's health and well-being," Haddox teased.

"But apparently you're thinking only about yourself. As usual," Eli scolded.

"Me, worry about a six-foot-seven black Adonis and a lethal former Army Ranger? If anybody can take care of themselves, those blokes can."

Eve and Eli just stared at him.

Haddox grinned. "You're thinking that I really am a cold-hearted bastard. But maybe you don't give me enough credit. Maybe I just figured something out. Something important." He tilted the computer screen to show them.

Mace drew his Glock. His heart hammered hard inside his chest. His muscles tensed, bracing for a fight, as he kept moving. Ahead of him, shadows swayed along an empty stretch of the wall.

All seemed quiet. Then there was a faint scraping.

He didn't dare shine his flashlight beam.

Mace moved in silence, his broad shoulders just brushing the wall. His gun in his right hand, at waist level.

Seconds passed.

Mace stopped. Stared into the dark. The stone-and-brick utilitarian room had something odd in its corner. Instinctively, he hugged the wall.

Then he took four steps forward. The odd form was taking shape. The slight scraping noise was growing louder.

Even so, he almost cursed when he heard a faint moan.

Haddox was keeping his eyes open. "You see that?" He went into the time-lapse record and pointed to a shadow along the Cathedral's uppermost windows.

Eli squinted, then shook his head. "What am I supposed to see?"

"That." Eve tapped the end of her pencil at a flash of red.

"I don't have Superman X-ray vision," Eli complained. "I can't see what you're seeing."

"Let me try to zoom in." Haddox refocused on the fragment of red. Slowly, it took better shape. It was a shadow.

Except shadows didn't wear a lucky red bandana around their neck.

Whereas Frank García did.

Mace knew: Sometimes offense was the best defense. Not just on the courts, but here in the uppermost reaches of Saint Patrick's Cathedral.

He took a soft breath, and with his Glock ready in his right hand, he reached out his left. Grabbed his Maglite and shined it—right into the astonished face of Frank García and a hostage bound to a chair.

# Chapter 80

Eve kept her focus trained on the video, watching. And listening—as though something in the silence itself might give her the answer she hoped for so desperately: the reassurance that García was fine.

She was distracted by the trill of the Hostage Taker's phone.

When she answered, Sean sounded steadier. "Let's try this one more time. I want to question all four witnesses at once. Bring them online. Tell them: It's their last chance for redemption before all hell breaks loose."

She counted to five, nice and slow, before she responded. If they had truly seen García's red bandana, then he was close. Right in the Hostage Taker's lair.

There was no longer any room for error.

Next to Eve, Haddox was focused on a different problem. Something was not right.

He was poring over the notes Eli had left him about crimes the four witnesses may have seen. He didn't leap to conclusions. He supposed that asking New Yorkers if they'd ever witnessed a crime was like asking an Irishman if he appreciated a pint of Guinness. But there were some odd discrepancies.

Among the four of them, they'd casually witnessed subway gropings, cellphone thefts, and a number of car accidents.

One incident caught Haddox's attention. He wasn't sure why. Not one of the four had described what they saw in exactly the same words. Of course, he knew witness testimony was notoriously unreliable. Human memory was an exceptionally fragile thing. Susceptible to prejudice. Riven with error. That was why the papers were filled with cases where DNA evidence exculpated people wrongfully convicted due to eyewitness testimony.

So Haddox didn't focus on the differences—even though each of the four named a different location. A different date. A different time. And described a completely different scenario.

He concentrated on the similarities.

A crime had occurred in the subway station underground.

A woman had been hurt.

García was leaning over the hostage. Mace recognized her from the steps of the Cathedral earlier in the day: The woman with cropped gray hair and the nasty scar on her left cheek. The one who wore men's shoes.

She was bleeding. Moaning softly in pain. And García was covering the wound with his red bandana—the one he'd worn for luck since the operation began.

"What's going on here?" Mace demanded. "She gonna be okay?"

"It's only a scratch." García tightened the bandana. Tied it off. "Do me a favor?"

"Go to hell," Mace said, glaring. "I was actually worried about you, man. I heard a shot."

"That would be the scratch. She thought *I* was the Hostage Taker coming for her and made threatening sounds. She startled me. My weapon went off. She got lucky."

"Meaning you were trigger-happy."

"Meaning you didn't cover me like you promised. So I had to look out for myself." García fixed him with a stony glare.

"Looks like we *all* got lucky." Mace gazed down at the explosives García had already defused and removed. "You're a damn fool. This is a danger zone, not target practice." The hostage's hands were shaking as Mace untied them.

She was dirty. Her wrists were bleeding, too.

"You okay?" Mace asked.

She managed to nod. He removed her blindfold and her gag. "The guy who did this to you. Is he around?"

She blinked, struggling to orient herself. She failed. She was either in shock or she didn't understand the question.

Mace tried again. "Have you seen him pass by?"

She nodded. Mumbled something.

García grabbed the water bottle that was beside her and offered her a sip. She drank from it greedily.

"That way," she croaked, tilting her head left. "I saw him headed that direction. Don't know how long ago." She pointed to her feet, which were still tied. "Can you please let me go? I gotta get out of here."

Haddox's eyes were locked on the file on the screen in front of him. Was it possible he was finally staring at the elusive connection between Sean Sullivan and the five witnesses he had demanded?

It wasn't filed under Sean Sullivan's name—although in the file he was listed among the investigating officers. He had been summoned late to help manage the scene. He had worked crowd control. He had not interviewed the witnesses.

The information was far from perfect.

Haddox was pretty sure the witness listed as Anna Leigh was actually Cassidy Jones. She admitted to having used the name in the past as her stage name. She didn't actually remember the incident. It was shortly after she first arrived in New York. She had delved into the party scene, she remembered, and might've been drunk that night.

He was also pretty sure that Louis Ramon was Luis Ramos. His name had been misspelled. That sort of thing happened all the time.

According to the report, all had been present when a subway mugging had gone bad. The victim had been severely injured, eventually dying three days later in the hospital. The mugger had never been caught.

Was this what Sean Sullivan wanted them to confess to?

*What are you guilty of?* he'd asked each one.

Not observing enough? Not preventing the assault? Not giving the police enough information? Not caring enough?

Or simply being there?

It was impossible to know.

But Haddox did know this—and it was what he told Eve: If the witnesses hadn't been able to give enough information to catch the perpetrator at the time, they didn't have a snowball's chance in hell of doing so now.

# Chapter 81

*Last July, I was waiting for the Bronx-bound D train—the Sixth Avenue Express—at the Bryant Park stop. It was a Tuesday night, about half past ten. The city had been baking all day, so it was hotter than a sauna underground. The lights were bright and seemed to add to the heat.*

*I remember it vividly—as though I am there now.*

*I am sitting alone on a wooden bench at the south end of the platform, which is deserted except for seven people. Two passengers are to my left; five are to my right. There is a subway map above me, next to a series of posters touting various summer blockbusters. Ahead of me, on the column near the edge of the platform, are a series of weekend and evening service announcements about work that will disrupt the lives of thousands. New York's subway system is well over a century old—and its tracks are in constant need of repair.*

*The waiting passenger closest to me is a Hispanic woman. She is built small and straight, less than five feet tall, and she looks overheated and bone tired. A battered leather bag is worn crossbody over her shoulders. She thinks about taking the seat next to me, but she's too high-strung. She keeps leaning over the tracks to check for an approaching train.*

*About eight feet away from her is a man leaning against one of the columns. He isn't relaxed; he's just too tired to stand up. He is Hispanic, too—short, with coppery skin and dark hair. His leathery face is lined with exhaustion.*

*On the other side of me is a woman I immediately peg as Caribbean. She wears a colorful orange-and-yellow cloth over her hair; her long dress is in the same bold hues. She is humming to herself, and the supermarket bag draped over her wrist bulges with knitting needles and yarn.*

*All are impatient. Ready to be on their way.*

*The next waiting passenger is different. She is petite, with glossy black hair in a twist, and she's dressed to the nines: black skirt, patent leather sandals, a strapless sequined top. She carries a tote bag with musical notes all over it. I guess that she's bound for either Lincoln Center or Carnegie Hall.*

*About fifteen feet away, there's another bench where a woman with curly platinum-blond hair is sitting. Her curves are tucked into a skin-tight red dress, but a pale blue waitress's uniform pokes out of her bag. She wants to be Marilyn, but she's stuck as Alice at Mel's Diner, I decide.*

*The sixth waiting passenger is a man about thirty-five, dressed like he's headed for the golf course, though he's probably returning home from dinner. He is glued to his smartphone, though he looks up at regular intervals. He remains alert, aware of his surroundings.*

*The last passenger can't stand still. He's jittery, and I remember he's wearing a skull ring with a diamond in each eye socket. He's probably fortysomething, white, just shy of six feet tall and two hundred pounds. His jeans are ripped and he's sweating through his red, white, and blue Captain America T-shirt. He zigzags past everyone, all the way to the end of the platform. His eyes are alert, taking in everyone. Noting their body language. Their clothes. The items they carry.*

*He turns back.*

*Walks past the guy with the smartphone. Past Marilyn Monroe and the dark-headed musician. Past the Caribbean woman and the tired Hispanic man. He stops one short pace away from the petite Hispanic woman.*

*He moves so quickly I almost don't believe what I'm seeing. With one arm he pulls the woman against him; with the other, he yanks her leather bag over her head.*

*He is agile and smooth. Confident. Like he's done this many times before.*

*So I get up and do my best to make sure he doesn't do it again.*

*Before he takes his hand off the woman's shoulders, I come up behind him.*

*"Give that back," I say.*

*"Mind your own fuckin' business." He keeps hold of the woman. Seconds earlier, she was frozen still; now she is struggling against him.*

*"Right now." I take another step closer.*

*The woman is saying, "Just take my money. Please let me go!" She whimpers in fear.*

*"You heard the lady. Let her go!" I've been home on leave for more than a year, but I'm still a Marine, and my training kicks in. I feint like I'm going to hit him, but I actually knee him hard in the gut and he staggers, falling. In that instant, I snatch the woman out of his arms. He regains his balance, but before he can rise, I launch my boot into the side of his head.*

*It is a solid hit. He seems unsteady and disoriented; I think he's down for the count.*

*With the woman still sagging against me, I kick her bag out of his hands, launching it beyond his reach. He offers no resistance.*

*Hindsight is perfect, of course. Looking back, I see that my taking the bag was the act that set him off.*

*Suddenly his anger boils over and he is back on his knees, then up on his feet, charging like a bull. I block him with my left hook, but my action isn't what the woman is expecting. She loosens her grip on my arm.*

*Spins away from us.*

*And teeters.*

*I watch, suddenly helpless, as she sways backward onto the track.*

*I cannot help.*

*Her mugger grabs me, smashing his fist into my face. The punch lands harder than I expect.*

*I struggle to break free of him—and cannot.*

*"HELP!" It may be the first time I've uttered the word in my life.*

*After several bloody minutes, he finishes pounding my face. He drives his knee into my ribs.*

*"HELP!" I say it again.*

*Bursts of pain flash through my body. Now I am screaming. Begging for help.*

*I see the others standing there. Gawking.*

*Finally, he shoves me down, hard—and I hear the sound of my own skull breaking.*

*Then he picks up the woman's bag and saunters away.*

*No one stops him.*

Afterward, they all *stand, frozen in place. Deaf to my pleas for help.*

*Ignoring my outstretched hand. Ignoring the half-dead woman on the tracks.*

*It's like we have become invisible. Or they have been turned to stone.*

*Later, I learn: Twelve and a half minutes pass before anyone dials 911.*

*A Japanese tourist makes the call. Not one of the original five.*

*Don't they know what they're guilty of?*

*Am I the only one who cares about justice?*

*Today they're all going to fucking pay attention. They're going to notice me for the first time. Today people are going to thank me for what I've done.*

# Chapter 82

García sent word that they had a line on the Hostage Taker—in effect authorizing Tactical Operations to enter the Cathedral and begin rescuing hostages and defusing all remaining explosives.

The hostage from the attic—who gave her name as Ellen—didn't know exactly where the Hostage Taker was located. Just the general direction.

She did confirm she had seen only one man.

García still worried they were facing more than one opponent. But he had combed the downstairs of the Cathedral, to no avail. The Hostage Taker—or Takers, if more than one—had to be here, in the upper reaches of the Cathedral.

The key would be to neutralize him before he had the chance to trigger any explosives.

García led the way. Mace followed. They stayed close to the wall, stepped onto a catwalk that spanned the length of the attic above the choir loft. It was essentially a tower passage, enabling access from the south tower to the north. The spire with the bells.

García tried to remember what he'd learned about the Bell Tower in preparation for this assault. It wasn't regularly used—and it hadn't been since the electronic age, when the bells were rung by a player at a miniature piano downstairs. Today they had remained silent.

The tower struck him as a perfect place for the Hostage Taker to establish the advantage.

García entered, suppressing a shiver as a gush of cold air—and a few stray snowflakes—managed to surge down the spire.

Mace was close behind.

There was a spiral staircase in the center of the tower. They began to climb, steadying themselves with handrails.

The spiral stairs gave way to ladders.

Inside the spire, everything was transformed. The lights of the city melted into an unearthly glow. The thrum of a helicopter circling above reminded García of a call to battle.

They inched toward the landing beneath the first bell room. The hanging straps of the bells swayed around them.

*In here,* García mouthed.

García checked his watch. Downstairs, the Tactical team would already be securing the Cathedral.

Soundlessly, drawing his Randall #1 knife, he climbed the remaining steps of the ladder. Moved into position, entering the first bell room with a catlike leap. The bell room was shaped like an octagon and illuminated by a single sixty-watt utility bulb. There was dust everywhere—but blurred and scattered by multiple footprints. Three of the Cathedral's nineteen copper and tin bells loomed just ahead of him. Named the Saint Patrick, the Blessed Virgin, and the Saint Joseph. Notes corresponding to B♭, C, and D. They hung from a crossbeam. There was a flashlight resting on top of that crossbeam. And snow was blowing in, from the open louvers.

It could almost be a postcard for the tourists: bells glistening with snow, illuminated by a magical, diffused light.

He heard someone moving about. Then saw the shadow slipping between the bells. A single figure. Dressed in fatigues.

The shadow's footsteps boomed and echoed. They seemed to come from all around.

It was the moment of truth. Decision time. Live or die.

García thought the odds were in their favor. The figure was distracted. Speaking urgently into a telephone. *Eve, I don't want to hear another word of this BULLSHIT!*

The ID was solid.

Now he needed a visual on the hands. He had to confirm that the Hostage Taker wasn't holding a dead man's switch that would set fire to the Cathedral the instant he was killed.

So he waited—and watched.

*Five seconds. Ten seconds.*

It took twenty-seven seconds before García made a clear determination. Sullivan's left hand was holding the phone. His right hand was gesticulating. There was no contact switch to worry about.

He whispered to Eve through his secure headset. *Do I take the kill shot?*

The reply came within a second. *Affirmative. Do it.*

He nodded to Mace, who eased himself soundlessly into the bell tower. Moved along an empty stretch of floor behind the bells. No sound at all. All García could hear was the wind, whistling between the louvers.

He focused his eyes. Pointed to his Glock, then made a thumbs-up.

Mace had a clear shot.

García nodded. *Go for it.*

Mace moved left, fired between the bells, moved left again.

Sullivan's body jerked, then fell. The injured man tried to reach something in his pocket, but his arm responded only with a spasm of movement.

García moved in to finish the job.

The man was trying to crawl. He couldn't. There was blood coming from his mouth. He looked at García and said, "'bout fucking time."

García hesitated.

Mace didn't.

He fired one more shot and Sullivan said no more.

# Chapter 83

The fellows overseas always said the end was just pretty pink mist. Quick and painless. A descent into nothingness.

They were wrong.

The pain in his chest was intense. A confused vision filled the blackness of his consciousness. He opened his mouth to ask for Eve. He wanted so desperately to explain.

But it was too hard to breathe—and he could think only of Georgie.

*Suddenly it was 7:53 in the morning again, the day before yesterday, and the snow was coming down in a fast, furious squall. Thick, fat flakes covered tree branches and patches of grass, but the streets remained wet and sloppy. Beside him, Georgie was light-footed, almost buoyant, as she moved. She wasn't talkative most mornings, but the first snowfall of winter had put her in a good mood. Snow was exciting—even though a New York City kid like Georgie would rarely ever see a day off because of it.*

*"Did you know that snowflakes aren't actually white?" She stuck her tongue out to catch a giant flake.*

*"They sure look white." Especially against Georgie's new black wool hat.*

*"It has to do with how ice reflects light and how our brain perceives it all wrong," she told him.*

*The crosswalk showed five seconds to go. She was about to go for it, but he caught her arm and held her back. His reward was the roll of her eyes that said "overprotective." Most of her friends got to school by themselves in eighth grade. But he passed by her school on the way to work, and Georgie walked with her head in the clouds, so for now, they stuck together.*

*It wouldn't last; he already knew. She was growing up too fast, so he clung to the last signs of her childhood. The way she still slept with her favorite stuffed bear. The fact that she let him kiss her good night every evening. These morning walks together to school.*

*"I need to get that application in," she said. "If I'm gonna go."*

*She wanted to go to acting camp next summer, but he and her mother had reservations. The Berkshires were a long way from home, and she'd be in a dorm with kids as old as eighteen. It was a daunting prospect. Even if she was thirteen-going-on-thirty.*

*"Sophie's going. I could room with her," she added, reading his thoughts.*

*He nodded and said nothing. Sophie was a nice enough girl, but she was part of what his ex-wife diplomatically called the fast set.*

*"We'll talk over the weekend, Georgie," he had promised.*

*"It's Georgianna now, Dad," she reminded him, with another roll of her eyes. She was grateful that they'd had the foresight to give her a suitably dramatic name. She could imagine it emblazoned on a Broadway marquee or engraved in a Hollywood star. She was annoyed that they never used it.*

*They reached her school.*

*"Goodbye." She had blown him a hasty kiss before she turned and brushed past him, darting up the stairs to the door.*

*"Bye," he'd answered, watching her, a flash of purple and gold and black in the swirling snow. The school's motto hovered over her image.* Consectatio Excellentiae. *The pursuit of excellence. Then she disappeared into the building, other kids crowding behind her, gossiping and talking and laughing.*

*He remembered thinking how in another eight hours, she'd emerge the same way, and his heart would bounce that funny way it always did every time he saw her.*

*Except nothing had gone as planned.*

*He'd seen her for the last time.*

*His worst nightmare had become reality.*

*He clutched his fingers to his heart and prayed Eve would figure it all out.*

NEWS NEWS NEWS NEWS NEWS

# HOURS 15 AND 16

10:14 p.m.

We have just received word from the New York FBI office announcing that the hostage crisis has ended.

We repeat, the hostage crisis that has gripped New York City has been resolved.

Early reports indicate that six lives have been lost. Their names are being withheld pending notification of family members.

The identity of the man responsible is being given by unofficial sources as Captain Sean Sullivan—a police officer recently suspended while under investigation by Internal Affairs. We have no information as to what may have motivated Captain Sullivan to commit the terrible acts of today.

Stay tuned. The mayor and governor will be holding a joint news conference soon with the police commissioner and FBI director to give us more details . . .

# Chapter 84

Sirens filled the air. The Cathedral swarmed with different operations teams. Not just FBI, but NYPD. FDNY. Homeland Security. HRT. Bomb Squad. EMS.

The former hostages were being checked.

The Cathedral was being secured.

Snow fell harder. As though Mother Nature was desperate to cover all traces of the day's violence with a coat of white. As though that would restore the holiday spirit—and help people forget.

Eve had been among the first to rush to the bell tower room, with Haddox and Eli close behind. They waited on the landing outside. But Eve wanted to see inside.

Inside the room where Sean Sullivan lay dead.

It was odd, not having seen the shots that ended Sean's life. She had heard them, though.

She felt relief that the remaining four hostages had survived unharmed—though her emotions were mingled with regret. She knew that Sean Sullivan had given her no choice. And yet . . .

*What had he wanted, really? Not absolution. Not understanding. Not even justice.*

The great injury of his life had been done at the hands of a Church teacher. Yet he had focused on questioning individual witnesses in a minor case. One that never seemed to have affected him deeply. Because if it had, surely he would have asked different questions. Made different plays.

During their long verbal dance, only twice had Eve felt the genuine ring of truth.

Once when he had spoken of the abuse he suffered as a child.

Again, when he talked about his daughter. Whatever had damaged him, his love for his daughter seemed unfeigned. Something true and untainted. If he had brought her to the Cathedral, then he would have kept her in a space he was certain was safe. A place where, whatever happened, she would survive, unharmed.

A forensic tech was working over Sullivan's body, bagging specimens of evidence. Eve watched, but her mind was spinning elsewhere.

"We need to organize a search," she said abruptly. "Mace, we need to check the Crypt as well as both Towers. García, I want to clear the Parish House and Cardinal's Residence. Eli, can you make sure we've missed nothing on the main floor and choir loft?"

Haddox brushed the snow off his jacket. Donned a pair of latex gloves. "I'll see what I can do with the different phones he used." He reached up to grab a shopping bag full of mobile units that Eve passed down. It had been found next to Sullivan's body.

"We need to send officers to check his home as well," Eve said.

The forensic tech finished with the phone Sullivan had been holding when he was shot. "Want this, too?"

Eve took it, passed it to Haddox, thinking that for all the scientific advances designed to help solve the tough cases, sometimes you still couldn't understand human behavior. It wasn't something that could be quantified, no matter how rigorous your analysis of call patterns or social networks or money-spending habits. Stolen weapons didn't explain it. Nor did a series of dead hostages. Sometimes you just couldn't figure out who someone was.

He'd done monstrous things. But was he a monster?

He'd been a father who loved his child.

A husband who—at one point—had loved his wife.

A man who had found life was hard. Who couldn't make his car payments. Or fix his teenage daughter's pain. Or even put his belt on with the engraved initials right-side up.

"You need anything up here before we go, Eve?" Eli asked.

She was only half listening.

*The belt.*

The realization danced at the edge of her mind for several seconds before taking hold. Several seconds during which she noted other things.

Small things.

Like the way he had organized his supplies so they flowed back to front. His drink was to the left. The half-eaten granola bar was on the left side of a plate. The cellphone he had been using had fallen to the ground on his left. He'd been looking out the louvers, but the dust was smudged only on the left. He'd set up two laptops—on his left—to monitor activity from the cameras he had strategically placed inside and outside the Cathedral.

In fact, Sean's final hours in this room had been spent only on the left-hand side of the room. Eve knew that because the right side was still coated in a thick layer of dust.

"You want this, too? I've dusted it already. I found it in his breast pocket." The tech handed Eve a small flash drive.

Automatically, she passed that over to Haddox.

She gazed at the crossbeam. And the single item that was the exception to everything else she'd noticed.

That was where Sean Sullivan's sniper rifle lay. Smack in the center. Neither right nor left.

A distant memory from her own days at Quantico became a thought. "García—the best snipers are usually right-handed, correct?"

"Most of the time, sure. Because sniper rifles are built for right-handed people. But it's really more about which eye is dominant, not which hand is dominant."

"Does it usually correspond? So right-handed people are right-eye dominant, and vice versa?"

"Again, usually. Why?"

"Can you look at that rifle and tell whether it's set up for a right-handed or left-handed person?"

García received clearance from the forensics tech, who had already dusted the rifle for prints. He lifted it down. Looked it over. "Remember, there's no such thing as a left-handed rifle. But I can say, this particular rifle was set up with a scope mounted for a right-handed person. Wasn't Sullivan right-handed?"

"You know," Mace suggested, "maybe Sullivan was ambidextrous. My left-handed layup is every bit as good as my right."

"Sniper shooting is a whole different game," García said.

"I agree." And Eve explained what she had noticed. The catalog of clues that had suggested Sullivan had been left-handed. She said: "I don't think Sullivan was the shooter."

At first, nobody questioned her.

Then Mace erupted. "Are you telling me I shot dead a man who wasn't a killer?"

"Sullivan was the Hostage Taker." García matched his anger. "You heard him when we entered the room. He was right on the phone, talking to you, Eve."

"We've got four hostages who now swear he was the man responsible," Eli reminded them. "They *all* positively ID'd his photo—and testified how this man hauled each one of them into the confessional, making them admit the worst things they'd ever done."

"We got our guy. Stopped his vigilante justice mission. So how come you don't think he shot that sniper rifle?" Mace was furious.

García's eyes were pure ice. "You think I've got all the answers? Maybe he had help. Maybe he forced one of the hostages."

"You think he forced one hostage to shoot another? With the kind of aim only an elite sniper can brag about?"

García took a step forward. The space in the tower was already tight. His movement made it tighter. "Calm down and stop your whining. So what if he wasn't the shooter? He was involved. He terrorized hostages. He almost certainly stole the explosives that still threaten this Cathedral. So you shot a bad cop. What do you care?"

"I ain't trigger-happy. I've got a thing about killing guys for shit they didn't do."

It was like watching a lion face off against a hyena. Until Eve stepped between them. "Everyone needs to calm down. This is *my* case. The kill shot was *my* decision. This information complicates everything but changes nothing."

Haddox had something in his hand; he held it up, like an offering. "Turns out we have another complication."

# Chapter 85

Back at the MRU, Haddox believed he had untangled the complication.

Eve had spent hours trying to figure out why Sean Sullivan was not worth trusting. Problem was: She was looking in all the wrong places. She believed that people's communication style—everything from their facial expressions and body movements to their tone of voice and choice of words—betrayed what they really meant.

What Haddox trusted was bits, bytes, and data. People lied, but their digital fingerprints always betrayed them. It was all pretty simple. And today he was convinced that they'd find the answers they were looking for on the flash drive found in Sean Sullivan's breast pocket. He told Eve as much.

She agreed. "Not because I think data has all the answers, though."

"Then why?" He shoved the drive into his secure machine. Touched a few keys to begin running the background diagnostics.

"Because it was important to him. He kept it right next to his heart."

There were two files on the flash drive. One was a .JPEG image. Its time stamp was forty-eight hours old. It was a digital copy of a scrap of paper.

*What are you guilty of?*

*I already know.*

*View the files on the enclosed flash drive. They will apprise you of the situation and what you personally have at stake.*

*Your first instinct will be to call the police.*

*DON'T.*

"I'm confused," Eli said. "Did Sullivan send this—or receive it?"

"Just wait," Haddox replied. "And keep an open mind."

"But Sullivan *was* the police," Eli mumbled.

*Your next impulse will be to call a friend.*

*That would be unwise.*

"Let's see the file," Eve directed. She crouched close beside him.

The time stamp read 15:53 hours. The date was two days earlier. The girl was sitting on a bed. She wore skinny jeans, a red cardigan, and socks with glitter sparkles on them. Her hands were tied behind her back. Her feet were bound in front of her. A long stretch of duct tape covered her mouth, stretching all the way around her long chestnut hair.

"Georgianna," Eve breathed. "This was taken right after she disappeared from school."

"This is what Sean Sullivan personally has at stake," Haddox told them. "Assuming we believe he was the recipient of the note, not the sender."

There was no audio on the drive. Just a second image.

In that one, the girl was lying down. The sun cast a shadow on her figure.

A crisscross image. It reminded Haddox a little of the Holy Cross. It also reminded him of the bars of a jail cell he'd once had the misfortune to sit in.

"Go back to the message," Eve directed.

Be assured of three things:

1. *I don't hurt those who do as I ask.*
2. *I won't kill the undeserving.*
3. *Obey my demands, and I will protect what you hold precious.*

"Annie Martinez didn't do as he asked. According to the hostages, he made them confess their worst—and those he eventually killed 'deserved it' from his point of view." Eve was thinking aloud.

"It's like he thinks he's being reasonable." Eli shook his head.

"That's always the key," Eve said. "It doesn't matter if someone's reasoning would seem preposterous to ninety-nine percent of the world's population. When you understand how that single person justifies their actions, then you've taken a major step toward understanding their motive. Haddox, was there any evidence of this in Sean Sullivan's email accounts—either as sender or recipient?"

"None whatsoever," Haddox confirmed. "I think we can assume this was a personal delivery." He clicked over to his diagnostic report. "The time stamp is accurate. The file was generated from pictures uploaded from Georgie's own computer via the public Wi-Fi at Bryant Park."

"Where, with the Christmas shops all over the park, they get several hundred thousand visitors every day," Eli remarked sourly.

"Let's focus on what we can assume." Eve pushed her hair behind her ears. "If Sean Sullivan *did* receive this message, how does that explain his actions—from around fifteen-fifty-three hours, day before yesterday, when Georgie disappeared from school?"

"We assume the flash drive was delivered to Sullivan almost immediately," Eli said.

"So what does he do?" Eve thought aloud. "He searches frantically—but can't find her. Then he receives instructions. He had no choice but to follow them. With his daughter kidnapped, he is completely under the Hostage Taker's control. Doing whatever he's told—even before he shows up at Saint Patrick's. Starting day before yesterday, the instant he learned Georgie had been taken."

"First things first," Haddox said. "I'm putting out an Amber Alert for Georgianna Murphy now."

But there was no separate bulletin issued for her abductor. He was still unknown.

"Why Sean?" Haddox wondered. "If you're the puppetmaster pulling the strings, why not handle things yourself?"

"Because you might end up dead," Eli pointed out.

"Because your real goal is something else," Eve said. "And the hostage-taking is just the means to an end."

"He was also the perfect scapegoat—for the hostage-taking and the weapons theft," Eli added. "Problems at home. Problems at work. A history of theft. Everyone would believe he'd done this because he was desperate and losing control of his life."

The alarm on Haddox's computer station beeped. It was eleven o'clock.

Outside, snow was falling fast, and church bells were tolling. It sounded like the Angelus. Had someone on staff been allowed back inside the Cathedral? Or was one of the Feds a good Catholic?

Haddox watched as Eve followed the sound over to the window, apparently lost in thought. The bells were ringing the Siren's song of normalcy. A promise that the world was right again—or as right as it ever could be. Floodlights once again bathed the Cathedral in hues of magical yellow and blue. Saks to the South was a fairy-tale concoction of red and gold, lit up again by seventy-one thousand lights. The Olympic Tower to the north shone a brilliant white.

The bureaucratic show where credit and blame would be sorted had already begun. A press conference was slowly taking form. A select few news organizations had been invited to return to Rockefeller Center. The mayor was standing in the middle of Fifth Avenue, microphones in his face and news crews trailing him with a camera. Traffic was still blocked within a two-mile radius, but forensics was working double-time to process the evidence. The mayor had already announced that he intended to reopen traffic by morning rush hour. This was the holiday season in New York, and that meant opening access to the thousands who flooded the city's sidewalks and shops—and the cabs and buses who shuttled them down Fifth Avenue.

The mayor walked over to the rescued hostages, who had apparently received their medical clearance—standard procedure after a crisis. The mayor paid particular attention to Penelope Miller, whose arms never left her son, Luke. Cops and security personnel surrounded them all. Doing their jobs, eyes alert for anything amiss.

Not fifty feet away, NBC had set up a tent where any of the witnesses who wished would be interviewed, together with a police officer who had to be the designated NYPD spokesperson.

It always amused Haddox how spokespeople were chosen based

on who was the most media-savvy. Rather than who actually understood the information to be conveyed.

Eve turned back to the computer station. "Tell me again about that case—the one tangentially linking Sean Sullivan with the witnesses."

"Not much to tell. It was July. The Bryant Park subway station. A woman was mugged. She suffered injuries and died. They never caught the guy responsible." Haddox clicked on the keyboard, pulled up the file. "Three witnesses on our list are confirmed to have been present. Each was interviewed. Based on the officer's notes, we believe Cassidy and Luis were also there. But they either gave false names or the interviewing officer made a mistake taking their names down."

"Why were two ambulances sent to the scene?" Eve asked.

"Where do you see that?" He squinted.

"Down here." She pointed to a scribbled sentence in the *Notes* field.

"Why don't you see if the main investigating officer remembers?" Eli piped up.

"A thirteen-year-old girl is still missing," Haddox reminded them grimly. "You really think this old case leads us to her?"

Eve slid her finger down more of the fine print on the computer screen. "I think it's all we've got. If she's not hidden inside the Cathedral, identifying the mastermind who used Sean as a pawn is our only chance of finding the girl."

Eve made the call to a lieutenant named Oliver Pryor. He was working, stationed at Rockefeller Center. One of the hundreds of officers pulling overtime duty in Midtown that night.

No-nonsense and plain-speaking, Pryor had two blunt questions for Eve the moment she identified herself. "Is it true the guy inside was one of us? A dirty cop?"

"It's complicated—but that's a working theory," she answered. "Did you know Sean Sullivan?"

"*That's* the guy? No way. No fuckin' way."

"How well did you know him?"

"Not well. But he never struck me as a wacko. *Jesus . . .* "

"I need to ask you about a case you investigated with him." Eve explained the details of the subway incident. "The NYPD file states that Captain Sullivan provided general support and crowd control."

"If it says so, then sure. I don't remember him."

She heard the doubt in his voice. "So safe to say he wasn't an integral part of the case?"

"No. And to be honest, there really was no case. Some street punk robbed a woman. Things escalated. She got hurt bad. Punk got away. We didn't have enough evidence to catch the bastard. End of story. I could tell you a thousand of 'em, just like it. Your own New York City fairy tale."

"I saw a notation that the victim suffered a traumatic brain injury."

"She got shoved onto the tracks," he informed her. "Train came into the station and ran over her. Didn't kill her right away, but she later died."

"Sounds like more than a routine mugging."

"Yeah. I'd forgotten about it 'til now, actually. There was even some crazy eyewitness on the platform who tried to fight off the mugger. Failed, of course. That was how the victim got shoved around. She would've survived the mugging just fine. What she didn't survive was her rescue."

"So the second ambulance was for her rescuer?" Eve pressed.

"Yeah. Think the eyewitness got beat up pretty bad. Don't recall what happened after."

"I don't see a name in the report. Just a notation: *J.D.*"

"That means your basic John Doe," he explained. "We go easy on those types. They don't give their name because they don't have health insurance."

Or, in this case, because they're ashamed. Embarrassed. Disappointed. Because they wanted to be the hero—but discovered that no good deed goes unpunished.

*You bring headlines, Eve.* Sean had been a convincing liar. He'd had to be, with his daughter's life on the line and the real Hostage Taker listening in on his every word. And like the best of them, Sean had known: The best lies always contained a shard of truth.

"There's no report of the case in the papers—not even the *Post.* Any idea why?"

"We didn't squelch it, if that's what you mean. But no one was a hero, no one caught the bad guy, and the victim's family requested total privacy. As a story, it missed all the key elements reporters pee in their pants over."

"There's no other file that might give the name of the would-be rescuer?"

"You want me to call the hospital?" Pryor offered. "They'll have records."

"It's okay," Eve told him. "I can figure out the rest from here."

# Chapter 86

*Not long ago, I read about a man who was mugged at the Port Authority Bus Terminal during early-morning rush hour. There were dozens of people around.*

*The man screamed for help as his mugger chased him through the station.*

*No one summoned a security officer.*

*No one dialed 911.*

*No one intervened to help.*

*The mugger caught up with his victim, knifed him, and robbed him.*

*Later, police were dumbfounded by how many videos of the incident appeared on YouTube. People were watching . . . recording . . . witnessing.*

*But not helping.*

Around the same *time, I heard about a woman in Liverpool, England, who was attacked at 4:30 in the afternoon on a busy street. She fought off a man who tried to drag her into his car.*

*She screamed loudly for help.*

*There were dozens of people around.*

*But not a single person came to her aid or called the police.*

Nothing has changed *since 1964, when Kitty Genovese was attacked outside her apartment in Kew Gardens. Thirty-eight neighbors heard Kitty's screams as she was stabbed multiple times—and raped—over the course of thirty-two minutes.*

*No one called the police. Not until it was too late.*

. . .

News reporters have *a name for this indifference. Psychologists call it the Bystander Effect. When I think about these things, I can't sleep. I lie awake at night and think of Stacy. I worry that all sense of morality and justice has disappeared from this world. That's what happens when no one gives a damn.*

*When not just your enemies look at you and wish you harm.*

*But when the decent people among us are at fault.*

*Are we all nothing but a lost cause?*

*What are we guilty of?*

*I am about to find out. This is my gift to the world.*

# Chapter 87

The official response had been immediate. In a show of interagency cooperation, the FBI, NYPD, FDNY, and Homeland Security had dispatched their Bomb Squad and Hostage Rescue and Antiterrorist Units to clear Saint Patrick's Cathedral. Everyone remained on high alert.

When the all-clear message finally arrived, it was tempered with bad news: There was no sign of Georgianna Murphy.

Eve moved fast to the rear of the Cathedral, where the mayor and his entourage were smiling for the cameras in front of the Cardinal's Residence on Madison Avenue. Snow was falling lightly, and someone had placed an evergreen wreath with a red ribbon on the door behind him, making for the perfect photo op. It was as though the mayor had rescued the holiday season itself.

Eve pressed herself against the concrete barricades that still protected the perimeter. She felt their icy-cold smoothness through her jacket.

She saw the rescued hostages some thirty-five feet away, talking with an officer to the mayor's left. One of them pointed to the slope of gray slate shingle that covered the back roof of the Cathedral.

*Where are the witnesses?*

She finally saw them, clustered with a group of photographers. Except for Sinya Willis, all appeared to be enjoying the attention.

Vast numbers of news personnel swarmed the scene: journalists and television crews, flanked by their news camera and photographer teams. It would be so easy to fake a press pass—and gain complete access to this event.

Eve scrutinized them carefully. But right now, everyone seemed to be doing his or her job.

"What's the plan?" Haddox stood at her elbow.

"I don't know yet," she answered, eyes scanning the gathering crowd.

"You? Without a plan?" He raised an eyebrow. "Isn't that like peanut butter without jelly? Laurel without Hardy?"

"Fred without Ginger? I actually agree with you. They balanced each other's strengths. Like the two of us. Now look at the people in front. What do you see?"

"I see your mayor, no doubt taking all the credit for averting a larger crisis. I see Monsignor Geve and the Church contingent, looking a wee bit less dour now their precious Cathedral is secure."

"Does anyone in the news corps look unengaged?"

"Um . . . no."

"What about the hostages?"

"They look tired. Like they've been through a long ordeal and just want to go home." He peered at Eve. "Why are we looking at these people? They're just politicians and journalists. Witnesses and hostages."

"Because something isn't right. So I have to look at everybody." She pressed forward. Studying the faces of those in front of her. Knowing her own powers of observation were good, but not infallible.

Penelope Miller looked flushed and exhausted, but relieved. She had not yet let go of her son, Luke. The boy was half-asleep in her arms.

Ellen Hodge hung back. Like she wanted to be anywhere but here.

Father DeAngelo seemed frail. Eve thought she saw him trembling slightly.

Ethan Raynor seemed to be enjoying the attention.

The mayor turned toward the front door. The TV crews and press photographers leapt into action, gathering their tripods and lights. They were going into the Cardinal's Residence.

Eve clicked on her headset. "García—have you cleared the Parish House and Cardinal's place?"

*Yeah. Mace caught up and slowed me down, but it all looks clean. We're returning through the Sacristy now.*

"A group of people is coming inside. Take a look—and be alert for anything that seems off."

Eve dodged a news crew, then a cluster of photographers, jockeying for position as they made their way inside.

"I thought we had to find the girl. Sean's daughter," Haddox whispered.

"We do. That's why we're here." She began moving to the front of the line.

He kept pace with her, ignoring the protests of others. "How do I help you?"

"Look at those in front of us. Help me find someone who seems okay on the outside, but is completely broken up on the inside."

"Sounds pretty abstract to me."

"Then let me make it concrete. Why do you think a kid like Sullivan's daughter hurts herself?"

"Because she's gone mental?"

Eve shot him an admonishing glance. "Because she's in pain. She has more pain bottled up than she can bear, and she's searching for a way to release it."

"Are we still talking about Sean's daughter?"

Eve's eyes widened. "You're brilliant. Absolutely brilliant."

"Not to mention a handsome devil. But damned if I know what you're talking about."

"It's similar, isn't it? Sean's daughter takes to the most public of stages, the Internet, to deal with her pain. Because she needs people to notice, because they don't in real life. I believe what we've seen here today is the flip side of the same coin. Played out on the most public stage in the city."

Everything is proceeding *according to plan. I still have a Cathedral and multiple souls under my control, and America's largest city under my thumb.*

*Only they don't know it.*

*I blend into the crowd. We all follow the mayor and his entourage into the dining room of the Cardinal's Residence. The room is designed to accommodate large state dinners, but that's inadequate for the number of people here tonight, anxious to hear the mayor's remarks.*

*Still, I make it through. I have no choice.*

*I am hidden among the masses of people. I lean down, as if to tie my shoe. I drop my gym bag.*

*Then I straighten and walk tall.*

*Since I was last here, someone has lit votive candles along a console on the right side of the room. Their glow casts a pink warmth onto the walls; every part of the dining room seems to glow. It is beautiful—for now.*

*I see Agent Rossi across the room. She looks confused.*

*I breathe a sigh of relief.*

*"We need her," Sullivan had pleaded. "She'll get headlines for you."*

*Later, he'd had another request. "Let the boy go. If your moves are unpredictable, they'll have a harder time figuring you out."*

*Yes, I chose the right man from the many officers listed in that police report. Captain Sullivan served his purpose with honor. From the moment I framed him for the weapons and explosives I stole—to the instant he took his last breath, doing my work—I could ask for no better assistant.*

*The time has come.*

*News reporters and sociologists blame the Internet, movie violence, and video-game culture for creating this out-of-touch generation. A generation with the moral sense of a baby killer.*

*Now is the ultimate test. Let's see what these people are made of.*

*Let's see if anyone—besides me—can step up and be the hero this godforsaken world so desperately needs.*

# Chapter 88

Eve's team made it in and fanned out. Eli snuck in first; he took a seat front row and center. Eve went to the left. García went right. Haddox and Mace stayed deep inside the crush of people.

The room was overflowing, packed beyond capacity. The mayor walked to the center of the makeshift stage and gripped his hands on the lectern. An audience of exhausted faces clapped. This wasn't exactly a victory celebration—but the crisis had ended. The collective relief was palpable.

*Who are we looking for?* Mace's voice crackled in Eve's headset.

"Anyone who might disrupt the moment," she replied. "We need to cover all the angles."

Henry Ma joined the mayor on his right, all smiles and handshakes. He was accompanied by Monsignor Geve and another Church representative Eve had not met.

*You sure something's about to go down, Eve?* Mace demanded.

"Believe me, I hope I'm wrong," she replied tersely.

More political officials walked to the front of the room, taking their positions near the mayor. She recognized the deputy mayor. The NYPD police commissioner. An interpreter for the hearing-impaired. The five former hostages—the four they'd rescued, in addition to the boy who'd been released—were in the place of honor to the mayor's left. The witnesses filed in, finding space to the mayor's far right.

Again, Eve tried to build an image of the person she was looking for. The demand for witnesses had been bizarre. Had he really wanted only to shame the men and women that he'd summoned? And the selection of hostages was worrisome. With little or no provocation, he had killed those who had sinned the most. The hostage-taking had involved a huge risk—and tremendous planning—but with no real reward.

Since the end game still didn't make sense, she couldn't relax.

Every seat was taken. The walls were lined with people who spilled into the parlor room next door. The camera crews had muscled their way to the front, taping microphones and recording equipment to the front edge of the dining room table. All the usual suspects were represented: NBC. CBS. ABC. CNN. Fox. Not to mention the local stations.

The lights turned on and cameras flashed.

A junior face initiated the briefing—a young official in uniform with spit-shined shoes. "Ladies and gentlemen, thank you for coming. This is a briefing from the mayor's office, not a press conference. That will come later, after the governor arrives." He began stating the facts, but was immediately interrupted with a barrage of questions.

He answered none of them—merely nodded and smiled and sidestepped the issues in a slightly patronizing manner. Then he introduced the mayor.

There were murmurs that went silent the moment the mayor started talking. He thanked everyone involved. He reiterated how Albany and Washington, D.C., were grateful, too.

Candles flickered. Too many people were cramming themselves closer to the mayor. Trying to see better, hear better, feel more part of the gathering.

A group of people in the parlor room next door had knelt down and appeared deep in prayer.

"See anything yet?" Eve asked.

*Nothing here,* Mace drawled.

*Or here,* Eli said.

Haddox concurred.

Eve started tapping her foot, her earpiece pressed so hard against her ear that it ached.

*How long was this going to take?*

The mayor was certain to talk for at least fifteen minutes—and that was assuming he didn't turn the microphone over to Henry, or the Tactical Ops director, or someone from the Church. Or all three of them.

She couldn't just stand there, helpless. Not while a teenage girl was being held captive—and a final threat loomed.

She studied the faces in the front rows. Then those crammed by the walls. What did she *see*?

There were clear-skinned, attentive faces. Lined, weathered faces. Bored faces—stiff as a piece of cardboard. Not one of them suspicious.

She felt for her Glock, confirmed it was in position, and backed up toward the parlor room door. She was about to retreat through it, search the overflow room, when she stopped short.

She'd heard a noise. A chirp. Someone had received a text.

It was followed by a second.

A third. A fourth.

Then more than she could count. A roomful of incoming texts, creating a burst of noise.

She reached for her own phone. Pulled it from her pocket.

Read: *Do I have your attention* NOW*?*

The sender was a five-digit number. *183-45.*

A gasp sounded.

"Haddox! What's going on?" she demanded.

*He's managed to text every single person in this room.* Haddox's voice came over the wire. *I'm gobsmacked.*

"How's that possible?"

*Through the carrier, by manipulating location data. I've seen it before. When I visited Jordan, the instant we crossed the border, everyone on the bus received a text message saying "Welcome to Jordan."*

Another chirp. Followed by another. Then a whole chorus of them.

Every person there had received a second text: *No one leaves. If anyone tries, we all die.*

"We need to stop this," Eve snapped. "Who's typing?"

Her eyes scanned the faces around her again. The attentive faces and the weathered faces and the stiff faces. It was even harder this time. Every single person in the room was hunched over his or her phone.

Watching. Waiting. Frightened.

Even the mayor.

The members of his security detail formed a protective barrier around him. NYPD officers did the same for the other officials and political dignitaries and former hostages.

*The messages may have been prearranged to send at specified times,* Haddox explained.

Penelope Miller was weeping. Father DeAngelo's eyes were closed. The priest appeared lost in prayer.

Another round of chirps. *There is a bomb in this room. You must do exactly what I say.*

Eve shoved her hands in her pockets to keep them steady. A rumble of noise rose from the crowd. People were talking, but not moving. They had gone stiff with panic.

*Yo—Mace! You see anything?* García demanded.

*Nothin' so far,* Mace replied.

*Do we even know he's in this room?* Eli's voice quavered.

"Don't think he'd dare miss it." Eve stood on her tiptoes, straining for a better view.

Another text chirped, a hundred times over. *SA Rossi needs to come to the front of the room.*

Eve's heart was pounding. It didn't matter that the room was packed as tight as a can of sardines. The moment she began moving, a path opened in front of her. The mass of people parted, just like the Red Sea.

More chirps. Then: *Find my witnesses. Tell them to spread out, so they can see and be seen!*

Now Eve's heart thudded an irregular beat. The witnesses had clustered together, not far from the mayor and his entourage. In a spot close enough that he could honor them with a special word. Let them be recognized. To a one, they had their phones out. They were reading the texts, too.

Sinya Willis let forth a long, keening wail. Blair Vanderwert was trembling like a leaf.

Eve caught Alina Matrowski's eye. "Please do as he says. I'm working on this."

Alina nodded. She had enough presence of mind to help the others move. Until they formed a half-circle in front of Eve.

The text came again. *Plenty of law enforcement types in this room. Plenty of people who are decent shots. That includes you, Eve.*

"No!" Eve protested.

*The moment one of you puts a bullet through one of their heads, we all go home. That's what ends this crisis, once and for all.*

Someone shrieked. A few women began crying; others began praying.

*Five min. Or the bomb blows.*

Eve heard Mace through her headset. *Is there really a bomb? Wasn't this room thoroughly screened?*

*'Course,* García's voice crackled. *But all these people with bags and news cams and mikes? We can't be sure something didn't slip in.*

Eve could hear the sounds of Christmas outside. The bells of Saint Patrick's pealing. Revelers—probably just allowed to return to their homes and businesses—were shouting in the streets.

Another text, another demand. *Their lives hang in the balance. At least one of you is going to die. Who in this room is going to help?*

Eve's eyes scanned the room. Searching for the guilty one responsible for these messages. These messages were for her, but everyone in the room continued to receive them. Some still cried and prayed, but many had grown quiet. Their voices strangled by panic.

Eve focused on Alina. The only witness who seemed to have any presence of mind. Cassidy jerked right and then left; her flight instinct had fully kicked in. But the room was jam-packed; there was no place to go. The others stood, stiff and unmoving—their faces blank with terror.

*Tell them to beg—and bow their heads like the confessors they are!*

Eve didn't have to ask. Alina and Cassidy immediately assumed the pose of the confessional. Blair nodded awkwardly. Sinya continued to sway back and forth, keening. Their words were a whisper at first—then they slowly gained volume. "Help. Help me! HELP!"

Eve heard Eli over the headset. *Just shut down the cell tower. Make the bastard talk to Eve, direct!*

*No can do,* Mace broke in. *Assuming there's a bomb, disrupting the cell signal could automatically trigger it.*

Eve cursed. There were no good options. "Just ID the carrier and shut down these texts!"

*Working on it,* Haddox muttered.

Cameras were still rolling. All eyes were on her. Expecting her to fix this situation, if only because she was the one at the front of the room. Because the sender of the text messages had mentioned her by name.

The mayor's security team was huddled tight. Planning their exit strategy.

The former hostages stood awkwardly behind a cluster of cops. Penelope and Luke Miller were locked in a tight embrace. Ellen Hodge stood stoically, blinking up into the lights. Father DeAngelo still prayed. Ethan Raynor was texting furiously on his phone. Except he wasn't a threat. A cop was proofing his every word, right over his shoulder.

Another text: *4 minutes.*

Eve's heartbeat was racing, but she knew how to keep her cool. Her strategy was simple: She imagined the Prelude of Bach's Cello Suite in G, a piece her mother had played. Its steady rhythm kept Eve's sense of time from spinning out of control. A mind trick—one that allowed her to become calm and focus on what was most important.

She caught a glimpse of Director Ma and the police commissioner, arguing heatedly. Monsignor Geve and his companion were attempting to edge toward the door, without success.

Everyone's phone beeped. *Someone must step up. Shoot just one witness. Save the rest in this room!*

The messenger had to be here. Had to be watching—gauging the effect of these words.

Eve spoke in a clear, loud voice. "Is that what this is about? The fact that these witnesses didn't help you that day on the subway?"

No answer.

Just the sounds of people in the room: keening and crying and nervous breathing. An elderly man was mumbling the *Our Father.* People behind Eve were praying the rosary.

A chorus of phones beeped. *3 minutes. Kill one witness—or my bomb explodes.*

The room rustled in panic.

"Don't you want them to explain?" Eve demanded. She locked eyes with Alina. "Last July. The subway station. You witnessed a mugging. The victim needed help. So did the eyewitness who intervened. Tell us what happened."

Tears were streaming down Alina's face—creating ugly dark rivers of black mascara. "I remember the mugging. I remember it was awful. I remember watching. But I froze. I wasn't scared, exactly. I just couldn't move."

"Me, too," Sinya chimed in. "It was like a bad dream. Like my body and my brain were trapped in a nightmare. I couldn't move. I couldn't stop watching."

*2 minutes.*

"Please!" Cassidy begged. "I don't want to die! Somebody stop this!"

"Where's your SWAT team now? Where's the police? The FBI?" Vanderwert found his voice. "It doesn't look to me like anybody's doing a damn thing! We're all just standing here, and this bastard says one of us has got to die for the room not to blow, and no one's lifting a finger! Can't *somebody* do *something*?"

What he had said wasn't true. Every pair of law enforcement eyes was working double-time.

Watching. Observing.

Cops had managed to return two bomb-sniffing dogs to the room.

García was eagle-eyed. Mace muscled his way through, checking the perimeter. Eli was alert in the thick of it all. Haddox was isolating the cell carrier that was enabling these damn texts.

Eve's eyes continued to probe every individual. Searching for the body language that would betray the architect of this madness.

*Sixty seconds. fifty-nine, fifty-eight . . .*

One bomb-sniffing dog was working the left side of the room. The other was checking the right.

*Forty-four. Forty-three. Save yourselves. Save this roomful of people. Just kill a witness.*

Time was running out. People began mumbling. Then shouting. Screaming.

The mayor's security detail pressed tighter around him. Eve watched their coordinated movements. They were preparing to break the mayor out of there.

*Thirty-two. Thirty-one. Will no one step up? Be a hero? Save the many?*

"Why not you?" Eve called out. "*You* can save all of us. *You* can be the hero. Instead of standing by like a coward, exactly like the witnesses on that subway platform."

On the left side of the room, people were moving. Away from the wall. The bomb-sniffing dog had given a signal.

All eyes went there. Searching.

"That woman! That bag! Right there!" One of the cops pointed to a woman in a cream coat who looked completely bewildered. Who had an olive-colored gym bag sitting by her feet.

"You're right!" A man with an egg-shaped shiny head opened the bag. Revealing something electronic inside.

Panic consumed the room. The warning that the bomb would go off if anyone moved was forgotten. A crush of people moved toward the door.

*Twenty-three. Twenty-two.*

"JUST SHOOT ONE OF THE DAMN WITNESSES!" The egg-headed man charged, tried to take the gun from the officer nearest him. Another cop tackled him. They ended up flailing on the floor.

The mayor's team was pushing forward. Eve could no longer see Henry. Three of the witnesses were trying to join the mass exodus—except the room was bottlenecked.

Only Vanderwert still stood—trembling, completely paralyzed.

The texts were still coming. *Nineteen, eighteen.* But the shouting and screaming were now so loud, no one could hear the chirps that announced them.

People were pushing. Everyone was trying to flee. This had all the hallmarks of a stampede.

Except Eve noticed: One person was moving differently.

"García," she breathed. "Do you see what I see?" She was remembering what Sean Sullivan had said. *Not the obvious answer.*

Sean had been right—though not quite in the way Eve had imagined.

One person was moving toward the lectern. Eve recognized the haircut and bearing as military. She saw the steady sense of purpose amid the panic. But that didn't explain it. There was something more.

In the corner of her eye, Eve saw Mace angling for position, trying to see what still eluded him. *Do you see a gun? A detonator? What kind of threat are we looking at?*

"It's in the body language," Eve replied. She knew what she saw, but how could she put in words what she understood? Some mental leaps were a matter of intuition—made in the space between the mind and the gut.

*I've got the shot,* García confirmed.

*No, Eve—not again,* Mace warned.

She ignored him. García understood. "Take the shot," she ordered.

Eve forced herself to focus on the moment. *This* moment. Ignoring past decisions that went wrong.

The mayor's security team was moving. The hostages were moving. The witnesses were moving.

Across the room, she looked and saw the metal glint from the gun in García's hand.

There was a chorus of screams. People shouting *No! He's going to shoot a witness!*

A lone voice countered *LET HIM!*

Four witnesses shrunk into the wall. There was no escape.

García fired.

The sound was amplified by stone walls, and the flash was brighter than a camera's.

One of the hostages fell to the ground.

And the Cardinal's Residence erupted into a panicked exodus.

# Chapter 89

Eve went from standing still to moving faster than lightning. She fought her way through the panicked crowd. She flashed her FBI shield at the security detail who'd closed ranks around the mayor.

The hostage's body had jerked backward from the impact. It landed just eight feet away from the mayor.

Eve heard the sound of running feet. In the tight quarters of the Cardinal's Residence, it sounded like a thousand steps.

Someone was yelling commands—ordering paramedics and summoning an ambulance for another victim with a GSW.

There was a scuffle ongoing in the west side of the room. It took five guards to subdue García. He wasn't taking it well.

"What the hell, Eve?" Henry Ma's face was twisted with fury. "*Your* guy was the shooter? The ex-Ranger—the one who's lost his marbles?"

"You can thank me later, Henry," she said, her eyes scanning the floor.

"*Thank* you?" he sputtered.

"For giving the order that saved lives." Eve searched behind the lectern.

"You *never* shoot one to save the many." The vein running across Henry's forehead was throbbing, threatening to pop. "You *never* take a nutjob demand like that seriously. García shot a *hostage*."

Eve saw cords and mikes and news camera cables. Hidden among them, she found the proof she wanted.

She didn't touch it.

She pointed it out to Henry and the mayor's security detail.

"Bring the Bomb Squad over here," she ordered. "The woman's bag out there? It's just a distraction, probably filled with trace explosive. *This* is the real thing. Get this building cleared."

"What the hell?" The mayor had elbowed his way through the crowd.

It was a detonator. Of a slightly different style than the others used throughout the Cathedral.

"You're saying someone tried to kill me?" The mayor was ashen.

"No more than anyone else," Eve replied. She was so cold, she felt she might be shaking. "The goal was to make us all bystanders. To make us literally *stand by*—and witness our own deaths."

"I don't follow," Henry said.

Eve was just putting it together herself, but she understood now. The hostage-taking—and the bringing of witnesses—had been a play. Sean Sullivan had been cast as the sacrifice. And it had all been designed for this moment—this scene. In order to replay a crisis where the Bystander Effect would come into play. Just like on the subway platform—with the same witnesses on hand to see it. With even higher stakes: the lives of the mayor and city leaders and hundreds of onlookers.

Not just to punish those original witnesses—the ones who refused to help.

Not just to illustrate a moral lesson for the world—which was corrupt and unfeeling.

But because re-creating the pain—and sharing it with the world—was the only way to manage an unbearable hurt.

"Who is she?" Mace was now right at her side.

Eve almost answered *The sniper.*

Or *The person who kidnapped Sullivan's daughter.*

Or simply the name on the woman's New York State Driver's License. *Ellen Hodge.*

Instead, she answered, "A Trojan horse."

As Eve said the words, Ellen Hodge lifted a bloody hand and wiped the scar that ran across her cheek.

# Chapter 90

Inside the ambulance, Ellen Hodge was hovering at the edge of consciousness. The attending medics shook their heads when Eve approached. The prognosis was not good.

But Eve didn't need much time. This wasn't going to be a long discussion. She had no interest in the woman's justification or rationale. She didn't care that Hodge was mumbling something about sins of omission and commission.

Eve just had one question. "Where is the girl?"

"Why should I tell you?" The words slurred together.

"Absolution. For all you're guilty of."

"Don't need it. Don't want it."

"Not from the Church. From Society."

Ellen Hodge tossed, moaning. In extreme pain.

"Tell me where the girl is," Eve repeated, "and you'll be the hero you wanted to be. The headlines will affirm it. That you stepped up, and didn't just stand by. Isn't that what you want?"

The only answer was a hoarse, choking sound.

A remembered phrase echoed in Eve's mind. "Otherwise, what will *you* be guilty of?"

Ellen Hodge tilted her head toward Eve. She opened her mouth to say something. But no words came out, only a bright trickle of blood. Her eyes went blank.

NEWS NEWS NEWS NEWS NEWS

# HOUR 17

After Midnight

We return to our continuing coverage of the astonishing hostage drama that unfolded today at Saint Patrick's Cathedral.

The source who had identified New York Police Captain Sean Sullivan as the Hostage Taker responsible for today's events has since retracted his statement. We await further word on the person or persons responsible.

In a situation that may or may not be related to the crisis, we are receiving reports that several streets in a Queens neighborhood have just been evacuated, as SWAT teams converge on a residence there.

There continues to be no word as to when the area around Fifth Avenue in the Fifties will reopen to the public. Stay tuned, right here, for all the latest developments.

# Chapter 91

Ellen Hodge's house in Queens was on a street filled with small Cape Cods, Queen Annes, and Tudors—almost all of them decorated for the season with lights and green wreaths. But this house was a forlorn place—surrounded by skeletal trees and neglected flower beds.

Eve and Haddox watched via live video feed as officers in protective gear opened doors, foraged closets, and explored the attic.

They watched together in silence. There was no audio. The only sound Eve heard was the thump of her own heartbeat.

Haddox kept one eye on the video feed. Another eye on the in-depth background profile he was generating. "She was forty-seven. A widow; her husband died in Afghanistan. Awful situation—she was deployed with him." He went on to explain all the details.

"So when Stacy Hodge died, and nobody stepped up to save him—when even *she* wasn't able to save him—Ellen became obsessed with the failings of bystanders," Eve surmised. "The incident following the subway mugging tipped her over the edge: Suddenly she was a victim who needed help, and no one stepped forward to help *her.*"

The search team smashed open a basement door secured by a padlock. The door swung wildly on its shattered hinges.

Inside, the stairs were dark. Mops and brooms and dustbins hung on the wall.

At the bottom, the floor was nothing but compacted dirt.

The search team split into three groups.

"Looks like Hodge's family was connected to Saint Patrick's," Haddox explained. "Her father, grandfather, and great-grandfather were all laborers—stonemasons who worked to build the Cathedral."

"Explains why she chose it," Eve agreed.

"Why did she choose Sullivan?"

"Ellen knew that it was only a matter of time before we'd uncover the link among her witnesses—how they were all bystanders who witnessed that subway mugging where she was the failed hero. To ensure their connection didn't point to her, she must have researched all the investigating officers. In Sean, she found the perfect pawn. He had a young daughter she could use to control him. And she *did* control him—he was all hers, at her beck and command, from the moment she took his child. He was a combat veteran like her, with enough military expertise that we'd believe him capable of handling a rifle and explosives. Best of all, he already had significant personal and professional problems—which made him easy to frame when she stole the weapons-grade materials she needed."

They watched as one team probed the storage area, filled with stacks of old board games, plywood, tar sealant, and a wet/dry vacuum so ancient it probably no longer worked.

Another scoured the utility room, searching behind the boiler, the washer and dryer area, and the massive oil tank.

"One other thing I still don't understand," Haddox said. "Why did Ellen Hodge ask for you?"

"I don't think she did," Eve answered. "Best I can tell, that was an ad lib on Sean Sullivan's part. Sean trusted me to find the real truth—and rescue his daughter. Somehow he sold Ellen on the idea."

The team began using their crowbars, shovels, and giant irons. They were going to pull down a wall.

Behind the wall there was a hidden room.

Inside the room was a cell.

Inside the cell huddled Sean Sullivan's daughter Georgianna—alive and unharmed. But Georgie had company. A sixty-seven-year-old woman who gave her name as Muna Hodge.

Muna told her rescuers that her son, Stacy, had been killed fighting overseas. And that her daughter-in-law, Ellen, had been unhinged by that loss.

Ellen Hodge was going to get her headlines.

But not the way she wanted.

# Epilogue

Six days later

It was a perfect winter day, where the snow fell but did not stick more than enough to coat the grass and trees with a crisp sugary layer of white that was starkly beautiful. Beyond the stretch of trees that was Riverside Park, the Hudson River was glistening like ice under cloud-filled skies.

A car pulled up in front of the marble townhouse at the corner of Riverside and 107th Street.

After saying something to the driver, Mace got out—followed by a black-and-tan five-year-old German shepherd. The dog bounded down the walk, up the stairs, and past two stone lions before sitting at the door.

"I brought you a present," Mace said when Eve opened the door at 350 Riverside Drive.

"Come in. The rest of them are already here." She knelt to hug the dancing, overexcited dog. "I'm surprised you're giving him up. You got tired of babysitting?"

"Nah," Mace chuckled. "We kept each other busy. Even got therapy training."

"No way." García had entered the room. "You are *not* giving me no therapy dog. I am not a dog person."

Mace shot García a look of annoyance. "That one statement probably sums up the whole reason we don't get along. Get over yourself already, Frankie. The dog is Eve's." He caught her eye. "Nothing like taking care of someone else to help you stay grounded. Plus, he'll help you remember the good times, not the bad."

*Zev's former home, now hers.*

*Zev's former dog, now hers.*

"Zev loved him," Eve said, burying her face in Bach's fur.

Mace hung the dog leash on a wall hook—strategically placed for that purpose. "This place ain't bad. Even got its own tunnel, huh?"

Eli and Haddox joined them. They'd all come to help Eve clear out and pack up Zev's things. She hadn't asked—but they'd insisted it wasn't the sort of job she ought to do alone.

"Can I ask you something?" Mace said.

"Sure." Eve gave a final pat to Bach's head.

"You gonna keep the house or sell it?"

The question gripped Eve's heart with an icy vise. "It's definitely too much house for me. What am I going to do with eleven bathrooms?"

"Do you know how much eleven bathrooms gets you in today's market?" Eli rolled tape onto cardboard, creating the lower half of a box. "You could retire to some tropical island. 'Cept you oughtta take the Steinway. It plays a mean chopsticks."

"I'd miss the snow." Eve raised her face to the chandelier above them. It was like a jewel, studded with dozens of brilliant diamond lights. Beautiful—but not her own.

She saw the antique bench and mirror. The Persian rug Zev had brought home from Iran. The silk paintings and jade statues from China and Korea and Japan. She still regarded this as Zev's home. No words in a last will and testament were going to change that. Maybe it was legally hers—but she couldn't imagine herself here, watching movies and unloading groceries, paying bills and shoveling the sidewalk.

"You know," Haddox said, "if you wanted to make it your own, all you'd need is a new coat of paint."

"Too much history." She gestured to the box Eli was filling with Zev's eighteen different chess sets. But she was thinking of Zev's final moments. He'd lost his life by the banks of the Hudson, not far away.

Haddox shrugged. "Some paint and your own stuff. It's enough for a fresh start."

Her eyes narrowed. "Why is everything with you about a fresh start?"

"'Cause that's what keeps us going, luv. Why we get up every morning. Every new day is the perfect do-over."

"I dunno. Most days I feel stuck in the same rut. Like Bill Murray in *Groundhog Day*," Eli said, shaking his head.

"What would John say about that?" Haddox teased.

"No clue. We're on a break."

"I thought you liked John," Eve said.

"I did. But he got mad when I ignored his calls. And his family? You have no idea the number of obligations these people expect. Four family events—a wake, two Christmas parties, and a dinner—this week alone. Too much for me."

"Too many expectations," Haddox agreed.

García was busy looking around. "You know, I'm not going back to the hospital. But I'd come here to work. If you wanted to do something with it, that is."

"This place?" Mace frowned for a split second; then his face broke into a grin. "You know what—I see what you mean."

"What are you talking about?" Eve felt like they were moving forward and making plans, while she stayed mired in the past.

"Zev used it as a CIA outpost for over a decade, right?" García jabbed his finger against the security panel in the front hall. "Why not make it the center for your own work? Either in the FBI—or not."

"I don't know what I want," Eve said honestly.

"That's 'cause you don't color inside the lines," Mace told her. "Maybe you did once—but now you don't. Not anymore."

"Not sure I've colored since I was ten." Eve ripped a long stretch of tape off the roll and sealed up a box.

"I hear it's like riding a bike," Haddox told her. "Think about it. Maybe over dinner."

She tossed him a new roll of tape. "You want a dinner date, ask Olivia Foley from Forensics. From the way she looks at you, I'm pretty sure she'd say yes."

"Which is why I don't ask. Where's the challenge?"

After the guys left, she curled up on the sofa. Bach settled in beside her like he owned the place. Just outside her door, the city was teeming with activity. Taxi drivers blared their horns. Punk teenagers yelled obscenities. Dogs barked.

That was what she loved about this city: how she could be alone, but never lonely.

She had expected to return to her own apartment. But she was surprised to find herself comfortable here with Bach. There were good memories here. And for the first time since Zev's death, she found them a solace and not a torment. Running her fingers across the keys of the baby grand, she felt surprisingly content. Was this—finally—the fifth stage of grief?

*Acceptance.*

Her phone beeped.

A message from the Irishman.

*Speaking of fresh starts: You know I'm a sucker for a good pizza. How about tomorrow night?*

Forty-seven blocks uptown, in an Irish section of the Bronx, Corey Haddox pulled up a stool at the Dead Rabbit and ordered a pint of Guinness. For the first time since leaving Dublin, he was in luck: the bartender knew his stout. Which was to say, the bloke knew a thing or two about timing.

He filled the glass in one continuous pour and let it rest for 119 seconds.

Just shy of two minutes.

Exactly the right amount to let the head rise just proud of the rim.

Haddox's phone beeped. Eve had responded. *Can't plan that far in advance. Let's stick to your 8:18 rule.*

It was all in the timing. He'd thought he had it right—but Eve was tricky. And this was one case where, he admitted, bits and bytes didn't do the conversation justice. All context was missing: The lift of her chin, the expression in her eyes, the thousands of ways she managed to communicate while saying nothing at all.

Mere words on a screen couldn't capture the half of it.

Then seven seconds later, she surprised him. *Better make it tonight. I'm starving.*

He smiled before he lifted his drink and savored his first sip—long and slow, a mix of bitter and sweet.

# Author's Note

The idea for this novel came to me shortly after Saint Patrick's Cathedral began its massive renovation project—and I first saw the Cathedral buried in scaffolding. Observing the chaos and upheaval, I began to think: *what if?* But while this landmark is real, my story is fictional: I've incorporated rumor and myth, legend and imagination, to create a blend of fact and fiction in keeping with the spirit of this historic treasure. Likewise, while some characters may share official titles with religious and city leaders, they are entirely my own creation and not based on any real individual.

It was the year 1809 when the notorious forger, thief, and master-of-disguise Eugène François Vidocq—a man no prison had managed to hold—walked into the offices of Monsieur Henry, the head of the French Prefecture. Tired of living life on the lam, Vidocq made an astonishing offer: He would deliver up France's most wanted thieves and smugglers in exchange for a clean slate.

The unique arrangement worked so well that Monsieur Henry had an epiphany: sometimes it takes a thief to catch a thief. He would give Vidocq a clean slate, but only if he took a permanent job with the police. It was a compelling offer: a chance to spend his life stalking criminals rather than wasting it in jail or on the run. So Vidocq took the only true option presented and went on to use his considerable talents in a very different manner, developing an innovative approach to police work. Vidocq rose to become head of the Sûreté—and when he handpicked those men who would staff his most elite units, he turned not to the best men on the force, but to the streets. He assembled a crack team of criminals just like himself. Their successes were legendary—even if questions about whether they were truly law-abiding dogged Vidocq for all of his career.

Many have studied him.

A number have followed him.

And—just maybe—a select few continue his legacy.

# Acknowledgments

No writer ever succeeds in publishing a book without significant help from family, friends, and dedicated professionals. I want to give special thanks to those who helped me most with this one.

Thanks to Kate Miciak, my editor, who has an unfailing instinct for story. To Anne Hawkins, my agent, who reads, suggests, and believes. Together, you both understand exactly what I need as a writer—and I'm grateful for your enthusiasm and support.

I'm grateful to everyone at Random House, including Libby McGuire, Julia Maguire, Lindsey Kennedy, Maggie Oberrender, Nancy Delia, my copy editor Amy Brosey, Victoria Wong, and all the other people whose contributions have made this book a reality. Special thanks to cartographer David Lindroth and cover designer Carlos Beltram.

Both the FBI and St. Patrick's Cathedral are formidable institutions—ones that I've slightly reframed and reorganized in the interest of telling a better story. I hope those who helped me with the research behind this novel will forgive me for the liberties I took: Charles Muldoon, Jacqueline Delaney, Evelyn Vera, and all those I had the privilege to meet as part of New York's FBI Citizens Academy; and Bob Grant and countless others at St. Patrick's Cathedral who answered my questions with patience and good humor. For additional reference sources, I'm indebted to Thomas G. Young, author of *St. Patrick's Cathedral* and *A New World Rising*, and Gary Noesner, author of *Stalling for Time: My Life as an FBI Hostage Negotiator*.

To David Hale Smith, for starting me on the journey.

Thanks to Mark Longaker, Natalie Meir, Cecilia McAveney, and always, to MacKenzie Cadenhead.

To Maddie, whose imagination inspires me.

Finally, heartfelt thanks to Craig, my partner in all things.

## About the Author

STEFANIE PINTOFF is the Edgar Award–winning author of three novels. Her writing has also won the Washington Irving Book Prize and earned nominations for the Anthony, Macavity, and Agatha awards. Pintoff's novels have been published around the world, including the United Kingdom, Italy, and Japan. She lives on Manhattan's Upper West Side, where she is at work on the next Eve Rossi thriller.

# About the Type

This book was set in Sabon, a typeface designed by the well-known German typographer Jan Tschichold (1902–74). Sabon's design is based upon the original letter forms of sixteenth-century French type designer Claude Garamond and was created specifically to be used for three sources: foundry type for hand composition, Linotype, and Monotype. Tschichold named his typeface for the famous Frankfurt typefounder Jacques Sabon (c. 1520–80).